Praise for
Sloan Parker's Other Books

"…I loved everything about this story—especially the level of intensity and connection that crackled between Grady and Mateo. I'd sum up my reading experience with this book in one word—unputdownable!"

—Hearts on Fire Reviews on I SWEAR TO YOU

"…I have loved every one of Sloan Parker's books and this one is no different. …exciting, suspenseful and most importantly, romantic. The love story between Walter and Kevin is so sweet and real. They have a connection that can't be denied by either one of them."

—Literary Nook on HOW TO SAVE A LIFE

"Vargas and Seth have an incredible love story. Totally amazing…"

—Amazon Reviewer on HOW TO HEAL A LIFE

"So sweet and romantic and incredibly well done in such a short format."

—Joyfully Jay on SOMETHING TO BELIEVE IN

"…seriously one of the most romantic books I have ever read."

—Books Laid Bare Boys on TAKE ME HOME

"You do not want to miss this AWESOME story… I highly recommend…"

—Whipped Cream Reviews on BREATHE

Other Titles by Sloan Parker

More (More Book 1)
More Than Most (More Book 2)

How to Save a Life (The Haven Book 1)
How to Heal a Life (The Haven Book 2)

Breathe
Take Me Home
More Than Just a Good Book
Something to Believe In
I Swear to You
The Break-In
Swept Away
A Lesson in Truth

More Than Ever
(More Book 3)

SLOAN PARKER

Published by
Sloan Parker Press
www.sloanparker.com

More Than Ever

Chapter One

"Oh God. Just hang on. I'm coming to get you. Just hang on. Please, God."

I awoke with a start, those words still echoing in my head, the feel of the harsh ground and sharp tree limbs still jutting into my back. It took a moment for the soft mattress and warm comforter of our bed to overpower the nightmare.

It was the same dream as the night before.

And the night before that.

I exhaled a long, shattered breath.

I didn't want to think about that dream—or who was featured in it—for one more second. I lifted my head off the pillow to check the clock on the nightstand. 5:00 a.m. Too early for Luke or Richard to get up, but there was no way I was drifting off to sleep again.

Now for the hard part.

The best thing about being in a gay polyamorous relationship? Sleeping between two gorgeous men every night.

The worst thing? Sleeping between two men when I had to get up first. It was hell slipping out of bed without waking either of them.

With my hands propped on the mattress beside me, I shimmied my ass up the bed until I had my back against the headboard, then folded the blankets down as far as I dared. After I had my knees tucked to my chest, Luke shifted beside me.

I paused, waited, making sure he hadn't woken. It took some awkward bending, but I managed to get my feet out from under the blankets one at a time without straining something.

When the three of us had first moved in together, I'd suggested we ditch the top sheet and each sleep under our own blanket so it would be easier for me to get up during the night without disturbing them. Richard had merely grunted out the word *no*, and that was the end of that discussion. He was all about the touching, and each of us under a different blanket would get in the way of that.

Not that I minded one damn bit.

Luke and Richard were the first men I'd met at the Haven who made me feel like I didn't have to hold back, like I could kiss and touch and simply be close to them as much as I wanted without it seeming desperate or needy or clingy. From the very beginning, they'd both loved to stroke and kiss and caress every inch of me as often as they could as if they needed that contact—needed *me*—to survive.

If only they were awake now, distracting me from that dream with their touches, their kisses.

I squeezed my eyes shut and, with my elbows propped on my knees, covered my ears. Such a childish thing to do. As if that could make the words rushing through my head disappear, could make the sound of that voice fade from my memory.

My entire body trembled.

All this time and my reaction to his voice, to that day I'd nearly died, was still so visceral.

Or maybe I was just cold.

Maybe the fresh fruit I'd eaten at dinner hadn't been so fresh.

Maybe… nothing.

I glanced down at Richard. With the bright moonlight seeping in through the bedroom windows, I could see him clearly. He lay on his back, the blankets folded down to just above his groin. One hand was propped on the hard cuts of muscle across his abs. Trixie lay curled up at his hip. His other hand was resting on her side as if he'd fallen asleep in the middle of petting her. His eyes were closed, lips slightly parted. Stubble covered his jawline, a hint of gray in the blond facial hair that hadn't been there when I'd first met him. His eyebrows were lifted ever so slightly, as if being asleep allowed him to relax in a way that his waking hours didn't offer.

I smiled at him. He was always so focused and meticulous, always in control. Except when he slept.

Leaning over him, I brushed the tip of my forefinger along one of those blond brows. Even after all this time, I couldn't believe he was mine, that they both were.

I dropped a soft kiss on his forehead and then carefully turned toward Luke.

His brown hair was a disheveled mess, jutting out all over on the white pillowcase. He wore his hair longer now than when we'd first met. A lot of things about him were different now. He was less guarded and enjoyed life more. He also slept in longer, slept heavier, even without having sex beforehand.

He lay on his side facing me, one hand tucked under his chin, the other resting on my pillow beside the indent where my head had been. I bent over him and pressed my lips to his forehead in the same soft kiss I'd given to Richard, taking in the warmth of him, the masculine scent, wanting to crawl back under the covers and pull them in close until I was wrapped up in them, in their touches.

And their love.

But I didn't want to wake them. Or scare them. If they got up right then, there'd be no hiding the flood of anxiety rushing through me.

That would just freak them out.

It was nothing to worry about.

Nothing.

Reluctantly I turned away from Luke, got on my hands and knees, and carefully crawled down the center of the bed. Trixie lifted her head to watch me, then got up and followed, stopping to lie beside me at the foot of the bed.

Since we'd gotten her several months earlier, she'd grown significantly, but she was still very much a puppy with long legs and giant paws. She had yet to find that balance of agility and speed that looked graceful on other dogs her size. The majority of her coloring pointed to the German shepherd side of her lineage, but her ears were as floppy as they'd been when we'd brought her home.

"Shh," I whispered as I patted her on the head. "Go back to sleep, baby girl." I gave her another stroke and a kiss on the top of her snout, then got moving for the bathroom.

Once I had the door shut behind me, I flipped on the low lights over the bathtub, hoping that wouldn't clue either of my men in on the fact that I was awake this early. Leaning against the closed door, I dropped my head back to the surface behind me and drew in a deep breath. It was the third time that week that I'd had the dream. Nightmare. Memory. I wasn't sure what to call it. I just knew I wanted to be done with it.

I'd tried so hard to move past that part of my life, to leave it all behind.

Yet here I was, engulfed by it once again.

Well, no more. I wasn't letting anger or pain or anxiety run my life. Not today of all days. I had too much at stake.

My meeting later had to go well.

I stood taller. "You can do this."

Wearing only my underwear, I went to stand at the bathroom sink.

I cranked on the faucet and splashed my face with cool water, exhaling a long breath as I straightened. Droplets of water dripped from my hair and chin to the sink below. My dark wavy hair was longer than I normally wore it. That, along with the additional curls from the extra length, had me looking eighteen, not twenty-four. I needed to do something about that soon. I'd just been so swamped lately with my college classes and work and everything else.

I shifted back a step and examined myself in the mirror again, trying to imagine how I appeared to other people.

Young. Naive.

Inexperienced.

Maybe someone would see past all that and give me a break.

"Yeah, someone will. It's just stupid hair." I laughed at my reflection. "You got this. You can do this."

But…

What if I fuck it all up?

Racing through everything that could go wrong, I bit at the edge of a thumbnail, then forced myself to stop the habit I'd had since I was a kid. I couldn't ease the rapid breaths pouring out of my chest, though. If I didn't knock it off, I'd be hyperventilating before long. I'd probably pass out right there in the bathroom. Richard would walk in later and find me with my ass in the air and my face pressed into the bath mat. Talk about freaking him out. That was all I needed. To scare the hell out of him, give him a heart attack or something.

I couldn't stand that thought.

I returned to the sink and cranked on the water once more. I scrubbed my face and the back of my neck, then grabbed a hand towel and buried my face in it, trying to slow my erratic breaths.

"Hey."

That deep voice immediately cut through the unease.

I lifted my head from the towel and there was Richard's reflection in the mirror, concern evident in those bright green eyes gazing back at me.

When he got a good look at my face, he came forward without delay. Stepping up behind me, he laid his hands on my shoulders and studied me in the mirror. "It's going to be okay, Matthew."

I stared back at him, as in awe as I ever was. At forty years old and well over half a foot taller than I, he was one of the most unbelievably gorgeous men I'd ever met. All broad, hard, muscular flesh and focused strength, wearing only a pair of snug black boxer briefs.

He kept those compassionate eyes locked on mine as he circled both thumbs over my shoulder blades, working the knots from my stiff muscles. "You're going to do great today."

His words, his touch, they all brought to life a shiver.

I smiled at him in the mirror, then tossed the towel on the counter, spun around, and wrapped my arms around his middle, the side of my head connecting with his bare chest.

With a heavy sigh, as if he'd been dying for me to do that very thing, he enveloped me in those strong arms. "They'd be crazy not to want you."

"You really think so?"

"I do."

"Okay. I'll try not to worry so much." I wasn't just referring to my appointment later that day. I was talking about the three of us. I think he got that.

After everything we'd been through together, he knew what I meant.

We continued with the quiet embrace, his warm hand caressing my back. I was so very aware of him. Of his touch. His scent. His heat. His heartbeat.

His hand stilled. "It might help if you talk about it."

Before I could say anything, Luke staggered through the open bathroom doorway, his eyes half closed. I turned to face him as he squeezed between us and the vanity.

Richard pulled me backward to lean against his chest, and together we watched Luke make his way to the toilet. He didn't say anything or even acknowledge us. He wrenched up the seat and did his business, all the while his head tipped backward, his eyes closed as if he was falling asleep standing right there with his dick out, pissing in the toilet. When he finished, he tucked himself back into his underwear, stumbled to the sink, and washed his hands.

Richard bent to whisper in my ear. "Do you think he even sees us?"

I laughed. "No."

Luke lifted his head and squinted into the mirror as he dried his hands. "Very funny. I'm not unconscious." He chucked the towel aside and spun to face us, resting his ass against the counter, his arms folded across his chest. "What the hell are we doing up so damn early? It's the weekend."

"We're up," Richard said, "and we're staying up. I don't think Matthew's going to be getting any more sleep until this interview is over. He's really nervous."

I sighed and sank back against him. "I'm okay."

Despite my words, Luke stepped forward, instantly awake. Holding my face, he lifted my head. "You're gonna do great." He searched my eyes, then ran his fingers through my hair, studying the movement of his hands as if getting to touch me like that was the most amazing experience of his life. "You have such a good heart, Matthew. Just be yourself, and they'll be impressed."

Richard tightened his arms across my chest and kissed the side of my head.

Luke stepped closer. I laid my head on his shoulder as he slid a warm hand tenderly across my upper back.

And just like that, the last of my unease slipped away as they held me. It was always that way with them.

"I really love what I've read about this place. It's different than anything else I've applied for." I lifted my head. "I know it's only an internship, but I want this so much."

Luke nodded. "I can see why. Seems like they do good work."

"Yeah," Richard said. "They sound right up your alley."

I figured he also thought it would be dangerous, but he had yet to comment on that aspect of this particular job.

Instead he added, "You went above and beyond with all the studying this past week. You're ready for this interview." He turned me to face him. "But no matter what, you've accomplished a lot already. You should be proud of yourself."

I shrugged. "It's just one year of vet tech school."

"Don't belittle that. You worked your ass off, both at your classes and the kennel." He swept the backs of his fingers over my cheek. "You're doing an amazing job."

Without thinking about my actions, I launched myself at him, standing on my toes and circling my arms around his neck in a fierce embrace. I needed him to know how much those words—and the physical contact they'd both offered—meant to me.

When we eventually parted, Richard dropped a quick kiss on my lips. I wanted more than one kiss, but I couldn't get the words out. Or make a move that would clue him in.

Apparently I didn't need to say anything. One look in my eyes, and he stepped closer. Cupping my face in his large hand, he kissed me again, more passionately, more deeply this time.

The mix of strength and tenderness in the press of his lips was exhilarating. I wanted more.

He understood. He always did.

He parted his lips and swept his tongue across my lower lip. I whimpered at the contact. In response, he deepened the kiss, tugging me closer, drawing me against his solid body with desperate urgency. His tongue brushed mine, and that was all I needed. I was instantly aroused, aching for him, wanting—*needing*—for us to take things further.

It hadn't been like this between the three of us for weeks.

Who was I kidding?

Not since that night at my mom's months earlier.

We'd had sex since then, but it was different. Strained. Restrained even.

Luke's hands were at my hips, his strong body coming in close to mine again. The feel of both of them against me brought out the raw truth. It always did. The anxiety slammed into me once more. It battled with the desire.

Richard jerked back, his eyes scanning mine. "What do you need to feel better about the interview? You want to do some practice questions? Or forget about it for a while, maybe watch TV to take your mind off everything? Crawl back in the bed and talk?"

I tipped my head forward until I had my forehead pressed to his chest, right over the wide, grim scar from his college days. I blew out a huff of air. "I don't know."

He ran his hands up and down my arms. "Why don't you hit the shower while Luke and I fix breakfast? We'll indulge ourselves, make chocolate chip pancakes. After we eat, we'll see how you feel, maybe go over the questions you have for them."

"Okay." I raised my head. "That sounds good."

He gave me a last kiss and then went to turn on the shower while Luke got towels out of the cabinet and laid them on the vanity. When they had everything ready for me, they headed for the open doorway.

Luke ticked off items on his fingers. "You make the pancakes, cut the fruit, and start the coffee. I'll set the table."

Richard snorted sarcastically. "Yeah, that sounds fair."

"You're right. That's not going to work." Luke pointed at him. "You should set the table too. I'll just watch that fine ass of yours move around the kitchen." He smacked one of Richard's underwear-clad ass cheeks and took off.

"Hey." Richard hightailed it after him.

I laughed as I watched them go. How the hell did I get so lucky to be a part of them, to be a part of what we all had together?

I would never—*ever*—take that for granted.

I knew part of the reason for the distance between the three of us lately was how busy we'd all been, but the rest of it... I blamed myself for that. They said I shouldn't, but something had changed that night Richard said I'd lied to him about what I wanted in bed, or more precisely, what I didn't want.

I could still hear his wounded voice when he'd said, *"How can I trust that everything I've done to you—every time I've touched you— that it was something you wanted, not something you were doing for me?"*

I also knew neither of them could stop picturing that moment I'd flinched from his touch.

Chapter Two

Showered and dressed, I headed downstairs. One look in the kitchen and I came to a sudden stop in the doorway, the breath catching in my throat.

Even after all this time, seeing them together, spotting any physical contact or intimacy between the two of them, left me spellbound.

Luke stood at the stove, a spatula in hand as he inspected a pancake cooking on the griddle before him. Richard was directly behind him, his arms encircling Luke's waist, his chin resting on Luke's shoulder. He also had his focus on that pancake on the stovetop as if there was nowhere else he'd rather be.

I knew the truth. It wasn't the pancake that captivated Richard.

Both men were still clad in only their underwear. The entire front half of Richard's solid, muscular body was pressed against the back of Luke's, his groin nestled against Luke's ass. Luke had his free arm snaked around behind them, his hand splayed across one of Richard's ass cheeks, holding him close.

Damn, they were beautiful together, obvious passion and devotion and love passing between them as they stood there doing something as mundane as cooking.

Those same emotions washed over me, had me feeling like a part of the moment—a part of them—even from across the room.

Richard turned his head and kissed the side of Luke's neck. In return, Luke raised his arm and laid a hand across Richard's nape. Then they were kissing over Luke's shoulder. A wild, frantic kiss right from the start. Their mouths open, tongues brushing in greeting again and again, the rough, unshaven skin of their chins scraping as they kept the kiss going, Richard slowly, deliberately circling his hips, grinding his body against Luke's ass.

This wasn't their first kiss since they'd come downstairs.

Luke ditched the spatula on the stovetop and spun around, wrapping both arms around Richard's broad shoulders. With that move, Luke's hip hit the handle of the griddle pan, and the entire thing went sliding off the burner and along the front edge of the stovetop. They didn't even notice. They just continued on with that electric kiss, Richard tightening his hold on Luke, pinning him in place against the edge of the stove.

I laughed and started forward.

After rescuing the pan so it didn't fall to the floor or burn one of them, I picked up the spatula and flipped the pancake. It was ruined, the entire surface as black as charcoal. I moved the pan aside and reached around them to click off the burner.

Beside the stove sat two platters, each with a stack of pancakes. One pile looked edible. The other not so much. It was a sloppy mess of charred and uncooked batter that we'd have to throw out.

I laughed again.

Without a moment's hesitation, or a break in their kiss, Richard reached out for me. Wrapping a hand around the back of my neck, he tugged me to him. Only then did he tear himself from Luke's mouth. "Come here."

He brought our mouths together. His lips were warm and wet from the kisses with Luke. He slid his hand around to the side of my neck, then up to cup my cheek, never breaking the contact of our lips as his thumb caressed my skin.

Luke gripped me by the hips and drew me sideways so I stood between them, just how we'd been in the bathroom earlier. Only this time, Luke leaned over my shoulder and ran his lips up the side of Richard's neck, Richard moaning into the kiss. Luke clutched my hips tighter, and Richard tugged me even closer, both of them erotically, blatantly rubbing their bodies against mine, urgency building between us.

Richard kept kissing me, drawing out each swipe of his lips, each brush of his tongue against mine. It was exquisite, beautiful.

When he pulled back, I leaned forward, my body instinctively following his. He gave me several soft, sweet kisses. Then he went right from my lips back to Luke's, kissing him in the same drawn-out, sensual way he'd been doing with me, still cupping and stroking my cheek as he loved on Luke.

He also ended the kiss in that same tender press of his lips, one chaste kiss after another, on Luke's lower lip, then his upper, then his lower again. He held Luke's gaze for a moment. Then he looked to me. "Thank you."

Luke snorted out a laugh.

I asked, "For what?"

"Not giving up on me. I know I can be a controlling ass who worries too much."

That brought out another sputter of laughter from Luke.

I shook my head. "You're worrying too much about how much you're worrying."

"Oh my God!" Luke tipped his head back. "Are you two trying to kill me here?"

That had all of us laughing.

But I wasn't done with this conversation. I waited until Richard met my stare again. "I'm serious. You don't have to worry so much about doing the right thing or saying the right thing. Every moment doesn't have to be perfect. We just have to talk about stuff when there's an issue, and everything will be fine."

"I know. I'm working on it."

"I am too," I said.

Leaning in, he rested his forehead against mine and let out a long breath. I heard the relief in that exhale. "I could still spend all day kissing you."

"Uh-huh. I want more."

"Me too. Tonight?"

I nodded. "Yeah. Tonight."

We held the stare for a lengthy beat. I knew what specifically we'd be doing before the weekend was up. Or at least, I hoped that was what he'd been implying. It was definitely what I'd meant.

He straightened. "We better eat before the food gets cold. It took us forever to cook the pancakes. Luke kept burning them."

Luke's jaw dropped. "It was hardly my fault. You kept distracting me."

"I certainly did not."

"Well, then your hands and mouth did, whether you wanted them to or not."

"Are you saying I have no control? Because I thought we've established I try to have too much control. You're not making a lot of sense here, Luke." Richard grinned at him. "But you're right." He grasped Luke around the waist and dragged him forward in one swift move, then ground his groin against Luke's in a blatant lust-filled motion like he'd been doing when they'd kissed earlier, only this time they were facing each other.

Richard repeated the action once more, the taut muscles of his ass clenching as he rotated his hips. Then he held still, his body tight against Luke's. "Since the day I met you two, I've had no self-control when it comes to wanting you." He gave Luke a last smoldering kiss. Then he let go of him and reached for the stack of more appetizing pancakes. "Now let's eat, and then we'll go over Matthew's questions for today." He started for the table they'd set earlier, leaving Luke standing there, panting, the bulge under his underwear impossible to miss.

I threw a pointed look at the stretched fabric. "You shouldn't tease him."

"Yeah." He gulped down a hard swallow. "When the fuck will I learn that?" Choking out a laugh, he shook his head, then went for the bowl of fruit and the syrup sitting beside the stove. Before heading to the table, he paused at my side. His blue eyes held a more serious note as he whispered, "Those were some unbelievable kisses."

I ran the tips of two fingers over my lips. "Yeah."

"It was different, like it used to be."

"It was."

"It seems like he's really letting it go."

"It does." I drew in a frustrated breath but held back on saying more.

Luke turned toward me. "What?"

"Nothing. You're right. It was great."

"I told you. He just needed some time."

"Yeah. I guess so."

He went to join Richard at the table.

It was hard to admit, even if only to myself, but despite what those kisses had been like, something was still wrong.

Something very wrong.

I just couldn't get the words out, couldn't make myself say it to Luke.

There'd been a noticeable difference in both of them since that day several months earlier when I hadn't exactly been truthful about not wanting Richard to fist me in bed. Despite talking it over on several occasions, Richard admitted that moment still left him feeling uneasy when it came to intimate contact with me. He'd promised me that nothing had changed between us. That we just needed some time, that *he* needed time and distance from that moment.

The one good thing was that he hadn't altogether stopped touching me. In fact, sometimes he seemed to go out of his way to reach out for me, offer a caress or a kiss. It was like he wouldn't allow himself to put too much distance between us.

I appreciated that, but...

There was still one moment when everything about his touch—both of their touches—felt wrong: in bed.

I could see it in their eyes, feel it in the brush of their lips, the little hesitations, the clasp of their hands as if they were holding back. They were afraid they'd do something I didn't want, afraid they'd hurt me.

I had done that to us. By letting them think I wanted something I didn't, I'd broken a part of us that I'd come to rely on more than I realized.

Which left me aching for more of their touches, for them to grab hold of me and kiss me, touch me, fuck me with that same passionate intensity they'd had since the day I met them, like they couldn't wait to get inside me and make us both feel so damn good.

I tried repeatedly to show them how much I wanted that—wanted them. I wasn't sure what else I could do to fix things for us. But I knew there had to be a way, something I'd missed, something I hadn't tried or said yet.

And I was going to find it.

Because everything was going to be okay between the three of us. More than okay. I wouldn't accept anything else.

Chapter Three

"Here, put these gloves on. They might try to bite, even at this age."

I took the padded gloves from Dr. Vega and slipped them on. "Where do you want me?"

"By the exam table. I'll put the carrier right on top, and we'll take them out one at a time and get a look at what we've got."

"Okay."

Dr. Vega set a towel-lined box on one end of the stainless-steel exam table and the carrier with his newest residents on the other side. He removed the first little guy from the crate.

The litter of red fox kits had been brought to Windtree Wildlife Rehabilitation Center a few minutes earlier by a park ranger who'd live-trapped the animals. Windtree was a nonprofit center that cared for injured and orphaned wildlife from the surrounding area, including Majestic Falls State Park, one of the largest state parks in the Midwestern US.

Located southwest of the park, the wildlife center took in over three thousand animals per year, releasing more than seventy percent back into the wilderness. The thirty percent that couldn't be returned to their homes in the wild due to an injury or the incapacity to care for themselves became education ambassadors, helping the center's volunteers teach the public about the importance of wildlife and conservation efforts.

With spring well underway and the local wildlife population more active after the long winter months, Windtree was currently in their busy season.

Dr. Vega—or Alex, as he'd asked me to call him—had been telling me about the center's setup and its volunteer program when the park ranger shuffled in with the dog carrier full of mewling, squirming fox kits.

"Perfect timing," Alex had said to me. "I like seeing anyone I'm interviewing work with the animals. That okay with you?"

"Definitely."

"You did some hands-on workshops during your wildlife course at the school, right?"

"Yeah."

"They had you get a rabies vaccine?"

"Yep. I'm all set there."

"All right." He stood. "Let's go check out some foxes."

With that sentence and a smile of encouragement from Alex, I couldn't have been more excited by the chance to show him that I could handle the job. I'd spent the past couple of weeks studying as much as I could about the native animals the center typically took in, as well as basic wildlife emergency procedures. I was ready for this.

Alex flipped the first fox kit onto its back. "This one's a female." He righted her and inspected her legs by feeling down the length of each. "She doesn't appear to have any swelling or broken bones. No signs of trauma. Here. Feel the belly." He handed her to me. "What do you think?"

"She's too thin."

"Right. And feel along her spine. She's not been eating enough lately." He reached over and pinched the skin on her back. It stuck together for a second or two before slowly lowering to her body.

"She's dehydrated," I said.

"Yeah. They've definitely been on their own for too long. It's possible that fox the ranger said he found dead along the road the other day was their mother."

"She was hit by a car?"

"He thought so. It was clear she'd been nursing, so he went back today to see if he could spot the den or maybe hear these little guys."

"Any sign of the father? Sometimes they'll care for the kits if the mother dies."

"That's right." He sounded impressed. "If they're far enough along on solid foods. I'm guessing his instincts told him these guys weren't, though." He had me turn the kit his way. He checked her face and ears. "She appears to be five or six weeks old. You know how I can tell that?"

He hadn't examined the kit's teeth yet, so I said, "Well, her eyes and ears are open, and the muzzle is beginning to lengthen. And the fur color is starting to change."

"Right. Anything else?"

"The eye color."

"Exactly. They start out blue and turn golden-brown as they age." He retrieved the kit from me and took a look inside her mouth. "You can also tell by the eruption of her teeth." He nodded. "Yeah, I'm guessing about five weeks, maybe slightly older." He set the kit into the box and pulled another one out of the carrier. This one was squirming more as he started the exam. "We've got another female."

He passed her to me. She was snorting and growling, trying to bite my thumb, but the gloves were specially lined. Her teeth couldn't puncture them. "She sure is a feisty little thing."

He laughed. "Yeah. She looks as thin as the other, but she's got some serious fight left in her. That's a good sign."

"Will they be okay?"

"Should be. They don't seem too bad off. They're bright and alert and responsive. No sign of a respiratory infection. I think we got them soon enough. We'll give them subcutaneous fluids today and start bottle-feeding them, then see how far along they are in eating solids. They should bounce back pretty quickly."

"Will you be able to release them at some point?"

"That'll be the plan. We'll keep them until they're older and have been on solid food for quite a while. It's good that there's several of them. Makes it less likely that they'll imprint on us. We'll limit human contact as much as we can as they grow. Then after they're big enough, and we've made certain they can catch their own food, we'll release them back into the wild. Do you know how we can tell a red fox from a coyote or a gray fox? They all look pretty similar before the adult color of the coat starts coming in."

"The tail," I said. "Red foxes have the white tip."

Alex nodded, looking pleased.

Before he moved to put her in the box with the other kit, I patted the top of her head. "It'll be okay, little one."

"Yeah, she'll be fine." Alex smiled at me. Every time he did that, his eyes lit up with genuine delight. He had a thoughtful gentleness to him that seemed to have many of the animals at Windtree at ease around him.

When we finished the intake exam on the kits, Alex got them situated with a volunteer who started them on fluids, and we moved on to another room lined with plastic crates and covered clothes hampers. "This is our recovery room for birds and owls." He introduced me to the various feathered residents at the center and asked me to help him do some physical therapy on one of his patients.

We worked together for another half hour. Then he finished giving me a full tour of the place, including the outdoor pens and enclosures where they kept the larger animals and the ones closer to release. Windtree currently housed two older foxes, several opossums, squirrels, minks, ducks, a red-tailed hawk, a pair of mourning doves, and even a bald eagle, among many others.

When another volunteer arrived for their shift, Alex suggested I get a better look around on my own while he discussed a case with the volunteer.

After walking through the treatment rooms, surgical area, and the interior kennels, I exited into the front offices. We'd been talking there at his desk before the ranger arrived. Similar to many of the other areas inside the facility, the walls were lined with stacked cages that housed all types of injured and recovering wildlife. As Alex had mentioned earlier, the center was in desperate need of an expansion, as well as updated office equipment.

It was clear from the way Alex had talked that the center didn't have the necessary money to do the expansion or to purchase the upgraded computers. He said the majority of their funds were spent on medical equipment and related supplies for animal care, as well as the salaries for the staff who were responsible for running the clinic.

He and one other staff member were currently the only full-time employees at the center. There were also four part-time support workers, but the rest of the people who helped out were volunteers, including Alex's wife and son. Alex had asked me to come in for an interview on a Sunday because he had more volunteer help on the weekends and could take the time to talk with me.

I returned to wait near his desk in the corner of the room. Four cages were situated beside the desk, each housing an injured squirrel. Stacked on the surface of his desk were research texts, medical supplies still in their boxes, various equipment used for capturing wildlife, and an open map of the park marked with hand-drawn gridlines. A nameplate sat on top of the books. It read: *Alejandro Vega, DVM, Wildlife Veterinarian.*

Beside the books were several framed pictures of what appeared to be his family. On the wall behind the desk hung photos of various animals at the clinic, as well as outdoor shots of wildlife in the park.

One of the pictures featured a white-tailed deer. A substantial buck drinking from the edge of a river. The setting sun was ablaze behind the deer, casting swaths of golden light across the wide expanse of hemlock trees along the river. The sunlight turned the ripples of the water a brilliant shade of orange. Several yards from the deer sat a dock lined with wooden posts. It looked like the exact spot where I had stood years earlier.

I'd been thirteen the last time I was at Majestic Falls State Park, and I hadn't been back since. Until today.

I stepped closer to get a better view of the photo. It *was* the same dock. I wasn't sure how I knew, but I did.

I squeezed my eyes shut, blocking out the picture before me—and the memories it brought back. I didn't want to think about that day. Or the horribleness that followed.

"My dad took those," came a young voice from behind me.

I turned toward the kid. He was about twelve. He carried a gray-and-white pet rabbit in his arms.

I gestured toward the picture. "He's a great photographer."

The boy nodded. "He loves taking pictures of the park and all the wildlife. Are you the new intern?"

"Not sure yet. I'm here for an interview today."

The kid gave another nod.

"Is Alex your dad?"

"Yeah."

"Your name's Tomas, right?"

The kid took a step forward. "Dad talked about me?"

"Sure. He said you're a big help around here, and this year when you head back to school in the fall, he's really going to need someone to fill in for you."

Tomas's face brightened for a moment. Then he focused on the rabbit in his arms. "We live next door. Usually my mom comes to help too, but she's gonna have a baby in a few weeks. She's gotta rest." He petted the bunny along its side.

"Is that your rabbit?"

"Uh-huh. Dad promised to help trim her toenails today. They grow super fast."

"What's her name?"

"Maggie."

I moved in closer and raised my hand. "Can I?"

"Sure. She's a real sweetheart."

I stroked the rabbit's fur. "Wow. That's the softest animal I've ever petted."

"I know, right?" He regarded me with curiosity. "You've never pet a rabbit before?"

"Nah. I volunteer at a humane society, but they mostly take in dogs and cats. How long have you had her?"

"Three years. My dad found her in the park. He says people from the city are always coming to Majestic Falls and dropping off animals they don't want anymore. They leave them along the river, thinking they'll be okay because there's fresh water there and lots of plants and other animals. But Dad said a pet rabbit would never survive long out there on its own. They're different than wild rabbits."

"So he gave her to you?"

"He asked me if I'd take care of her. He says that when you take in a sick or homeless animal, you're responsible for them for the rest of their lives and you have to take that responsibility as seriously as you would your own life."

"He's pretty smart."

Tomas's face lit up again. "He is."

The front door of the center opened, and a very pregnant woman entered. She had long dark hair pulled back in a high ponytail. She stood an inch or two shorter than her son and was petite in every way, except for the large, round belly. She stepped up to Tomas. "You forgot her toenail clippers." She gave them to him.

"Thanks." He showed me the clippers. "These work best on her nails."

His mom smiled at me. "Are you here about the intern position?"

"Yeah, I'm Matthew Stewart."

"Natalie Vega."

Tomas pointed at her. "This is my mom."

We shook hands. "It's nice to meet you."

"You too." She rested a hand on top of her belly and slid her other arm around her son's shoulders. "I hope Tomas isn't keeping you from something. When he gets to talking about his animals, he tends to go on and on." She shot a look his way. "And on and on. Just like his father."

"Not at all," I said. "He was nice enough to introduce me to Maggie."

She gave the rabbit a scratch between her flattened ears. "One of his many critters."

"You have more?" I asked.

"Yeah. I've got a dog, a turtle, a hamster, a guinea pig, and a goat. Oh, and a potbellied pig."

"Wow. That must be a lot of work."

He shrugged. "It's not bad. It's totally worth it."

"It is," his mom said as she ran her fingers through Tomas's hair above his ear. "Listen, hon, I've got to get back before your dad catches me walking around and gives me another lecture about staying off my feet."

"Yeah. Sorry I forgot the clippers."

"It's okay. Despite what your dad says, I do need the exercise." She looked to me. "It was nice to meet you, Matthew. I hope it works out if you want the job."

"Thank you."

She left, and Tomas laughed as soon as the door was shut behind her. "Why does she always do that?"

"Do what?"

"Put stuff like that off on my dad. Like he's the only one who's worried."

Before I could think of anything to say, the door to the back rooms opened and Alex entered the office area. "All done." He stopped beside his son. "Sorry, Tomas. We're not quite finished with our interview. Why don't you take Maggie back to one of the exam rooms to wait? I'll wrap up here and then we can work on her nails after that."

"Okay." Tomas headed for the hall door.

I called after him, "It was nice to meet you. And Maggie."

He smiled back at me. "Yeah, you too."

After he left, Alex stared off at the closed door separating the office area from the rest of the rehab center.

"He's a great kid," I said.

"He is." Alex turned to me. "You have kids?"

"No." But that reminded me of what I hadn't told him yet, what I'd made myself say to every person who'd already interviewed me for the other internships where I'd applied.

Alex considered me as if he knew I had something important to tell him. Maybe he got that I needed a minute to bring it up. He gestured to the chair opposite his desk. "Why don't we pick up where we left off before the ranger got here?"

"All right." I had a seat, and he did the same across from me.

He asked me a few more standard interview-style questions. Then he sat back in his chair. "Thanks again for the help with the fox kits and the physical therapy. We're pretty busy here. You can see why we need to hire someone."

"It doesn't seem like it'll be boring, that's for sure."

"I'm glad you see it that way. I deal with a new challenge practically every day. As I mentioned before, the intern position will include some paperwork, answering phone calls, but I guarantee you'll get to work with all kinds of animals, and you'll get to assist me with surgeries, so it should be some great experience. Definitely more diverse than what you'd get at a regular animal clinic in the city." He drummed a closed fist on the desk as if nervous to ask me the next question. "So what do you think?"

"I really like the work you're doing here. I'd love to be a part of it."

"Good." He smiled, that genuine delight lighting up his face again. Then he grew quiet, examining me as if he was thinking something over. "You're done with school for this semester?"

"Yeah. Classes finished a week ago."

"You could start anytime?"

"Whenever you'd need me."

"All right." He leaned forward, elbows propped on the desk. "Not making any promises here, but the center is on the short list for a grant that will allow us to add another full-time staff member. If you did get the internship, and you liked working here, it could turn into a regular position after your schooling ends. Would that be something that might interest you?"

"Based on what I've seen so far, yeah, I really think so."

"Good deal." He looked over my résumé once more. "So you had that one class on wildlife care. Anything else?"

"Not yet. I'd liked to take the more advanced one next year. Neither class is a requirement for my program, but I thought they sounded fascinating."

"That's a good sign. If you were to work here after you graduate, would you be willing to go to some additional training specifically on wildlife rehab? The cost would be covered by the grant."

"Definitely. I'd love that."

"Okay. Are there any other questions you have for me? Or is there anything else you'd like me to know about you?"

I drew in a deep breath. "Yeah, actually." I had said the same thing at each of the other interviews I'd gone on, but somehow it wasn't getting any easier to tell someone. Not with a job this amazing on the line.

"It's something very personal, but I'd like you to know before you consider me for the job. In case there's any reason it would be an issue for you or your staff. I want to work in an environment where I can feel comfortable being myself, where I don't have to monitor my words when I talk about my life."

Alex sat back and folded his hands over his stomach. He smiled and tipped his head my way. "Okay. I like what you're saying so far. Go on."

He was the only one who'd reacted that way. Every other person had stiffened and gaped at me with trepidation like they were watching me come unhinged. Alex just kept the grin going.

I chewed on my lower lip and then made myself stop the nervous habit. "I'm in a relationship with two people. Two men. We all live together. They're both my partners, and they are the same with each other. All three of us are in the relationship together." I stopped and kept my focus on him. I had nothing to be ashamed of. I was proud of the three of us, and I didn't want to work for a boss who wouldn't, at the very least, respect that my private life was my own business, and definitely not for someone who'd think less of me for it and then treat me that way.

He pointed at one of the cages beside us that held a single squirrel. "See him? A hiker found him in the middle of the road five days ago. He had a broken leg, a severe cut along his back. The park is loaded with eastern gray squirrels like him. Some people would say that it wasn't worth the time or money to help him, that he's vermin and I should've put him out of his misery and been done with it." He watched me for a moment. "What do you think about that?"

From inside the cage, the squirrel stared back at me, eyes wide as he gnawed on a walnut shell that he held between his two front feet. "I think if he could communicate with us, he'd say he just wants a chance to survive. It's what any living creature would want. No matter how many of his kind there are."

Alex smiled again. "That's the kind of answer I care about. Seems to me a person who can love two people the way you described, without jealousy or resentment, might have exactly the right kind of compassion to do this job well."

I swallowed down the flood of emotion, trying to keep it from seeping into my voice as I said, "Thank you."

He nodded. "Besides, what you do in your personal life is no one's business but your own. If you end up working for me, and any of the staff or volunteers here at the center don't get that, or they don't treat you with the respect and courtesy you deserve, then they won't be working here much longer." He looked to one of the framed pictures on his desk. I couldn't see who was featured in the photo. "And just so you know, I'm a big supporter of gay rights, and not only because I'm fairly sure my son is gay." His eyes lit up again as he kept his focus on the picture. Then he looked my way. "But because I strongly believe in equality. For everyone."

I smiled back at him.

He stood. "Now that we have that settled, we have a release scheduled for today. If you don't mind hanging around while I help Tomas with his rabbit, you could come along and give me a hand with the release afterward."

"I'd love that." I got up as well. He towered over me, but I didn't feel small next to him.

Three hours later, I couldn't contain my excitement as I drove

Richard's car along one of the main roads through Majestic Falls State Park, captivated by the beauty that surrounded me. The lush, green, forest-covered hills, golden rock formations, cliffs, gorges, and waterfalls. The rushing water of Windtree River and all its tributaries. It was one of the most amazing places I'd ever been, and I wanted to work at Windtree Rehab Center more than any of the other facilities where I'd applied.

Alex had said there were a few more applicants he had to interview before a final decision was made, but I had a really good feeling about this one.

As I drove toward the northern exit of the park, I spotted Windtree River again where it ran along the road. A flock of mallard ducks dotted the surface, the iconic brilliant green heads of the males glowing in the sunlight. The classic piercing quacks of the females echoed in the air. I was transfixed by the sights and sounds.

Then the memories I'd been trying to keep at bay all day slammed into me without warning. I gripped the steering wheel tighter and did my best to stay focused on the road ahead.

It would be weird to work there, at least at first. I knew that from the moment I'd seen the position listed on my school's website as a possible internship.

But I wasn't about to let anything ruin this experience for me. Especially not *him*.

He'd already done enough damage.

He still was in some ways.

He was part of the reason Luke and Richard and I were struggling.

He was part of the reason I was afraid to show them something I'd hidden from them in our house.

Because what I hadn't wanted to see before now was that deep down, in a place I tried to ignore most of the time, I was afraid of losing them. Terrified.

Which meant... I had to find a way to let this go. Or else I'd spend the rest of my life living with that fear.

Chapter Four

The house sat still and quiet as I stepped inside. Before I got the door shut, Trixie was barreling down the hall toward me. She skidded to a stop in front of me.

"Hey, baby girl. Did you have a good day?"

As usual, her tail wagged with such vigor I thought she might topple over at any second. I crouched down and gave her some love behind her ears. In response, she flopped onto her back so I could rub her belly.

"You here all by yourself? Where's Luke?"

She immediately scrambled to her feet and thumped up the stairs, her long limbs flailing as she made her way. She was the sweetest and smartest dog I'd ever met, but she was also the most uncoordinated. I laughed as I trailed up after her.

The hall was as dark and silent as the downstairs had been. Sometimes when I headed up alone like that, with the house quiet all around me, I was right back to the night Richard had given us a tour of the place when we'd first moved in with him. Following him up those stairs, I'd been both excited and scared.

It wasn't that I didn't trust him or Luke—although I probably shouldn't have since I barely knew either of them, and what I did know from previous experience was how hurt I could get trusting the wrong man—but with Richard and Luke, the anxiety hadn't come from being afraid of them or what they might do to me. It was about being scared I'd say or do something that would put an end to whatever was building between us.

I'd known from that first night at the Haven that they were different, that *we* were different together. They'd always been the only people in my life I'd ever felt completely comfortable being myself around. I relied on that now even more.

I found Trixie waiting in the open doorway of Luke's office. Luke sat at his desk, working, his complete concentration on the computer screen before him. He hadn't shaved, and the dark stubble, ripped jeans, and tight black T-shirt he wore gave him a rugged bad-boy look. Like he belonged on a Harley instead of in front of a laptop. Incredibly enticing. And sexy as hell.

He'd been assigned a new high-profile programming project at the IT consulting firm where he worked, and it had been kicking his ass lately, as he described it. There were a number of new twentysomething employees in his department, and I got the impression that, at thirty-five, he was starting to feel old and outdated. He'd even signed up for some online training to get up to speed on a new programming language.

I hated that he felt inadequate in any way.

He was so focused on his laptop, he didn't hear me approach. I laid both hands on his shoulders and began working my fingers and thumbs over his muscles. He groaned in pleasure and tilted his head back, his eyes closing. "God, that feels good." He opened his eyes and beamed up at me. "Hey."

"Hey."

He held my stare for several beats, his expression full of hunger and longing. There'd always been an intensity to the way he looked at Richard and me, the way those blue eyes took in the sight of us as if we were the only two people in the world and that single moment between us was all that mattered to him.

He sighed. "Damn, you have the right touch." His eyelids fell shut once more as I continued the massage, digging my fingers in deeper. His muscles were incredibly tight and stiff.

"You're working too hard. You need to take some time off soon."

He grunted, and I wasn't sure if that was in agreement or not.

"Richard still at his meeting?" I asked.

"Yeah. Said he wouldn't be too long."

Richard had been putting in as many extra hours as Luke lately. He'd cut back on his investment business months ago and instead he'd been focusing nearly all his time on the renovations to a famous estate he'd purchased. The remodeling project had resulted in the Griff Harrison Community Center, which had officially opened a few weeks ago, but there were still a lot of details Richard wanted to make certain were handled correctly.

I dipped my head and kissed the spot where Luke's neck met his shoulder, brushing my lips along his flesh to aid in easing his tension. "You never told me," I said as I switched to his other side, offering another kiss. Then another. "How did things go with the new guy last week?"

He groaned again, this time the sound containing far more frustration. "He's such a total dick. He thinks he's the only one who knows anything about object-oriented programming."

I straightened and kept my fingers moving over him. "I bet he's just really nervous. I mean, this is his first job out of college, right?"

"Yeah."

"You're a senior programmer. He might be trying to impress you, show you that he's not as green as you think."

Luke opened his eyes and tilted his head back to study me. "How do you always do that?"

"Do what?"

"See the good in people. See things from their perspective."

"You don't think it's naive?"

"I guess it can be. But it seems way healthier than the alternative. I hadn't thought about him being nervous. He just comes across as an arrogant jerk."

I laughed. "I might not be right about him. I'm just saying give him a chance. He might actually be intimidated by you and even look up to you and that makes him overcompensate."

"Maybe. I'll keep that in mind." He considered me again. His voice warmed as he said, "The world would be a hell of a lot better place if everyone thought the way you do, if everyone saw things the way you do."

That meant a lot coming from him. He could be cynical sometimes, sarcastic about stuff like this. "Thanks."

He closed his eyes as I worked the tension from his shoulders again. Another ten seconds of the massage, and his eyes shot open. "Wait." He sat up with a start and turned to face me. "How'd the interview go?"

"Fantastic."

"Yeah?" He got up from the chair and perched his ass on the desk beside his laptop, propping his feet on the seat of the chair. "What'd they say?"

Before I could reply, the front door opened downstairs.

Luke held up a hand. "Might as well hold that thought."

I laughed. "Yeah."

A few seconds later, Richard came barreling up the stairs. He didn't hesitate at the office door. He came up behind me, wrapped his arms around my chest, and spoke against my ear. "How'd it go?"

I laughed more as I faced him. Leaning against Luke's leg, I rested my forearm on his thigh. "It was great."

"Yeah?"

"You should've seen it. The park and the center were both amazing. I really want to do my internship there even more now, but I won't know anything for at least a week, maybe two. There are other people he's meeting with."

Richard caught my chin and lifted my head. "I've got a good feeling about this one."

"Me too. I really want this to work out. And not just because I need an internship lined up before the fall semester. I just think it's so neat how they're helping all these animals that have no one else looking after them. I got to touch a fox today."

Richard's expression momentarily fell, but he dialed back the reaction and didn't say anything. I knew this was hard for him. He thought working at a wildlife rehab center would be far riskier than the domesticated animal clinics where I'd also applied.

I tipped my head forward until he looked my way again. "It wasn't dangerous. She was just a baby. I wore special gloves, and the rabies vaccine I had before is still good."

He nodded.

Luke asked, "Was she hurt?"

"No. It was a litter of orphaned kits. They think the mom died. They're about five weeks old."

"How small?" he asked.

I showed him the size with my hands.

"Really? That's so cool."

"It was. I also got to help with some physical therapy on a northern saw-whet owl."

Luke looked impressed. "An owl? Sweet."

"She had a broken wing that had to be kept wrapped for weeks. Now she needs therapy so she can expand the wing all the way out again."

"What happened to her?" Richard asked.

"They weren't sure. Maybe hit by a car. A park ranger found her along one of the main roads through the park. Oh, and I also got to help the vet release a peregrine falcon back into the wild. You should've seen him fly off. I could feel the rush of freedom as he spread his wings. It was incredible." I couldn't hold back my excitement. My body vibrated with it.

Richard eyed me with a pleased expression. "I'm glad it went well."

"He was just so cool. I really liked him, and I liked everything he had to say about the center and the job."

"The falcon talked to you?" Luke teased.

I nudged him in the side. "No. Dr. Vega, the vet who runs the place. His name's Alex. He's smart and compassionate and he knows so much about caring for wildlife." I shrugged, trying to play down my next words but knowing full well how they were going to sound. "He was really nice when I told him about the three of us."

Luke straightened, his entire body tensing instantly. "You told him? About us?"

I nodded.

He kept gaping at me, then gestured between the three of us. "About... our relationship?"

I nodded again.

"Why?" He dropped his feet from the chair to the floor and folded his arms across his chest. "It's no one's business but ours."

Luke had always been a private person. He'd spent years hiding from everyone, keeping secrets about nearly everything in his life. The fact that his initial instinct was still to hold back the truth about us made me uneasy. Especially about sharing with him what I'd hidden in the bottom drawer of our bathroom vanity. There was no way Luke was ever going to understand.

I opened my mouth to explain why I'd told Alex anything about us, but nothing came out. My chest grew heavy. I hadn't had such a panicked reaction to what they'd think about me, or something I wanted, for such a long time. It felt like a piece of my old life prior to meeting them was slipping back into place, and that frightened me. Was I trying to force something that I should leave alone?

Without a word, Richard took my hand and led me to the couch on the opposite side of the office. He didn't say anything as we sat beside each other. He just studied me with that customary thoughtful concern locked on his face.

I shook my head, wanting them to drop the whole thing, but instead I said, "I don't want to lie to the people I work with."

He laid a hand across the back of my neck. "I get that. But you're not lying if you don't tell people something like this. Especially people you work with. Not everyone is going to be as tolerant as we'd like or treat you with the respect you deserve. Luke was right. It really is none of their business."

"But you tell everyone now."

"I do. Because it didn't feel right for me not to. We each have to make our own call on this. If you feel uneasy keeping our relationship to yourself at work, then you did the right thing."

"Did I?" I pointed to Luke, who was still leaning back against the desk with his arms braced across his chest, his lips pursed, brow furrowed. "I freaked him out again."

Richard chuckled. "He's just processing. Give him a minute. He hasn't gone on a job interview since before he stopped hiding. It's a new world for him."

Luke rolled his eyes. "I can hear you, you know? I'm not in a coma." He breathed deep, then uncrossed his arms and came forward to kneel before me. "It's not that I want to keep our relationship a secret from anyone. I just thought it was a weird thing to bring up at a first interview. What if the guy was an ass about it? What if he doesn't want to give you the job because of this?"

"That's just the thing. If he was a jerk about it, then I don't want to work there."

"That makes sense. But you need an internship for school, and you've got to get one this summer or you'll never get enough hours in to graduate with your class next year. I don't want people discriminating against you and fucking up your future over this, over *us*. I couldn't stand that." His jaw clenched.

"I'd rather go an extra semester, even an extra year, than work for someone like that."

A slow smile formed at the corners of his lips. "I know you would." He settled his hands on my thighs. "I'm glad you said something, then. And I'm glad he was cool with it."

"Me too," Richard added. "Sounds like the entire thing went really well."

"Yeah." My voice wavered with my next words. "My hopes are really up about this."

Richard cupped my face in one hand and encouraged me to look his way. "I know."

I leaned into his touch. "I just loved being there so much. It felt like such a good fit for me, and I'd get some really amazing experience. They had hawks and swans and red and gray squirrels and bats and turtles, and Alex has this really neat kid who helps out there." I was rambling, but Luke and Richard were just grinning at me, so it was okay. "I think Alex and his family liked me."

Luke ran his warm hands up my thighs. "Who wouldn't?"

Richard stroked the back of my neck again. "Exactly."

"See?" Luke pointed at me. "I told you there was a reason those other jobs didn't work out. You're meant to get this one."

"Maybe."

Richard slid his hand from my nape and let it fall to his lap. "It's a long drive every day."

"It only took forty-five minutes."

"Each way. That's a lot of time away from your schoolwork come this fall."

"It'll be worth it."

He paused for several seconds. "You'll be working around a lot of wild animals there."

"Yeah." I waited for him to press the issue of how much more unpredictable wildlife could be and the inherit risks in the job, but he didn't say anything about that. He placed his hand on my thigh next to Luke's. "I'm very proud of you, Matthew."

"Ditto," Luke added.

I laid a hand over both of theirs. "Thank you. For everything. I never could've—"

"Nope." Luke shook his head. "You did this, kid. Not us."

"He's right."

I smiled at them in thanks.

Richard gripped my thigh tighter. Those green eyes studied me, and he visibly swallowed as if he were struggling with something.

"What?" I asked.

"This morning in the bathroom and in the kitchen... That meant a lot to me."

I nodded. "Me too."

"Me three."

We turned to Luke.

"What?" he asked, clearly baffled by us.

Richard's brows rose. "We're being serious here."

"I know." Luke tossed his head back and let out an exaggerated sigh. "God, you two are such drama queens. I really don't know what to do with you sometimes."

Richard snorted out a laugh. "You're saying we're the ones who bring all the drama into this relationship?"

"Oh, yeah, definitely. Before I met you two, my life was sailing along real calm and steady." He made a slow sweeping gesture. "Not an ounce of drama."

"No, just your psycho dad having you followed every second of your life, installing listening devices in your apartment, and then threatening the three of us before trying to kill you. No big deal."

I burst out laughing. Richard turned to me. He ran his thumb over my lower lip, his complete focus on my mouth. "Luke thinks he's hilarious. What are we going to do with him, Matthew?"

I wanted to make a joke of it because teasing Luke had become one of my favorite pastimes, but I needed something else right then.

And with the way Richard watched me, touched me, heady anticipation rolling off him in waves, I got that he did too. So I simply said, "Love him forever."

"Hell yeah, we will." He kept tracing my lip with his thumb.

No one said another word for several breaths. Then Luke spoke, his tone carrying far more significance this time. "Tell him, Matthew."

Richard's eyes searched mine. "Tell me what?"

Chapter Five

I opened my mouth to answer him, but nothing came out. Kissing him, touching either of them, had always been the easy part for us. To know that had shifted to be one of the aspects of our relationship that we were struggling with—along with the fact that I was having trouble sharing how I felt with them—had my heart aching in a way I'd never known possible before.

I blurted out, "I want you to want me again."

As soon as the words were past my lips, Richard's face held the same stunned pain as the night I'd flinched from him. "I do, Matthew. God, so much."

He slid forward along the couch, and I did the same. He enveloped me in his arms and kissed me with soft reverence and affection that immediately eased the ache in my heart.

I whispered against his lips, "Kiss me again. And again. And again."

He did, his tongue repeatedly sweeping out to meet mine.

Clasping his head in both hands, I relished the slow, sensual, passionate kiss like it was the first time.

He smelled of his usual cologne, a sharp, woodsy scent that sent me back to that first night he'd sat at our table in the Haven. I breathed in the scent, letting it wash over me as the kiss became something far more intense.

With his arms circling my waist, he drew me closer, kissed me deeper. An urgent, restless need built in his touch that I hadn't felt in months. I wanted more of that fervent contact. So much more. I wound my arms around him and brought our lips together again, offering him the same passion and desire he was showing me.

His hands settled at my lower back, and he hauled me against him. Then he swept his warm lips down the side of my neck, pausing at the base of my throat. "I love you, Matthew." His voice was raw with emotion. "I love you so damn much." He held me tighter, burying his face in the crook of my neck. His shoulders shook, and his next breath hitched around a strangled, hoarse cry.

"Richard?" I'd never seen or felt him this vulnerable. Not even the night we thought Luke had gone to the Haven to be with another man.

When he still said nothing, just kept a tight hold on me, I laid a hand at the back of his head and looked Luke's way. He was eyeing Richard with a mix of concern and panic. Then he met my stare, and the panic vanished. He mouthed: *Talk to him.*

I ran my fingers through the back of Richard's hair as I whispered, "Do you know how sorry I am?"

He lifted his head. His eyes were moist with unshed tears, making the green of his irises darker, almost emerald. "God, I am too."

"I wish I could take back that night."

"I know. I know you do, but you don't have to. We've talked about it. Everything's okay."

"It doesn't feel okay."

"It is." Despite those two words, he shook his head. "It's killing me to think you don't get it."

"Get what?"

"I want to be with you. More than you'll ever know."

"Then what's wrong? Why are you still hesitating?"

He opened his mouth to speak but stopped short. So very unlike him. He tried again. "I'm afraid."

"You won't hurt me." I held his face until he looked me in the eyes again. "You won't hurt me. And I promise I'll be honest with you. Always."

He lowered his gaze as if thinking that through. Then he exhaled a long breath. "You're right. I won't hurt you. And I trust you. Completely." He tugged me forward again.

With the press of his mouth to mine, I tried to let the worry and fear drain away. We'd been good at this part. We could be again.

I pushed my weight against him until he lay on his back on the couch. I straddled him, and we continued with those amazing kisses. Long, slow, deep meetings of our mouths that brought to life a desire I'd only ever known with him and Luke. Arousal grew heavy in every part of me. I slid my groin along his body, needing to feel that sexual, lustful connection between us.

With sudden urgency, he thrust up under me.

Yes! There it was. That primal need I'd been dying to feel from him. I matched it with my own movements over him.

When I thought I might explode from that contact alone, he

encouraged me to sit up. He unbuttoned my dress shirt and jerked it off and onto the floor, then followed with my undershirt. I did the same for him. As soon as his torso was bare, he lay back down and swept his palms along my body from my lower abs up over my pecs, taking his time, loving me with that sweet simple stroke of hands over flesh. When he made the trip back down my body, he undid my belt buckle, then the front of my pants. He threw the fabric open as if he couldn't wait another second to feel more of my skin. But he must've also felt the same about kissing me. He gave up on the pants and flung back into the kiss, tugging me even closer this time.

Luke chuckled. "Come here, kid." He hauled me off the couch.

"No." Richard sat up in a rush. "Come back." He grabbed my hand and tried to pull me back down to him.

Luke laughed more. "Just hang on a second, big guy. I'm gonna get the rest of his clothes off."

"Yeah, yeah, you do that. But make it fast." He draped one arm across the back of the couch as he swept his gaze up and down my body, devouring the sight of me, and Luke hadn't even gotten started on the rest of my clothes yet. "Damn, you're gorgeous, Matthew."

"He is." From where Luke stood behind me, he reached around my hips and gradually lowered my pants down my legs, teasing both me and Richard with his unhurried movements. When my pants were at my knees, he took the time to cup my ass, then skimmed his palms along the backs of my bare thighs before making his way down the rest of my body. He let my pants gather at my ankles, then repeated the entire action with my underwear, slowly, erotically stripping away the fabric, sending goose bumps racing over my flesh and making the hair on my legs stand up. Kneeling behind me, he kissed one bare ass cheek, then the other, his hands sweeping up the front of my thighs.

Richard watched my every reaction to Luke's touch. "He's good at that, isn't he?"

"Which part?"

"Getting us naked. The way he makes you feel about your body when he takes your clothes off, it's like there's nothing in the world— no one else—he'd rather be touching."

"Yeah. It's like—" My breath caught as Luke ran his tongue down the crack of my ass right as he brought his hand around to fondle my dick. He cupped and stroked my length, intensifying my hard-on. "It's like he's worshipping me, like he's never experienced anyone like me before."

Richard nodded. "That's how I knew in the beginning."

"Knew what?"

"That he was special. Do you know how lucky we are? He could've run from us after that first night, could've walked out of the Haven and never looked back. It's what his brain was telling him to do."

"But it wasn't what he really wanted. He wanted us."

Richard grinned up at me. "Yeah, he did."

Luke let go of me and worked my pants and underwear over my ankles and feet. He got up to stand behind me, the heavy bulge of his erection insistent at the top of my ass. "Would you two just shut the hell up and fuck already?"

The grin grew on Richard's face. "We're embarrassing him."

I shook my head. "We're turning him on with all the talking. I can feel how hard he is."

Richard raised a brow. "Talking is turning Luke on?"

"Uh-huh. He loves it when we talk before sex."

That had Richard laughing. He held out a hand for me, then brought me back down onto him so I was straddling his thighs. "You know what else he loves?"

"What?"

He gripped my ass and slid me up his body until we were plastered together, my aching cock trapped between us. "He loves watching us." He dived in for another kiss, his warm hands splayed across my bare back. I ground down on him while the kiss went on and on. He explored the side of my neck with his mouth, cupping my naked ass and helping me move against him as he nipped and sucked on my flesh.

It was all driving me crazy.

Except I was missing one thing.

Luke.

I reached back for him.

He moved in behind me and straddled Richard's thighs too, pressing his front half against my back once more. "Is this what you wanted?"

"Uh-huh," I said around a moan as Luke's mouth traced a path up the other side of my neck.

I melted under their combined touches. With an arm over my shoulder, I laid a hand at the back of Luke's head so I could hold on to them both, shifting my body between them. "Please." I needed to feel more of them, to be touched by them in far more intimate ways.

Richard lifted his head and traced my bottom lip with his thumbs. "What do you want?"

"Luke to kiss me."

He hadn't kissed me in days.

I expected Richard to tell Luke what to do, but there was no time. Luke laid his fingers against my chin and turned me toward him. It was a near perfect replica of the sensual, erotic way Richard had kissed me earlier, only with a slight touch of the animated enthusiasm that was all Luke.

When we parted, he was breathless. "Fuck. Your kisses are amazing."

I tipped my head farther back, not wanting him to go. "Kiss me again."

A grin hit his lips, and then his mouth was on mine, electric heat passing between us once more. This was what I'd been aching for. The three of us desperate for each other.

"Now," Luke said. "Tell Richard what else you want."

I turned to Richard. "Touch me."

"That's not very specific." He flashed me the same easy smile as Luke's. "But I can make it work." He held a hand out at my side, palm up. "Luke."

Without a moment's hesitation, Luke spit in Richard's hand. Then Richard grasped my shaft, using Luke's spit to lubricate my length. The complete raunchiness of that move had my breath coming faster. Not to mention that large fist working over my dick.

Luke whispered in my ear. "Lean back against me."

I did. There was nothing better than feeling both of them at the same time.

Richard tightened his grip on my cock and squeezed to the top in a slow drag. "Feel that?"

"Uh-huh." I licked my lips.

"That's me. Wanting you." He massaged the head of my cock, then glided his hand up and down my length, his eyes locked on mine. The deliberate, sure strokes blended with a teasing tenderness in each movement of his hand was intoxicating. He knew how I liked it as well as I knew myself. Maybe better. The scent of my own arousal grew heavy in the air.

Luke reached around me, and the heat of their combined hands engulfed the length of my dick with each stroke as they jerked me off together, moving their hands as one.

I squeezed my eyes shut and arched into it. "Oh God."

"That's it." The sound of Richard's deep voice was like a caress against my skin. "Let go, Matthew."

I groaned. They sped up. It didn't take long, and I was close. So damn close. My body on fire, a rush of release working its way through me.

Then everything stopped. Their hands were gone.

I threw my eyes open.

Richard gestured at Luke to shift back, and Luke stood, grasping me by the hips and pulling me up with him to stand before the couch again, steadying me with the press of his body to mine. Richard also got up. He drew me close again, lifting me up onto my toes as he kissed me, taking my mouth harder than before, his wet, warm tongue seeking out mine again and again. I humped against him, needing to come so badly. The fabric of his pants scraped against my sensitive cockhead in the most delicious way. He seized my ass in both hands. "Hold on to me."

I pushed off the floor, my arms around his neck, my legs around his waist. Spinning us, he faced the couch and lowered me down so I was the one sitting. He pressed his entire body against mine as he gave me another toe-curling kiss, but he didn't stay there long. He shifted to kneel on the floor before me. He grasped Luke by the wrist and encouraged him down so they were kneeling side by side, both of them completely focused on me, though neither was touching me any longer.

Richard studied me for another moment, the look on his face filled with longing. Then he turned to Luke and whispered in his ear.

Luke licked his lips and nodded.

"What?" I asked.

There was a glint in Luke's eyes. "You'll see."

Then the two of them were kissing. A wet, sloppy kiss, mouths open, tongues tangling, desire like a live current passing between them, just like that morning in the kitchen. I was captivated, soaking up every detail: the wild touch of their lips, the glimpse of their tongues coming in contact, Luke's stubbled chin rubbing against Richard's smooth clean-shaven face, the way Luke swept his palms up Richard's chest.

Watching them together, locked in that erotic moment, was so powerful. I felt like I was a part of it, like I was touching them, their lips on mine, their arms around me, their hands gliding across my skin, their bodies moving against mine.

To avoid taking myself in hand, I grasped the edge of the couch cushion on each side of me. I wanted the two of them to be the next touch that brought me pleasure.

When they parted, both panting, Richard cupped Luke's cheek as he'd done to me earlier. Luke lowered his eyelids and turned into the touch, planting a soft kiss on Richard's palm. That simple, affectionate act went straight to my heart. No matter what Luke was like when we first met him, he now loved the tender moments with us. He needed them, craved them, ached for them more than anything else that went on between us.

Seeing them like that together, the two of them mostly dressed while I was laid out on the sofa naked, my dick hard as a rock, my balls aching, it all kicked my arousal up another notch.

Richard turned Luke's head so they were eye to eye again. "Do it exactly as I say."

Luke nodded.

"Slowly."

He nodded again, but he made no move.

Richard tilted his head my way. "Go on. Touch him. I know you want to, *need* to."

"Fuck, yes." Luke faced me and crawled forward, settling his body between my spread thighs. He grasped my shaft in one hand. "He wants to watch us together first."

I whimpered at his touch. I couldn't take my eyes off Luke as he lowered his mouth over my cock. I groaned. "Oh God." It had been far too long since I'd felt this.

"Just the head," Richard said in a commanding tone.

Luke sucked on the head of my dick, following Richard's instructions and not moving a fraction of an inch lower, using his tongue, one agonizingly seductive swipe after another, around my glans and over the slit. I threw my head back and groaned once more. Louder. Longer.

From where Richard was still kneeling on the floor, he laid a hand in the middle of Luke's back. "Now stroke him with your hand too. Lightly."

Luke did, and it was torture barely feeling the tunnel of his fingers on my shaft.

"More," I groaned.

Richard shook his head, the hint of a smile at the corners of his lips.

Despite that Luke hadn't seen Richard's response, he kept the touches featherlight, never taking his mouth off the head of my cock.

"Just your tongue now."

Luke opened wide and let my dick slip from his wet lips, a string of saliva hanging from his bottom lip to the head of my dick for a second. Then he swept his skilled tongue over and around the tip again. That, combined with the soft touch of his teasing fingers holding my shaft, had me breathing in rapid pants I couldn't control. My hips moved without my consent as I instinctively tried to get Luke to take me back into his mouth.

"Not yet," Richard said from where he still knelt next to Luke. He moved his hand to settle on the back of Luke's head, lovingly petting him. "Make him sit still."

Keeping hold of my dick with one hand, Luke placed his other on my lower abs. He gave just enough pressure to keep me glued to the couch.

I whimpered.

Richard chuckled. "Wait for it. You know it'll be good."

I nodded. "Uh-huh."

Luke was still using only his tongue, driving me crazy with tantalizing sweeps across my swollen head. I clutched the couch cushion on both sides of me again and arched up as best I could with Luke pinning me to the couch.

"All right," Richard said with another laugh. "Go ahead, Luke. Swallow him down."

Luke did just that, immediately and with urgency, going all the way to the base and burying his nose in the hair above my dick.

I threw my head back. "Oh God. Oh God. Oh God."

"Only once," Richard said. "Then hold still."

Luke drew the wet heat of his mouth to the tip once more, sucking with the perfect amount of pressure. He held there, his warmth wrapped around the head of my cock. No movement, no swipes of his tongue this time.

"Just like that." Richard sounded breathless. I met his stare. He cupped the front of his dress pants and squeezed his substantial bulge. "The things you two do to me." Massaging himself through his pants, he laid his other hand on Luke's back again, then ever so gradually ran that hand down to the crack of Luke's ass, not stopping until I was certain he was teasing Luke's asshole through the jeans. "Do it now. Fuck him with that beautiful mouth of yours."

Without a moment's hesitation, Luke went to town on my dick, his head bobbing, his hand flying over me, his eyes locked on my face before they eventually fell closed as if giving me head was pure ecstasy for him.

Richard watched it all, his breathing racing faster, his gaze now switching between my face and Luke's activities on my dick. It was like he was living vicariously through the blowjob. Either from my point of view or Luke's. Maybe both.

He let go of Luke and stood. Rubbing himself with one hand through his pants, he used his other to undo his belt buckle, the muscles of his taut biceps flexing as if he were lifting weights. I loved when he showed off like that for me.

Luke granted me no respite. He kept caressing me with the heat of his mouth, his cheeks drawn in as he sucked and slurped and tongued my entire shaft. When he'd gone down on me at the Haven that night we'd met, he'd been the first guy to give me a blowjob in more than a year, and it had been the best damn one I'd ever had up to that point in my life. His blowjobs had only gotten more intense since then. He could deep throat a guy like no one I'd ever known. But that wasn't the only thing that made them so powerful. It was the sheer enthusiasm of the way he went about it. Like he'd been waiting years for this moment, waiting years for my dick.

Now I knew for sure, he'd been missing this as much as I had.

That thought sent me over the edge. I bit my bottom lip. "I'm gonna—"

Richard shook his head. "No. Not yet." He opened the top button on his dress slacks, then slid the zipper down.

I did my best to fend off my orgasm. Not easy with Luke sucking me off like a vacuum hose attached to my dick. I swiped my tongue over my lower lip, waiting for Richard to shove his pants down and show me his thick, hard shaft.

He didn't. He held still and said, "Nice. Do that again, kid." I ran my tongue over my lips again, and he groaned as he slid his hand inside the front of his own pants. "Luke, do what I told you next."

Luke moaned around my dick. It was clear that Richard telling him what to do, ordering him around, was really doing a number on him. He pulled off me. "Spread your legs. Wide."

I grasped my legs behind each knee and lifted them up and open as Luke sucked his forefinger between his moist lips, drawing it in and out, really getting his finger wet. Then he let it pop from his mouth and drew my shaft between his lips again. He ran that wet finger along the skin behind my balls, teasing my hole with each swipe.

"Oh. My. God."

Just when I thought I couldn't take one more second of him wetting and stroking my taint, he slipped his finger inside me. My body jerked forward in response, and I sank deeper into his mouth. He didn't gag or relent. He fucked me with that finger while he sucked my cock faster and faster.

Then, when my body tensed and my dick was ready to explode, Richard dropped to his knees beside Luke. He leaned in, placing a hand on Luke's upper back. At that touch, Luke removed his lips from my shaft, and without a moment's hesitation, Richard took over, his mouth sliding down my spit-slick length as Luke moved lower to lick and suck my balls.

"Oh God. Oh God." I moaned, loudly, forcefully. My toes curled. My hips shifted into their touches.

Richard pulled to the tip, sucked on the crown, his head bobbing over me in short, powerful bursts. Then he took me all the way in again. My entire body went taut, and my hips jerked forward, sending my shaft farther into the heat of his mouth. I held on to him by the back of his head and let loose, nearly shaking apart as I came.

He held me there until I relaxed back onto the couch.

"Fuck." He wiped his mouth with the back of his hand. "I love feeling you lose it like that."

"Uh-huh," Luke said as he sat up. "It's a fucking beautiful thing."

I needed them closer. I grabbed on to Luke first, then Richard, and tugged them onto the couch with me, holding them in a strong embrace. I couldn't stop every part of my body from shaking.

"Hey." Richard laid a hand on the back of my head. "Hey, you okay?"

"Yeah." I was more than okay. I shifted back so I could see him. "I love you. I love you both so much." I rotated us so Richard was the one sitting with his back against the couch, Luke kneeling beside me.

I tugged Richard's pants and underwear down and off, threw everything aside, and grasped his solid cock. I stroked him, nothing light or tentative, jerking him off with abandon right from the start, and then I took him into my mouth. I didn't hold back. I got him wet all over, exploring his shaft with my hand and lips and tongue, giving his balls just as much attention too, using every trick I had in my arsenal, wanting him to feel as out of control as they'd had me.

He groaned and whispered words of encouragement. "Shit, Matthew. That's it. Oh fuck. You're so damn good at this."

Luke sat back on his heels, his focus locked on us, lips parted, chest rising with each surging breath. Richard was right. After all this time, Luke still loved to watch us together. His own private porn show. I loved seeing that lust-filled expression on him, but I also could never resist getting him involved once I'd seen that look from him.

I took a quick breather, keeping my hand moving over Richard as I leaned to the side and kissed Luke. He eagerly kissed me back, like it was his dick I stroked.

"Damn," he said when we parted. "I love when you taste like him."

"I'm going to taste like both of you in a minute." I indicated the empty spot on the couch with a tilt of my head. "Sit there."

Luke stripped down to nothing in seconds and moved to sit beside

Richard, their bare hips and outer thighs touching. I shifted sideways to kneel before both of them, my knees straddling one foot of each man. With one hand still on Richard, I grasped Luke's dick and slid my mouth down his length to get him nice and wet. Then I stroked them both, looking from one to the other.

Richard had a hand on Luke's thigh, squeezing his muscular flesh over and over again. Luke grasped Richard's hand in return as he arched up into my strokes.

It was beautiful. The way they always needed to touch each other, a reminder that, no matter what position we were in, moments like this were always about all three of us. It had been that way from the start.

It was also incredible to have all that sleek flesh and hard muscle on display before me, to see their looks of admiration and desire focused on me.

I still couldn't believe they were all mine.

"How'd I get so lucky?"

Luke laughed, but then I must've squeezed just right at the tip of his cock. His laughter cut off, and his head dropped back to the couch behind him. A low groan tore from his chest.

Richard kept eyeing me. "You're not the only one who's lucky here."

Luke lifted his head. "Yep. So fucking lucky."

Keeping my hand on Luke's shaft, I sank my mouth down the length of Richard's cock again. His reaction was just as pronounced as Luke's, his every breath rapid.

I took turns going down on them, never letting up with the swift stroke of my hand on whomever I wasn't taking into my mouth, using the same speed and technique on both of them. Back and forth, jerking them off with mouth and hand.

Luke groaned again. He turned to Richard. "Kiss me."

Without delay Richard let go of Luke's thigh, gripped him by the back of the neck, and hauled him forward. Their mouths met, lips parting in a fierce exchange of carnal need.

I kept my focus on that kiss as I took Luke deep. Richard had moved his other hand to Luke's chest. He plucked a nipple between two fingers. Luke arched his back, the movement sending his cock to the back of my throat. I couldn't hold him there for long, but I didn't care. There was nothing like the burst of adrenaline that came from taking one of their dicks that far. I sucked harder.

Then I switched focus again, shifting my mouth to Richard's erection. He gave one last flick to Luke's nipple. Then he dropped his hand and let it hover over the back of my head. The hesitation was brief, but it was there. I squeezed my eyes shut, wanting, needing him to touch me. Then his hand settled on my head. He wasn't grabbing or pulling me forward. He was just there, holding me.

But then his hand was gone in a flash.

It didn't matter. That short contact had been amazing. It had been months since he'd done anything like that when I'd been blowing him. I had to wonder if he was afraid holding me like that was the same as coercing, even forcing me to go down on him.

He had no idea. I craved this. The feel of him, either of them, in my mouth, giving them pleasure in this way, was more than need and desire. It was like feeding an unrelenting hunger, like finding harbor after being lost at sea, like coming home.

I kept sliding my mouth down his shaft until Richard's body tensed under my touch, his thick thighs straining.

I let go of Luke's dick and stayed focused on Richard with both my hands and mouth. Without hesitation this time, Richard tunneled his fingers through my hair. *Oh God.* I moaned around his length, moving my lips faster, cupping his balls and jacking him with everything I had.

He thrust up into it. "Shit. Matthew!" He bent over me, his fingers buried in my hair. "Holy fuck." He shot.

And shot.

And shot some more.

I avoided swallowing all of his cum, holding the last of it in my mouth on purpose. When he relaxed back onto the couch and opened his eyes, I let some of his release dribble out of my mouth, then swiped it away with my tongue.

"Jesus, kid. You are something else." He smiled at me, but then, without warning, that amazed look faded.

"What?" I asked.

He leaned forward and brushed his thumb over my wet lips. "That was okay? What we did?"

"It was perfect."

Luke let out a desperate moan. He'd been watching our exchange while he jerked himself off, one hand on his shaft, the other clasping his balls.

Richard laughed. "Was that some good porn, Luke?"

"Best." Another grunt as he continued working himself over. "Ever."

I shifted to kneel before him and shook my head. "Stop. That's all mine."

"Uh-huh." But he didn't quit stroking his dick. He moaned again.

"Here." Richard encouraged Luke to turn and lean back against him so they were lying along the length of the couch, Luke cradled between Richard's thighs, his back to Richard's bare chest. "Let's give you a minute to calm down. Draw this out a little longer." He grasped Luke's arms and held them along his sides so he couldn't touch himself again.

Luke bucked up and let out a frustrated whimper, but Richard had a secure hold on him. He laughed at Luke's eagerness. "Patience."

I sat back, my hands resting on my own thighs, trying to be patient too. I couldn't stand it any longer. "Now?"

Richard shook his head. "Not yet."

Luke turned and buried his face in the side of Richard's neck. "Please."

"Soon. Just hang on. It'll be worth it. Trust me."

"I do." Luke panted around the words. "Always."

Richard let go of one arm, grasped the back of Luke's hair, and tilted his head back. He covered Luke's mouth with his own in a fierce, scorching kiss. When they parted, Richard tipped his head my way. "Go for it." He held on to Luke by both arms again, keeping him pinned down.

Luke threw his head back to Richard's shoulder. "God, yes!" I wasn't sure if that was because he was about to get my mouth on him again or if it was the way Richard had him restrained that Luke was loving.

Maybe it was both.

I scrambled onto the couch to straddle Luke's legs. I took him in hand again and frantically lowered my mouth down his shaft. I knew I had to seem desperate for this, but I didn't care. This was Luke and Richard. I could always be myself around them. That hadn't changed.

I eased up on the pace and teased Luke with a swirl of my tongue over and around his slit.

Richard said against Luke's ear, "Don't you love the way he does that? He knows just when to tease and when to go at it harder."

Luke grunted out something that sounded like an agreement. Then he whimpered again. His hips restlessly shifted from side to side. Richard stilled him by squeezing Luke's hips between his thick thighs.

That encouraged me on. I swallowed Luke down.

But then Richard said, "Don't let him come yet. Tease him some more." He pressed his lips to Luke's ear again. "You like being teased. I know you do."

Luke nodded energetically.

I planted openmouthed kisses down the side of his shaft, then worked my lips lower toward his balls.

Richard spoke more forceful. "Say it, Luke."

Luke threw his head back again. "I do love it. Tease me more, Matthew."

I swept my tongue all over his sac, wetting and sucking each testicle in turn, keeping the touch light, ignoring his cock completely until Richard spoke again.

"Now tongue him all the way to the tip."

I did, working my way up his shaft once more. I drew the swollen head of his dick into my mouth and sucked on the crown, using just the right amount of pressure to drive Luke nuts.

"More. God, more, please."

"No," Richard said. "You'll take what he's giving you, and you'll thoroughly enjoy every single second of it."

"I will. I do." Luke's words were practically unintelligible between the rapid exhales streaming out of him.

I loved when he got to that point, a desperate ball of energy about to explode, his every molecule focused on what we were doing to him.

"Oh God. Matthew! Richard! Please!"

"Now, kid." Richard's voice was both breathless and commanding. "Finish him off."

I slid my mouth over Luke, taking his cock hard and fast, picking up the pace and matching the rhythm with my hand.

"Jesus." Luke's legs shook. "Oh God." He arched up under me and came while Richard kept hold of him as if he were tied down to the couch. It was explosive and powerful, and Luke moaned through the entire thing.

When he'd offered everything he had, I drew back, mesmerized by both how satisfied and shattered he looked.

He blew out a huff of air. "Goddamn, Matthew. There is nothing like your mouth."

"No, there isn't." Richard reached out for me with one arm and tugged me forward so I lay over them.

Luke held on to me and breathed deep again. "Holy hell."

"Yeah." Richard held me closer to them and whispered, "That was perfect."

"Uh-huh," Luke said, sounding halfway to snoring. A few more deep breaths from him, and I could tell he was drifting off. If we didn't move soon, he'd be out for the rest of the night.

As if Richard was thinking along the same lines, he asked me, "When's she getting here?"

"Seven." It seemed like a silly thing to celebrate—finishing my first year of school—but it was sweet that they wanted to do something special, and even more so that they'd included my mom in the dinner.

"All right." Richard shifted his weight under us. "Time to get up."

Luke groaned and held on to me tighter. "One more minute."

I laughed and sat up. "Nope. Now." I smacked him on the hip, then scrambled off the couch and took off for the door, feeling light and free like I hadn't in weeks, months.

Before I made it into the hall, Luke nabbed me from behind. "Not so fast."

I squirmed, trying to get away, laughing more. "I gotta take a shower. I can't smell like sex when my mom gets here."

He tickled me along both sides. "You're not going anywhere yet. It's my turn to tease you."

Richard slid by us and headed for the bathroom. "You two go right ahead and torture each other. I'm hitting the shower. I'll try to leave you some hot water."

As if he'd ever stick us with a cold shower. By the time Luke and I had gotten fresh towels out of the cabinet, Richard was washed, rinsed, and out of the shower. He left the water running and made quick work of drying off. "I've got to run out for something, but I'll be back in a few minutes. Then I'll help you get dinner ready, Luke." With the towel wrapped around his waist, he exited the bathroom.

Luke and I exchanged a look.

I called after Richard, "Where are you going?"

He returned to stand in the open doorway, already wearing a pair of jeans, a grin on his lips. "It's a surprise."

"For me?"

His eager smile grew. "For all of us."

Luke glanced my way again, then looked back at Richard. "What is it?"

"Well..." Richard went to him. "If I told you that, it'd take away the surprise part." He kissed him, long and hard. Then he gave the same to me.

I loved the way he held me by the back of the neck, the way that hand slid forward and his thumb slowly caressed my chin as he kept the kiss going for another beat.

He whispered over my lips, "I'll show you guys the surprise as soon as I can." He gave me a shorter, sweeter kiss, then pointed at the shower door covered in steam. "Shower. I'll be back soon."

After he was gone, Luke leaned back against the vanity. "What do you think he's up to?"

"I have no idea."

Did it matter? I'd already had the best surprise. For the first time in months, they had touched me sexually without that look from either of them like they were afraid of what I did or did not want. And it had been perfect.

Except for one thing.

One very specific thing.

After Luke and I were showered and Luke had left the bathroom, I went to the vanity and got out my shaving kit from under the sink. As I'd done dozens of times before, I removed the narrow plastic case from inside and tugged open the lid, then set the case on the countertop before me. I moved back and sat on the edge of the bathtub. Propping my elbows on my knees, my chin in my hands, I stared at the contents of the case.

I knew I'd work up the nerve to show it to them eventually. I hated keeping something this important from them, but now didn't seem like the right time. Because what was in that case would either bring us closer or put more distance between us.

Trusting my gut, I stood and closed the case, then stashed it away inside my shaving kit again.

I'd know when it was the right time.

Chapter Six

I was sitting on the couch waiting for my mom to arrive when Luke came into the living room and asked, "Richard's not back yet?"

"No, not yet."

He stopped on his way to the couch and glanced toward the hallway leading to the front door, anxiety radiating off him.

I couldn't help but laugh. "You really don't like surprises, do you?"

"What?" He gave me a puzzled look. Then the unease slipped away as if something in my eyes reassured him. He came to sit beside me. "Not after spending fifteen years hiding from my nutjob father. Surprises were never a good thing."

"I get that." I gestured toward the front door with a tip of my head. "I think this one is."

"Yeah." He considered me for another moment. "Hey, are you okay?"

I shrugged. "I guess."

"What'd you think about this afternoon in my office?"

"It was wonderful."

"Yeah, it was." He leaned in, and using his thumb, he tugged my bottom lip free from my teeth. I hadn't even known I'd been biting it. "But you're not feeling better about you and him?"

"No, I am. It's just…"

He lifted a knee onto the couch and turned to face me. With the way he was focused on me, I knew he wouldn't let this go.

"It's better, but it's still not the same as it used to be."

He laid his arm on the back of the couch between us. "Maybe you're overthinking this. I saw the way he was with you today. He was more relaxed, more in the moment with us. Now that the Harrison Center's open, I think he'll be less stressed out with work. That should help."

"I guess."

Luke raised his hand from the couch and tunneled his fingers through the hair above my ear. He repeated the action in a comforting stroke. "You don't think so?"

I didn't say anything.

"What is it?"

"It's just that—" I cut off and shook my head. "It's nothing. I just need to be patient."

Luke stilled his hand in my hair. "What aren't you saying?"

"I just feel like... maybe he doesn't completely trust me anymore."

"But he told you he did."

"I know, but..." I focused on the couch cushion between us, wishing I hadn't said anything. Maybe Luke was right. Things had been different upstairs. Maybe we'd continue down that path, and everything would be back to normal soon.

"Matthew." Luke's voice was filled with concern.

I shook my head again.

"Matthew, you have to tell me."

"I can't. I can't say it."

He placed a hand under my chin and brought my head up. "It'll be okay. Just tell me. You're kinda scaring the shit out of me here."

My breath caught in my throat. I swallowed hard, then blurted out, "He hasn't fucked me."

Luke dropped his hand and sat back, gaping at me. Then he turned toward the front door as if he could see Richard standing there. When he swung his gaze back to me, the shocked expression had morphed into a level of distress I'd rarely seen from him. "Since when?"

"Since before that day when you got hurt at the Harrison estate. The same night he thought I wanted him to fist me." The day he said I'd lied to him.

"Jesus." Luke shot off the couch. I thought he was going to do his usual agitated pacing thing he did whenever he was pissed off or felt uncomfortable about something we were discussing, but instead he moved to kneel in front of me, his hands on my thighs. "That was *months* ago, Matthew. I know he said at first that he needed time to forget that night, but I thought... I get that things have been strained lately, but it's not like we haven't been doing stuff. We've had sex a number of times since then."

"Yeah, but..."

"But what? I thought you said he was just holding back, hesitating until things got started, and then he seemed okay during the sex. I didn't realize that—" He blew out a frustrated exhale.

"He almost always positions us so I'm the one blowing you guys or you and he are the ones fucking each other."

Luke's eyes widened. "Today was the first time he's even sucked you off since then?"

"Yeah."

Luke shook his head and stared at my chest as if he was mentally running through the past few months. He looked ready to panic.

"It's getting better. I mean, now he's the one who starts things sometimes. And today, upstairs in your office, that *was* amazing, like when we first met. But he still won't..." I bit my bottom lip. "Not once since that night." I wanted to say more, tell him the rest, admit the worst part, the part that was hurting me the most, but I couldn't force those words out.

Luke sank back on his heels. He held still for a moment. Then he abruptly stood and ran a hand over the top of his head. "Fuck." He paced the room. "I know I'm not the most observant person, but how the hell did I miss this?"

"It's not your fault."

He glared down at me. "It's *no one's* fault." Then, as if he regretted how he'd spoken to me, he came to kneel before me again and laid his forearms on the couch on either side of me. Holding on to me by my hips, he gave me a slight shake. "You two have to talk about this. I mean..." He gestured toward the front door. "This is Richard. He doesn't want to hurt you. But everything is not fine, and he needs to hear that from you."

"Luke..." I breathed deep and leaned forward until our foreheads were touching. "I'm scared."

He stroked my upper arms in a soft caress. "Of what?"

"What if I broke us? What if it's never like it was before?"

"That's not possible."

The front door opened. I sat up and shook my head, trying to tell Luke without words that I didn't want him to say anything to Richard right then. Richard would push us to talk about this until I had answers to my questions, and I wasn't sure I was ready to hear them.

Maybe Luke didn't get that.

Or maybe he did, and it didn't matter because he'd already made up his own mind on how to handle this.

He called out, "Richard, get your ass in here. Now!"

I gave Luke another pleading look. "Please don't."

He scoffed. "Richard!"

Richard entered the living room in a quick stride, but as soon as he saw us, he stopped in the middle of the room. "What's wrong?"

Luke gestured between us with a frustrated swipe of his hand. "The two of you."

"What?"

"Why the hell didn't you say something?"

"What do you mean?"

Luke got on his feet and stalked to him. He jabbed a finger at Richard's chest. "You lied. Whenever I asked about you and him, you said everything was fine. It's not fucking fine. You're not the same with him, and you should've said something. He told me three weeks ago he felt like you were still holding back with him, and now I find out it's even worse than that."

This was crazy. I couldn't stand to hear Luke yell at Richard like that. I'd probably been overthinking things, seeing stuff that wasn't there. Maybe it was just a coincidence that the three of us hadn't been positioned in that one way during sex. After all, that night we'd fought had been about fisting, not fucking.

Luke continued, pointing back at me. "You've been purposely avoiding him in bed. No blowjobs until today. No fucking. This has gotten ridiculous."

Richard's jaw clenched.

I couldn't stand that they were fighting. I just wanted it to end. And the only way that would happen was if I told them the whole truth. "It's not Richard."

They both turned their heads my way.

Luke's furrowed brows demonstrated his confusion. "What do you mean?"

"It's you. You're the one who won't tell me why you can't be with me like that."

"Me? What about all that stuff you were just saying about Richard?"

"I was talking about you. I thought maybe it would help you figure things out if we were saying it about Richard."

He looked floored.

I gestured toward Richard. "He's been taking things slowly. He hasn't fucked me either, but he's also been talking about it to me, talking about how he feels. You're the one who's different with me and not telling me why you won't touch me. I get why he's been holding back, why he's scared. I don't understand why you are."

Luke remained silent.

Richard watched him for a moment, but when Luke still didn't say or do anything, Richard came to the couch and sat beside me. "I'm sorry. I completely missed this. I was so wrapped up in what I was

feeling, I didn't realize that Luke..." He sighed. "I should've seen
how things were between you two. How long has this been going on?"

"Since that night at my mom's."

He asked Luke, "Why?"

Luke answered Richard but spoke to me. "I was waiting until..."
He let his words fade away.

When he said nothing more, Richard asked, "Until what?"

Luke shifted his focus to Richard. They held the stare for several
weighty breaths, and then Luke finally looked back at me. "Until I
could stop picturing that night. Until I could stop seeing you flinch
like that in our bed."

Oh God. My stomach turned.

Richard must've seen something in my face. He laid an arm over
my shoulders and drew me closer to him. "It wasn't you he flinched
from."

"I know. It doesn't matter."

Richard nodded as if he got that. "You do other stuff with him."

Luke gave a sharp nod, but he didn't say anything more right
away. After a series of deep breaths, he moved in to sit at my other
side. He reached for my hand and held it on his thigh, his focus on our
combined hands. "I couldn't stop touching you altogether." He ran his
thumb over the backs of my fingers. "I need to make you feel good. I
need to be one of the ones who give you that kind of pleasure. But
every time I think of taking it further..." He closed his eyes for a
second and shook his head. "What if I do something you don't want? I
can't stop thinking that maybe I've already done something you
weren't into and you just didn't want to tell me. I can be pretty pushy
about sex, pretty selfish sometimes."

"No, you're not. You've never been. I've loved everything we've
ever done. And I promised I'd tell you guys the truth."

"I know. And I trust that." He looked up at me. "I trust *you*. I do."

"Then why?"

"I don't know. It's just still there. In my head. I can see the look
on your face when you pulled away from him." He turned my way. "I
want to move past this. I do."

"I wish you would've said something."

"I should've. I kept thinking if I pretended it didn't bother me, it
would go away." He squeezed my hand. "I need you to know that how
I feel about you hasn't changed. It never will." He leaned in and
kissed my cheek. Before he could pull back, I turned toward him so
his lips almost touched mine. He held still. I did too.

I said, "I want us to be the way we used to be. So bad."

He sucked in a sharp breath and reached up to hold my face in his hands. "Me too." He leaned in without delay and kissed me, softly, tenderly, like a first kiss between two men who'd just realized they were falling in love with each other.

I fell into the sweet press of his lips.

He stroked my cheeks with his thumbs as he pulled back and searched my eyes. "I'm trying to let it go. Every day I try to forget it. Forget that moment." He lowered his hands as his eyelids fell shut. "I can't stand that I'm hurting you. I can't stand that things are different. I want what we had back. More than anything." When he opened his eyes, desperation shone in those blue depths.

I cupped his face the way he'd done with me. "We *can* have it back. Because it's what we all want. Richard's trying. I am too. We get to decide how things are going to be for us from here on out. It's a choice we can make."

His mouth turned up in the slightest smile. His lips were still moist from the kiss. "You're always so damn wise, I actually forget that you're years younger than us."

"If you think I'm wise, then you should listen to me."

He laughed. "Yeah, I should."

I couldn't take my eyes off his lips. "You both used to fuck me like there was nothing that could stop you. Like there was something driving you, something powerful that you couldn't control. I miss that so much." I bit my lower lip, then met his stare.

With desperate urgency, as if my words had unfurled a buried part of him, he slid to the floor before me, gripped my hips, and hauled me off the couch onto his lap. "You have no idea how much I want you like that." Desire blazed in his eyes. With his hands on my hips, he rocked my body forward over his, and that had me instantly aroused.

He kept his gaze locked on mine as he reached for the front of my jeans and ripped the button open, his breathing picking up speed.

Richard shot off the couch and knelt beside Luke. He nuzzled the side of my neck. "I think he wants you, Matthew."

"God, yes." Luke skimmed his hands up under the back of my shirt, stroking my skin in long, slow sweeps.

Maybe hearing me say how much I missed being with them was just what they needed to hear. Maybe I needed to be more assertive. After all, I was never one to hold back in bed. That was the guy they'd first met at the Haven. The one they fell in love with.

I wrapped an arm around each of them and moved over Luke, grinding our bodies together in a raw, primal building of lust and passion. "I want you both to fuck me." I leaned in. I was going to give

Luke, and then Richard, the most erotic, mind-blowing kiss I could manage.

Luke sucked in a sharp gasp as our lips drew closer.

The doorbell rang.

I froze. "Shit." My mom was there for dinner. I had completely forgotten she was coming. I dropped my forehead to Luke's shoulder. "You gotta be kidding me."

Richard laid a hand on my back. "Why don't you guys head upstairs? I'll distract her, take her for a walk or something."

"No," Luke said with urgency. "We'll all pick this up later when we have more time."

I sat back so I could see him. "You're sure?"

"Definitely." That flirtatious smirk I'd loved about him from day one was back. "Besides…" He looked to Richard, his expression now beyond serious. "We do that part together. Always."

I loved hearing those words from him, loved knowing he still wanted to keep to that one rule we'd set when we first started dating.

Not because of jealousy or distrust.

Now, for all of us, it was for far more sentimental reasons, something special to do as a threesome, a reminder that this relationship was never just about any two of us.

Chapter Seven

"Mom, can I ask you a personal question?"

"Sure, honey." She set her cup on the coffee table before her and turned my way.

We'd just finished dinner, and the two of us were seated on the couch in the living room while Richard and Luke cleaned up in the kitchen.

The stuffed peppers with risotto they'd prepared had been delicious, but the best part was the cake they'd made while I was at my interview earlier that day. Luke had handled the baking, and Richard did the frosting. It was a lopsided, leaning tower of chocolate, but it was one of the sweetest things they'd ever done for me.

I really didn't want to ruin the night with the conversation I was about to have with my mom. I didn't know for sure whether or not it was a good idea to bring this up. The last thing in the world I wanted to do was remind her of something painful from her past. But there were things I needed to know. Especially with the dreams I'd been having.

Every single time I dreamed of that moment from my childhood, I couldn't keep from hearing him scream out my name. There was so much fear and panic in his voice.

And love.

Why did he have to love me? It made everything worse.

As if sensing my unease, Trixie got up from where she'd been snoozing near the fireplace and came to sit at my feet. I patted her head as I casually threw out the question, hoping it wouldn't send up too many red flags with my mom. "Do you ever talk to Dad?"

She gaped at me for a moment. When she recovered from the shock, she composed herself, but I knew I'd hurt her feelings by bringing him up, or perhaps because I'd implied she'd keep something like that from me, and that about killed me.

She didn't get a chance to say anything before we heard the guys laughing as they came our way from the kitchen. When they reached the living room, Richard stopped in the archway. He put a hand on Luke's arm, indicating without words that they should wait a minute.

I gestured for them to join us. "It's okay."

Luke started forward again and sat next to me, but Richard waited at the edge of the room. Luke nudged my shoulder with his. "So, you liked the cake, huh?"

I smiled at him. Just having that contact had the anxiety fading. "It was great."

"First time I've ever made one."

Richard chuckled from across the room.

Luke rolled his eyes. "Okay, the one we ate was my second attempt. I dropped the first one when I tried to put the pans in the oven." He pointed to Richard. "But since it was never actually baked, I don't think it counts."

"You should've seen it," Richard said. "Cake batter was everywhere. On the floor, inside the oven, underneath it, along the crack between the stove and the cabinet, in Luke's hair. We had to move the stove all the way out, wash everything, and he had to take a shower before we could try again."

Luke nodded. "It was not pretty."

I laughed with them. Individually they could be a bit of a disaster in the kitchen. Put them together, and it was worse. I could picture them laughing their asses off through the entire thing.

My mom looked at each of us in turn, her eyes lit with affection.

"What?" I asked her.

"This is nice. The three of you together." She patted my leg. "They really love you."

"They really do." I turned to Richard, then Luke. "Which means we can get through anything together."

Relief shone in Luke's eyes. "We can."

Richard came forward and cupped my chin. "We can."

I placed my hand over his, and we held that simple touch for several breaths before he moved to sit in the chair across the couch from us.

The four of us chatted for a bit. Then my mom squeezed my leg. "Well, I better get going. We can finish our talk when you come for dinner this week. I promise I'll answer any questions you have, okay?"

I nodded. "Okay."

She reached for my hand. "I'm so very proud of you, Matty."

"Thanks, Mom."

We stood, and she gave me a hug and a kiss on the cheek. She did the same with Luke and Richard, thanking them for dinner. After she left, the three of us returned to the living room. This time Luke dropped into the chair across the room, and Richard came to sit beside me on the couch.

He asked, "Everything okay with her?"

"Yeah."

"Good. You're very lucky to have her. We all are. She's wonderful."

"She is."

"I like that she's so accepting of us and gets how much we care for you." He stroked my thigh with an open hand and then leaned in and kissed me. It was like that moment earlier had changed everything for him. He was more affectionate, more confident and determined with his touch than he'd been in weeks. Months. He really was trying to let go of the past. I hoped Luke could do the same.

Richard ran his hand over my thigh again. "You look tired."

"I'm okay. Just thinking about the job at Windtree. I want to do some more studying tomorrow. In case I get a call."

"Sounds like a good idea." He gestured toward the hall. "Why don't we head up to bed, then?"

As he did every night, Richard locked the doors and set the house alarm, and then we made our way upstairs. I changed into pajama pants and used the bathroom down the hall while Luke and Richard got ready for bed in the master bath. Back in our bedroom, I lay horizontally across the middle of the bed, propped my chin on my folded arms, and watched them through the open bathroom door. Luke was brushing his teeth, Richard flossing his. Both were down to their underwear. Neither noticed me.

Luke paused the brushing and removed the toothbrush from his mouth. "If I promise not to ruin the surprise for Matthew, will you tell me what it is?"

Richard snorted out a laugh. "Are you really going to keep a secret from him?"

"No." Luke went back to energetically brushing his teeth. Then he stopped again. "I bet I can guess what it is. Just tell me, is it bigger than a shoebox?"

Richard momentarily paused the flossing and studied Luke in the mirror. He sighed. "Yes."

"Is it a car?"

"No."

"A motorcycle?"

"No."

"A boat?"

"It didn't cost me a dime. Not yet anyway."

"You got us a surprise that didn't cost anything? Did you make it?" Luke pointed the toothbrush at him. "Wait. Did you take one of those pottery classes that we got a flyer about in the mail?"

Richard tossed the floss into the trash. "Would you stop asking me questions?" He headed out of the bathroom, grinning at me when he spotted me lying on the bed. He went to the dresser near the closet and got out a pair of pajama pants.

Luke rinsed his mouth, then turned out the bathroom light. "So I'm close, huh?" He folded back the blankets on his side of the bed and sat. "Is it erotic pottery?"

Richard stared at him. "Erotic pottery?"

"It's a thing."

"No, it's not erotic pottery. It's not any kind of pottery."

Luke seemed to be genuinely racking his brain. "Is it something we've talked about getting before?"

Richard came to the bed and lay alongside me, positioning me between them. "No. Well, sort of."

"Sort of?"

"Yep." He laid a hand across my lower back and asked me, "You okay?"

"Yeah."

"Sort of?" Luke repeated. "What does that even mean?"

"You'll see."

"When?"

"Soon, I promise."

Luke groaned and flopped onto his back, his head hitting the pillow in an exaggerated thump.

I giggled, looking from one to the other, certain another guess would come from Luke at any moment.

Richard ran his warm hand along my spine. "Hey."

I glanced up at him.

"What is it? What's wrong? And don't say nothing. I can hear it in your laugh."

That got Luke's attention. He sat up.

"I guess I'm just distracted, thinking about stuff."

"About our conversation earlier?" Richard asked.

"A little bit. And something else."

He got up and crawled over me to sit against the headboard. "Come here." He held his arms out.

I moved up the bed and sat between his legs, my back to his chest. He held me in his arms, his chin resting on my shoulder. "What is it?"

I laid my hands over his strong forearms. I wanted to talk to them about what was going on with me, but I didn't want to upset them or worry them. Not after our talk earlier. Things between us were just starting to feel better.

"Talk to us," he whispered against my ear.

I drew in a deep breath and let the words tumble out. "I've been to Majestic Falls State Park before today. When I was a kid. My dad took me there."

Richard's entire body stiffened. Luke's eyes widened.

Before either could say anything, I added, "We only went camping there the one time. It was before he..." I flipped a hand through the air. I didn't need to say the rest. They knew what he'd done to me when I was a teenager, how he liked to smack me around whenever he was drunk. They didn't know the specifics, but enough to get the gist of how much he'd hurt me, both physically and emotionally. "Going there just brought up a lot of memories, mostly the good stuff with him. I guess thinking about that part of our relationship always makes it..." I wasn't sure what words I wanted to use.

"Hurt more." Luke said.

"Yeah. That trip to the park was when I first realized something about him, and I can't seem to let it go. I keep thinking that maybe I should've talked to my mom about it back then, that I made a big mistake keeping it to myself. Maybe I could've saved myself a lot of pain if I'd just talked to her."

I could feel the unease building in Richard's body, but his voice was soft when he spoke. "You want to tell us about what happened with your dad in the park?"

"I don't know if I can. I never talk about him. I never let myself think about him. Or that trip. He was different after that week. The way he was with me in that park when I..." I shook my head, not sure I could say more. "He was never like that again." Which explained the recent dreams. Consciously repressing a memory didn't always keep it buried. It could do the exact opposite.

Richard lovingly laid a hand over my heart. "Might do you good to talk about it."

Luke nodded.

When I said nothing for a moment, Richard added, "We're right here with you."

"Okay." I started the story where the dream always began.

* * * * *

The ground under my feet felt wrong. Harsh. Uneven. Like I was about to slip and fall on my ass at any moment.

Which was a stupid thought. I wasn't usually the clumsy type. We'd been hiking the roughest trails of the park for two days now, and I hadn't fallen once.

I'd probably just jinxed myself.

Everything about the moment felt wrong, epically wrong, and I had no idea why. Maybe it was one of those things thirteen-year-old kids couldn't understand.

It had been hours since we'd left the rented boat at the dock and started the trek through the dense forest. I couldn't stand the silence anymore. The longer it went on, the more time seemed to drag on and on.

I just had to say something.

"Dad?"

He didn't say a word in return. He'd never been big on talking, the total opposite of me. But this quiet hiking all day was pushing it, even for him.

If he was mad, it was my fault. Why couldn't I have been excited about the stupid fish I'd caught? Why'd I have to stare at the tiny thing in my lap, watching its wide eyes as it gulped in air instead of the water it desperately needed to survive?

I thought he'd been okay about my reaction. Despite our plan to cook any fish we caught, he just said, "It's okay, Matty. Throw it back in."

So I did, relief washing over me as the fish swam to safety with sharp swishes of its tail.

I always liked how I didn't have to explain stuff to my dad. He just got me.

After I'd thrown the fish overboard, I looked up at him, and he simply smiled. He hadn't done that the entire trip. I thought he'd been proud of me for caring about the fish, or something along those lines.

So why the rushed hiking like he had to get away from something? Or someone? Maybe me. And why the silence?

I sucked in a deep breath and continued trudging along the trail, my complete focus on his back as I tried to keep up with him and not lose the backpack that kept sliding down my arms every five minutes.

Another twenty steps, and the need to speak again was overwhelming.

"Dad?"

He sighed and said, "Yeah." He didn't stop, though, just kept on pushing forward like we were running late for something. Which didn't make sense. We were in the middle of nowhere. What could we be late for?

I hopped over a rock in the path. "Where are we going?"

"To find someplace to camp for the night."

"Do you know somewhere special?" He said he'd never been to this state park before, and we'd already passed several designated camping areas, so I was more than a little confused.

"No." He rounded a substantial oak tree and started up an incline, following a narrow dirt path that led away from the top edge of the gorge we'd been hiking along. "Just looking for what feels right."

I trudged around the tree after him and began climbing the hill, both hands holding my backpack in place on my shoulders, my focus on my feet so I wouldn't slip and complicate the journey for him. The ground, still damp from the rain that morning, made the tennis shoes I wore not the best idea.

"What do you mean?" I asked.

He sucked in another ragged breath, then finally halted. He turned around, towering over me, not only due to his height advantage, but also because of the incline. "I just needed to do some thinking before we stopped for the night." He spun on his heels and started trekking up the hill again, this time going at an even faster pace, his strides more agitated.

I hurried to catch up, which made talking more difficult, but I couldn't stand not knowing. "Is the walking helping? With your thinking?"

At my words, he came to a sudden stop and whirled to face me once more. There was a shocked look on his face as if what I'd said had somehow snapped him out of the intense focus he'd had for the past several hours. For a long moment, I gaped up at him, trying to remember what the heck I'd said. Then he started laughing. I didn't get what he found so funny.

I kept staring at him, hoping he'd explain.

Eventually the laughter died off, but the relaxed grin remained, just as he'd been right after I'd let go of the fish. "No, Matty. It's not the walking that's helping." His smile widened. He scanned the surrounding area and gestured with a tilt of his head toward a flat spot on the ridge at the top of the incline. "Up there. That's a good spot, don't you think?"

I shrugged. "Sure."

He started up again, and I followed. This time we hiked at a more leisurely pace. Not that it mattered. I didn't get far. With my next step, my foot landed on the edge of a rock, and I faltered, my ankle twisting. I fell onto my ass with a thump that reverberated throughout my body. No time to react. I instantly tumbled down the steep slope in a backward somersault.

I tried to grab for the thick brush alongside the trail, but I couldn't get a hold of anything. Vines and twigs scraped my forearms and hands. I kept flying down the hillside, barely avoiding slamming the side of my head against the moss-covered boulders and massive tree trunks lining the trail.

I heard my dad running after me. "Matty! Oh God. Just hang on. I'm coming to get you. Just hang on. Please, God."

Another few seconds rushed by, and then I finally slowed enough I managed to dig my fingertips into the damp earth. I came to a crashing stop, lying flat on my stomach, my face half-buried in a puddle of mud.

My dad was there in a heartbeat, helping me sit up. "Are you okay?" His voice was shaking. "Jesus, you could've smacked your head on one of those rocks or fallen over the edge into the gorge and..." He swallowed down the last of his words.

Died. I could've died.

That was what he'd meant.

That hit me with a shock I'd never known in my thirteen years. I guess kids mostly figure they have a whole lifetime left, that everything and everyone they knew and loved would always be there. I was no different.

"I'm okay." The ankle wasn't bad, and nothing else hurt all that much, but I was covered in mud and sweat. My backpack had slipped off one of my arms and was open at the top. Strewn along the path up the hill were my favorite Green Day sweatshirt, a pair of sweats I'd worn for pajamas at night, and four pairs of the extra underwear my mom had insisted I bring. Everything was wet and muddy.

There was no stopping the frustrated, embarrassed tears. I batted at them with the heel of each hand. Why the hell did I always cry at the drop of a hat? "I'm sorry."

He sat beside me and slid an arm around my trembling shoulders. "It's okay. Everyone falls at some point in their lives. It's that you get up and try again that matters. Are you sure you're okay?" He examined my head and face, wiping away some of the mud.

"Yeah. I'm fine."

He gave up on checking me over and looked up the hill at my scattered clothes. "Why don't we just throw those muddy underwear out? Otherwise your mom's going to think I literally scared the crap out of you by bringing you out here." I gave him a wide-eyed look, and he nodded. "It's totally going to look like skid marks once they dry out." He burst out laughing. I did too. We sat there for several minutes, laughing and joking about what she'd think if she found those stained underwear in my bag.

When our laughter died off, I stood. My right ankle already felt better. I could put pressure on it.

He got up and pointed to an area at the base of the hillside, closer to where I'd landed after my stellar fall. It was another designated camping site with a fire ring. "Why don't we camp there instead?"

"We don't have to. I can keep going."

"I know you can. But this is good."

He gathered my stuff and then kept his eye on me as we made our way to the area he'd indicated. He had me sit on a log from a fallen tree while he pitched the tent and started a fire. The sun was setting, and the forest around us was coming to life with the glow of fireflies and the nocturnal song of crickets. A single firefly landed on the sleeve of my muddy sweatshirt. Its light dimmed, then flickered on again. It was the first time I'd seen a firefly in person. I watched it crawl down my arm. Then it flew off, its body producing that brilliant, beautiful glow again, adding its light to the dozens of others in the sky. It was the most magical thing I'd ever seen.

I decided right then and there that, despite my trip down the hill, I loved Majestic Falls.

An hour after the sun had disappeared behind the horizon and we'd finished eating our bowls of chili, we settled in on tree stumps on opposite sides of the fire. My dad fiddled with the line on his fishing pole, and I stared into the orange and yellow flickering flames, thinking about what he'd said about getting up after a fall. I got that he wasn't just talking about physically falling down, but I wasn't exactly sure what he'd been trying to say. Had I done something he thought I'd failed at? Or was he saying he had?

I didn't think I could ask. Which felt so strange.

Despite that he'd never been much of a talker, he also never seemed to care how much I rambled on. In fact, I was old enough now to get that he sometimes asked me questions just to get me going. But sitting by that fire, he was even more subdued than normal. That had me back to wondering what his silent frustration and the long walk through the park had been about. What had he needed to think over? Was it related to something he thought he'd failed at?

"Dad?"

"Hmm?" He didn't look up from the fishing pole.

Something told me not to mention his need to think again. Instead I asked, "Did you and your dad ever go camping when you were a kid?"

At first, he didn't say anything. He set the pole aside and picked up a stick to stoke the fire. There was no missing the tight clench of his jaw as he focused on the growing flames.

Great. I was fucking up the entire weekend.

He finally said, "No, Matty. My dad wasn't a very nice man. He didn't do anything like this with me."

"Oh. Okay." My mom had mentioned on more than one occasion that my dad didn't like to talk about his family or his childhood and that I shouldn't bring up either topic.

I should've listened to her.

He kept jamming the stick into the fire, anger rolling off him, directed more at the flames than at me.

I felt so stupid for asking. I'd just always wondered what my grandfather was like. He was my only living grandparent, and I'd never met him. I muttered, "I'm sorry I brought him up."

My dad stopped with the stick, his focus locked on me across the fire, his eyes serious and steady. "It's not your fault." There was a pointed resolve to the way he watched me that I'd never seen from him before. He gestured at me with the burned end of the stick. "Don't you ever think anyone else's problems are your fault. A person's anger comes from the inside." He tapped his chest, then jabbed the stick my way again. "No matter what happened to a man in his life, it's his choice to let it go or to hold on to it and let it change him."

I had no idea what he was going on about, but I got that it mattered to him that I understood. "All right."

"I mean it, Matthew."

He rarely used my full name, so I just nodded.

In a move that seemed odd given his words, he smiled at me. "And don't worry about that fish today. You have a big heart, and I don't want you to ever feel bad about that. No matter what."

"Okay."

"You're a good kid, Matty, and you're going to be one hell of a man when you're all grown up." He watched me for a moment more, then went back to gazing into the fire, his fist clenched around that stick. When he spoke again a few minutes later, the words were said so quietly I almost missed them. "I don't ever want you to feel the way my dad made me feel."

I didn't think he planned to say anything more, but then he added, "He died this week."

"Your dad?"

"Yeah."

"Oh. I'm sorry."

"It's okay." He dropped the stick to the ground and propped his elbows on his knees as he stared into the fire once more as if lost to another time and place. "It's all going to be okay now."

I wasn't sure how I knew, but despite his words, I had a feeling nothing would be okay again. For either of us.

Chapter Eight

After I finished sharing what happened that day with my dad, I grew quiet. Having gone through the whole thing, I realized now that the dream version wasn't exactly accurate when compared to my memories of that day. In the dream, my dad sometimes morphed into an older or younger version of himself, the younger depiction looking disturbingly like I did now. Sometimes I didn't fall down the hill. Sometimes he pushed me.

It felt good to tell them what had actually happened. It made the dream seem less powerful.

"Matthew?" Richard's voice held a soft, patient tone. He was waiting for me to say more.

"I'm okay. It's just that as much as I loved my dad, that was the day I realized he hid something very dark and damaged beneath the surface."

Richard kept his arms wrapped around my chest.

I laid a hand over one of his. "The next day after we got home, I found out from my mom he'd gotten a call about his dad right before we left for the park. He ended up going alone back to his hometown for the funeral. That camping trip is one of the last good memories I have of him. He changed after that. It took some time, but I could see it happening. At first, it was just the drinking, the anxiety. Then came the anger, the rage. Eventually he directed all that at me."

Richard's body tensed beneath mine again, but he held me with that same gentleness he'd used the entire time I'd been telling the story.

I shook my head as if that act alone could somehow make the words stop pouring out of me. But I *wanted* to talk to them. I wanted to move past this once and for all. "When I fell that day in the park, I knew he cared about me, that he loved me. I heard it in his voice."

"I think," Richard said, "that makes it all the harder on you. Harder to reconcile the bad shit he put you through."

"Yeah."

"But Matthew, you did nothing wrong. No matter what you realized about your dad, it was not your fault that he hurt you."

"I guess I know that. Logically. I just wonder what would've happened if he had talked to somebody about what he went through as a kid. Maybe things would've been different for him. Maybe he wouldn't have become so angry. Maybe he wouldn't have started drinking."

"A lot of people drink, and everybody gets angry sometimes, but they don't beat on their own kids because of it. It was all on him to get help, to stop himself from hurting you. You did nothing wrong." He paused. "Why didn't you tell us all this before you went on the interview?"

"I didn't want to make a big deal about it. I wanted to go, and I thought you might try to talk me out of it if being in that park was going to remind me of him."

We were all silent for a brief moment. I thought maybe they were waiting for me to say more, but then Luke blurted out, "Hell yeah, we would've tried talking you out of going." It was the first time he'd spoken since I'd finished telling them about the camping trip. He was sitting up now, his legs tucked underneath him, arms folded across his chest. "I don't think being anywhere near that park is good for you."

"But I really want this job."

"I get that, but…" He shifted his gaze to Richard as if hoping he'd say more on the subject.

Richard encouraged me to sit up and turn to face them. "He's right. I would've tried to talk you out of going." He held up a hand before I could respond. "But maybe that wouldn't have been the right move. This needs to be your choice. You know what you can handle. You wouldn't put yourself in a position where you'd feel miserable all the time."

I nodded. "I think it'll be okay. If I get the job, it won't be long before I'll have all kinds of new memories there." I hesitated, but I needed to say the rest. "I never told you guys, but I thought I saw him once."

"Your dad?" Richard asked.

"Yeah. After we first moved in here. I went to leave for work one day, and there was a guy across the street. He just stood there, sort of off to the side, staring toward our front door."

Richard's eyes narrowed.

I shook my head. "It wasn't him."

"You sure?"

"Yeah. And now that I think about it, I'm guessing it was someone watching Luke. That was back when your dad was having you followed."

Luke's expression morphed into a guilt-ridden one. "I'm sorry."

"Don't be. I'm just glad everything with your dad is over." Although the minute I said the words, I wished I could take them back. Things with Luke's dad might never truly be over for him. They weren't for me with my dad. At least not in my own head.

"You're sure it wasn't your father?" Richard asked again.

"Yeah."

"Okay." He let out a relieved breath, but the aggravated lines across his forehead weren't going away. "I just couldn't take it if he…"

"I know."

"If that man ever comes near you…"

"He won't."

"How do you know?"

"I guess I don't, really. I always figured if I ever did see him again, it would be because I looked for him."

Richard reached for my hand and held it between his. They were quiet for several beats. I expected Richard to push, ask if I wanted to find my dad, ask if I'd been considering that lately, which was the truth. Instead he asked, "You want to tell us what happened after that camping trip? You've never really talked about what he put you through."

I wasn't sure I could get the words out, even to them. "I rarely think about that part anymore. Even after going to the park, I'm not sure why he's been on my mind so much lately."

"When a memory resurfaces, it can open old wounds."

"Yeah, I guess. What's bothered me the most is that I never told my mom what happened."

"She doesn't know?" Luke asked. "I always assumed she was the one who made him leave because he was hitting you."

"She knew he'd been drinking. But the yelling, the slaps, the shoves, all the times he hit me, that all happened when I was alone with him. She said she didn't like how he was starting to change, to drink heavily, becoming more like *his* dad, so she told him he had to get help or he had to leave. Those were his only options. I guess he didn't want to get better. He just walked away. He didn't even consider getting help. She thought she was saving me from the kind of violence my dad lived through when he was a kid. She didn't know it had already started. I'd gotten good at hiding the results of our fights from her."

Richard's voice was stern but caring as he said, "They weren't fights, Matthew. He abused you."

"I know."

"Do you? Because I'm beginning to wonder if maybe you never really dealt with all this."

"No, I have."

He didn't look like he believed that. Luke either.

"I'm okay about it. Really, I am. It was a long time ago. I just... there's a part of me that hates that I've kept this from my mom for so long. I feel like I'm lying to her."

Luke said, "It's never too late to say something to her, if that's what you want to do."

"Right," Richard agreed. "Might do you some good to talk about it with her. You've been keeping this inside for far too long."

"Yeah, I guess. But I don't want to hurt her. She'd want to know the specifics, what he did, how he hurt me. I couldn't tell her all that. It would break her heart."

Richard nodded, then lowered his eyelids as he sucked in an unsteady breath. "I hate both of your fucking fathers. With everything I am. If I could—" He shook his head in frustration. When he opened his eyes again, they held a haunted look of despair, and the aggravated lines were back across his forehead.

I reached up and ran my thumb over that furrowed brow as if I could smooth away the hurt and anger with just my touch. And maybe I could. His expression softened, and he smiled at me in thanks.

I wanted to drop this conversation and pick up where we'd left off before the dinner with my mom, but I also wanted—*needed*—one of them to make the first move the next time. So instead I asked him, "Do you think I look too young?"

"What do you mean?"

"Maybe that's why no one wants to hire me."

Luke snorted. "That's ridiculous."

"Maybe not." I picked at a loose thread on the comforter beside me. "I think I should get my hair cut. Just in case. So I look more professional."

Now it was Luke's forehead that was all scrunched up. "You don't need to cut your fucking hair. You look great the way you are."

Without a moment's hesitation, Richard reached out and tugged me to him again so I was snuggled against his chest, my head tucked under his chin. "He's right. You're perfect. And you're going to get a job soon. The right job for you. So try not to worry so much."

He'd barely finished the words when Luke slid in close, his arm around my waist. "You know it's gotten bad, Matthew, when Richard's giving advice about not worrying so much."

I laughed. "Yeah."

He kissed my cheek, and with his lips against my skin he said, "Any place will be lucky to have you."

I sighed and settled into their warm embrace. "I don't know what I'd do without you guys."

Luke grunted a low sound. "Good thing you never have to find out."

"Exactly," Richard agreed.

I reveled in their touches as much as their words, until we were all yawning and ready for sleep. We climbed under the covers, and they held me between them again. Exhaustion from talking about my dad drew me into sleep quickly.

* * * * *

The next morning I awoke to find Richard leaning over me. "You sleep okay?"

"Yeah."

He gave me a soft look. "Good. I made breakfast."

"Is it burnt?"

"No."

"Is it gross?"

He snorted out a laugh. "No."

"Did you order takeout from Happy Larry's?" It was his favorite place to have breakfast.

"I may have."

I laughed again.

He traced a path across my forehead, swiping several strands of my hair aside. "It's not fair. You know all my secrets."

"Do I?"

He nodded with another laugh, but then he must've got that I was serious. "Yeah, you do."

"Do we know Luke's?"

"I think so. And if not, it's not intentional." He supported the back of my head and lifted me up for a long, drawn-out kiss.

After we parted, I said, "We better wake him and go eat your home-cooked breakfast before it gets cold." We both looked Luke's way. Still asleep, he lay on his stomach, his arms wrapped around his pillow.

We shifted so we lay facing him, Richard spooning me, an arm across my chest. He rested his chin on my shoulder. "How should we wake him?"

"Hmmm. How about..." I reached for the comforter and slid it down Luke's upper body, revealing the taut muscles of his shoulders and back. "Let's tickle his feet."

Richard chuckled and held me tighter to him. "Perfect."

Just then Luke groaned and stretched, tightening his hold on the pillow, his eyes still closed. "You guys suck."

I shook my head. "Nope, we said nothing about sucking any part of you."

"Especially not your feet," Richard added in disgust.

I turned toward him and buried my face in his neck, laughing more. A second later Luke snuggled in beside me, their warm bodies holding me close, just like the night before.

We were all quiet for several breaths. Then Luke lifted his head. "When are we getting our surprise?"

"Soon."

"Soon? Not now?" He groaned and rolled onto his back. "Seriously? We still have to wait?"

I laughed more. I had no idea what Richard wanted to surprise us with, but it didn't matter. Not really. Because I already had the best life anyone could ask for.

Richard was right. I really needed to stop worrying so much.

The three of us were going to get things back on track, we already were in some ways, and I'd done the best I could at my interview. If I didn't get this internship, I'd eventually get another one. Everything else was in the past. And the past didn't matter anymore.

It was the future that did.

Which had me thinking about what was hidden in a drawer in our bathroom.

Why couldn't I show it to them? What was I afraid of? Did I really think it could ruin things for us? Was that even possible?

Chapter Nine

As I stepped inside our house, I dropped my backpack by the door, and it thudded against the hardwood floor. I had checked out half a dozen books at the public library. Maps of Majestic Falls State Park, information on the care and rehabilitation of local wildlife, and various guides on hiking and how to navigate by map and compass. The latter Alex had mentioned during my interview as a necessary skill, since one of the job's requirements would be to hike through the park to recover injured wildlife. I'd also found loads of new articles and videos online. I couldn't wait to dig into the rest of the materials. I'd read a ton of information before and since my interview, but it didn't feel like enough. I wanted to learn everything I could in case I got the job.

Although, I wasn't sure that was still a possibility. I hadn't heard back from Alex at Windtree yet. It had been two weeks since my interview, and every excruciatingly slow day since then, I'd been at home alone, waiting for the phone to ring.

Most mornings I put in a few hours at the kennel, but with my classes finished for the semester, I was left with all kinds of free time. At first, I tried to distract myself by taking Trixie on long walks, playing Real Racing on my phone, and reading wildlife rehab articles online.

That lasted three days. Then I was left waiting again.

The nights were agonizingly long too. For the past two weeks, either Richard or Luke, or both, had to work late, getting home just before we usually turned in. We hadn't had a chance to talk all that much, let alone anything else. We also hadn't gotten to see Richard's surprise yet.

Feeling disheartened, I decided to skip dinner with my mom for the second time in a row. As I made the call to her, I tried to tell myself that I wasn't avoiding her, but by the time I'd hung up, there was no denying it. If I went over there, she'd want to talk about my dad. Despite that I'd been the one to bring him up, I wasn't sure I wanted to have one more conversation about him.

I tried to ignore that thought as I closed the door behind me.

As usual, Trixie greeted me in the front hall. I gave her scratches behind the ear, and together we headed into the living room. Luke lay on his side on the couch. He had his eyes closed, one arm tucked under his head and his other hand slid between his knees. His laptop sat open on the coffee table. He'd probably dug right back into his work as soon as he'd gotten home. He really needed to take some time off.

I went to the hall closet, got out one of the afghans my mom had made for us, and returned to lay it over him. There was a vulnerability to Luke when he slept that I rarely got to see when he was awake. Richard and I were the only two people who ever saw him like this, so I just stood there for a minute, taking it all in.

Eventually I made my way to the back of the house. I took Trixie outside and played with her in the backyard until even her nearly unending puppy energy was spent. When we returned to the kitchen, I found a pot of vegetable soup—the only completely homemade dish Luke ever made on his own—on the stove. Beside that was a cutting board with a pile of veggies that hadn't made it into the soup yet, like he'd left in the middle of making dinner so he could get back to work. He'd probably had an idea for something he wanted to add to his latest programming project.

The burner was off. I turned it on and added the vegetables. Standing at the sink washing my hands, I heard the front door open. A few seconds later Richard came into the room.

He wound his arms around my shoulders, snuggling up behind me. He kissed my cheek. "How was your day?"

"Good. I learned a lot."

"Yeah?"

"I really want to work there even more now."

He kissed me again, then let go of me and leaned against the counter beside me. "I think you'll get the chance. I've still got a good feeling about this one."

I dried my hands on a towel. "Thanks. But I'm thinking he would've called already if I was the top pick."

"Don't give up hope. Not until you find out for sure."

"Yeah. Guess there's no point in worrying. I can't change anything now."

He kissed my cheek again. "Where's Luke?"

"He's napping on the couch. He started dinner."

Richard tilted his head toward the hallway. "Come on." He took my hand and led me to the couch where we stopped and did the same as I'd done earlier, just stood there watching Luke sleep. Richard whispered, "He's pretty cute when he sleeps."

"Yeah, he is."

"He's been so exhausted lately."

"He's working too hard."

"I think it's more than that."

I gave him a questioning look.

"He's been worrying a lot."

"About what?"

"You."

"Me?"

"Sure. You've been under a lot of stress the last few weeks. What causes you anxiety affects him."

I looked back to Luke.

Richard moved around behind me so he held me as he'd done in the kitchen, his cheek pressed against the side of my head. "Don't you get stressed out when he is?"

"Yeah." There was a hitch in my voice I couldn't control.

"Hey. It's okay. I wasn't trying to make you feel bad. Just wanted you to know that you've been on his mind a lot. He loves you."

I nodded.

"So if he's sleeping more or seems on edge sometimes, try not to worry. It's temporary."

"Okay." I had a feeling he wasn't just talking about Luke. I laid a hand on the arm he had across my chest. We stayed like that for a minute, saying nothing. Then I had another thought. "Stress doesn't just make him sleepy."

Richard laughed, a deep rumble I'd never tire of hearing. "Nope. Not just sleepy."

"It also makes him horny."

"Yep. That's our Luke. Sex is his security blanket."

I laughed too. "I don't mind. But…"

"What?"

"You really think sex can go back to the way it used to be for us?"

"Absolutely. I'm sorry I didn't realize he was struggling with this."

I peered over my shoulder at him. "You were too."

"I'm not anymore."

We exchanged a long look. Was he just saying that to make me feel better?

Before I could ask, Luke drew in a deep breath and shifted to lie on his back. Slowly his eyes fluttered open, then widened as he took in the sight of us standing beside the couch, watching him. "Creepy much?" He lifted up onto his elbow and scrubbed a hand over his face. "Were you watching me sleep again?"

"Yep," I said.

He raised his brows at us. "How often do you guys do that?"

Richard and I exchanged a glance.

"What do you think, Matthew? Three times a week?"

"I think it's more like four or five."

"That's right. I forgot about all the mornings we set the alarm early just so we can get up and watch him."

Luke rolled his eyes. "Great. I married a couple of freaks."

We both stood there in shocked silence, beaming down at him.

He squinted up at us in return. "What?"

Richard pointed at him. "Don't ever stop saying shit like that."

"What shit?"

With a huge grin still plastered on his face, Richard started for the hall. "I'm going to set the table for dinner."

"What shit?" Luke called after him.

I bent down and gave him a kiss. "You called us married."

"Oh jeez." He dropped back down to lie on the couch. "I really need to think before I speak."

I shook my head. "Nope. No thinking. You're at your best when you don't think." I laughed as I headed for the kitchen.

$$* * * * *$$

When we were wrapping up dinner an hour later, Richard set his napkin on the table and asked, "So, you guys ready for your surprise?"

Luke sank back in his chair with an exaggerated groan. "Finally!"

Richard got up from the table. "Close your eyes."

Luke shot a curious look to me, then one across the table to Richard. "Is this about to get kinky?"

"No." Richard folded his arms across his chest. "Are you going to close your eyes or not?"

"Only if you promise to do kinky shit to me while they're closed."

This time Richard silently, stoically stood there, eyebrows raised.

I leaned in to Luke's side. "You better quit teasing him."

Richard nodded. "You want your surprise?"

Apparently Luke wasn't done playing. "You going to make me beg for it?"

Richard's brows climbed higher. He lowered his arms and sauntered around the table. Then he pulled Luke to his feet and backed him to the kitchen wall. Grasping Luke's wrists, he raised his arms over his head, pinning them to the wall above Luke's head. "Would you like that? Because you know I can make you beg all night. I'll make you beg and squirm and scream, and then only I'll decide when and how you get to have it. You want that?"

"Yes." Luke bucked his hips, seeking out contact.

"Well…" Unrelenting, Richard leaned in, pressing his groin against Luke's. He rotated his hips in slow circles, mercilessly rubbing their clothed cocks together. "We'll need to see what we can do about that. Soon." He held there for a few seconds more, then let go of him and stepped back. "But right now, the surprise. Wait here." He headed out of the room, leaving Luke leaning against the wall, panting, his eyes wide, an obvious bulge at the front of his slacks.

I shook my head. "Told you. You gotta stop teasing him."

"Yeah. When the fuck will I learn that?" He sucked in a deep breath but made no move away from the wall.

I got up and went to him. Standing before him, I said nothing. Just licked my lips, teasing him by keeping my lips parted as I ran my tongue over them again. "Is there something you need, Luke?"

"Touch me."

Taking a single step forward, I softly ran the tip of my index finger over the front of his pants, slowly, tantalizingly tracing the bulge of his hard cock. He jerked his hips forward, seeking out more pressure. I shook my head, then dropped my hand and stepped back. "Can't get distracted. We've got a surprise coming."

I took my seat again.

He stood there for another few seconds, taking shallow, uneven breaths. When he'd composed himself, he returned to sit beside me. "You know you do that teasing thing as good as he does."

I arched a brow his way. "Do I? Huh." I struggled to keep a straight face. "I'll take that as a compliment."

"You should. No one's ever got me worked up the way you two do."

"And no one else ever will again." I met his gaze once more, feeling confident in a way I hadn't in months. "Don't you forget that."

"Never."

Despite my confidence, I searched his eyes, trying to read if there were any doubts behind that one word.

Before either of us could say anything more, Richard came back into the room. He didn't appear to have anything with him, and he didn't take a seat. "Close your eyes."

We did. No smart-ass remarks from Luke this time.

"Okay. Take a look."

The first thing I saw was the huge grin on Richard's face. He was beaming.

On the table before us sat a single sheet of paper: a printed web page from a real estate site. Pictures and information about a house for sale. A two-story blue Cape Cod–style home with white trim and white shutters.

"What's this?" Luke asked. "You want us to buy that house?"

"Well, maybe not this specific one, but yeah, I'd like us to talk about getting a new place, something we all pick out together. I thought showing you what I was thinking would be a fun way to bring up the topic. We could take a drive there and see it tonight. I met with a real estate agent and told her the basics of what we'd need and a price range, and she suggested this one and a dozen others that all have pretty much the same space we have now. Unless you think we need something bigger." He asked me, "Are you going to be bringing a lot of stray animals home that you'll need to nurse back to health?"

I shook my head, utterly speechless. He wanted us to live somewhere else? The blue house in the pictures seemed nice enough. It had a flower-lined walkway bursting with the striking purple of English lavender. The path led from the front sidewalk to a substantial porch that had a swing, and the house had a series of interesting peaks that I found charming. The exterior was a combination of stone and brilliant blue siding that I also liked.

But it wasn't *our* house.

Richard still stood across the table, the tips of his fingers tapping his thighs at his sides, excitement radiating off him. This was important to him. I gave him a tentative smile.

Luke was examining the various pictures of the house's interior. "It's nice. I'll miss the basement bedroom, though."

"Huh." Richard glanced toward the basement doorway on the other side of the kitchen. "I hadn't thought of that."

I had. It was where we had some of our most meaningful moments, in and out of bed.

"If we want," Richard added, "we can add a playroom to the basement in whatever house we buy."

Luke lifted his head. "I'd like that." They held the stare for a moment, but when Luke focused on the paper again, there was a slight sadness to his expression. Was that about the bedroom in our basement? Or was he anxious about the idea of moving? I waited for him to bring up whatever was on his mind.

He didn't.

Or maybe I was reading him wrong. He continued surveying the bullet points that highlighted the house's features, nodding as if he liked what he read about the new place.

Before I could stop myself, I blurted out, "I don't want to move!"

Richard stood motionless for a beat, eyeing me with surprise. Then he pulled out the chair on his side of the table and sat across from us. He didn't say anything. Just calmly, silently sat there and waited for me to go on.

I bit my lower lip and tried to assemble the jumble of thoughts into a coherent string of words. I didn't want to hurt him or keep him from doing something that was this important to him. I knew part of the reason he wanted to buy a new house. We weren't there when he'd bought the townhouse, and that bothered him. He wanted the place where we lived to feel like it was ours too. We'd already told him it did, but if this was going to be one of those things that would eat away at him, then I wanted to do whatever necessary to make him feel at ease. After everything we'd gone through, maybe he needed a fresh start. I just wasn't sure how different he needed things to be.

"Matthew?" He was looking at my hands where they were clasped together on the table, one thumb rubbing the back of the other.

I tried for a deep breath and unfolded my hands. The words came tumbling out, only not the ones of support I'd intended. "You're trying too hard."

"What do you mean?"

"You said you're putting the past behind you, but you're still trying to make up for stuff that you don't need to worry about. You still feel bad about what happened to Luke and me at the Harrison estate. You blame yourself because we were in danger, so you're trying to fix things by buying us a house. You said you'd let it go, but you're not." I wasn't only referring to what had happened at the Harrison estate, and we both knew it.

He nodded. Was he agreeing with me or just trying to tell me he heard and understood me?

"I love where we live," I said. "And it's not like we need more space or anything. We each have an extra room, plus the basement. And—" I forced myself to stop. I hated the incensed sound of my voice. It wasn't me. I didn't talk like this to the people I cared about.

That was what my father did.

Richard searched my eyes. "What?"

More calmly I said, "This house is special." I shook my head. I needed to stop this. I was being overly sentimental, but I couldn't keep the rest from spilling out. "It's where we had our first date, where we got to know each other, where you asked us to move in, where Luke told us about his past, where we—" I shook my head again before the tears could start. What the hell was wrong with me? Was this really about a house?

With sudden urgency, Richard got up. He grabbed the back of the chair he'd been sitting in and dragged it around the table to sit beside me. Moving in close, he cupped a hand over my nape. "Where we fell in love."

I nodded. "It's not just where we live. It means something to me." I glanced at Luke, and I knew I'd been right. "For Luke too."

He offered a nod in agreement.

"You're right," Richard said. "This place *is* special. It always will be. But I want the home where we spend our lives together to be a place we all have a say in. Together."

"It doesn't matter to me that I wasn't here when you bought it. This is still my home. *Our* home."

He gave me a considering look. "The idea of moving really bothers you this much?"

I gestured to the printout of the blue house. "That place looks great, really, but when I think about moving, I just get really sad. Even if it's something you want, something that's important to you, I can't shake the feeling that it's not the right move for us."

He gave a nod. "Okay."

"Okay?"

"Then we won't move." He looked toward Luke on my other side.

"Sounds good to me."

"All right." Richard smiled. "Then it's settled."

"Just like that?" I asked.

"Yep. Just like that."

"You were so excited about this."

"Because I thought it would be something fun we could do together. It isn't a good idea unless we all want the same thing."

"That doesn't sound right. We're not always going to want exactly the same thing."

"That's true. But with the big stuff, I think we all need to agree." He caressed the back of my neck. "I wanted to do this because I felt bad that you weren't here when I bought this house. But that's all it was. Nothing about feeling guilty or anything else. I was just worried you guys might feel like this place was more mine than yours. If that's not true for either of you, then I won't let it bother me anymore. I'm letting go of my guilt." He ran his palm along my cheek. "I am."

I reached up and laid my hand over his, leaning into his touch. "I know that. I don't know what's wrong with me."

"I think everything that's happened lately has shaken your confidence."

I let go of him. "No."

"It has, and I hate that. I hate that I was a part of that. I want to help you get back to where you were headed before that night we fought. You told Luke he needed to talk to us, but you need to also. You have to tell us what you're feeling so we can help. Don't hold back because you're embarrassed or you think something shouldn't bother you."

"I'm trying not to."

"Good." He stroked my cheek again, with his thumb this time. "I want you to have everything you want out of life, everything that makes you happy. But more than anything, I want to be a part of that happiness."

"I want that too," Luke added, sounding both full of misery and fear, like he was afraid of the same thing I'd been lately, that he'd somehow broken us.

I tried to show him with a single look all that I felt for him. "You are. Don't you guys get that? Being with you two, it makes me feel strong and brave in a way I've never felt before. Having your support is the most amazing feeling."

Luke leaned in and offered a long, chaste kiss. Then Richard slid in closer and kissed me too.

When we separated, he said, "It is amazing." He tugged me out of my seat and onto him so I was straddling his lap. He kissed me again, his large hands cupping my ass, holding me close, and I felt the truth in his touch almost more than his words.

"It is amazing," Luke echoed after a brief moment watching our embrace.

Without letting go of each other, Richard and I turned our heads his way.

"You know," Richard said, "you're back to doing that thing where you just repeat everything we say."

"Am I? Really? Huh." Luke sounded genuinely surprised.

"And we're going to keep calling you on it. Aren't we, Matthew?"

"Yep." I held Richard's face in my hands, turning his head toward me. No matter how much I loved teasing Luke, I needed something else right then. I pulled Richard in for another kiss. I didn't hold back. And neither did he. The kiss was sensual and explosive all at once, his wet, warm tongue sliding over mine again and again as he hauled me closer.

When Luke spoke again, his voice was rough with need. "You always think you're the one in charge, big guy. But really? It's Matthew. He's got us wrapped around his little finger."

Did I?

Richard drew me even closer. "Yeah, he does. And I wouldn't have it any other way."

Maybe they were right. In a way. Maybe I was the real reason things had been so strained between us. Because I'd been timid, holding back more than them, and that had thrown everything out of whack for us.

I leaned forward, grasping the top of the chair behind Richard in both hands. I rocked my body over his lap as I whispered in his ear. "I know what you want, and it has nothing to do with buying a new house." I ground down over him again, feeling the swell of his cock through his dress pants. "You know what I want too." Another tantalizing rock of my hips. "And you're going to give it to me. You and Luke. Right now."

His breath caught.

When I sat back, he glided his hands around to my front, up my chest, brushing my nipples through my T-shirt with his thumbs, then taking a path down my body, lower and lower. Confidently, assuredly, he tore open the front of my jeans.

He glanced at Luke.

Without a word exchanged between them, Luke inched his chair closer and slid a hand inside my pants. He cupped my cock through my underwear, rubbing it sensually at first, then mercilessly. I thrust up into the touch in no time. Richard kissed me again, almost matching the movement of his tongue with each swipe of Luke's strokes along my aching dick.

Then all at once, Richard pulled back. He shot Luke another look.

As if that communicated everything, Luke got out of the chair and dropped to his knees beside us. Without moving my underwear out of the way, he took the head of my cock into his mouth.

How the hell had they gotten so good at that silent communication thing? Or was it lust-filled instinct driving them on?

The thin fabric of my underwear was no match for that hot, wet mouth. I groaned, begged, pleaded for more.

And Luke gave it to me, his saliva and my precum leaving a growing wet patch on my briefs. Inside me a swell was building. Surging, rising, trying to find its crest.

Luke let go of me and sat back on his ass. His lips were wet. His chest rose and fell with each deep breath that surged out of him. "I want you guys to give me a show."

Richard ran his thumb over Luke's lower lip. "You got it." He bent down and kissed him, all moist lips and slow swipes of tongue against tongue.

Luke stood before the kiss had ended. "Come on." He hauled me up, then Richard next.

"Yeah," Richard said. "Upstairs. Bed. Now." He took my hand and then Luke's and led us into the hall.

Before we made it to the steps, as if he couldn't wait another second, Luke tugged me tight against him. His hands at my lower back, he brought our lips together. I groaned and clawed at the dress shirt covering his upper arms, trying to drag him even closer. I couldn't get enough of him. My body was on fire, alive with an energy I hadn't felt in months. I swayed under the wave of desire, but that was okay. He had me.

When we parted for air, Luke leaned sideways and whispered something in Richard's ear. I couldn't hear what he said, but Richard nodded as Luke let go of me and took a step back. Richard undid the top two buttons on his dress shirt, along with his cuffs, then drew the entire shirt off over his head in one motion. God, he looked amazing. All sculpted muscular flesh, a light dusting of blond hair on his broad chest. He came forward, an almost predatory look in his eyes, and kissed me again. That same powerful, passionate, consuming kiss as in the kitchen.

But I wanted more. So much more.

I backed him toward the base of the stairs until I had him flattened to the wall. He stared down at me with such intense desire I thought I might lose it from that look alone. Then he grabbed my ass, lifting me off my feet. With my legs wrapped around him, he spun us so my back was against the wall. His lips found the skin below my ear. He nibbled and licked and stroked my flesh with his tongue as his body ground against my heavy, full cock again and again.

I arched into him, giving him more to rub against. That had him groaning in my ear. "Fuck, Matthew. Do you have any idea what you do to me?"

"Oh God. Do you have any idea what I want you to do to me?"

Richard grunted in response, his hips slamming against me faster. "Bed. Now." He held on to me and started for the stairs.

I tipped my head back and laughed. It wasn't often he became nearly incoherent. I heard Luke laughing too. He stood close, enjoying the show Richard had promised him.

Richard carried me up four steps but then stumbled on the next.

"Careful," Luke said with a grunt. "I don't want to spend the night in the ER."

"Fuck it." Richard stopped and laid me down on the stairs. He knelt before me and scrambled to get my still-open pants down.

I laughed again. God, it felt so good to be like this with them. I reached out and grasped his shoulders.

He started working my jeans past my hips. I had to let go of him so I could prop myself on the step above and lift my ass up. When the pants were at my thighs, he gave up on them and cupped my bulge through my underwear, massaging my cock, stroking and teasing me until I could barely stand it.

Apparently he was teasing himself too. He groaned again. "I want this. It's mine."

"It's yours. All of me is yours. You know that, right?"

He nodded.

"And Luke's," I added in a rush.

"Yeah. Luke's too."

Luke snorted out a laugh. "As long as we all remember that, then we'll never have an issue."

Richard turned toward where Luke leaned against the hall wall, watching us through the banister rails. "That has never been an issue."

And I loved that. Richard hated the thought of sharing us with other men, but he didn't have any issues with Luke and I being just as important to each other as he was to us.

"Do you know…" I had to stop and catch my breath.

He kept jerking me off through my underwear, his focus now locked on my face. "Do I know what?"

"We wouldn't be here without you. You're the one who—" I groaned and arched into his touch again. "Fuck, that feels so good."

His hand stilled. "I'm the one who what?"

"Kept us together in the beginning."

The lust-filled expression on his face shifted to something far more heartfelt. "I've never regretted that I was so pushy."

Luke came up the stairs and slid in to sit beside me on the same step. "Yeah, yeah, we're all glad you're a pushy bastard. Now…" He snaked an arm around Richard's waist and brought him forward toward me again. "Where's my show?"

Richard settled his body over mine, but he planted a heated kiss on Luke. "Talk about pushy." He kissed him again, turning it into something even more sensual and hungry.

When the kiss ended, Richard kept his gaze locked on Luke. "We're not doing this without you."

"You better not."

Richard sat up with a start. That strength and confidence he usually exuded was back. He got my underwear out of the way. As soon as my cock was free of the fabric, he shimmied down the stairs and dropped his mouth over my length.

I bucked up under him. "Yes!" I loved watching him go down on me, his wet lips sliding along my shaft, my full length glistening with his spit, his cheeks sucked in as he worked to make me feel so damn good.

"Shit, that's beautiful," Luke said.

"Uh-huh." I wasn't going to last long. I grasped Richard's head in my hands and tugged him off me. "Now. Please." I reached for the front of his pants.

"Wait." He snatched my wrists, stopping me. He tucked my dick back into my underwear. "Lift up." Despite my confusion, I raised my ass off the step. He hauled my jeans over my hips again, then wrapped my arms around his neck. "Hold on." He picked me up and carried me up the stairs without strain, calling back behind us, "Get up here, Luke."

In our room, he laid me on the bed and followed me down, lying half on the mattress beside me, half on top of me. He slid a hand into my open pants, stroking my wet length, his biceps flexing as he jerked me off. The stare he directed at me was electric. I wanted to touch more of him, all of him.

Instead I asked, "We're not moving to a new house?"

"We're not going anywhere."

"Okay."

"But we *are* missing something."

For a panicked second, I gaped up at him. Was he talking about the two of us? Was this not good for him? Did it not feel as right for him as it did for me?

He gave me a wink, then shot a look across the room. "Luke, get your ass over here."

Luke smirked back at him from where he stood near the bedroom door. "Thought you were giving me a show."

Richard shook his head. "Not today. We're doing this together. All of us."

Luke came forward and lay on the bed alongside me, opposite Richard. Then he tugged Richard in close, and they kissed over top of me. Their lips parted, tongues tangling, all while Richard kept massaging my cock like it would hurt him physically to give up that contact.

God, I loved when they did that. Kissed while one of them touched me in such an intimate way. It made me feel closer to them.

Watching them also fed something primal in me that drove my arousal higher, had me desperate in seconds, and made me love them even more. It still amazed me that I got to be a part of them, that I was as important to them as they were to each other.

Richard asked Luke, "Help me with him?"

"You got it."

They shifted their focus to me.

Together they undressed me, getting me down to my underwear as they kissed and licked and sucked on my skin everywhere from my neck to my knees. Two sets of lips. Four hands. Caressing and stroking and branding me with hot kiss after kiss, each man loving on me until Luke hauled Richard off the bed and started undressing him. When he had him naked, Luke took a step back and stripped off his own clothes. As if he needed that thick, full shaft in his mouth or he'd die, Luke hit his knees and took Richard's cock between his lips. Watching Luke's enthusiastic blowjobs were almost as good as feeling them on my own dick. Almost.

Richard held Luke by the back of the head as he kept his gaze locked on me. "Damn, he's good at this."

I nodded. "He is."

Luke took him deep and paused, and I knew he was swallowing around the head of Richard's cock. Richard gasped. He dug his fingers in Luke's hair. "Stop. Stop."

Luke released him. "What?"

"I'm not coming until I'm inside him."

"Yeah. Definitely." Despite those words, Luke leaned in again and slid his mouth down Richard's shaft once more, sucking him like crazy, his head bobbing, his fingers stroking Richard's balls. He moaned around the dick in his mouth. I couldn't help but smile. Richard absolutely loved when Luke did that last bit.

"Fuck." Richard jerked his hips forward. Then he grasped Luke by his hair and tugged him off his dick. He hauled Luke to a standing position. Holding him by the back of the head, he dominated the kiss, the angle, the pressure.

With their lips still touching, Luke grinned. "Yeah. There you are. That's the man we first met."

Richard scoffed. "Haven't gone anywhere."

"Yeah, but you were hiding a bit, holding back."

"Apparently you were too." He turned Luke my way, and together they came forward and got onto their knees on the bed. "We're not holding back now."

"Fuck, yeah, we're not."

Richard hooked an arm around me and pulled me up to straddle his lap. He kissed me, never taking his lips from mine as he shifted us around so he lay on his back, me on top of him, with Luke stretched out beside us.

I sat up and rocked my groin over his, and we both moaned at the sweet slide of our bodies.

"Christ." He reached up and held my face. "Kiss me again." He didn't wait. He sat up and plastered our lips together. One beautiful melding of our mouths after another.

Then I moved lower, kissing along his skin, down the base of his throat, along his collarbone. He fell back against the bed, one hand petting the back of my head. There was no hesitation in his touch this time, and I reveled in that contact.

I felt Luke's warm breath against my ear. He tongued and nibbled my earlobe, then joined me in loving on Richard's body.

Richard held us both by the backs of our heads now as we made our way lower. I kissed his stomach, his right hip, his left. I breathed in his scent as I ran my lips along his flesh. It all felt so unbelievably good. I needed to taste him, to feel his hard length, feel how much his body wanted mine.

I took hold of his thick shaft. Luke joined me and together we ran our tongues all over the flared head, kissing each other as much as we were his cockhead. The sleek slurping sounds and Richard's guttural moans filled our bedroom. Then Luke pulled back and took over with his hand around the base of Richard's shaft, his other hand teasing his balls. He threw me a grin. "You got this."

I so did.

I sat up higher for a better angle and slid my lips over the head of Richard's cock, loving the sleek feel of the crown, the moisture at the tip, the pulse of need flowing through him. I sucked for all I was worth, then dropped my mouth over his full length.

He buried his fingers in my hair, cupping my head in both hands.

I groaned. God, how I'd missed that. I liked knowing that he craved my mouth on him more than anything else in that moment, that he wanted to stay buried inside my wet heat until he came.

He moaned again. His abs tightened. He was close. If he was going to fuck me, we needed to stop. I just wasn't sure I could pull off him, wasn't sure I could make a move that would turn the moment into something else, which felt so odd. I didn't need to be nervous. This was Richard. And it was sex. I'd always felt comfortable in bed with them.

Always.

Well, except for early on that first night at the Haven. I'd been so afraid he and Luke would find me boring or annoying or clingy. I didn't want to drive them away before we even got going. But the minute I'd kissed them both, everything else faded away. I was at ease and confident with them in a way I hadn't been with any other men I'd met at the club.

I wanted that feeling back.

Luke's breath brushed my ear again only a second before he said, "Stop. Don't let him come yet."

Right.

I moved up Richard's body again as Luke got in behind me so we were both straddling him.

"Hold out your hand," Luke said, and when I did, he squeezed lube into my palm.

Richard laughed. "That's our Luke. Always prepared. Such a good sex scout."

I laughed too, and the tension eased as Richard met my stare.

"Yeah," Luke said. "And you love it. Don't pretend you don't."

Richard nodded. "Yep. From day one."

I looked over my shoulder at Luke. "From day one."

He snorted out a laugh. "How come I'm the only one who gets busted for repeating shit?" But then he must've seen something in my eyes, some last bit of anxiety. He gave me a long, sweet kiss. "It's going to be great. I promise."

"I know." I returned my focus to Richard. Grasping his cock, I slowly stroked his length with both hands, trying to show him how much this moment meant to me, how much I wanted to feel that thick, full shaft buried inside me. Richard exhaled sharp breaths, his eyes locked on mine as I slathered the lube over his dick.

"That's right," Luke said as he slid off Richard and lay beside us again. "Just like that."

I kept on stroking Richard, far longer than necessary, my nerves battling with the desire blazing through me.

"Stop," Luke said again.

I looked his way.

"You want him to fuck you?"

"Yes. God, yes."

"Okay, but..." He sat up and ran a hand tenderly through the back of my hair. "He needs you to take the lead for the next part. We *both* need you to take the lead this time."

Richard was now looking at me with silent anticipation, and I knew Luke was right.

"What?" I slid off Richard and got up from the bed, my body vibrating with frustration. "Then everything's not all right between us. Because you don't really trust me."

"No." Richard rushed to sit up. "That's not it. At all. I just wanted to feel it some more. *Really* feel it."

"Feel what?"

He opened his mouth to respond, but Luke beat him to it. "How much you want us."

"Oh." I looked from one to the other. The fact they both had stayed on the bed, neither moving to follow me when I'd pulled away, and the quiet way they were watching me now said more than their words. They both looked so... vulnerable. Just how I had felt a few minutes earlier, and the night before when I wanted to get something started with them but also needed them to make the first move.

I shook my head. "I don't know what's wrong with me. You're allowed to feel things, to need things from me."

Richard turned so he had his feet on the floor, "So are you. I think you need the same thing we do." He reached for me and pulled me to stand between his legs. "No hesitations. No overthinking things. All of us just in the moment together."

He was right.

My phone sounded with a new text message. Maybe it was Alex, setting up a time to call. I rushed to the bathroom to wipe the lube from my hands, then retrieved my phone from my jeans that were lying on the floor. I checked the phone's screen.

Shit.

"I have to go." I gathered my clothes and started getting dressed.

"Now?" Luke asked as he shot off the bed.

"I need to go talk to my mom. She's really upset. She knows I've been avoiding her. She said she needs to see me tonight." I did up my jeans, then turned away and crossed the room.

"Hey." Richard came to me in the doorway. "I'm sorry about..." He gestured toward the bed.

"No." I wrapped my arms around his middle and laid my head against his chest. "You don't have to be. I want to know what you need, what you're feeling. I'm sorry I overreacted."

"It's okay." He slipped his arms around me. "Everything's okay."

"Yeah." I pulled back right as Luke stopped beside Richard. I added, "We're going to get there again. Right?"

"We are," Luke said, then leaned in and kissed me.

When we parted, Richard gave me the same sweet kiss. "We are."

Then they both held me.

I didn't want to pull away again, but after a minute I said, "I really do need to go see my mom. I can't stand that I worried her."

"All right," Richard said as they let go of me. He held my stare, and I knew he had something important he wanted to say before I left. "Whatever you decide to tell her or not tell her about your dad is okay. It's your decision to make, Matthew. There's no wrong move here. Whatever you need."

"Right," Luke said. "Whatever you need."

Chapter Ten

"Are you sure you want to do this?"

I nodded at my mom. "I think I have to."

She remained seated across the kitchen table from me for another moment as if unsure she could do as I'd asked. Then she finally said, "Okay. I'll be right back." She got up and left the room.

As I'd suspected from reading her text earlier, she'd been worried about me after the question I'd asked about my dad and then the cancellation of our last two usual dinners together.

I'd gotten to her house a half hour earlier, and we casually chatted over coffee until she finally mentioned my father. She told me she hadn't seen or talked to him since the night he left us, but that led into a far more serious discussion about why I'd brought him up.

She returned to the kitchen and took her seat. I could feel her gaze on me as she silently slid a piece of paper across the table. She seemed like she wanted to say something. I wasn't sure I wanted to hear it.

I spotted the old worn wooden rocking chair in the corner of the room. She'd always loved that chair. She had rocked me in it when I was a baby and hadn't been able to part with the chair since. I really needed to get it fixed for her. With several of the spindles broken, she couldn't even sit in it now.

The rocker had started to fall apart when I'd been in high school. At the time, my dad said he'd fix it, but then a week later he'd taken off. I didn't want to examine too closely what it meant that I'd never gotten that chair repaired for her, or what that said regarding any unresolved feelings about my dad and his exit from my life.

"Mom, would you mind if I worked on repairing that?"

"The rocker?"

"Yeah. I'd really like to."

She looked lovingly at the chair, then gave me a similar expression of affection. "I'd like that too."

"I'll come by later this week with Richard's car so I can take it home with me, if that's okay with you."

"That sounds perfect." She reached across the table and held my hand in hers. "Thank you." When she let go, she got up and came around the table. She kissed me on the top of the head, just how she used to do when I was little. "I'll get us some coconut pie."

As she crossed to the counter, I stared at the piece of paper she'd left on the table. Did I really want to make this call? Could I deal with the consequences when I did?

An alert for a new text message sounded on my phone. I dug it out of my pocket and read the message. It was good news, just not for me. I couldn't ignore the pangs of jealousy and anguish. I stood. "Mom, I'll have to take a rain check on the pie. I've gotta get going."

"All right." She came back to the table and offered an embrace, remaining quiet as she held me. It was uncharacteristic of her not to smile and request that I be careful.

When she let go of me, I picked up the piece of paper.

She studied me for a long moment. "I gave you that because I trust you to do the right thing for yourself, but I want you to promise me something." She hesitated for a long moment, then finally broke the unusual silence, her voice stern. "If you decide to use that number, and you find what you're looking for, do not go alone."

"Okay."

"I mean it, Matthew. Either you tell Richard and Luke, or I will. I know I'd be interfering in your relationship, but I'd do it to make certain you have the emotional support you need."

"I know. I wouldn't keep this from them."

"Good." She gave me another hug. "Try not to worry about the internship. I'm sure you'll hear something soon."

I nodded and didn't share with her that another clinic had called that day and said they'd already filled their internship slots, or how I was guessing that I hadn't been selected for the Windtree internship since the deadline was long past. And here I'd thought Alex really liked me.

I'd also thought my instincts were telling me that I should say something about my relationship with Luke and Richard up front at every one of my interviews, but maybe I'd just been messing things up for myself.

Maybe I'd lost the best job opportunity I was ever going to have because I'd been overthinking things, being too emotional and wrapped up in my own feelings.

I wanted that job. So much. But most of all... I didn't want to feel like a failure. Or feel the sting of rejection one more time in my life.

* * * * *

I watched the cab pull away from the curb until I could no longer see the taillights in the distance. I was stalling. As if those extra few minutes would make a difference.

When the cab's lights were gone, I turned toward the house.

Time to face the music.

I hiked my backpack higher on my shoulders. After I had the front door unlocked, I tugged on the handle, but the door wouldn't budge. I tried again. Nothing. What the hell was wrong?

As I attempted once more to get the dang door unstuck, my keys slipped from my fingers and landed on the stoop. As I bent to pick them up, my head spun and my stomach turned. The next thing I knew, I was on my hands and knees, swaying from side to side.

"Whoa." I did not like this feeling. And it was only getting worse. I wasn't sure I could keep from face-planting right there outside our front door.

Eventually I was able to slide a leg under me and teeter my way to solid footing. I tried again with the door but had no success.

"Stupid fucking door." I couldn't remember it ever sticking before. Just my luck that it'd choose right then of all nights to do something like this. I tried again, giving the door handle a tug with both hands, and only then did I remember the door opened inward.

"Duh." A laugh surged from my chest, a series of low giggles I couldn't control as I pushed the door in and stumbled inside the house.

Even with the hall light on to guide my way, my foot caught on the edge of the carpet runner, and I pitched forward, ramming my gut into the hall table. I managed to keep the table upright, my hands clasped on each side of it. If only the two sets of keys lying on top weren't sliding across the surface. I scrambled to catch them, but I was too late. They clattered to the floor, making a racket.

I held still, lying over the table in the silence that followed.

There was no way Richard and Luke had missed all that noise I'd made coming into the house. And then there was the annoying chirping sound behind me. What the hell was that? Had some kind of big-ass bird gotten inside? The chirping was getting louder. I covered my ears and glanced around, spotting no bird or other wildlife on the loose.

"What *is* that?"

A red flashing light caught my eye.

Oh, right. The house alarm.

I probably only had a minute left to get the dang code entered.

I slipped my backpack off my shoulders, swung the front door shut, and approached the control panel. Without giving it too much thought, I punched in numbers on the keypad, hoping muscle memory would do the trick. It must've. The red light turned green, and the chirping halted.

Thank God.

The tiny green light on the panel seemed to glow more vibrant the longer I focused on it, growing brighter and brighter in the darkened house. I felt dizzy again, nauseated.

Then the giggling returned. I hated the way it made me sound. Who giggled when they were feeling sick?

Who giggled at all?

No men I knew. Richard sure didn't. His deep, sensual laugh was sexy as hell. That sound alone always drove me crazy. So did his toned, tanned body. Every inch of him was masculine and strong. A man's man. So was Luke. Just the opposite of how I looked and sounded.

I shook my head and spoke to the alarm's display panel. "What do they even see in me?"

The glowing green light didn't answer.

I closed my eyes and dropped my head forward until I had my forehead pressed to the wall beside the alarm. Something wet nuzzled my hand at my side. Without opening my eyes, I said, "Hey, baby girl. Did I wake you?"

Trixie licked my fingers, and I laughed again.

No, *giggled*.

"Matthew?" That deep voice cut through the humor like a shot. Even with my eyes closed, I could tell lights were turning on, could hear two sets of footsteps on the stairs. Then a hand slid across my upper back. "Are you sick?" Richard asked.

"Maybe. I don't feel right." There was no missing the slur of my words. I opened my eyes in time to see Luke lift a hand to my forehead.

"You catch that flu going around?"

I swiped his arm away. "No." I laughed again. Why the hell couldn't I stop laughing? Then I got a good look at them, and the amusement was gone. They were serious as hell, wearing only their underwear and two concerned, confused expressions.

"I'm sorry I woke you guys up." I pushed away from the wall. Only I didn't come to a stop soon enough. I started to pitch backward. "Whoa." I tried to catch myself but found nothing to grab on to. My arms weren't cooperating anyway.

"Hey." Richard caught me with one hand around my forearm and his other at my back, steadying me. "You okay?"

"Matthew," Luke said in an incredulous tone. "Are you drunk?"

I understood his surprise. I never drank. Never. I usually hated being around anyone who did. I had major trust issues after the way my father hit me every time he tried to find whatever he'd been missing in life at the bottom of a bottle.

With a hold on my upper arms, Richard turned me to him. He searched my face, his eyes wide.

I stared back. "Your eyes are so beautiful. I wish I had green eyes." I shook my head. "No. I like that we all have different colored eyes. That's probably silly." Something a stupid kid would say. The dizziness was back. I dropped my head forward to his chest. "I don't feel so good."

A rush of breath hit the back of my neck as he let out a long, uneven exhale. "You going to be sick?"

"I don't think so."

"All right. Come on." He wrapped an arm around my shoulders and got us moving for the stairs. "You're getting in bed."

That brought the giggling fit back. I laid a hand on his chest and leaned into his side. "I like our bed." I tripped on the first step.

"Jesus," Luke said.

"I got him." Richard swooped me up into his arms.

I laid my head against his shoulder as he started up the stairs. "You're so strong."

Once in the bedroom, I thought he'd deposit me on the bed, but he kept us moving into the bathroom. He set me down on my feet and held me by the upper arms again as I swayed. "Hang on." He shifted me backward, and there was Luke behind me, holding me up.

"I got ya," he whispered against my ear.

Richard went to start the shower. I turned my head so I could see Luke. Those sharp blue eyes were intently watching me. I smiled at him. "I love you so much." He opened his mouth, but I raised a finger to his lips to stop him. "It's okay. I know you really don't like to say it all the time."

His forehead scrunched up, and he reached for my hand, moving it away from his mouth. "You think I don't like telling you that I love you? You think I don't say it enough?"

I turned my whole body to face him and slipped my arms around his waist, burying my face in his neck. "It's okay. I know how you feel. I know you love me."

"Hey." That was Richard. I thought he was talking to me until I opened my eyes and found him standing beside us, his gaze fixated on Luke, the palm of his hand splayed across Luke's nape. "You don't need to change anything about yourself. We know how you feel about us, every time you touch us."

I nodded. "Uh-huh. That's what saying I am." I reached up to pat the side of Luke's face but miscalculated and caught Richard's cheek instead.

"Great," Luke said. "We'll be lucky if we can understand him in a few minutes. What the hell is going on?"

Richard started tugging my T-shirt over my head. "Let's get him in the shower first."

When the shirt was off and Richard had a hold of me again, Luke crouched down and worked my pants and underwear off my legs. "I can't believe he drank, let alone got drunk." He was talking so low I could barely hear him over the running water.

I wrinkled up my nose. "I don't like the taste of beer."

Richard opened the shower door. "Good. Get in." He guided me inside. Then he slipped off his underwear and followed me in. He gripped me by the biceps and turned me so the steady spray of water pounded my shoulders and upper back.

I yelped. "It's hot."

"Uh-huh." He reached for the bottle of shampoo. "And when we get out, you're drinking a glass of water and taking some aspirin. You'll thank me in the morning."

I closed my eyes as he wet my hair and lathered it with shampoo. "You're so good to me."

He just grunted in response as he rinsed the shampoo from my head, his fingers working through the strands of my hair in tender sweeps.

I heard Luke moving around, opening cabinet doors. "Got towels and the water and pills," he called out from behind the shower door.

Richard shifted us around so his back was to the water as he went for the shower gel on the shelf beside us. He ran his large soapy hands all over my body, working in slow, careful swipes across my chest, my back and shoulders, along my arms, and down over my hips.

I pulled him in close. "I love the way your hands feel on me.

Thank you for touching me like this again." I stood on my tiptoes and kissed his neck. With the steam trapped in the shower stall and the hot water warming our skin, I felt like we had slipped into a private oasis. The heat of his solid, muscular chest against mine was electric, sending desire surging through me. I couldn't stop myself from shifting against him in a seductive slide of wet body over body.

I pressed another kiss to his neck, adding a swipe of my tongue. "Tell Luke to come in here."

"We're not having sex when you're drunk."

A low whine came barreling out of me.

Luke chuckled as he entered the shower behind me. The space was tight for three people, but that was okay. It kept us all close. He pressed into my back. "Was he trying to make out with you?"

"Pretty much."

"I am not." I reached back with one hand and gripped Luke's ass, tugging him closer so his groin was smashed against my lower back.

That had Luke laughing again. "Who knew he could get more affectionate?"

But Richard wasn't laughing. "Stop." He held my face in his wet, soapy hands. They smelled of my fresh-mint shower gel. His voice was hard, somber. "You're going to get some sleep, and then you're going to tell us what happened tonight and why you got drunk."

I rolled my eyes. "We were just celebrating my friend's new job. Sheesh."

"Don't sheesh this. Drinking is not that simple for you. It never will be."

I shoved at his chest and then pushed Luke backward with my elbows. "Let me out of here." I flung the shower door open and stumbled out, grabbing a towel on my way by the sink and wrapping it around my waist. "I'm not a fucking child."

Suddenly feeling sober and alert, I stormed out of the bathroom, water dripping from my hair onto my shoulders and back. I heard the shower cut off, then the two of them getting out. I stopped in the center of our room, three feet from the foot of the bed. I wanted to take off, head downstairs to get the bottle I'd brought home with me. It was tucked away in my backpack. But I didn't want to look at it again until I understood why I'd purchased the damn thing in the first place.

Richard spoke but didn't approach. "I didn't mean to treat you like a child."

"I know." I couldn't face them. I shivered, despite the warmth from the water that lingered on my skin.

Richard asked Luke, "Can you get him something to wear?"

"Yeah, sure."

But Luke must not have moved.

"Luke." There was a long pause. Then Richard added, "It's going to be all right."

"Yeah, okay."

Out of the corner of my eye, I spotted Luke as he went to the dresser we shared. He dug through one of my drawers.

I felt Richard's presence behind me before his arms came around my chest. "Come to bed with us."

Unable to say anything, to do anything else, I leaned into him.

He walked me to Luke's side of the bed, and Luke brought me a pair of underwear and pajama pants.

I took them from him. "I don't feel so good."

Luke ran a hand down my arm. "You gonna be sick?"

"I don't know. I don't think so."

He toweled me dry, then helped me with my clothes while Richard returned to the bathroom. When Richard came back with the glass of water and aspirin, I sat on the edge of the bed and took the pills.

Luke peeled back the sheet and comforter, and I crawled in. He followed me down, tucked the blankets over me, and spooned me along my back. Richard got dressed in a pair of his sweatpants and then climbed into the bed on his side.

He didn't say anything. He slid close to me, one arm tucked under his head as he scanned my face. Without moving my lower half away from Luke, I rested my forehead against Richard's chest, taking in the faint scent of my shower gel combined with his own woodsy cologne that lingered on his skin. He petted the back of my head.

My body started to relax, the adrenaline fading.

"I just want it to stop."

"Want what to stop?" Richard asked.

"The thoughts. The dreams. I just want to move on. I just want to stop falling."

"Falling?"

"Down that stupid hill."

Chapter Eleven

I awoke in the middle of the night with two warm bodies pressed against mine, two arms wrapped around me, two men holding me close.

Despite their comforting touch, I couldn't shake the lingering feel of every branch and clump of dirt digging into my back, the sound of my dad's panicked voice as he called out for me. There was compassion and worry and love in those cries.

Why couldn't I stop reliving that day?

I slid out from under their arms and then the blankets so I could work my way to the foot of the bed. Sitting on the edge of the mattress beside Trixie, I bent forward, clutching my spinning head until my stomach decided it was done holding on to its contents.

I dashed for the bathroom, swung the door shut behind me, and dropped to my knees before the toilet. The vomiting didn't stop until long after my stomach was empty and I was left dry-heaving.

I sank back against the wall opposite the toilet. The tile floor, chilly even through the pants I wore, felt like heaven against my heated skin. A part of me wanted to lie down right there and press my cheek to that enticingly cool surface. Instead I forced myself to get up.

When I had my face washed, teeth brushed, and mouth rinsed with mouthwash, I felt slightly better. At least physically. I studied my reflection in the mirror. No matter what anyone said, I knew the truth. My hair *did* make me look young. Too young. Like I was still in high school.

Just a stupid kid.

I dug in the bottom left drawer of the vanity and removed the electric shaver. It didn't take long before my head was covered in dark fuzz instead of the wavy hair I'd had all my life. The sink and most of the countertop were obscured by my curly strands.

I stared at myself in the mirror again. I looked different.

A lot different.

"Oh God." *What did I just do?*

Tears welled in my eyes.

I shook my head and forced myself to stop. I was not going to cry or get upset. Not about my hair, the internship, or my father.

Swallowing down the tears, I stared at myself again, hoping I at least looked older. I wasn't so sure. I sort of looked like I was going into the military.

Like a man.

With a nod, I said, "Okay." Then I undressed and climbed into the shower. I was rinsing the stray hairs off my shoulders when I heard the bathroom door open. My stomach churned.

A second later the shower door cranked open. A very audible gasp followed. "Matthew!"

Luke.

"Kid, what did you do to your hair?"

Oh God. Oh God. I looked stupid. My body started to shake, despite the warm water cascading over me. I covered my face with my hands, but that did little to muffle the strangled squeak that escaped my chest.

Luke stepped in behind me and tugged me around, pulling me against his chest. He wore a pair of underwear. The fabric was quickly soaked through. He didn't seem to care. "What happened? What's wrong?"

"I thought maybe I'd look older, more responsible, if... Oh God." I wrapped my arms around his waist. "Richard's going to hate it."

"What are you talking about? Your hair?"

"He's going to hate it like this." I stepped back and held the top of my head in both hands. "He loves to run his hands through my hair when I'm sucking him off." They both did, actually, but saying it about Richard to Luke seemed easier.

"Matthew, he's not going to give a shit about your goddamn hair. He's going to be worried because you're this upset."

"I'm not upset!" I squeezed my eyes shut and shook my head. I was *not* going to cry.

I. Was. Not.

I heard the bathroom door open, then the shower door, but I couldn't bring myself to look at either of them. "I'm fine." I shoved at Luke and turned away from him toward the spray of water. "I'm fucking fine!" The shouted words bounced off the shower walls and rang in my ears, leaving behind an unbearable, painful silence.

"Matthew." The nervous sound of Luke's voice was a new one for him.

I couldn't stop the frustration and despair racing through me. "Just leave me alone. Please. I just want to be alone."

I wasn't sure if I expected Luke to step out of the shower or Richard to get in. Then a moment later, Richard was there with us.

I thought he'd try to get me to talk the way Luke had done, but he didn't. He maneuvered his way under the spray of water to stand in front of me. He held me by the hip with one hand and ran the other over the top of my head. A slow smile spread across his lips. "You look hot."

"You don't hate it?"

He shook his head. "Not at all." He swept his palms all over my cropped hair. When he let up, he held my face with his hands and stepped in closer so we touched along our bare lengths, his thumbs repeatedly sweeping over my skin. He bent and kissed my right cheek, then my left, and finally my lips. "It's not your hair that makes you so damn sexy."

I sucked in a sharp breath and held on to him.

He offered another tender kiss. Then another.

I wanted more, but the water was growing cold.

He took my hand in his. "Come back to bed with us."

"Okay."

He held my hand as we stepped out of the shower. Luke didn't follow. He just stood there under the tepid water, his mouth hanging open. He gestured to me. "You're not going to make him talk about this?"

"Not now. He needs something else right now."

I drew in another deep breath and nodded. I wanted it so badly. I needed to feel them, needed to know everything in my life wasn't completely fucked up, that what we'd been working to fix between us was okay. I wanted—*needed*—to feel something other than the anxiety and disappointment and aggravation surging through me.

When Richard had us both dried off, we went to the bed. I crawled to the middle of the mattress and lay down while he went around to his side. Luke moved in to lie beside me, his damp underwear still on, his wide eyes watching me with concern. No matter what I was feeling, I got how lucky I was to have them, to know I wasn't going through this alone.

Richard got in the bed. "Come here." He drew me to him. He didn't try to kiss me or get anything sexual started. He held me with my head pressed to his chest as we'd been earlier when I'd fallen asleep.

When he made no other move, I said, "I thought we were going to do something."

"We are doing something. We're holding each other."

I laughed. "I meant sex."

He caressed my bare shoulders and back. "We're going to stay right like this until you can breathe without sounding like you're running a marathon, until you can think about what you're feeling without trying to avoid it. Then you're going to talk to us."

I shook my head. "No." I buried my face in his chest. "Please, don't." I kissed his skin. Once. Twice. "I need you."

He caught my chin in his hand and lifted my head up. "You got me. You got us."

Luke slid in closer behind me and wrapped an arm around my waist. "Always." There was a slight shake in his body. I could feel the fear in the clench of his arm.

I didn't want to disappoint them or hurt them, but... "I don't want to talk anymore. I don't want to feel like this anymore. Everything was just starting to get good again."

"I know," Richard said. "You don't have to talk until you're ready. Just lie here with us."

I breathed deep. "Okay."

"No." Luke lifted up. "I want to know what's going on. Right now."

"Luke." Richard's voice was patient but determined.

"What? Why are you picking now not to be so damn pushy about shit?"

I hated that they were arguing again because of me. I couldn't stand to hear it. I sat up, crawled over Luke, and headed for the bathroom again. I got dressed in the pajama pants I'd had on earlier. On my way back through the bedroom, I avoided looking at them.

I didn't stop until I was down the stairs and at the front door. With my backpack in hand, I went into the kitchen. I had the bottle out on the table in front of me, an empty glass beside it by the time Luke and Richard entered the room. Richard wore his sweatpants again, and Luke was in a dry pair of underwear. They stopped at the table but didn't sit or say a word.

I clutched the bottle of Jim Beam, letting the base scrape the surface of the table as I spun it around and around. "This was my dad's drink."

"What are you doing with it?" Luke sounded even more anxious than he had upstairs. When I didn't answer, he added, "Why did you drink tonight?"

"Because my friend Kimberly got a job and she asked a group of us to go out celebrating with her."

"So? You've gone out with your friends from school before. You never had a problem being the one who wasn't having a drink."

"I do when I'm the last one in my class without an internship, and I'm feeling kinda shitty about it. People have a drink after a crappy day, right?"

Richard swiped the bottle off the table and pointed it at me. "You keep telling me not to hold back on what I'm really thinking, that I shouldn't worry if it sounds too controlling, so here goes—"

Before he could say more, Luke seized the bottle of bourbon from him. "Well, I don't give a fuck how I sound." He aimed the end of the bottle my way the same as Richard had done. "You are *not* drinking this."

I snatched the bottle back from him. "I know I'm not. That's not why I bought it." Despite my words, I opened the bottle and poured some into the glass.

Richard breathed deep, a shaky, uneven sound I tried to ignore. He stepped around my chair and sat beside me. "Matthew, you don't need to drink this—or *not* drink it—in order to prove you're a better man than your father."

"Jesus." Luke reached out and cupped my chin. He tilted my head back. "Is that why you bought this? Is that why you drank tonight? To prove something?"

I shrugged. "I don't know. I guess." I sighed as I faced the glass of booze again. "Which is fucked up. I know that. It's the reason my dad started drinking. After he left, my mom told me about my grandfather. He was an angry drunk who hated my dad. He abused him from the time my dad was two years old until he left at seventeen. He burned him with cigarettes, whipped him with his belt, beat him every day, sometimes until he was unconscious. My dad had scars all over his body that he hid from me. He was a broken, damaged man before I was born, before he ever had a single drink. From what Mom said, returning home for his father's funeral brought up all the pain he'd tried to bury. I guess he started drinking because he wanted to prove he was nothing like his father. But instead, it released all the rage he'd never let out." I picked up the glass of bourbon and tipped it back and forth, watching the slosh of gold liquid. "I just don't understand. If he loved us, why wouldn't he at least try to get help?"

"Because," Luke blurted out from where he still stood beside the table, his arms crossed over his chest, "he was a selfish prick."

Richard nodded, but then he added, "Or maybe he did what he thought was right for you. You're better off without him. Maybe he understood that."

"I guess. But I don't get how he could walk away. How could he hurt me like that and then just leave?"

"You don't get it, Matthew, because you could never understand a man like him. You are nothing like him."

I didn't want to give that serious thought right then. Instead I told them, "I decided not to say anything to my mom about what he did to me. It would destroy her if she thought she didn't send him away soon enough. I won't—*I can't*—do that to her. It was never her fault."

Richard cupped my cheek. "I get that, but Luke and I want you to do what's best for you with all this, not what's best for your mom."

"I am. I think going over it with her would just make me feel even worse. When I was at her place earlier tonight, I realized something. I don't tell her everything about my life, everything the three of us do or say or about our sex life. It's okay to keep things from someone you love if it's what's best for both of you."

"It is," Luke said. "But Richard's right. You need to talk to someone about what happened to you."

I held the glass, squeezing the hell out of it as if I could make everything disappear if I could just shatter that glass with my bare hands. "My dad loved me when he was sober. I knew that. It was the main reason I didn't say anything to my mom when he started hitting me. Why I pretended it never happened. Why I couldn't blame him at first and told myself it was just the booze. But it *was* his fault. He was the one who drank, who let the alcohol give him a reason to take all his pain and anger out on me."

I couldn't stop the frustrated words.

Maybe they were right. Maybe I needed to talk about this. But why? Why did this still bother me after all this time? Because I'd never allowed myself to be angry, to really let it all out. I had buried it down deep inside.

Like my dad had done.

I sucked in a sharp breath.

There was no way I would let myself become him. I was not keeping this inside any longer.

Forcing the words out, I said, "I remember every detail of the first time he hit me."

Luke quietly moved to sit on the other side of the table facing me. I could feel Richard's hand on my back, but I couldn't make myself look at either of them. If I did, I might stop talking. I needed to do this. I'd never told anyone this story.

"My mom was working nights. He'd spent hours at a bar near our apartment that night, and when he came home, he was already drunk, which wasn't anything odd at that point. Like usual, I started helping him to bed. He tripped, and we fell into the hall wall. I guess he thought it was my fault. He shoved me, and when I tried to help him again, he hit me across the face with the back of his hand. He struck me so hard, the other side of my face smacked into the wall. When I turned to him, he did it again. Harder. That time I landed on the floor, blood from my lip dripping down onto my T-shirt. There was so much rage in his eyes. I couldn't believe what I was seeing. I couldn't believe he'd done that to me. I thought it was a nightmare. I thought I'd wake up at any moment, and it would all be over. Because that wasn't my dad. That was someone else's father."

I lifted my head. "And you know what?" I grabbed the bottle of bourbon and the glass and stood. "It's not ever going to be me." I marched across the kitchen to the sink, poured the entire contents of both the glass and the bottle down the drain, then jammed the empty bottle into the recycling bin below the sink. The abrupt movements had my head spinning. I whirled around and sank back against the edge of the sink, covering my hands with my face.

The next thing I knew, I was on the floor, both of them there with me, one on each side of me.

Richard pulled me against him. "It could never be you. Just because you have that man's genes doesn't mean you are—or ever will be—anything like him."

"I know that. I do. I don't know what's wrong with me." I shook my head. "I'm just so mad at him. He needed help, and he chose to run away instead. He never once tried to get in touch with me. Or Mom. He never sent us any money. She had to work so hard just to pay for food and rent. He left all that on her shoulders. He left—" I let my head fall back to the cabinet door behind me, trying to push aside the rush of emotions. I was so tired of feeling this way, of thinking about this, talking about it.

I wasn't that scared, defenseless kid anymore.

I was a grown man.

Richard sighed. "Maybe you shouldn't have gone to that park."

"No. It's not the park. I really like it there."

"But," Luke said, "maybe it's too much."

"I think maybe it's exactly what I need. I have to find a way to let this go."

Richard stroked my buzzed hair at the back of my head. "You will."

I nodded. "I will. I have to."

We were all quiet for a long beat. They sat there on the floor with me, Richard still holding my head, Luke's hand on my knee, his thumb rubbing in comforting circles.

Then all at once it hit me what Richard had said earlier about the bottle of booze. I turned to face him. "I don't want you to stop saying what you really think. I'd rather you were honest with me more than anything else."

"I know. We all need to be honest with each other. About everything."

"I want that too."

He searched my face. "You sure?"

"Yeah, of course."

He gave a nod. "Then here goes. I don't want you drinking again. Not because I want to control you or tell you what to do, but because I don't think it's healthy for you. It'll always be something that's mixed up with your father and what happened to you as a kid. And it's also pretty clear alcoholism runs in your family. If you ever feel like you did tonight, you don't go out drinking. You talk to your friends or your mom, or you come home and talk to us."

"I will. I promise. I feel better just talking to you guys about it."

"I'm glad."

We grew quiet once more.

"Matthew." Luke hadn't said anything for several minutes. "I'm sorry."

"For what?"

"That you had to go through all that when you were a kid. That your dad hurt you. I wish—" He stared at his bent knees, his jaw clenched.

I waited for him to continue, but he said nothing more. I looked to Richard.

He said simply, "Luke."

Luke jerked his head up as if surprised to hear his name. His eyes were moist. He exhaled angry huffs of air as he looked my way. "I hate your father. I want to find him and end him." He shook his head in agitation. "But mostly, I wish I'd known you then. Wish I'd been your friend. Someone you could've hung out with, been safe with. You shouldn't have had to go through that alone."

"Yeah." Richard leaned into me and rested his forehead against my temple. "What he said."

I sighed around a laugh. That was usually Luke's line. Which was funny, considering how good Luke had gotten at saying what he thought and felt lately. He had so much passion inside him, so much devotion and kindness and love, and when he said something intimate and sweet, it always blew me away. I was honored that he'd let us see that man he'd tried not to be for so long. His words about my dad had been one of the most honest, beautiful things he'd ever said to me.

He tugged me against him, and I buried my face in his neck as Richard wrapped his arms around us both.

Chapter Twelve

When I could finally speak again, I sat up. "Thank you for what you said."

Luke ran his fingers over my cheek as he whispered, "I'd give anything—*anything*—if I could make everything better for you."

I sighed at those words, at his touch. "I know you would." Now that the adrenaline had faded, I felt sick again. "My head hurts."

Richard stood and gingerly pulled me up. "Let's get you back to bed."

Luke stood behind me and kissed my bare shoulder. "You can sleep in tomorrow, and I'll wake you up with a nice long blowjob."

I smiled back at him. The sweet words from him were amazing, but the sex stuff he said was pretty dang good too.

I hadn't thought it was possible to love them any more than I did before that moment.

We headed up the stairs and got into bed. I wasn't sure when I drifted off to sleep, but I awoke sometime later with my head on Richard's chest, his arms around me and one of Luke's arms draped across my middle. Without opening my eyes, I could tell the sun was up, but I didn't want to move. Not yet.

A moment later the bed shifted as Luke sat up behind me. He leaned over me like he was trying to get a look at my face. Then he asked in a hushed whisper, "He's been asleep this whole time?"

"Yeah." Richard swept a warm hand across my upper back. I was just about to tell them I was awake, when he spoke again, his voice strained. "I hate seeing him hurting like this."

Luke shifted closer. I heard them kiss, and then Luke said, "I know." He pressed in close again and offered another kiss. "You think this is all about his dad?"

"A big part of it, yeah. But maybe it's a lot of things all at once."

Luke gingerly ran a hand over the back of my cropped hair. "What are we going to do?"

"I think he needs to see someone."

"Like a therapist?"

"Yeah. But I'd really like him to come to that conclusion on his own."

"Is that because you don't want to tell him what to do?"

"It's not that." At first Richard didn't say anything further. Then when he did, I heard the hesitation in his voice. "I think the only way he's really ever going to heal is if he finds a way past this on his own. I don't think you or I can try to pick up the pieces for him. As much as we'd like to."

I couldn't imagine how hard it was for him to admit that.

Luke rotated to sit up against the headboard. "That call earlier this morning should help."

"Yeah. I think so."

I shifted my head on his chest to give them some warning. "I'm not asleep anymore."

Richard chuckled, his upper body jostling under me. "You been listening to us?"

"Maybe." I lifted my head. "You don't have to worry about me so much."

Luke laughed at that. "Seriously?"

Richard threw him a pointed look. Amusement laced the expression.

I laid a hand over his heart and propped my chin on the back of my hand. "You were right when you said it was just a lot of stuff at once. I don't have a job yet and going back to that park brought everything up with my dad more than I thought it would, but I'm okay now." I paused, thinking over the night before. "I shouldn't have had anything to drink like that."

I lifted up and turned to sit between them with my back against the headboard. They were studying me with concern. I knew what they needed to hear from me: that I would go see someone about this. I just didn't want to talk about my father anymore. I didn't want to rehash it with another person. I wanted to be done with it.

They watched me for another minute. Then Luke said, "You got a call this morning. On the house phone." He grabbed the cordless phone from the nightstand. He hit the speaker button and played the message.

"Hi, Matthew. This is Alex Vega at Windtree Wildlife Rehab Center. Sorry to call so early, but I wanted to let you know as soon as I could. You are our top pick for the internship, and we'd like to offer you the position. Give me a call as soon as you can, and we'll discuss

the specifics. I really enjoyed talking with you at your interview, and I'm looking forward to working with you. Talk to you again soon." The message ended.

"Oh my God." I bounded up onto my knees. "I got the job?" I crawled to the end of the bed and swung around to face them. "I got the job? Really?"

Luke laughed. "What? You think we faked that message to make you feel better?"

Richard laughed too. "Congratulations, Matthew."

"Yeah, kid, congrats."

I smiled at Luke, then Richard. "Thanks." The giant dopey grin grew. I couldn't believe it. "I got the job." A joyful laugh surged out of me. "I got the job!" I barreled forward and flung myself at them. They caught me in their arms and held on to me.

A comforting peace settled over me. Maybe what had been wrong with me lately, the unease and uncertainty, had more to do with feeling like I'd been failing than anything to do with my past.

Yet even as that thought ran through my mind, I knew it wasn't that simple.

Chapter Thirteen

Sitting on the couch in the living room three days later, I heard two sets of footsteps coming down the stairs. One pair was solid. The other trudged along like he'd been awoken from a deep sleep.

I had every light on in the living room, the coffee table before me covered in an array of books, articles, and my open laptop. I'd been too excited to sleep, so I'd slipped out of bed at four in the morning and got started on more research. I wanted to be as prepared as I could before I returned to Windtree Wildlife Center.

Richard entered the living room first and came to sit beside me on the couch. Luke followed, sprawling out on his back so his head lay on the book I had open on my lap. He stared up at me with heavy-lidded blue eyes. I was certain the only reason he'd gotten up was because Richard had woken him and told him I wasn't in the bed with them.

I smiled down at him.

"What's with all the books?" he asked. "I thought you already studied up on everything possible about taking care of wildlife."

"Hardly. There's so much to know." I shrugged. "I want to make a good impression."

"You will. You have almost two weeks until you start, right?"

"Yeah." The board at the center had to officially approve the new intern, so I had to wait until after their next scheduled monthly meeting.

Luke lazily kissed his index finger, then pressed it to my lips. "You're gonna do great."

"Thanks."

"What were you reading?" Richard asked as he gestured to the book on my lap.

I slid the book out from under Luke's head and showed Richard the cover. "*A World of Wildlife in Our Backyard*. Alex wrote this one."

"Alex?" Luke sat up beside me. "He's the vet at the center?"

"Yeah. The book's all about Majestic Falls and the different types of animals there. Most people who live nearby don't even get how amazing the park and the surrounding national forest are. Alex has had some really interesting cases. Listen to this." I sat up taller, opened the book to the part I'd been reading, and read aloud.

"*My assistant and I had been tracking the coyote for an hour, trying to get close enough to sedate it with a blowgun. When I finally got a good shot, the coyote was more than a hundred yards from the river. After the dart hit his side, he took off. When the sedative started to kick in he was too close to the edge of the river, and he fell into the water face-first. That was disastrous. The worst possible thing that could happen. We were trying to help him, and we might've just killed him. He could drown in seconds. We had to get to him and lift his head, but we were nearly the length of a football field away from him. He could also still be partially awake and claw and bite at us if we touched him too soon. Nevertheless, we raced for the water. When I was a few feet away, I could see that his head was turned slightly and his muzzle was above the waterline. He was breathing fine. We had lucked out. I let out a deep sigh of relief. Then we got started on situating him for the procedure. The surgery to remove the dead tissue and suture his wound was the easy part that day.*"

"Wow," Luke said.

"He had to perform the surgery right there along the river too, trying his best to set up as sterile an environment as he could."

"Very cool."

"Yeah." I flipped to the colored photos at the center of the book. I pointed to one with Alex. "That's him." I indicated the boy next to him. "And that's his son, Tomas. He's a couple of years older now. And this is his wife, Natalie." I flipped more pages, each depicting various animals and the spectacular cliffs and waterfalls of the park. "He took all these pictures."

Luke got a closer look. "Dang, it's gorgeous there."

"Yeah." Richard indicated a photo taken from the top of a cliff overlooking one of the falls. "Look at that. I had no idea it was so remote or so beautiful. I've heard about that place for years, but I've never been there."

I nodded. "The entire area is this incredible mix of forest, hills, meadows, caves, and gorges. It's a huge tourist attraction. Lots of campers and hikers and climbers go every year. Did you ever go camping as a kid?"

"Nah," Richard said. "My parents were never the outdoorsy type. Camping wasn't their thing."

I looked at Luke.

"Sure." He flipped a hand through the air. "My dad and I went all the time, whenever the senate had a recess. We'd canoe, go fishing, roast marshmallows over the campfire, tell ghost stories." He rolled his eyes. "Not. The only thing he ever did with me was throw the ball around on our front lawn when he wanted a good photo op for the press."

I bumped shoulders with him. "Sorry."

He shrugged like it didn't matter, and maybe it didn't anymore, at least not the way it used to. He eyed me with regret as if it had been rude for him to make a joke about his dad in front of me.

"It's okay," I said. "Part of moving past the issues with my dad is finally accepting that I actually have issues. But you know what? Everyone has shit they hold on to. Everyone. Dealing with it and trying to move past it is a lot more than some people do."

"Yeah." He searched my eyes. "You're figuring that out a lot younger than I did. How the hell did you get so smart?"

I scoffed. Smart? "I feel like I don't know anything lately. I feel like I have no idea what I'm doing."

"You do, kid. You really do." Before I could say anything in response to that, he added, "Thanks for talking to us about your dad."

"Yeah." Richard's hand came to rest at the back of my head, stroking my shorn hair. Since I'd cut off the curls, he'd been touching me like that even more than he used to. He offered a couple more strokes. Then his hand stilled on my head. "I've been thinking about everything you said about that trip with your dad." He looked toward the lighthouse painting that hung above the fireplace. He remained quiet for a moment, his focus locked on the image of the raging, choppy water beating against the rocks in the painting. "This isn't easy for me, but…" He hesitated again, then returned his attention to me. "If you need to see him, I'll go with you. And I'll help you find him in any way I can."

Luke's jaw dropped. "What?"

I gaped at Richard. "How did you know?"

"It was a hunch. I'm right, though, aren't I?"

"Right about what?" Luke swung his gaze from Richard to me, then back to Richard.

"He wants to find his father."

"And you think this is a good idea?"

"I think it doesn't matter what you or I think about it."

"The hell it doesn't."

"Luke."

They held the stare for a moment. Then Luke sat back and ran a hand through his hair. When he dropped his hand, it made a loud slap on his thigh. He shook his head in frustration, but the scowl faded when he turned to me. "This is what you want?"

"Maybe." I refocused on the book on my lap that sat open to the pictures of Majestic Falls State Park, the last place where my dad had been a loving father to me and not someone I also feared. "I'm not saying I want a relationship with him, at all, but there are things I need to hear from him. And things I need to say to him. I want him to see how good I turned out without him, to see that I didn't need him." And deep inside, in a place I tried very hard to pretend didn't exist, lurked a part of me that wanted my father's approval, that also wanted to hear him say he was wrong for hurting me and then leaving us.

Would I ever stop being that insecure kid?

As if Luke sensed something about where my thoughts had gone, he bolted upright and spun my way. "You listen to me, Matthew Stewart. There is nothing you need from that man. You are so much better off without him in your life."

"I know. But I need closure. My mom said she looked him up online a couple of years ago, out of curiosity, but she couldn't find anything. No address, phone number, social media accounts, nothing. It was like he disappeared. She gave me the name and phone number for the attorney who sent her the divorce papers. He was the brother of one of my dad's friends. She thought he might know how to get in touch with him. I haven't called yet. I wanted to talk to you guys about it first." I paused and forced out the next part. "But I did call Kevin after I left my mom's house. He said he and Walter could probably contact the lawyer and find my dad for me."

Since Luke's friend Walter was an ex-cop, and his boyfriend Kevin still worked as an investigative reporter, I figured they'd know how to go about something like that.

"Okay." Richard took my hand in his. "Sounds like a good place to start. They'd certainly handle it however you felt comfortable."

It meant the world to me that he was giving me the space to make my own decision on this, but... "Why are you doing this? You said you never wanted him near me."

"Because you need to work through this, and you're the only one who knows what will help you do that."

I shook my head. "I'm not sure what I want to do yet."

"It's okay. Take your time. Think it through. When you know, we'll be there for you."

"Yeah." Luke sounded reluctant, but when I looked his way, he said, "Richard's right. It's your decision. I can't say I feel good about you having that man in your life in any way, for any amount of time. In fact, I'm not exactly sure how I'd keep from beating the shit out of him if I ever saw him near you." He slid an arm around my shoulders and kissed my temple. "But I get needing closure. I really do."

"Thanks." I just wasn't certain I'd ever know the right thing to do. I waited until the flood of emotion passed. Then I bumped elbows with Richard. "How do you always know what I'm thinking?"

"I don't, trust me. I wish you'd talk to us more."

"Yeah," Luke said. "Same here."

I gave him a quick kiss, then one to Richard.

When I shifted to lean back against the couch, something dug into my ass cheek. The TV remote. The sound of the local news filled our living room.

Luke laughed. "Your ass is very talented."

I turned to him to offer a comeback but stopped short. A familiar image was on the TV: a picture of Alex Vega superimposed over a map of Majestic Falls State Park.

"Search dogs and a helicopter are being used to comb through the park in an attempt to locate the veterinarian or his remains."

Chapter Fourteen

"What?" I spun toward the TV, focusing on what the reporter who stood near an entrance to the park was saying.

"The sheriff has given no indication as to whether they believe foul play could be a factor in the veterinarian's disappearance. The sheriff did say that the doctor went into the park alone for a routine animal rescue on the day he vanished, and that their search efforts to locate him will continue throughout the day. We'll bring you more as this story unfolds. Reporting live from Majestic Falls State Park, this is your local Action News Team, on the ground and in the air to bring you the news you want most."

I grabbed the remote and clicked the TV off. "Oh my God."

Richard placed a hand in the middle of my upper back.

"What should I do?"

"I don't think there's anything you can do."

"Maybe I could call the center, see if they need anything."

He nodded. "Sounds like a good idea."

"What time is it?"

Luke checked the clock on the wall. "After seven thirty."

Before I could move, Richard got up and retrieved my cell phone from the end table. He handed it to me. "I think it's okay to try calling now, given the situation." He sat in the chair facing me, while Luke stayed beside me on the couch.

I clutched the phone in my shaking hand. This couldn't be happening. I stood and paced the room as I dialed. A man answered. I identified myself and told him I was supposed to start work there soon and that I'd seen the news about Dr. Vega.

"Ah, yes, Mr. Stewart. You're on my list of people to call. I'm the head of the center's board of directors. I'm sorry to say that we're temporarily closing the facility."

"They haven't found Alex yet?"

"No. We thought it best to close until we know more. Even with all our volunteers, it'll be hard to keep the place running without the doc. We're moving most of our seriously injured animals to other facilities in the state who've agreed to take them in. A handful of regular volunteers will care for the rest. That's really all I know for right now. I can call you when we have a more permanent plan in place on when we'll reopen. We'll understand if you need to make other arrangements for employment before then."

"Is there anything I can do? I could come in and help with the animals."

"The volunteer coordinator is organizing their care. I'll let her know you're available if they need assistance."

"Are the police asking for people to help with the search?"

"No. Right now they're using local law enforcement and the park rangers. They don't want anyone else to get lost in the park."

"You think that's what happened? That Alex got lost?"

"Probably not. He knows that park better than anyone. I imagine he was injured in some way and couldn't make it back to his truck, but they haven't found his vehicle yet either."

My heart sank. Would they find Alex in time? Or was it already too late? And what about Tomas? Would he lose his father? Would he ever know what happened to his dad?

The director added, "I probably shouldn't say more, but there's also speculation that this might not be about something happening to him in the park. I guess he and his wife have been hurting financially, and with the added pressure of a new baby... Well, the sheriff is looking into the idea that he just couldn't take it anymore and drove off."

"He doesn't seem like the type to leave his family."

"No, he's not. It's just that he's such a quiet guy, keeps to himself a lot. Hell, he spends most of his free time with the animals or alone out in the park. Most people in town don't know him all that well, so there's a lot of talk going around. I don't think the sheriff is seriously considering the rumors, but he's got to follow up on everything." He paused. "Listen, Mr. Stewart, I really need to go. There's a lot of press here. It was good of you to call."

"Please let me know if there's anything I can do to help."

"We will. Thank you."

We exchanged goodbyes and hung up. I returned to sit on the couch and relayed the conversation to Richard and Luke.

"Dang," Luke said. "I hope he's okay."

I nodded. "Me too."

Richard kept a concerned eye on me from where he sat across from us. "I'm sorry about the job."

I shook my head. "That doesn't matter. I just keep thinking about his family. They must be worried out of their minds. They have no idea what happened to him."

With an urgency I didn't see coming, Luke reached for me and wrapped me in his arms. There was an uneasiness to his touch, and Richard still studied me like he thought this might send me over the edge, like I was about to lose it or something. I'd really scared them lately. What with the drinking and cutting all my hair off and going on and on about my past.

"I'm okay." When neither said anything in response, I added, "Really. I'm just worried about Alex and his family. I wish there was something I could do for them, some way I could help."

Chapter Fifteen

The ringing of my cell phone pulled me awake. It was past eight. The bed lay empty beside me, Richard and Luke long gone for work. It was the morning I would've started the internship, nearly two weeks since the news of Alex Vega's disappearance.

I rolled toward the nightstand on Richard's side of the bed and grabbed my phone before it stopped ringing. I checked the caller ID. *Windtree Wildlife Rehabilitation Center.*

I sat up in a rush and answered the call. No one responded.

"Hello?" I tried again.

Nothing. I checked my phone. The line was open.

"Hello? Is someone there?"

Still no answer.

I hesitated. "Alex?"

I waited but heard nothing. I rechecked the phone. The call had been cut off.

Maybe the caller had a bad connection on their end, and they'd call back.

Or maybe I should.

I waited two minutes and then dialed. All I got was a recording stating that the center was temporarily closed and providing the number of another wildlife facility to contact for emergencies.

I returned my cell to the nightstand and lay down again, speculating on who might've called and why. Were they getting ready to open the center again? Did they need my help with the animals? Had they found Alex? Was he okay?

The latter two options seemed more and more unlikely with each passing day.

The search had officially been called off, and neither Alex nor his body had been discovered in the park. The local news indicated that the sheriff's department no longer considered Alex a missing person and that there was enough evidence to assume the doctor had left town of his own volition, adding that if the veterinarian had been in the park, they likely would've located him or his vehicle by now.

The entire thing was heartbreaking.

I sighed and rolled onto my back.

Waking up to an empty bed on both sides of me had become the norm lately. I slept in most mornings after tossing and turning throughout the night. I had given notice at my part-time job at the kennel as soon as I'd gotten the offer for the internship, so I didn't even have that job to go to anymore. I also had no classes scheduled for the summer semester.

Of all the résumés I'd sent out, only one remained, one place that I hadn't heard from yet, one more possibility.

I had nothing to do but wait.

Reluctantly I got up and then spent the rest of the morning on the couch, binge-watching one of my favorite shows, *Teen Wolf*. Then, determined to do something more active, I went to the basement to run on the treadmill and lift free weights. After lunch, I took Trixie for a walk and then picked out something for dinner that required a trip to the grocery store. I also decided to splurge and make a fancy dessert as a thank-you to the guys. Since news of Alex's disappearance, they had been bringing home a lot of takeout so I wouldn't feel like I had to cook.

I stood in the kitchen, staring into a pan of caramel sauce I'd just finished preparing when I heard the front door open. I wasn't sure if it was Luke or Richard until I caught the scent of his crisp, woodsy cologne as he stepped up behind me, pressing his solid, tall body against mine.

Richard.

He folded his arms across my chest and kissed my cheek. That simple touch sent a wave of contentment through me.

I reached up and laid an open palm at the base of his neck. He tenderly swept his hands down my abs, along the fronts of my thighs, then back up.

Everything between us felt normal, but I couldn't completely keep the doubts at bay. Did holding me like this come naturally to him? Or did he have to force himself to touch me? Was he so worried about me that he was burying his feelings of uncertainty when it came to physical contact between us so as not to hurt me?

"I'm so proud of you," he whispered against my ear.

"For what? Making dinner?"

"For how strong you've been. I know how much you wanted that job."

"I don't care about that. I'm just... sad." I turned and laid my head against his chest.

He stroked a hand up and down my back. "I know."

"Thank you. For everything, for touching me the way you used to."

He shifted me backward and bent until he had our foreheads pressed together. "It wasn't only you who'd been wanting that."

I heard the front door open, but Richard didn't move away from me. A moment later Luke sat on a stool at the kitchen counter, watching us. "That sauce is going to burn."

Richard kept his green-eyed gaze locked on mine as he stroked my cheeks with his thumbs. "I don't care." He moistened his lower lip and watched my mouth in return. With the subtle hint of end-of-the-day stubble on his face and that decisive look, he exuded masculinity and strength. I was vibrating, wanting him to kiss me so badly.

The doorbell rang, and he grunted out a curse. "Tell whoever it is to go away."

Luke laughed as he stood and crossed the room. "On it."

As if he hadn't been kidding, Richard leaned in and kissed me, sweetly at first, then deeply, passionately, drawing me against him. I clung to him and kissed him in return.

A moment later, Luke cleared his throat from where he stood in the kitchen doorway. "Matthew, there's someone here to see you."

Standing next to Luke was Alex's son, Tomas. He had a backpack over his shoulders, his eyes wide as he took in the sight of us.

I let go of Richard and shifted back a step. "Hi, Tomas."

"Hey." He gave a nod, never letting up with the stunned, almost embarrassed expression like he was still witnessing us kiss. "I was, um... I was wondering if I could talk to you for a minute."

"Yeah, absolutely."

Richard gestured to the stove with a tilt of his head. "Luke and I'll keep an eye on dinner."

"Thanks." I crossed the room and stopped before Tomas. "I'm very sorry about your dad."

"That's what I wanted to talk to you about." He glanced at the floor and forcibly swallowed. "I got your address from my dad's files at the center. I wasn't positive I had your name right, so I called this morning to make sure it was you. Sorry I hung up on you. I thought it'd be better to wait to say anything until I got here."

"That's all right. Does your mom know where you are?"

"Yeah. She dropped me off on her way to an appointment here in the city. I told her that you agreed to let me interview you about your vet tech training program for a school paper." He shrugged. "I didn't want to lie, but I thought she might not let me come if it wasn't about stuff for school. She'll be back in two hours to get me. But I uh—" He darted a look around the room, then pointed at the table set for three. "I don't wanna mess up your dinner."

"It's okay. We can go in the other room and talk." I gestured toward the hall, but he made no move.

"Maybe I shouldn't have come." He continued staring at the three sets of plates and silverware. Maybe he needed a minute before he could get to whatever it was he wanted to talk to me about.

I motioned toward the table. "Why don't you eat with us? We're having garden salads and enchiladas, and I made a chocolate cheesecake with caramel sauce for dessert. We could talk after."

"You don't mind?"

"Not at all."

He shrugged. "I am kinda starving."

"Good. Let's dig in."

Luke and Richard helped me get the food on the table. We all sat, and Tomas immediately scarfed down several bites. He had a mouthful of enchilada when he finally looked up at where Richard and I sat across from him. He slowed down and swallowed. "Sorry. I didn't eat much at lunch."

I shrugged it off. "I'm glad you like it."

"It's real good." He ducked his head again and had another bite. "My dad's enchiladas are kinda like this." He smiled. "But his aren't as good as yours."

I wasn't sure how much I should talk about his dad, but I went with my instincts. "Does he cook for you guys a lot?"

"Yeah. He usually makes dinner most nights. Mom doesn't really like to cook." He grew quiet after that and didn't say much more while we finished eating.

During dessert, Richard told a story about a mix-up at the Harrison Center where a set of football helmets for a local high school were delivered by mistake. Before sending the helmets on to the school, a group of the seniors living at the center started a new hashtag online: #NeverTooOldToRockTheHelmet. They wore the football helmets and shared photos of themselves posed in various states of play like they were in the middle of a game, sometimes in the middle of a tackle. The story held Tomas's interest, and he seemed grateful for the distraction.

When we were finished with the cheesecake, Luke and Richard

cleared the table, and then they headed into the living room so Tomas and I could talk alone. On their way by, I mouthed, *thank you*.

After they left the room, Tomas gestured behind him. "They're nice."

"Yeah, they're great."

"So you all live here together?"

"Yep."

He grabbed his glass of soda and stared down at the dark liquid. "When I got here earlier..."

"Yeah?"

"That was some kiss." He seemed to want to say more, but he remained quiet, taking a long guzzle of the soda instead, then staring into the glass once more.

Again I went with my instincts. "You ever kiss someone? Maybe a special guy at school?"

His head shot up. "You know? About me? That I'm—" He didn't say the rest. Which I understood. Especially if he'd never said it out loud before. The first time was the hardest.

"Your dad mentioned it to me."

His jaw dropped. "My dad knows?"

I nodded and leaned forward with my elbows on the table. "Sometimes our parents know before we're even sure ourselves."

"What did he say? Was he okay about it?"

"Yeah. He made a point of mentioning you because he wanted me to know that he was a big supporter of gay rights."

"Oh." Tomas set his glass on the table. "I wish he was here."

"Me too. You don't think he left, do you?"

"He didn't!" His eyes were filled with fierce determination. "I think he got hurt or something. That's why I wanted to talk to you. The sheriff needs to look for him again." Tomas sat forward, leaning his arms on the table in a replica of my pose. "No one will listen to me. I know where he probably was that day. He's still gotta be out there. He was upset, really upset. He and Mom had a fight the night before, and they never fight. He wanted time alone. Which means he went somewhere he loved."

"And your dad loves that park."

"He does. He knows all the best spots. Places far away from the touristy stuff."

"When we drove out to release the falcon, he told me about this one spot with a waterfall that wasn't as easy to get to as some of the other falls. It sounded amazing."

As if my words confirmed something for Tomas, he reached for his backpack that hung over the back of his chair. He pulled out a stack of photos and a map and set everything on the table. The map was marked with bold black circles. Each circle had a handwritten number and a notation beside it.

He pointed to the map. "I know he was at one of these places. I just know it. But the stupid sheriff called off the search too early. He said they had proof that my dad left town. Which is bullshit!" He abruptly stopped as if his mom was there and would scold him at any moment for the curse. He sank back in the chair. "I want to go find him myself, but I can't drive and it'd take me forever to hike out there. I'd have to walk for two or three days to get to a lot of these locations, and I..." He trailed off and shrugged.

"You can't do that to your mom."

"Yeah. She's gonna have the baby soon. She wants to go look for him too, but she can't go with how big she is now." He longingly stared at the map and photos he'd laid out between us. "I was hoping that maybe if I showed you everything, that you could... I mean, I could tell my dad really liked you when you were at the center, and you seemed to like him."

"I did. A lot. I was really looking forward to working with him."

He sat forward again and rushed to say the rest. "Maybe the sheriff will listen to you. I'm just a kid, and he thinks my mom's too emotional."

"Tomas... if your dad was in the park that day and something serious happened to him, then..."

He nodded. "You're saying he might've died. I get why you'd think that's true. But I know my dad. Even if he was hurt, he'd know how to take care of himself."

"I'm sure he would."

"And even if..." Tomas's voice faltered. "I know it's gotta seem stupid for me to still want them to find him in the park. I mean if he took off, then for sure he'd be okay. But that would mean..." He lowered his head again.

"He wasn't the dad you thought he was."

"I'm not just saying that I wanna *believe* he loved me and my mom and wouldn't leave us. I *know* it." He held my stare. "My dad is still in that park. And he's alive."

I gestured to the map and photos. "Show me what you got, and I'll talk to the sheriff."

Tomas smiled and sat taller, relief rolling off him. "Yeah?"

"Absolutely. And if he doesn't do anything or he won't listen to me…" I paused to make certain he got that I was serious. "I promise you, Tomas, I'll find out where your dad is and what happened to him."

Chapter Sixteen

I sat at the kitchen table, reviewing the map of Majestic Falls State Park with its handwritten numbers and black circles in seemingly random locations. I picked up the photos and leafed through them again. Some featured popular areas of the park—the boat launch along the river and another at the lake, as well as several famous rock formations, cliffs, and the various waterfalls for which the park had been named. Others were shots taken along the hiking trails, with hikers in the background. The rest of the images were of more remote locales deep inside the forest.

Each photo was labeled with a number and a date on the back. Tomas said his dad had started writing a new book about the park to raise awareness of land and wildlife conservation efforts. The photos Tomas had given me were ones his dad had left in his home office with his notes for the book. The numbers were probably Alex's way of keeping track of all the photos he wanted to use, perhaps coinciding with chapters he was writing. Tomas had used sticky notes on the backs of the photos to mark them with their corresponding locations on the map.

I returned the photos to the table before me and reviewed the map again. A few of the locations were not too far from one of the main roads that ran along Windtree River, close to the wildlife center on the west side of the park. The other locations were strewn all across the park. Several were smack dab in the middle of the vast forest. Only a few walking trails even went that far in. I could see why the sheriff's deputies and park rangers would've had a hard time searching for an individual in those areas.

I sighed and sank back in my chair.

A half hour earlier, I had walked Tomas to his mom's car at the curb with the promise that I'd do my best to help. He'd been adamant about not telling his mom the real reason he'd come to see me because he didn't want to get her hopes up that I'd be able to figure out what happened to her husband.

I wasn't sure that I'd actually be able to accomplish anything, but I had to try.

As I was going over the materials from Tomas again, Richard and Luke came into the kitchen and sat opposite me.

"Tomas thinks his dad got hurt in the park and is still out there somewhere."

Richard gave a nod. "He wants your help to find out for sure?"

"Yeah."

"So," Luke said, "what can we do?"

"You want to help?"

"Of course."

I looked to Richard.

"Absolutely. Do you have any ideas?"

"Tomas thought maybe if I talked to the sheriff, I could convince him to take another look at these locations." I indicated the map, then told them about Alex's fight with Natalie. "Tomas said he knows where his dad would've gone when he wanted to be alone after something like that."

"Did Tomas talk to the police?" Luke asked.

"Yeah, he tried to show this map to the sheriff when they first reported Alex missing, but I don't think the sheriff took him seriously. He told Tomas they were doing the search the way he and the park rangers thought it should be conducted."

Neither said anything for a beat. Then Luke spoke, his voice low. "So the kid thinks they missed finding his dad, alive or not?"

"Yeah. And the truck he drove and his red backpack. Tomas says Alex takes that pack with him whenever he heads out into the park."

Richard sat forward. Resting his forearms on the table, he clasped his hands together. "You going to contact the sheriff?"

"I called his office after Tomas left. I tried to be vague and not let on how I knew about the locations from the map, but the sheriff guessed right off that Tomas had talked to me." I shook my head in defeat. "I didn't want to lie."

"Of course not."

"But maybe I should have. Sheriff Emerson said they're not spending any more money or resources searching the park for someone who most likely ran out on his family. He said they'd already looked for days. They had teams with search and rescue dogs, and a helicopter doing aerial searches over the areas they didn't cover on foot. There was no sign of him or his truck. They went through

Alex's computer and personal items at the center and his home. They found evidence that he and Natalie were having financial problems."

Richard sighed. "Add in their fight, and it probably gave the sheriff more reason to assume Alex took off."

I nodded. "I believe Tomas. I think Alex was injured somehow." I was afraid they weren't going to like the next part, but all I saw from them was genuine support. "I want to go talk to the sheriff in person. Maybe if I put a little more pressure on him, he'll reconsider."

Richard tapped his thumbs together, then stopped. "If Alex got hurt the day he first went missing over two weeks ago, chances are good he might've died out there."

"He's alive. I don't know how I know that. I just do. He's still alive."

Richard studied me for a long moment. "Then why don't we all go talk to the sheriff? Together."

"You'd do that? You guys would go with me?"

"You bet," Richard said with a nod. "How about we head there first thing tomorrow?"

"Yeah," Luke agreed. "And if that doesn't work, we'll let the sheriff know that we plan to go to the press and tell them he ignored evidence from the family. Maybe that'll get his ass in gear."

Chapter Seventeen

Sheriff Pat Emerson sat behind his desk, not saying a word, just leaning back in his chair, hands folded over his stomach, the pads of his thumbs pressed together, a disapproving glare locked in place.

He was a big guy, burly, but not overweight. More of an athletic build that indicated he didn't spend all his time behind that desk. His forehead had the hard vertical lines of someone who scowled a lot. I wasn't sure if he could tell the three of us were gay and in a relationship or if he was trying to determine our intentions as he carefully examined me, then Luke and Richard on either side of me.

I didn't care what he thought of us. I'd come for his help, and I wasn't leaving without it.

He sat forward, his hands slapping the surface of the desk. "Let me see if I've got this right." He pointed at me. "You want me to waste more taxpayer dollars looking for a man and his truck when there's every reason to believe he took off on his own—stealing the truck from his employer, by the way—all based on the word of his kid?"

I went to answer, but Richard beat me to it. "We expect you to do your job."

That got Richard another hardened glare. Emerson eventually eased up on him. He slid open his top desk drawer, shaking his head, and removed a pack of chewing gum. He unwrapped two pieces and popped them into his mouth.

Despite the youthful nature of that move, Emerson had to be in his late fifties, detectable only by the gray in his hair and the lines on his face. He walked with a poised, assertive stride like he figured he'd have to jump in and break up a brawl at any moment. When we'd first gotten there and the clerk notified him about our arrival, he hadn't offered a smile or his hand in greeting. He was all about getting down to business, but not in an annoyed way. More like he didn't want anyone to think he'd missed something on this case. So without a word, he'd led us to his private office, which sat in the corner of a sizable open room filled with metal desks and hordes of computers, printers, and fax machines.

Along with his office and those of his deputies and the various support staff, the two-story brick building included a communications and dispatch center, a briefing room, the county's 9-1-1 call center, and the local jail. With all that, I would've expected the place to be jumping. It wasn't. It was strangely lacking in activity.

A lengthy hallway off the main room led to several other areas, but there were no signs on those doors marking what those rooms were used for. Overlapping faint voices could be heard in the distance. Nothing discernible in the dialogue. It all seemed eerily reticent and downright odd for an official county law enforcement building.

On our way to his office, we'd passed by several deputies, all standing stoically, quietly watching us follow the sheriff. I made eye contact with one of them. He had a stern face with sharp angles, and black hair that was slicked back with too much product. His judgmental glare made it seem like he knew why we were there and he wasn't happy about it. Maybe the sheriff had clued him in before coming to greet us.

After Sheriff Emerson had chewed the gum into a manageable clump, he spoke again. "I thought we'd settled everything over the phone, Mr. Stewart."

"I was hoping you'd reconsider and take a look at the map I mentioned. I figured you'd know better than anyone if it's possible Alex was at one of these locations that day."

He snorted, the wad of gum nearly slipping from his gaping mouth. "Like I said—"

"Just please take a look."

He huffed out a long breath. There was something very attentive and driven about the expression on his face, and it reminded me of how Richard looked at me when he was trying to understand what I was—or wasn't—saying.

"Listen," Emerson started, "I liked Alex. I really did. Despite what some people thought of him, I knew he was a good guy."

"He is."

"That's what I'm saying. I gave him the benefit of the doubt and did everything I could to try to find him. A lot of people in this county were pissed off at me for keeping the search going past the first couple of days, but I didn't give in to that pressure. Until I had to." Abruptly he stood and went to a file cabinet in the far corner of his office. He opened a drawer and retrieved a thick file folder. He dropped the file onto the desk with a loud slap. Tossing it open, he thumped into his seat, his loaded duty belt creaking.

He removed a map of the park similar to the one I'd brought. He unfolded it until the map filled the top of his desk, then jabbed a finger at the center of the park, nearly poking a hole through the paper. "My deputies and the park rangers did an in-depth search of this entire park. There was no sign of the doctor or his truck."

The map before him was divided into sections, with notations sprawled diagonally across the paper, as well as large black Xs that had been drawn through each section.

"But," I said, "maybe you could help us identify areas that weren't searched as thoroughly as the others. Tomas said there are a lot of places his dad drove his truck off-road, isolated spots he loved to hike to." I held out the map. "Please."

He hesitated, staring at me so long I figured he was waiting for me to give up. Then he snatched the map from me. He opened it and examined the notations Tomas had made. His expression softened for a brief moment as he scanned the map. Then his face hardened again. "These are the same ones he told me about. After the kid came here, I asked the park rangers to have another look at these areas."

"Then why didn't you tell Tomas that?"

He snorted out a low sound. "I didn't want to tell him we were searching again because I didn't want to get his hopes up."

"You didn't find anything?"

"No. Which is what I expected. I'm certain the search dogs would've found the doc the first time if he were out there."

Richard harrumphed. "Over that much land?" He didn't wait for Emerson to respond. "The park rangers don't work for you, right? They work for the state. Why didn't you send your own people out to recheck those areas? Did you even send the dogs back out there for another search?"

Emerson held his arms out at his sides. "It's not like a have a huge staff with nothing else to do. And the dogs came from the state police. I can't just call them up on a hunch and ask them to throw more valuable resources my way." He went for another piece of the gum as if that would help with his agitation.

After he had the new gum crammed into the glob already in his mouth, he said, "When Alex first went missing, I had loads of people out looking for him. Nearly every one of my deputies, the park rangers, and numerous state police officers. They found nothing. The search dogs couldn't even pick up his scent. It was like he was never in that park."

"But how's that possible?" I asked. "He told me he went out there nearly every day. Wouldn't they have found some sign of him from earlier, even if he drove out of town like you said?"

"A storm came through the area the night before. Lots of rain. It washed away his, and everyone else's, scent from earlier in the week. Trust me. He was not in the park that day."

Luke spoke for the first time since we'd sat down. "What makes you so sure he took off? Because of some money issues and a single fight with his wife?"

"No. One of my deputies said she'd seen the vet's truck heading out of town that morning, in the opposite direction of the park. Add that to their money problems and the fight, and it all tells me that Dr. Vega was a man who was under a lot of stress, a man who just decided to walk away from his life."

I shook my head. "He's not that kind of man."

"You knew him well, did you? I've known Alex for eight years, and I barely knew much about him. He was a quiet guy, kept to himself a lot. He's only got one friend that I can think of. One of the park rangers. Gus Cleary. Before Alex went missing, they were working together on a landscaping project at Gus's new house. Only thing I've ever heard of the doc doing that had nothing to do with the wildlife center or the park. I'd almost call Alex a recluse, except he had a family. Most people found him odd, different. I don't think it's a stretch to say that he might not have come across accurately to you at a job interview."

That had me feeling deflated. Had I been seeing something in Alex that wasn't there? Had I been subconsciously comparing him to my father, concluding that Alex was a better man and coloring him in a far too positive light?

Sheriff Emerson scrutinized me. He had that intent look on his face again, and underneath that there was a kindness to him that was difficult to see at first glance. He seemed to genuinely want us to believe him. Or maybe he was desperate for it.

He cleared his throat. "Look, Mr. Stewart, I took this case seriously, very seriously, and everything possible was done to find the doctor." He seemed like he might say more, but then the phone on his desk rang. He answered, listened, and then hung up. "I've got something to take care of, so if you don't mind…" He stood, and I did the same.

Richard remained seated. "We're not done here yet."

Emerson gave him a challenging look, then sighed and headed for the door. "I'll be back in a minute."

After he walked off, I sank into my chair. "He's not going to do anything."

Richard patted my thigh. "Let's give it one more try."

"Yeah," Luke said. "Maybe we'll annoy him into it. Or we can threaten him, tell him we'll go to the press." When I didn't respond, Luke asked, "What are you thinking?"

It used to be Richard who knew when I held back on something. Now Luke could read me nearly as well. I got up and perched on the edge of the sheriff's desk to face them. "You guys wanna go camping?"

They just stared back at me.

"There's a private campground north of the wildlife center, right outside the park. There are cabins for rent with a road nearby that leads into the park and to some of the hiking trails. We could stay at the campground a couple of nights while we check out the closest locations on Tomas's map. Then we could backpack farther into the park and stay out there for a few more nights." I smiled again. "Just the three of us. Might be kinda fun."

"Fun?" Luke gaped at me. "You want to go look for a guy the cops couldn't even find, a guy who might very well be dead, in a park as massive as Majestic Falls?"

I shook my head. "Alex isn't dead. But even if he is, or if we can't find him, we could try to locate his truck or the backpack he had with him that morning. That would prove he was in the park that day, prove that he didn't leave town. Then Sheriff Emerson would have to reopen the case and search for him again."

Luke exchanged a quick glance with Richard. "But the sheriff said they already went through the areas Tomas told him about. You think we can find something they didn't?"

"I don't know. But I have to try. I promised Tomas I'd do whatever I could."

There was a flash of uncertainty in Richard's eyes. "There's a lot of rough, hilly trails out there, gorges and cliffs too. We're not experienced hikers, Matthew."

"I know. We'll go slow, be careful."

He seemed to be mentally going over our options.

I waited, but they both remained quiet. "Tomas and Natalie don't know what happened to someone they love. That's a horrible feeling."

Luke glanced Richard's way again, and I knew he could see what I did. That Richard was considering my plan. Luke pointed at me. "Tell him this is crazy."

Richard said nothing to him, just kept his focus locked on my face.

"All right. But let's give it one more try with the sheriff. We'll see if we can get him to change his mind first."

"And if he doesn't?"

"We'll take it from there if we have to."

I wasn't sure exactly what he meant by that, but the sheriff was headed back our way so I took a seat again.

Emerson rounded his desk and remained standing, hands propped on his duty belt beside his gun and flashlight. "I'd love to sit and chat some more about how shitty you think I've done my job, but I have to help citizens of this county who actually bothered to stick around— unlike Alex Vega." He made a dismissive gesture. "So why don't you head back to your fancy, comfy condos in the city and let me get back to my work?"

Richard opened his mouth to respond. I laid a hand on his knee to stop him. "One more question, Sheriff Emerson. If you believe Alex left town, then there's no investigation for us to interfere with, right? There's no harm in us taking a look ourselves?"

"In the park?"

"Yes."

"The three of you?"

"Yes."

Emerson snorted out a laugh.

Luke leaned into my side. "I'm really not liking this guy."

I reached for his hand and held it on my thigh.

Emerson didn't bat an eye. "You want to have a look around? Fine. But let me give you some friendly advice." He pointed to the kid's map on his desk. "Do not go to any of those locations beyond the basic trails. The landscape out there is rugged. Even if you avoid the steep cliffs and ravines, it's dangerous. If you're not experienced hikers, it can be grueling. Even the marked trails are not always easily passable for the average person."

Richard stood. "Thanks for the concern, but we'll be fine."

Emerson continued to regard him with hostility. "To get to all the sections of the park that you want to check out, you'll have to travel through forest areas that even the park rangers don't spend much time in. Cell coverage is spotty at best, and if you don't know what you're doing—"

I stood and cut him off. "Like he said, we'll be fine."

"I don't think you understand." He jabbed a finger my way. "You need to stay out of those areas. I cannot afford to send more people out there to save your asses."

Richard motioned for Luke to get up. "We're done here." We all turned to leave.

"Wait." Emerson had a hand up. He held it still for a second more, then let it fall to his side as if in defeat. He returned to the file cabinet in the corner of his office and removed another folder. He opened it and took out a second map. "If you insist on going out there, take this. It includes several access roads that are not marked on any public map. The rangers use them. You can take those roads if you need to. If the rangers give you any trouble, have them call me."

I took the map from him. "Thanks. What kind of truck are we looking for?"

"A 2005 white Chevy Colorado. It has decals on both sides with the logo and name of the wildlife center." He picked up Tomas's map, refolded it, and handed that to me as well. "I'm sorry about your job there. It's a shame the place had to close."

"It is."

We started to head out again but stopped at the doorway when the sheriff spoke once more.

"If you do find that truck or anything else, you call me, and I'll come out there myself."

"All right."

Once we were outside and almost to our car, Luke jerked his thumb over his shoulder at the sheriff's building. "What a fucking asshole."

"Yeah," Richard agreed. "How the hell did that guy ever get elected to the office of sheriff?"

I stopped at the passenger-side door of Richard's car. "He wasn't that bad."

Luke scoffed. "Did you hear how he talked to you?"

"He was just being defensive. I think he actually feels bad that he couldn't find Alex."

Luke shook his head in disbelief. "There you go again. Seeing the good in people. Even complete asshats."

Was that what I was doing here? Or was I being naive? Did I just see what I wanted to see in people like Emerson? And what did that mean about my impressions of Alex?

"Well," Richard said, "I'll tell you one thing about our friendly neighborhood sheriff. I'm starting to wonder how well he and his people even looked for Alex."

"Yeah," Luke said. "That man is definitely hiding something."

That surprised me. "You think he knows what happened to Alex?"

"Maybe. Or maybe he doesn't want anyone to know how badly he fucked everything up."

Which meant this was all up to us. No one else was going to spend any more time looking for Alex Vega.

I opened Tomas's map and laid it on the hood of Richard's car. The map showcased the miles and miles of intersecting trails that cut through the park, each trail drawn in a different color. There were also icons designating specific areas for activities such as camping, bicycling, and sledding. Most trails allowed for hiking except for the few that were used only for cross-country skiing or horseback riding.

Richard came to stand at my side. "Emerson was right about one thing, though."

"Yeah?"

"This could be dangerous. Things happen to hikers all the time."

"I know." I gave him a pointed look. "But I *have* to do this."

After a beat, he said, "I guess we could hire a guide who knows the park, have them take us to the locations on the map."

"That sounds good. So you'll go with me?"

His mouth turned up in a clear smile. "Of course."

Luke gestured toward the sheriff's office again. "I guess somebody's got to do this asshole's job for him."

I couldn't hold back my relief. I lunged for Luke and wrapped my arms around him. Then did the same with Richard. "We'll be very careful. I promise. Can we get started right away?"

"I don't see why not," Richard said.

"What about your work? Do you have to be at the Harrison Center this week?"

"I'll make some calls, get someone to cover for me. It'll be fine. Besides, Dominic will keep everyone in line."

"Okay. Luke?" Taking time off from his work was a lot to ask of him, considering how many extra hours he'd been putting in at home just to keep up lately.

"I'm game. I've got a shit-ton of vacation days saved. It's about time I use them up."

"Thank you. I'll call Kevin, ask if he and Walter can go pick up Trixie and keep her for a few days. We could see if there's a sporting goods store here in town where we could get whatever supplies we'll need."

"Wait." Luke held up a hand. "Supplies?"

"Yeah." I ticked off items on my fingers. "We'll need a tent and boots and backpacks and sleeping bags and food and—"

"Wait. Sleeping bags? A tent?"

"Sure." I examined the map and pointed at one of the routes near Tomas's notations. "I think we should follow this road along Windtree River first. There are trails close by that'll take us right up to most of these initial sites." I indicated another cluster of four marks on the map. "Then we'll head east of the river after that, taking the tent with us."

Richard nodded. "Sounds like a good plan."

Luke still stared at me in that shocked way of his. "A tent? We're going to sleep in a tent?"

I nodded, afraid he'd change his mind now that we were going over the specifics.

Before I could say anything, Richard asked him, "You ever sleep outside under the stars?"

"No. You?"

"Nope." He stepped around me and moved in behind Luke. With his arms around Luke's waist, he spoke against his ear. "Kind of nice for Matthew to take us to do something we've never done before, don't you think? A new first for the three of us."

Luke rolled his eyes. "You can't play me that easily."

Richard raised his brows my way, then whispered in Luke's ear again. "Can you picture it? The three of us alone out there for an entire week? A few nights in a cabin and then a tent. Just think of all the ways we could entertain ourselves."

"Are you trying to use sex to get me to agree to this?"

Richard winked at me over Luke's shoulder. "Is it working?"

Luke laughed. "You know it is."

"Then you'll come too?" I asked.

"Of course. And *not* for the sex." He tossed another exaggerated roll of his eyes at Richard, then grew serious as he met my stare. "This is important to you."

"Yeah, it is."

"Then I'm in." He smiled at me and then turned to collect the map from the hood of the car. "Besides, you two would be lost after five minutes without me."

"Yeah," Richard said as he moved to the driver's side door. "We definitely would be."

Chapter Eighteen

"God, it's beautiful here."

Luke's astonished voice carried from the backseat, where he sat surveying the incredible view of Windtree River. We were driving along State Route 389, following a ridge just outside Majestic Falls State Park, heading for the private lodge and campground where we'd be staying for the next couple of days.

We'd rented the vehicle, a blue Jeep Wrangler, two hours earlier and packed it full of the supplies we purchased in the small town of Majestic Falls, which was located south of the park. When we'd left home earlier that morning, we each brought an overnight bag in case getting in to see the sheriff had taken longer than expected and we ended up deciding to stay the night in town, but we hadn't been outfitted for a backpacking trip. The woman working the camping store had been helpful. She loaded us up with the appropriate equipment and food for a week of camping and backpacking.

Now we had a three-person tent, battery-powered lantern, rope, compass, multi-tool, reusable filtered water bottles, bug repellent, binoculars, and various other supplies.

We'd already passed the wildlife center and the Vega home on our way to the campground. We decided not to stop and say anything to Tomas or his mom about what the sheriff had said or what we were up to. I didn't want to get Tomas's hopes up. I wasn't sure what the chances were that we'd find anything in the park. Although I'd just started to wonder if not keeping him updated had been the right decision when Luke spoke up about the view.

From the front passenger seat, I turned to look back at him. "Isn't it great? Wait until you see all the waterfalls."

"It's like a whole other world out here. Feels like we're way more than forty-five minutes from the city."

"It does," I said as Richard maneuvered the Jeep around a curve in the road. The setting sun cast a brilliant orange glow over the rock formations on the far side of the river. Beyond that, a stretch of forest containing a spectacular blend of coniferous and broad-leaved trees covered the hills and valleys. It all made for a stunning view.

I couldn't wait to see more of the park.

"Hey."

At the sound of that deep voice, I focused on Richard. He was carefully watching the winding road ahead.

"I'm willing to do this, Matthew, on one condition. No splitting up. We all stay together. No matter what."

"Sounds good."

"And, we take it slow. We drive as far as possible and then we stay on the trails as much as we can until we get close to those locations the kid showed you on the map. No veering off anywhere else."

"All right."

"I'm not trying to be an ass about this. I just want us to be safe. We're on our own out here."

"I know."

Earlier, after we'd loaded up the Jeep, we'd spent two hours in Majestic Falls trying to find anyone willing to serve as a guide to escort us into the park. Richard had talked to the woman who ran the camping store, but she hadn't been able to come up with the name of one person who might be willing to assist us. We also tried asking around at the local diner, hotel, hardware store, and bowling alley. We hadn't located a single person willing to help or a recommendation from anyone.

It was like there was some kind of conspiracy, like everyone in town had known we were coming and why, and they'd already planned to turn us away. Which was odd. Because most of them had also seemed regretful that they weren't able to help. Had the sheriff said something to them? Manipulated them? Threatened them? But why? Maybe I'd read him wrong. Maybe he was determined to keep us from looking into Alex's disappearance with even more vigor than I'd first thought, and for reasons I didn't want to fathom right then.

As if Richard could sense my frustration, he laid a hand on my thigh and gave a squeeze. "We'll be all right."

"Shit!" Luke called out from the backseat.

I whirled around. "What?"

He was rummaging through his backpack. He stopped and slapped his hands on top of the pack. "I can't believe I forgot it."

"Forgot what?"

"Lube." The disappointed look on his face was priceless. "I

thought I grabbed it before we left the house this morning." He smacked his pack again. "Dang it." He was so damn serious. I couldn't keep the laughter at bay.

Richard shook his head. "I'm here worrying about keeping us from walking off a cliff or drowning in the river or getting attacked by a bear, and you're freaking out about going five days without sex?"

"Hey." Luke pointed at Richard. "You were the one talking about fucking under the stars."

"That's not exactly how I said it."

"Close enough."

I laughed more, then said, "It's incredibly rare to see a bear in this part of the country."

Richard threw me a sideways glance. "Rare but not unheard of?"

"I guess. We're more likely to see a coyote."

"Really?" Luke sounded freaked. "Wait." He pointed at the back of Richard's head. "Don't try to change the subject. I saw you at that camping store. When we bought that tent, you were thinking the same thing I was. You love the idea of doing us in the great outdoors."

Richard turned the wheel to follow another curve in the road. After a minute of silence passed, he said simply, casually, "There are plenty of ways to fuck without lube."

"Ah-ha." Luke jabbed a finger in the air. "You *were* thinking about it."

That had me laughing again, despite why we were there.

But then a thought hit me. Was there more to Luke's words than he was letting on? Maybe this trip could be about more than helping Alex and his family. Maybe it could be exactly what the three of us needed.

"So?" Luke said.

"So what?" Richard asked.

"You going to admit it or not?"

"Admit what?"

"What you brought with you."

Richard sighed. "I don't have a clue what you're talking about."

Luke crossed his arms over his chest and fell back against the seat, keeping his gaze locked on the back of Richard's head.

Richard continued driving, his focus on the road. Eventually he glanced in the rearview mirror at Luke and then shrugged indifferently. "It's not a big deal. So I picked up some lubricant at the pharmacy in town. That doesn't mean I'm as sex-obsessed as you."

"Sure." Luke winked at me, and I smiled back at him.

I loved them all the more for doing this with me.

After we were checked in at the main lodge, we headed for our assigned cabin, following a narrow dirt road that brought us even closer to Windtree River and the park land beyond. Each of the cabins was at least a quarter mile from the next. There were utility poles lining the road, but other than that, there were no other signs of civilization. Nothing but trees and brush and rocks and the chirping of birds. It was one of the most remote backcountry roads I'd ever traveled on.

"Guess this is it," Richard said as he turned into a stone drive. He stopped the Jeep in front of a log cabin. The small building had a golden tone to the natural wood facade, which gave the place a warm, inviting glow in the fading sunlight.

We unloaded our overnight bags and went inside. The cabin's charming one-room interior included a kitchenette, living room area, fireplace, and a king-size bed. A colorful patchwork quilt lay draped over the back of the couch, and the fireplace mantel had several carved wood animal figurines. Bears and coyotes and wolves.

When we'd checked in at the lodge, the guy working the front desk had made a point of telling us about the two rollaway cots in the closet. It didn't occur to him that any of us would be sharing a bed. To him, we were probably a group of buddies, just hanging out, having some fun on a fishing trip for the week.

Well, at least he thought two of us were straight. It was obvious he knew Luke was gay, and the guy flirted mercilessly with him. Maybe living out there in such a rural area, he didn't get many chances to talk to another gay man. It made me wonder what it was about Luke, and not Richard and me, that had clued the guy in. I also couldn't let go of the idea that maybe Luke got that reaction from guys a lot.

Luke glanced around the cabin. "Hey, this is nice." He set his bag on the couch. "Even has a fireplace."

Richard deposited his bag beside Luke's. "Yeah, it's pretty great. Out here, I would've been happy with electricity, running water, and a toilet that wasn't a hole in the ground."

"And lube. Don't forget the lube."

Richard chuckled as he wrapped an arm around Luke's waist and tugged him backward until he had Luke's ass nestled against his groin. He kissed the side of his neck. "How about I make you a promise? I'll never forget the lube. Ever."

"So when you're eighty, you still plan to fuck my ass?"

"Hell yeah. Why do you think I work out every day?"

"To keep up with Matthew." Luke reached back and gripped Richard's ass in one hand. He rotated his hips, provocatively rubbing his ass over Richard's groin. "You know how young he'll still be when you're eighty?"

Richard let out a groan. "Don't remind me." He cupped Luke's chin and turned his head sideways, planting a powerful kiss on his lips.

"I won't care!" I practically shouted the words from where I stood across the room, clutching my duffel bag to my chest.

They both turned to me.

"I just want us all to be together. Always."

"We will be," Richard said.

"Yeah, kid," Luke added. "I was just kidding around."

"But…"

"What?" Richard asked.

"Does it bother you? Because it's not like I'm going to be in my twenties forever."

Richard let go of Luke and approached me. "The only thing that bothers me is that I don't want to leave you all alone someday."

I searched his face. "We don't know that's what'll happen. We don't know what will happen to any of us, or when."

"I know." He took my hand in his. "And we have a long time together before we have to worry about that."

"Yeah. A long time."

We said nothing more for a while, just stood there with our hands entwined.

As if trying to ease the apprehension or avoid the topic he'd brought up, Luke rounded the couch and flopped down onto the bed. "Nice mattress."

"Yeah?" Richard kept his focus on me, but he indicated Luke with a tilt of his head. "Did you notice how he was the one who mentioned us being together when I'm eighty?"

I nodded.

"I love when he says shit like that."

I nodded again. "Me too."

"Remember that first week you guys moved in with me, how casual he was trying to be?"

"Yep."

"But he was scared shitless."

"I was too," I said. "I was so scared it wouldn't work out."

He brushed my chin with the backs of his fingers. "Same here."

I studied him with surprise.

"I thought I was pushing too hard, and eventually Luke would leave. Then you would too."

"I wouldn't have left. I was way too obsessed with you already."

He smiled. "It doesn't matter now. He's still here. We all are."

"Yeah, we are."

He gave me a kiss, and any remaining unease faded away. When we parted, I went to the small round table that sat between the kitchen and the living area. Setting my duffel on a chair, I opened the bag and removed Tomas's map. I laid it out, covering the entire surface of the table. Dropping into a seat, I examined the map.

"You got a plan for tomorrow?"

Richard's voice startled me. I hadn't heard him step closer.

"I think we should start here first." I pointed to the location Tomas had marked that was closest to the cabin.

According to the map, the nearest trail ran along the road for a while, then veered off toward the middle of the park. It actually made little sense for us to explore the first few places on the map. The road, as well as the outermost trail, would've been heavily traveled by the sheriff's deputies and the park rangers throughout the search, plus by all the hikers and tourists that had been in the park since then. But I wasn't about to leave until I'd searched every spot on Tomas's map. Also, with our limited hiking experience, it seemed wise to start with the more accessible locations as a way to ease into things.

Richard laid a hand at the back of my head. "Whatever you think is best. You're in charge on this."

"Why me?"

"This is your show."

Luke crossed the room to us. He stood on my other side and placed his hand over Richard's. "Yep."

They waited for me to go on.

"Okay. Then we'll start here and hit these spots along the main road on the west side of the park first. Then head down this trail if we have time before it gets dark."

They both nodded in agreement.

"It'll be a long day," I added, "but I think it's doable."

Richard bent and kissed the top of my head. "Sounds good."

I gestured toward the bed. "I guess we should get some sleep."

Luke and I changed for bed and brushed our teeth in the kitchen sink while Richard used the small bathroom. Earlier that day in town, we'd purchased warmer pajamas as well as some more appropriate outdoor clothing, hiking boots, and lightweight waterproof jackets specifically made for keeping warm without adding too much bulk. The late spring days were getting warmer, but at night, the temperature dropped significantly.

Luke spotted me staring at him. He yanked the toothbrush from his mouth. "What?"

I flipped my brush through the air, scanning up and down his body. "You never wear this many clothes to bed."

He glanced down at the blue-and-white flannel pajamas. "I'm not about to freeze my dick off out here in the middle of nowhere."

I laughed and finished brushing my teeth. When Luke had done the same, we climbed into the bed. He moved in to lie close at my side, an arm draped across my waist. He nuzzled my neck. "This is nice."

"Yeah."

"If we have more time tomorrow night, we should get a fire going." He swept the tip of his nose along my cheek. Then he kissed the same path. "It'd be romantic."

I laughed again.

"What's so funny?"

"Just getting used to this new romantic, flannel-wearing Luke."

"Oh jeez." For a moment I thought he was going to do his usual tickle retaliation, but then he tightened his hold on me. Richard had been right about him. Every time Luke held me, I could feel his love for me.

Guilt hit me hard. I still hadn't told them about what I'd hidden in our bathroom cabinet at home. "Luke?"

"Yeah?"

"You know what we were talking about earlier? About growing old together?"

"Yeah." He sounded reluctant again.

I forced myself to go on. "Do you ever worry about being faithful to us? Long-term, I mean?"

He let go of me and shifted back so he could get a good look at my face. His eyes were wide, and they held a wounded note that seemed different than anything I'd ever seen from him.

Shit. I never should've brought this up.

Chapter Nineteen

"Why would you ask that? Is this about that night I went upstairs with that guy at the Haven? I told you nothing happened then."

"I know," I said. "I believed you about that. I guess I've just been thinking lately that..."

"What?"

"Forever's a long time."

The sound of running water in the bathroom shut off, and then the door opened. Richard came out and went to the couch to return his toiletry items to his bag.

"Hey," Luke called out for him. "Come here."

Richard came to the bed. He crawled in and lay on my other side, propping himself on one arm. "What's going on?"

"Matthew's asking weird questions."

"Weird how?"

"Wanting to know if I worry about being faithful to you guys."

Richard looked at me with stunned surprise, and I shrugged like it was no big deal. But I couldn't fool them.

"I guess I wonder if you've thought about it, really thought about what it'll be like. In five years, ten, twenty."

"If *I've* thought about it?" Luke asked.

"Well, both of you, really."

Richard asked, "You don't think the three of us can make it?"

"No, I do. I just... that guy at the lodge was really flirting with Luke. I guess it got me thinking."

"I didn't flirt back!"

"I know."

Regardless, he gaped at me, eyes wide, mouth hanging open in disbelief. "You can't tell me other guys don't come on to you sometimes, Matthew. You haven't been asked out at all since you met us?"

"Sure. Once."

"Who was he?" Richard asked.

"A guy in one of my classes."

"And you told him about the three of us?"

"I did."

"Did he keep on pursuing you, try to get you to change your mind?"

"No, he was cool about it. Thought it was hot that I got to be with two guys."

Luke scoffed. "Damn straight, it's hot."

Richard snorted out a laugh, but then they both grew quiet for a beat. Eventually he said to Luke, "That guy at the lodge *was* doing some serious flirting with you. He'd have gotten you guys a room and fucked you while we stood there waiting for the key to the cabin had you given him one sign you were interested."

"So?" The penetrating stare Luke directed at Richard was full of the emotions that he still tried to bury beneath the surface most days. Slowly that stare turned into a grin. "Were you jealous?"

"No."

He searched Richard's face. "You were."

I turned my head and buried my face in Richard's shoulder, barely stifling the laugh.

"Hey." He slid his hands along my sides and tickled me in the ribs.

I squirmed, moving out of his reach as far as I could between them.

"No. Don't go." He sat up against the headboard and pulled me to sit between his legs so I was leaning back against his chest, his arms around me. "Okay, maybe I was a little jealous."

Luke kept the smile going as he moved to sit up, facing us. Peeling back the blankets, he straddled my lower legs and ran his hands along the outside of Richard's thick thighs. He settled his ass on my upper legs, his gaze locked on Richard. "I'm not sure how I feel about that."

"You disappointed I didn't go all caveman and try to rip his head off the minute he started in on you?"

I laughed.

Luke did too. "He almost did, didn't he?"

I laid my head back against Richard's shoulder and looked up at him. "Nah, but it was close."

Richard held on to me tighter and spoke to Luke again. "You didn't answer the question. Did you want me to be jealous?"

"Maybe." He cocked his head to the side as if giving that thought. "Is that wrong?"

"I think it's a normal response." Keeping hold of me with one arm, Richard breathed deep and splayed his other hand over one of Luke's thighs. "It doesn't really surprise me. All those years before you met us, all those guys you were with night after night... I'm guessing not one of them really cared when you said it had to be just the one time."

Luke didn't say anything, but I could see it on his face. Richard had hit on the truth.

I reached out and placed a hand beside Richard's so we were both touching Luke. "I cared."

He looked to me.

I added, "That first night, before we went upstairs and you said no repeats... I knew, even then, that it wasn't going to be enough. The way you looked at me... I was already hoping that maybe it could be something more."

Luke's eyes softened. He took my face between his hands. "I was addicted with that first kiss."

"Same here," Richard said.

"And the first time you both kissed me at once..." Luke shook his head. "I was a goner."

I nodded. "It was amazing. All three nights at the club were like that."

He stroked my cheeks with his thumbs. "They were."

I leaned into his touch. "Will you tell us?"

Luke searched my eyes. "Tell you what?"

"If you ever find yourself wanting someone else? *Really* wanting them?"

He dropped his hands. "What?"

"I'm not saying I think you're going to. I just..."

He slid off me and sat back on his heels.

I sighed. "I don't ever want you—either of you—to stay because you feel obligated, or because you've made promises to us. I want it to be because it's what you want more than anything else."

"I'm staying because I love you. Both of you."

His words meant the world to me, but... I sat up and turned to face both of them. "What if something does happen someday?"

Richard folded his arms across his chest. "What do you mean?"

"What if one of us messes up? What if one of us cheats?"

Luke's voice rose. "I'm not going to—"

"I don't mean you. I mean any of us. What if we can't ever get things back to the way they used to be for us in bed? Or what if someday our sex life gets boring? What if we go through a dry spell and were hardly having any sex, and we can't figure out how to fix it?"

Luke said nothing at first, and I had to wonder if he was waiting for Richard to respond. But Richard remained oddly quiet, his focus locked on the open space of the bed between us.

The heavy silence stretched on. Then Luke finally spoke, meeting my gaze with intention and sincerity. "We may have gotten together in the beginning because of the sex, but it's not why I'm here now. It's not what defines our relationship. It's just a part of it. Not even the most important part."

"But what if one of us makes a mistake?"

That was met by silence again.

I really shouldn't have brought this up. Because before I could say anything else, Richard jerked away and got up to pace the room, his large body stalking back and forth in agitated strides. He stopped at the foot of the bed. I waited for him to speak. He didn't. He breathed deep and got moving again, storming into the bathroom and swinging the door shut behind him.

When he didn't come back out after a few seconds, Luke gestured toward the bathroom door with a tilt of his head. "Come on." He got off the bed.

I couldn't move. I stared at the closed bathroom door. "I shouldn't have said anything."

Luke opened his mouth to respond, but Richard called out from the bathroom first. "You can say anything, ask anything you want. Always."

Luke and I waited a moment, but Richard didn't return.

Luke gestured at me again, and I moved to get up. At the bathroom door, he didn't bother knocking. He turned the handle and pushed the door in.

Richard was leaning forward, staring into the sink, his hands braced on the edges of the narrow vanity. "Nothing like that's ever going to happen."

I said, "But what if—"

"Stop." He lifted his head. There was a hard edge to his scowl. "It's not going to happen. And I don't want to talk about this anymore."

Luke leaned against the doorjamb. "And you saying that is probably exactly why we should have this discussion. You not wanting to talk about shit is not right."

"And you wanting to is starting to get annoying."

Luke's eyes went wide. "Wow."

Richard shook his head. "I didn't mean that. I…" He spun back to the sink and hung his head again. "I can't stand thinking about this."

"Fair enough." Luke stepped forward. "But what if in five years, some guy at Matthew's work has a crush on him? What if Matthew finds it flattering, and maybe you and I are swamped with work and haven't been home much." He jerked a thumb at me. "And maybe he's lonely, and he finds himself thinking about this guy a lot. So much so that when the guy kisses him, Matthew doesn't stop it right away. What then?"

Richard straightened in a rush. He pushed past us and stormed out of the bathroom into the main room of the cabin.

I shook my head. "Stop, Luke. Please."

He didn't let up. He followed Richard out.

I rushed after them in time to see Richard swing around and point a finger at Luke, jabbing his chest with each word. "It's. Not. Going. To. Happen."

Luke swatted his hand away. "Stop saying that."

I approached them. "I'd never do that to us. I can't imagine I'd ever let anything get to that point." I wanted to end this conversation, but I couldn't stop the next words from spilling out. "But people mess up sometimes. What if it's like Luke says? What if I make a mistake? What if it goes even further? What if it's a blowjob or—"

Richard spun away and went for the other side of the cabin, moving with angry, heavy steps. He stopped and slammed his hands down onto the countertop that separated the kitchen area from the rest of the room.

A painful ache built in my chest with the strained quiet that lingered.

Luke crossed the room. He gripped Richard by the upper arm and forced him to turn around. "Say it. It would end us."

"God, no." Richard ran a hand over the top of his head. "No." He sighed and scrubbed that same hand over the bottom half of his face. "Look, I'm not going to break us up over one goddamn blowjob. It's just..." He shook his head again. "The thought of someone else touching you, either of you... I don't think..." He turned away.

When he finally faced us once more, his movements were less jerky and abrupt. "I'm not sure how I could let that go. How I could get it out of my head." He met my stare. There was desperation in his wounded expression. "But I'd try. If you were sorry and you wanted to stay, then I'd have to try. I don't ever want to lose either of you." The defeated look on his face made it seem like what we were discussing had actually happened.

"I'm sorry." I raced forward and wrapped my arms around his waist, my body slamming into him with such force, he took a step back. "I'd never do that."

He held me in return. "You don't have to apologize. You didn't do anything wrong. At all."

"You both need to relax." Luke's words ended on a heavy sigh. "It was a hypothetical question."

Richard scoffed. "So now you're the one wanting to talk about shit that hasn't happened?" He was referring to all my questions about our future I'd asked them months ago at my mom's house. He caressed my back in a comforting touch.

I shook my head, my face still buried in his chest. "I'm sorry I brought it up."

"Don't be." He pulled back so I could see his face. "Maybe talking about this will make it easier for one of us to say something if there's a situation brewing, so we can discuss it before anything ever does happen. If either of you start having thoughts about actually being with someone else, I'd rather know *before* it turns physical."

"I promise, I'll tell you. But it's not going to happen."

He smiled at me. "For me either."

Luke went to sit at the foot of the bed, groaning as he dropped to lie back on the mattress the same way he'd done when we'd first arrived at the cabin. "God, you two are so difficult."

"Luke?" Richard said in a gruff voice.

"Yeah?" He sat up. One look and he must've got what Richard wanted, what he needed him to say. Luke rolled his eyes. "I've gotta work out five times a week just to keep up with Matthew. He's a little sex fiend. Like I'd have the energy to fit a third guy into my life."

My jaw dropped.

Richard went to the bed and sat beside Luke. "He is a little horndog."

"Yeah, but he's our horndog."

"Yep. All ours."

Luke turned serious as he faced Richard. "That was my point. I didn't need to hear him promise he wouldn't cheat. I know he won't, unless..." He didn't finish the thought, just kept his focus on Richard as if he needed him to understand what he was saying without actually uttering the words.

"Yeah," Richard said. "I get it."

I didn't.

Richard gave me a slight smile. The gesture seemed sad and nostalgic all at once. He turned back to Luke. "We won't take him for granted or ignore him. We won't let our own fears get in the way again. We won't send him back to that miserable place he was trapped in before he met us, okay?"

"Okay."

"But that's why we have to talk about stuff. No more trying to deal with shit on your own."

"Gotcha."

"You—" My voice cracked. "You saw it? When we met?" I'd been trying so hard to hide that part of myself. Guys at a sex club didn't want to pick up a sad, lonely, clingy wreck.

Richard stood and came to me. He held me in his arms once more. "Yeah, we saw."

"And you still wanted me?"

"Oh yeah. You were also sexy as hell. I was driven to make you feel good. I wanted to see that smile of yours when it was one hundred percent genuine."

Luke waved a hand through the air. "I was so not that observant. That first night? I just wanted to get laid by the hottest piece of ass in the place." He shifted his attention to Richard. "And the most intense guy who'd ever looked my way. It seemed like the perfect combination for the mood I was in that night."

I laughed.

Richard didn't. "You thought I was intense?"

Luke snorted out a chuckle. "You wouldn't fuck me unless I stared into your eyes."

I laughed again, my body shaking in Richard's grasp. When he drew back to gaze down at me, I nodded. "It was pretty intense."

He took my hand and led me to the bed. Then with one move, he shoved Luke flat on the mattress. Leaning over him, Richard propped his hands on the bed on each side of Luke. "And you loved every minute of it."

"Every fucking second."

"That intensity brought you back for more."

"Yeah. That and Matthew's mouth."

"Fuck yeah." Richard grasped my arm and tugged me down onto the bed next to Luke. He laid a hand on the mattress beside me so he was bent over both of us. "The two of you *were* the perfect combination."

I stared up at him. "Are we still?"

"Absolutely."

"Good." I rolled over onto Luke so I lay on top of him, holding on to him. Then I reached back for Richard, wanting, needing him to press his weight into me so I could feel them both.

Luke groaned. "How come I always end up on the bottom getting squished into the bed?"

"Because," I said, "you're the biggest bottom I know."

"Yep," Richard agreed. "You just love getting fucked into the mattress." He rocked his hips against my ass, pushing me into Luke.

Luke groaned again, this time the sound more a moan of appreciation.

Laughing once more, I held on to him tighter, and Richard settled his weight on us. Who knew a conversation about cheating could make me feel even closer to them than I ever had?

Without lifting up, Richard stroked the top of my head, rubbing his palm all over my buzzed hair. "This is sexy."

"Yeah? You don't hate it?"

"There could never be anything about you that I hate." He shifted off me and onto the bed beside Luke. We all moved up to lie on the pillows, and Luke tugged the blankets over us. As soon as we were settled, Richard added, "And your age doesn't bother me, Matthew. I love you exactly the way you are."

I wanted to tell him that I loved everything about him. I loved that he couldn't stand thinking of another man touching me. I loved the way he cared, the way he wanted to protect us. I loved how dedicated and devoted he was. I loved his body and the way he touched me. I loved his mind and his heart. But before I could say anything, he breathed deep, and his eyes fell closed. The stress of our conversation had worn him out.

When it was clear he had drifted off to sleep, I rolled to face Luke. He was still awake.

"I don't think what he said is right," I whispered. "I don't think we'd make it."

"What do you mean?"

"If you or I had an affair, it would destroy him. We'd never be the same."

Luke lifted up to glance over my shoulder at Richard. "Yeah, I think maybe you're right." He watched Richard for a moment more, then lay back down. "Guess it's a good thing none of us have a reason to even think about another guy." There was a tender sincerity to his tone.

It was sweet, the way he was saying things I needed to hear. And since we'd gotten to the cabin, he hadn't really complained about all the talking. "You're weird in flannel."

I expected him to laugh with me. He didn't.

"I'm serious, Matthew."

I searched his face. "Yeah?"

"Yeah. So don't worry so much. We're going to be fine. No matter what comes up, our relationship will be there, and we'll deal with everything else together. Like we're doing out here in this park."

"Okay."

He snuggled into my side. "Now get some sleep."

For the first time in days, I nodded off without issue and fell into a deep, restful sleep, despite the reason we'd come to the park.

The next morning, we got up, made breakfast, and were ready to go by seven. Richard had a thermos filled with coffee and was the first one out the door, waiting for us by the Jeep.

As we all piled into the vehicle, Luke said, "I have a really good feeling about this, Matthew."

"Me too."

Or maybe I just couldn't fathom going back to Tomas with anything except the truth of what had happened to his dad.

Chapter Twenty

"Stop here." I pointed out the passenger window. "I think this is it."

Richard pulled the Jeep off the side of the road at an open area near a clearing in the trees. "You sure?"

"Yeah. We should be able to pick up the trail right through those trees."

"All right, then." He cut the engine. "Let's go."

We got out of the car. This far from civilization, the rush of fresh air was shocking to the lungs. We stood there for several seconds, basking in the golden rays of sunlight and the sharp scent of earth and pine. The sky was so very blue, the clouds perfectly white and fluffy, in all sorts of shapes and sizes. In one I spotted the image of a galloping horse, its mane flowing through the air. Another looked like a spaceship getting ready to swoop down over us. I could've watched those clouds all day, coming up with a perfect descriptor for each.

But I had a mission.

The three of us donned backpacks that were stocked with various items we'd need for a daylong hike: drinking water, trail mix, a first aid kit, and a few other emergency supplies.

Heading through the opening in the trees, we spotted the path right away. It had a yellow marker identifying it as Majestic Falls Scenic Trail. This was the main trail through the park that started at the lake on the opposite side and looped around in a huge circle. The trail ranged in complexity from easy-to-walk to far more challenging. Where we were joining it, the path followed the river for several miles, then cut through the forest.

Luke gestured to the sign. "Wonder how often we'll see these markers."

"I think it depends on the trail," I said. "Some are every quarter mile. Some are more often, especially when the trail makes a turn." I stepped onto the trail and led the way north as we'd planned the night before. We walked in a straight line with Luke directly behind me and Richard bringing up the rear. We didn't talk much as we hiked, but the world around us was far from quiet, filled with buzzing insects, chirping birds, snapping twigs under our feet, and the occasional rustle of a squirrel darting across the dirt path in front of us. A plethora of vegetation—shrubs, grasses, and ferns—bracketed the trail.

The ground under our feet was uneven, with tree roots that burst up through the dirt every few yards. Oddly for me, I had to concentrate with each step to keep from faltering. All very similar to that day with my dad. As hard as I tried, I couldn't keep thoughts of him from my mind.

After a half hour of hiking, the path made a large bend, and we reached an outcropping overlooking the river. It was the first of Tomas's markers.

I stopped. "This is it."

"Wow," Luke said as he came up behind me. "This is incredible."

Running along the rim of the ravine, the trail offered a view down into the gorge and the winding river below. A dense grove of chestnut oak trees covered the drier ridge areas where we stood, while hemlocks blanketed much of the slopes. A red-tailed hawk soared across the open expanse of sky above the gorge.

Richard joined us, stopping at Luke's other side. He shifted his sunglasses up to rest on his forehead. "Damn. I can see why this was one of Alex's favorite spots."

"I know, right?" I pulled out the map. "Tomas made a note that his dad would hike here after work sometimes." Which made sense. Of all the marked locations, it was the closest to Windtree Wildlife Center. I stepped closer to the edge of the ravine, keeping enough distance I wouldn't fall and tumble down the side of the slope if I lost my footing.

"Careful," Richard said.

"I'm okay." I slipped my pack off and took a seat in the open area overlooking the gorge.

Luke and Richard followed my lead, and we drank from our water bottles in silence as we watched the flow of the river below.

"Matthew."

I turned to Richard. "Yeah?"

"If this is too much for you, if it's bringing up too many painful memories, you need to tell us."

I considered that. "I can't say I'm not thinking about him at all, but it's okay. I'm okay. My dad's not why I came here."

He gave a nod. "All right."

But his question did help me make a decision about something else. I tugged out my phone and texted Tomas: *The sheriff was a no-go. I'm in the park with Luke and Richard. We're going to do our best to find out what happened to your dad.*

Five seconds later Tomas replied. *THANK YOU!!!*

I responded with, *I'll keep you posted.* Then I showed Luke and Richard the exchange.

"You sure that was a good move?" Luke asked.

"He needs to know someone is trying to figure out the truth."

"It's going to crush him if we don't find his dad alive out here."

"I know."

"But I guess if he thinks there's a chance his dad ran out on him, then he's already crushed."

I studied Luke's profile as he looked out over the river once more. There were a number of other rivers and streams in the park, but Windtree was the most significant. The impressive flow of water seemed to mesmerize him. All I could think about was what he'd said. Was it more awful to have your dad beat you and then take off like mine, or for him to be physically there and not give a shit about you, like Luke's? Maybe he'd had it worse than I ever did.

I smiled at him even though he was still turned away from me. "You're pretty amazing. You know that, right?"

He turned to me. "Huh?"

Richard was watching our exchange. I could tell by the glint in his eyes that he knew exactly where my thoughts had gone.

"You always talk about those fifteen years that you spent running from your dad like you made some kind of mistake, wasting all that time worrying about him. But whatever you did, it was the right move for you. Because no matter how jaded you thought you'd become, you never really let that anger and betrayal into your heart. You never let it destroy you."

Luke snorted out an incredulous sound. He swung his focus back toward the water. "I don't know where you come up with shit like that, kid." He shook his head, but when he turned my way once more, his blue eyes held genuine affection. "Thanks."

I smiled at him again. Then I picked up my pack and stood. "Let's get started."

For the next hour we scanned the area on each side of the trail and searched up and down an embankment farther down river where another marked trail led into the river valley, all the while looking for Alex's red backpack. We also walked along the river's banks and then hiked to another high point so we could survey the entire area using binoculars, hoping to spot likely locations where Alex could've hiked to, or a break in the trees where he might've been able to drive his truck off-road to park closer to the ridge above the ravine.

We found nothing.

We made our way back to the Jeep and spent the afternoon driving and hiking to the next three sites on the map, using the photos Tomas had provided as a comparison to make certain we were in the correct locations, then searching those areas as we had the first. At each stop, we uncovered no evidence of footprints or damaged vegetation anywhere off the trail. And still no trace of Alex or anywhere he might've driven his truck.

Continuing on to the fourth search area, the Jeep bounced along the rough, rocky dirt road. Tree roots had busted up through the road in several places, and the heavy rains and freezing winters had created numerous potholes. The off-road vehicle we'd rented had been a wise choice.

When we reached the next location, we searched along the trail until we spotted a break in the trees to our right. I stepped through the opening and came to an abrupt stop.

"Shit," Richard said as he halted beside me. "I didn't think this place could get more amazing."

The word *breathtaking* barely covered the vista before us. We were atop a cliff with a complete 180-degree view of the river valley below. This time the scenic landscape included the most famous waterfall in the park, Eagle's View. The eighty-foot waterfall tumbled over a massive rock wall, then plunged into a blue pool of water below. A large rocky area lay at the base of the falls. People often swam out there and sat on the rocks to enjoy the cool spray. Where we stood higher up, chain barriers at various drop-offs provided protection for visitors.

The bright sun streaking through the trees made the waterfall sparkle and gave the sight before us a magical quality. It took my breath away, just standing there, soaking in the absolute peaceful beauty before us.

We reveled in the stunning view for a moment more, then started scanning along the top of the cliffs before hiking down into the valley. We avoided the wet rocks on either side of the waterfall and instead descended via an embankment farther downriver where the incline wasn't as steep and stone steps had been added to provide a walkway.

Thousands of bluebells dotted the river's edge. They gave off a delicate, sweet fragrance that filled the air. That, along with the gorgeous view of the falls, made this a popular tourist spot at the park, and we encountered several people during our search. We also found loads of footprints, as well as multiple areas of trampled plants and dirt along the river. From that evidence alone, there was no way to know if Alex had been one of the individuals who'd walked through this area.

There was also no reason for us to look for his vehicle at this spot. With the dense trees on the ridge above the river valley, he wouldn't have had any way to drive the center's pickup truck to this area.

We ended our search on the flat sandstone overhang jutting out above the falls. The rocks there were dry, so we sat and took a break, taking in the unique sight of the tumbling water below. I didn't say anything to the guys, wasn't sure I could, but this was the exact location at the falls where my dad had taken me.

"Maybe his truck broke down." I blurted out the words so abruptly, I startled them. And maybe myself.

Luke set his water bottle on the ground between his legs. "The sheriff said it was a 2005 Colorado. That's a pretty old truck."

"Yeah. And maybe he got hurt trying to walk for help."

"Maybe."

We grew quiet. Then Richard said, "But then why didn't he use his phone to call for help?"

I shrugged. "Cell service sucks out here."

"Seems like he'd usually carry a radio, then. Something so he could get in touch with the wildlife center or the rangers?"

"I guess." We should've asked the sheriff that. Or talked to someone at the center about what Alex would've had with him.

"And," Richard started but didn't finish.

"What?"

"If it was just car trouble, someone would've found the truck by now."

"I guess."

I was guzzling down a long swallow of water, mulling that over, when I spotted something red inside the tree line at the river's edge, about fifteen yards from the falls. I jumped up. "Alex's backpack. It's right there! Come on." I dashed back the way we'd come. I heard Luke and Richard behind me, both yelling at me to be careful, but I wasn't about to stop.

I descended the steps into the valley, taking the stone stairs nowhere near as carefully as I'd done earlier, then sprinted along the river for the area where I'd seen the red object. My right foot slipped on a patch of damp vegetation, and I fell forward, flopping face-first into the dirt. I slapped the ground beside me in frustration.

"Matthew!" Richard and Luke simultaneously shouted as they sped down the last of the steps.

"I'm okay." I got to my feet and searched the ground nearby, sweeping aside the tall brush with my arms. I found it within seconds. Had I not spotted the red item from above and known where to look, I would never have seen it in the thick grass.

As I dropped to my knees, disappointment slammed into me. It wasn't a backpack. It was a T-shirt. A woman's shirt. Something much too small to have been Alex's.

"Dammit."

I got up and stalked to the river's edge. The flow of water from the falls slid gracefully over the edge of the sandstone rocks before plunging into the pool below. We were close enough now I could feel the cool mist on my heated face. A moment later Luke and Richard came to stand beside me. No one said a word for several minutes. The hypnotic rush of water as it breached the surface drowned out all other sounds from the forest.

Eventually Richard said, "We'll keep at it."

I nodded. "We should get going." I tilted my head toward the steps where we'd entered the valley. "Let's head back to the car."

By the time we reached the Jeep, the sun had begun to set. The sky had turned a deep shade of violet blue, and an arc in the colors of a rainbow lit up the horizon.

Richard opened the driver's side door. "What now?"

I started for the other side of the Jeep. "Guess we should go back to the cabin for the night."

"All right." We all got in, and Richard pulled out onto the road. "I'm sorry we didn't find anything today."

"We'll try again tomorrow."

"You got it."

After we were inside the cabin and I was showered and ready for bed, I wanted to make a new plan of attack for our search the next day. So while Richard and Luke were sharing the sink in the bathroom to brush their teeth, I used the time alone to go over the map. I laid it across the bed before me and surveyed the remaining locations Tomas had marked.

When Richard and Luke got into the bed on each side of me, I said, "I know I originally said we should try these spots on the west side of the park first, but I don't think we'll find anything this close to the road. Like you said, his truck, or even his backpack, aren't going to be out where someone would've seen them by now."

"Yeah," Richard agreed. Despite that, he seemed apprehensive.

I didn't want to give that too much thought.

"I think we should go here next." I pointed to an area farther away from the campground, near a different trail. "We could leave the Jeep here, where the river turns east, then head the rest of the way on foot. Since we won't make it back to the cabin by nightfall, we can take the tent. Then we could hit these three locations the next day."

Luke inspected the map. I wasn't sure if he was waiting for Richard to say something about the plan or what, but when the quiet lingered on and Richard didn't provide an opinion, Luke said, "Sounds good." He folded the map and set it on the nightstand. He lay down and held his arms out for me. I slid into his arms and laid my head on his shoulder.

Richard turned to sit on the edge of the bed, his back to us, his focus now on the dark fireplace. We'd all been too worn out from the day spent walking and climbing and searching that we hadn't bothered to light a fire. Richard had his elbows propped on his thighs, hands clasped together, his broad shoulders strained with tension.

I couldn't stand the weighty silence that had descended over us. "Richard?"

"Hmm?"

"You don't think we'll find anything, do you? You don't think Alex is still alive."

He sighed but made no move to face me. "I really don't know, Matthew. I just know I can't stand the thought of you coming all the way out here and being disappointed."

"I'll be okay, no matter what we find or don't find. But right now... I just need to keep looking."

He sighed again. "All right." He rotated around and slid under the covers. "I guess we're just getting started."

"Yeah. We can't give up yet."

I actually wasn't sure I'd ever know when it was time to do that. Or if I'd ever be able to walk out of that park without the answers Tomas needed.

I was just glad it was far too soon to make that call.

Chapter Twenty-One

The next morning, Richard drove us to the location I'd indicated on the map. We left the Jeep there and began our hike east. If all went as planned, we wouldn't return to the rented vehicle for several days.

As we made our way along the winding trail, we traveled through flat grasslands and low hillsides that were even more densely populated with massive oak and maple trees than the previous day's hike.

I had hoped to track our progress via GPS, but my phone wasn't getting much of a signal, and I figured it best to save the battery as much as possible, so instead I paid attention to the map and compass, making sure we were still traveling on the right trail and in the right direction. I also estimated the distance between each of our breaks and marked our current location on the map.

At noon we stopped for lunch and gave ourselves an hour's rest. The hiking was strenuous. Muscles all over my body were sore. Apparently I'd gotten far too lax with my workouts lately. The backpacks we wore were loaded down with more gear than the day before, making the trek even more taxing.

It took another five hours of hiking and two more short pauses before we reached the location I wanted to check. We were in a substantial hollow, surrounded by tree-lined hills on three sides. We searched in a zigzag pattern through a quarter-mile stretch along a stream. Again, there was no sign of Alex and nowhere a truck could've driven off-road to reach that location.

"Now what?" Luke asked. He and Richard looked as exhausted as I felt.

I checked the map. "Let's continue east. According to this, there should be several walk-in campsites along this trail. We could stop at one of those for the night."

We hiked for another hour until Richard halted and gestured to our left. "Is that it?"

He pointed to a flat, cleared section of ground perfect for pitching a tent about thirty feet from the trail. The campsite also included a fire ring and several tree stumps that had been positioned as seats around the ring. Another stream was visible through a wooded area past the campsite.

"Yeah," I said. "This one's good."

It was still light, but dusk was fast approaching. We'd have to hurry to set up the tent, get a fire going, and have something to eat before hitting the sack. I wanted to be up early the next morning.

We worked in near silence as we removed the gear from our packs and got the tent in place, thanks to Luke's persistence. None of us had assembled anything like that before, and the instructions included with the tent weren't all that detailed. Thankfully the woman running the camping store had provided us basic instructions on how to set up a campsite, as well as a few other necessities about primitive camping and the concept of backpacking without leaving a trace of our presence behind, as requested by the park service.

When Luke had finished with the tent, he held up a short pole and several nylon cords. "I'm guessing there shouldn't be extra parts."

Richard laughed. "Well, it's staying up."

"True." Luke shrugged and tossed the extra pieces back into his pack. "Let's just hope there's no rain or strong winds."

After we ate, we all crowded inside. Made for three people, the tent was still a tight fit. We each took off our shoes but kept our clothes and coats on to keep warm while we slept. Richard had opened up the three individual sleeping bags and laid one out like a mat for us to sleep on. The other two we used as blankets over all three of us.

Once we were situated, we lay in the relative quiet, listening to the near constant chirp of crickets, until Luke shot up. "Did you hear that?"

"What?" I asked.

"A wolf howl."

"Sure." Richard snorted out a laugh. "Except there are no wolves in this part of the country."

Luke pointed toward the closed tent door. "I'm telling you. That was a wolf. Wait. Shh." He held up a finger to keep us from speaking again.

We all listened.

"There it was again," Luke whispered.

Richard looked to me.

I shook my head. "I didn't hear anything."

"Me either." He gestured for Luke to lie back down. "You're tired. Come get some sleep."

Luke lay down beside me again. A minute of quiet passed. Then he asked in a soft voice, "Do wolves eat people?"

Without warning, Richard quickly shifted over me onto Luke. Grasping Luke's wrists, he pinned his arms above his head and spread out to lie over top of him. "Are you scared?"

"No."

"Because if you are, I want you to know one thing."

"What's that?"

"I'll protect you. Always."

"Sure. And who's going to protect you?"

"Matthew." Richard let go of Luke and returned to lie on his back on my other side, his hands folded behind his head. "If you haven't noticed, he knows far more about what he's doing out here than we do."

"Yeah, he does." Luke wrapped an arm around me.

I lifted my head and asked Richard, "You really think that?"

"Uh-huh." He shifted his hips from side to side as if he couldn't get comfortable. "I miss our bed."

I laughed. "Me too."

He rolled to his side and laid an arm over my waist atop Luke's so they were both holding me but also touching each other. "You're doing a good thing here, Matthew."

"Yeah," Luke agreed. "Not everyone would've bothered talking to the sheriff when the kid asked, let alone come all the way out here."

"Thanks."

Despite their words, Richard seemed reluctant. I had a feeling he really didn't think we'd ever find Alex alive, but he didn't say anything about that.

A half hour later we were all still lying awake, listening to the drizzle of light rain patter the top and sides of the tent. Within minutes, the soft rain became a downpour and the wind kicked up. I elbowed Luke in the side. "You jinxed us."

He scoffed. "The weather report said only ten percent of the county would get rain tonight. Who the hell knew it would rain right on top of us?"

Richard snorted out a laugh. "That deal was probably sealed the minute you started putting together our tent. You've got the worst luck."

Before I knew it, Luke lunged over me to get to Richard. He pinned him down the way Richard had done to him earlier. "I so do not. That's you."

"Nope. I live a charmed life. How else do you think I got the most reticent, closed-off, commitment-phobic man I'd ever met to move in with me after the first date?"

Luke rolled his eyes. "You fucked him into a stupor."

"Damn straight." Richard bucked up under Luke in a teasing attempt to dislodge him. Then the two of them were in the middle of an all-out wrestling match, the tent swaying under the thrashing weight of their bodies.

"Stop!" I called out. "Stop! You're gonna rip the tent, and then we'll all be sleeping in the mud and rain."

They halted the wrestling and turned their heads my way. Luke was straddling Richard, and they had their heads close, both breathing heavily.

Oh no. I knew what those looks meant.

Yep, five seconds later, they were tickling the hell out of me, and I couldn't stop laughing.

No, more like giggling.

But I didn't care. They both seemed to love hearing that sound from me.

Chapter Twenty-Two

"No. No. Matthew!"

I bolted upright. So did Richard.

I had awoken a few minutes earlier to find the rain had stopped. The sun was just starting to make an appearance, its golden rays warming the cool morning air. Outside the tent, the high-pitched squawk of songbirds punctuated the sorrowful call of a mourning dove. It had still been a little too early to head out, so I snuggled in against Richard's side and closed my eyes again. I was just drifting off once more when Luke called out and started frantically kicking at the sleeping bag covering our feet.

He hadn't had a nightmare in such a long time, not since he went to see his father in prison. I was unsure what to do. Once, when I'd previously tried waking him, he'd accidentally hit me, and it had left him feeling like shit for days after.

Good thing Richard was thinking clearly. He reached across me, laid a hand in the middle of Luke's chest, and gave a slight shake. "Wake up, Luke."

Luke clasped on to Richard's forearm and shot up in one motion. "What? What happened?"

"It's okay. You were dreaming."

"A dream? God." He let out an exaggerated exhale and sank back down onto the sleeping bag. He took another breath, and then he reached out for me and drew me into his arms, hugging me in a fierce embrace.

"Was it your dad?" I asked.

"No." He ducked his head and kissed the base of my throat, then kissed lower and lower until he had me lying on my back, his cheek resting against my chest. "You fell while we were hiking. You slid backward down an embankment and hit your head on a rock. I thought you were dead."

"Oh. That's sorta how I fell that day with my dad. Only without the hitting my head part."

"Yeah. I guess that story really stuck with me."

Richard shifted around inside the tent until he lay behind Luke, spooning him. "He's going to be okay. Nothing like that's going to happen now."

"Sure." Luke breathed deep once more. "He'll be fine." He lifted my sweatshirt and the T-shirt underneath. He laid his cheek against my bare flesh. His arms tightened around me.

"Hey." I ran my hand through his hair. "I'm okay."

"I know."

We lay there holding him for several breaths, then I said, "The sun's up. We should probably get going soon."

"Yeah," Richard agreed. But then he lifted his head. "Shh." He sat up all the way and listened intently. "Do you hear that?"

Luke's eyes widened. "The wolf's back."

The sound of footsteps crunching over fallen twigs came from outside the tent. "Park ranger here. Anyone in the tent?"

I grinned at Luke. "A wolf?"

"I *did* hear a wolf last night."

Richard laughed as he unzipped the doorway of the tent and slid out. Luke and I followed.

A man stood on the other side of the campfire ring. He wore a brown uniform that had the park emblem on his shirt pocket. He had a wide stance, his hands on his hips above his loaded utility belt. Park rangers weren't armed, but he still looked ready to pull out some kind of weapon at any moment. He stood in the dark shade of the trees. All that was visible of his face were the whites of his eyes. They were almost glowing.

He gave the three of us an apprehensive scan. "The sheriff said you folks might be on this trail. Figured you'd have to camp here for the night before you went any farther."

"And you are?" Richard asked.

"Gus Cleary. I'm Alex's friend. Not some *strangers* who barely knew him." He stepped forward into the light, his hands still bracketed on his hips. He had long dark hair, secured in a ponytail at the base of the blue Detroit Tigers baseball cap he wore. The cap looked out of place with the uniform. "Emerson said you're looking for Alex."

Richard spoke again before I could. "We're just trying to help if we can."

"Did you tell his wife and kid what you're up to?"

"Tomas knows."

He scoffed. "Did you even think about what that'll do to him, getting his hopes up like that?"

I stepped forward. "They need to know the truth."

"What? That the man they loved ditched them?"

"Alex didn't just walk out on them. He's here in this park somewhere, and they need to find out if he's still alive or not."

Cleary spun away and marched toward the stream. He stared out at the water flowing over the smooth rocks. Something about that reaction told me he didn't believe that rumor about Alex leaving town either.

I wasn't sure if he was going to talk to us again, take off, or what.

After a beat, he turned back.

Before he could speak, I asked, "Were you part of the original search team?"

"I was."

I retrieved Tomas's map from my pack inside the tent. "Could you take a look at this and tell us if you searched these areas?"

"I don't need to. I know where you're going. Tomas told me everything yesterday." Despite his words, Cleary came forward, moving more slowly than before. "All those areas have already been searched." His tone made it sound like he recited a memorized line.

"You sure?" Richard asked.

Cleary removed the cap he wore and ran his free hand over the top of his hair, smoothing the loose strands. He replaced the hat as he blew out a huff of air. "Hell, I don't know. All the places the park rangers checked out were searched thoroughly, but the ones that the deputies went over..." He shrugged as if it was anybody's guess.

"Did you look here?" I held out the map and indicated the next location where we were headed.

"I wasn't assigned that area. I'm not sure who was."

Richard spoke up again. "Then it doesn't hurt for us to take a look, does it?"

Cleary glared at Richard once more, but the look softened as he answered. "No, I suppose it doesn't. I just—" His words cut off sharply. He tipped his head back and remained silent. There was something he wasn't saying.

"Mr. Cleary," I started.

"Call me Gus."

"All right, Gus, do you think something bad happened to Alex out here?"

"I don't know. Maybe." He searched my face for a long moment as if trying to decide if he could trust me. Then his expression changed to something much more jaded and angrier. "But I will say one thing for certain. That asshole sheriff wouldn't know how to conduct a search out here if his own life depended on it. He also never gives a shit about anyone who gets hurt or lost in this park. The way he figures it, if they were stupid enough to head far away from the public areas, then they deserved what they got. He'd never publicly say that, of course. He's an elected official. But it's how he conducts business. He didn't care about what happened to Alex, except how the whole thing made him look on TV."

That surprised me. Sheriff Emerson didn't seem like the most cooperative guy in the world, but I hadn't sensed any true malice in him, not like what Gus described.

"The sheriff and his deputies," Gus added. "I'm not sure they tried all that hard to find Alex."

"Why would you say that?" I asked. "They were out here for days, right? They used search dogs, a helicopter."

"Well, they had to make it look good. The local news was on their asses. But they couldn't even find his truck, and I *know* it's out here." He jabbed at his chest with his thumb. "I've been trying to find that vehicle, find him whenever I have time off from work, so I really don't know what you all think you're going to be able to do in a couple of days."

"We're going to try our best."

He considered me with skepticism for several more seconds. Maybe he deemed me sincere. He gave a nod, then checked his watch. "I've gotta get going. We have a ranger meeting back at the main station. Just wanted to see for myself if you were really out here." He scrutinized me for a moment more, then marched past us. He stopped before reaching the trail, his entire body alert, ready to take off again at any second, but he didn't. He turned to face me. "Thank you for doing this."

Luke made an exasperated noise of disbelief. "You've got a funny way of showing your appreciation."

"Yeah, I know. I've got trust issues." Gus hesitated for a second longer. Then he started for the trail again without another word.

"Wait." I raced after him. Richard and Luke followed close behind. I didn't think either of them trusted this guy, but there was a genuineness to Gus Cleary that I liked. He stopped and waited for me to approach. I held the map out once more. "Where do *you* think we should look?"

He eyed the map but didn't take it. "The rangers searched south of

Springbrook Trail pretty good. I'd try where the kid said north of that. He knew his dad better than anyone."

"Okay."

Gus said nothing more at first, but he didn't take off either. "You're right about Alex. He didn't leave his family. I've known that man for years. He was the most loyal person you'd ever meet. He loved his wife and son. And the new baby. He lived for them and that wildlife center. I've never met a man who loved his life more." In contrast to his words, Gus took a frustrated step my way. He jabbed a finger at me. "He did *not* just walk out on them."

Richard bolted between us. "Watch it. We're not the enemy here."

I laid a hand on Richard's back. "It's okay. It's not me he's mad at." I eased around Richard to stand beside him. "We're going to do what we can to prove that Alex was here in the park that day."

Gus sighed as he tipped his head back, once more staring up into the canopy of trees. When he spoke again, it was in a more thoughtful tone. "You really shouldn't go much farther down this trail." He gestured to all three of us. "You guys don't exactly look like you're regular hikers."

Richard shrugged that off. "We'll be fine."

"It's dangerous if you don't know what you're doing." There was something ominous about that warning that made me think he wasn't only referring to the difficult hike or natural threats. Or maybe I was reading too much into things, wanting to see explanations and evidence where we were never going to find any.

Despite his warning, Gus said, "Fine. But just stay on the trails as much as you can." He removed a business card from his wallet and handed it to me. "Call me if you get into any trouble. Or if you find any sign of Alex or his truck. I can talk to my boss. He'll get the sheriff to open the search again."

I pocketed the card. "Thanks."

He didn't move. Didn't speak. When he finally did say something else, his voice was tight with emotion. "I tried to find him. Before it was too late. I really did."

"It might not be too late."

Breathing deep, he gave another nod. "Be careful out here." He took off again and was out of sight down the trail in no time.

"Well," Richard said, "he sure was helpful. I can't decide if he wants us to leave the park or keep looking."

"Yeah," Luke agreed. "What's up with that?"

"I don't know," I said as I stared off at where Gus had left. "If I had to guess, I'd say he wants both."

"Why?"

"Maybe he wants answers, but he also doesn't want anyone else to get hurt."

Luke studied me for a long breath. "So… are we still doing this?"

Richard waited for my answer too.

"Yeah. We are."

Chapter Twenty-Three

"No!" I gripped Richard's arm and jerked him to a stop. "Not here. Too dangerous."

After the first few steps, the path before us was startlingly steep. The grade would require some sort of rappelling gear. Especially for novices like us. "We need to find another way."

Richard gave a nod. Then instead of heading down the narrow, rocky dirt path that led into a similar valley as the day before, we hiked along the top ridge until we came to a more manageable slope.

Once down in the valley, we took a good look around but found nothing odd and no trace of Alex's backpack, so we continued on to the next location, trekking through a series of rock formations that created outcroppings and arches over the dirt path.

We weren't seeing many places where Alex could've taken his truck off-road, so we decided once we were done hiking the remote locations from Tomas's map, we'd return to the Jeep and head down each of the access roads to search for spots where Alex might have been able to drive from the access road into the forest.

We were in the process of making our way down another embankment that led to a shallow stream when my foot got tangled up in the underbrush covering the trail. I pitched forward.

Luke caught me before I went down. "You okay?"

"Yeah, just tripped."

"You've been doing that a lot lately." The furrowed brows demonstrated his concern. Probably because of his nightmare.

"I'm okay. It's this trail. It's pretty uneven."

"Sure. It's just not like you at all."

"Really, I'm fine. I just want to keep moving." I wasn't sure if that appeased him or not, but we continued on without another word on the subject.

We reached the third location, a heavily wooded area with

enormous pine trees that towered over us like skyscrapers and left a carpet of rust-colored pine needles covering the forest floor. There we found nothing yet again. Dusk was fast approaching. I was beginning to doubt we'd ever be able to locate anything helpful, even if Alex or his truck were out there somewhere in the park. It wasn't like we had experience conducting this kind of search. We could've already walked right by some sort of evidence that proved Alex was there that day and not had a clue we'd missed it.

As we wrapped up searching in that area, the sun was beginning to set, and the sky was growing dark. I'd already used the map to pick out a campsite for the night, one of the last park-maintained primitive sites we'd see for quite a while, positioned near a small waterfall. According to Alex's book, the falls spilled out over a series of rock steps into a sizable body of water, creating a stunning swimming hole that would be far more popular with tourists if it were in a more accessible location. I was anxious to see it.

It wasn't long before we found the site. Despite the numerous breaks we'd taken, we were all hot and sweaty, exhausted from another day of such an intensive, arduous trek with heavy packs on our backs. The spring day had felt more like summer, and the setting sun hadn't cooled the evening air all that much. Hopefully the humid heat wouldn't last all night. We needed our rest. The next morning we'd be heading into an even more desolate, isolated section of the park, and we'd be taking one of the most remote trails.

We got the tent set up, and then I sat on the ground and reclined back on my elbows to examine the evening sky. It was dark, startlingly dark. No light pollution from city streetlights or outdoor artificial lighting fixtures that people typically installed to feel safe from their own neighbors. The sky was a dramatic dark blue near the treetops, then grew black above that, illuminating more stars than I'd ever seen before. Hell, we barely saw the stars at home.

Richard came to me and took my hand. "Come with me. You too, Luke."

"Where are we going?" I asked as he helped me up and led me away from the tent.

"You'll see." He stopped at the edge of the water. "Strip."

"What?" I glanced around.

"No one's out here. Get naked. We're going skinny-dipping."

Luke grinned at Richard and immediately started peeling off his clothes.

Richard laughed before he eyed me with curiosity. "You don't want to?"

"I've never done anything like this before."

"Me either." He tilted his head at Luke. "And I'm guessing Mr. Speed Stripping over there hasn't either."

Luke stood naked now. "Nope. Never." He rubbed his palms together, then gestured to us, indicating we should get naked too. "Let's go."

Richard and I got undressed, and we all stepped into the pool of water. A couple of inches below the surface the water was bracingly cold this time of year, but the chilly liquid moving over my heated flesh felt amazing. I dived under the surface and swam away from the shore. When I emerged near the center of the pool, I found Luke and Richard had done the same. It was shallow enough that we could stand on the bottom, our shoulders and heads above the surface.

We swam and splashed around for a while.

Then Luke floated on his back. "Shit. This is awesome. Who the hell knew there were this many stars out at night?"

I floated too. The moon hung low in the sky, creating subtle beams of light that filtered down through a lattice of tree limbs to create soft swaths across the surface of the water. The waterfall's foaming cascade glowed in the moonlight. I let my eyes fall shut, and the sounds of the forest seemed to rise up around us: the soothing flow of the waterfall, the hoot of an owl, the chirping of crickets, and the rustle of wind through the tree branches.

I felt a hand settle at my lower back as if helping to hold me up so I wouldn't sink into the water and disappear. I opened my eyes.

Richard was standing over me. "Hey."

I smiled up at him. "Hey."

He lifted me up and into his arms.

I thought he was going to kiss me, but instead he ran his wet hands over my shorn hair, then down the sides of my neck, over my shoulders, my back, my hips, my ass.

Luke pressed in behind me and swept his hands across my chest while Richard reached around to my front. He cupped my cock and balls and massaged my flesh.

"What are you doing?" I asked.

"We're helping you wash up."

"You are not. You're teasing me."

"It's not called teasing if Luke and I have every intention of following through." Despite his words, he let go of me. "Let's get dry and have something to eat."

Luke laughed as he and Richard headed for the shore.

"See!" I called after them. "You were teasing me."

"And you loved every second of it," Richard said over his shoulder.

He was absolutely right.

After we were dry and dressed in clean clothes, we got a fire going and all took a seat, Luke and I on a downed tree, Richard on the ground facing us. We ate a simple freeze-dried pasta dish that only required boiling water. As we were finishing up with dinner, an alert sounded from one of our phones inside our backpacks propped near the tent. We hadn't had much of a signal for most of the day, and I thought all our phones were off, so it surprised me to hear the notification.

Luke searched through his bag, then mine next. "It's yours, Matthew." He brought me my cell. Apparently I'd forgotten to shut it down the last time I checked the phone.

I read the message. "It's from Tomas. He wants to know how it's going." I sent the kid a reply. *Haven't found anything yet. Just getting started on more remote locations tomorrow. Not giving up.*

He texted back: *Thanks. I owe you so much.*

No, you don't. I want to help.

We texted back and forth for a few more minutes. Tomas sent a photo of his pig and dog playing tag together. I told him I'd love to meet his animals, then made sure to add that my phone's signal had been cutting in and out and that I'd keep him updated when I could. I also texted Kevin to let him know we were okay and to check on Trixie. They were spoiling her like crazy, and she was enjoying all the trips to the dog park.

After the sky had grown darker, the three of us sat in the quiet for several minutes, the air filled with the scent of smoke from the campfire and the first signs of fireflies. It all reminded me of that night with my dad when he'd spoken about his father.

Luke leaned into my side. "Thanks for bringing us out here. I know we're not here for the view, but it's hard not to be impressed. It's so dang beautiful here. Peaceful." He looked out over the water and sighed with contentment. "It'd be awesome to build a cabin right by this waterfall, live out here, and never leave."

"You'd really like that?"

"Yeah." Then that relaxed smile faded, and his forehead scrunched up. "Until we ran out of lube."

"We could go to a store once a week."

He laughed. "Sounds good."

I stared at him as he kept on taking in the view of the starry night sky above the waterfall. I was more in awe of him than the beautiful blanket of stars. He was so amazingly gorgeous, but also passionate and thoughtful and so full of life. My chest ached with the thought of what Richard had mentioned the other night, that Luke could've so easily walked away from us and we wouldn't have gotten to see this side of him. He'd nearly sprinted out the door and never looked back that second night at the club.

Without a word, Richard stood. He came to me and encouraged me to my feet. Wrapping his arms around my waist, he pulled me to him. "He's pretty amazing, isn't he?"

"Yeah." I held him in return. "Some days, I can't believe he picked us."

"Me either. I was just thinking of that second night at the club."

"I was too."

He drew my lower body against his. "Remember when we sat there at that table by the stairs? I was trying to play it cool, but all I kept thinking was, *Dear God, don't let him walk away.* I wanted you both like I'd never wanted anyone else. Ever."

"Me too. You know how the other day he said we wouldn't be here if you hadn't kept pushing us all together in the beginning?" He nodded, and I continued. "Really, we wouldn't be here if it weren't for him. He held our entire future in his hands that night."

"He did. Good thing he's such a smart man."

I laughed. "More like, good thing he listened to his dick that night, instead of his brain. I told him the other day he's at his best when he doesn't think."

"God, that's so true."

Luke snorted. "Why do you two always talk like I'm not in the room?"

I reached down and patted the top of his head. "Oh, Luke, it's time to use that brain of yours again. I know you computer tech geeks don't get out much, but we're not in a room. This is called the outdoors."

Richard buried his face in the crook of my neck and held me tighter as laughter poured out of both of us.

"Lame much?" Luke stood and jabbed Richard in the side. "Why do you always encourage him like that?"

Richard straightened and met my stare. "Because I love his laugh."

Luke nodded. "That is a pretty sweet sound."

"Let's hear it some more." Richard ducked down and grabbed hold of me around my hips, hefting me over his shoulder in a firefighter-style carry.

"What are you doing?" I squealed.

"You'll see. Get a blanket, Luke."

Luke went to the tent. He came back with a sleeping bag. He barely had it spread out on the ground before Richard maneuvered us down onto it. He laid me out on my back and propped himself over me. Then he turned to Luke. "Tickle him." Luke went to do as instructed, but Richard held up a hand to stop him. "With only your mouth."

Luke's brows rose in anticipation. "I can do that."

Richard leaned on an elbow beside me, and Luke moved in on my other side. He raised my shirt, exposing the bare skin of my stomach. Bending forward, he brushed his lips along my flesh, sending goose bumps shooting across my skin. He hadn't shaved since the morning before, and the rasp of stubble lightly sweeping my skin tickled. I squirmed under the teasing assault. He repeated the action again and again. Then he tongued around my navel, and I laughed more.

The laughter died off the minute he started making his way south. My breathing kicked up a notch as he opened my jeans and pushed them and my underwear low so he could keep traveling down my body with his mouth. He stopped when he reached the hair above my cock. He blew a warm breath through the dark hair.

That tickled more. I laughed again.

"Nice," Richard said as he continued to watch us. Then his hands were on me, raising my shirt higher over my torso. "Lift up."

I sat up, and he peeled my T-shirt over my head. After I was on my back again, Luke lowered my pants and underwear the rest of the way off my legs. He tossed them and my socks and boots aside, and then I was naked again right there outside, under the stars. I exhaled deeply as a wave of lust engulfed me.

"He's not laughing enough," Luke said.

"No, he's not." Richard stroked one hand across my pecs, then followed that movement with his lips and tongue, teasing one nipple, then the other. Luke went back to running his tongue over me, this time lightly brushing the tip of my cock. It was just enough pressure to bring my dick to life.

I arched into their touches. "Oh God."

Luke groaned, a frustrated, playful sound. "We're turning him on, not tickling him."

"Yeah, guess we are," Richard said. "Time to change gears. I think he needs to be teased and turned on way more."

"Uh-huh," Luke agreed.

"More?" I whimpered. "Oh shit."

"Yep." Richard sat up. He reached for Luke and brought him up so they were face-to-face. "Take off your shirt."

After they both shed their shirts, Richard grabbed Luke again and laid a mind-blowing kiss on him. They continued kissing wildly, passionately, Richard showing his love for Luke's body the entire time. Luke plunged into the kiss with as much abandon as Richard. It was all so heady and erotic to see them like this outside, nothing but the dark sky and the canopy of trees and stars above. I reached for my erection and gave a squeeze, then a slow stroke.

When the kiss ended, Richard spied me fondling myself. He shook his head. "Hands above your head. Don't touch yourself again."

I followed his command as the two of them finished undressing each other.

Then they were both naked, leaning over me again, their lips on me, kissing me, touching me everywhere. Two mouths. Four hands. It was intoxicating.

Only, I wanted more.

I wanted them to take me right there, have their way with me and make me cry out in uncontrollable bliss.

Richard dropped a kiss on my right nipple, then tongued over and around it. His breath danced across my sensitive flesh as he spoke again. "On your hands and knees."

I could barely lift my head. "What?"

He grinned. "Trust me. Get up on your knees."

I sat up, and he helped me flip over as he'd requested. I swayed back and forth under the unbelievable desire thundering throughout my body. Richard got on his back perpendicular to me and positioned his head at my groin. He grasped my cock, and without delay, he sucked the head into his mouth.

"Yes! Fuck, yes!"

It was hot as hell watching him take my dick into his mouth from underneath me. There was always something very powerful about seeing him suck me off in that way. It drove me crazy. Every single time. Made me desperate to thrust into him, watch him swallow me down, watch him take my release down his throat.

Luke was behind me now. He spread my legs wide and swiped his fingertips over my hole, teasing, stroking, stoking my arousal higher. Then his hands left my body. When he touched me again, his fingers were wet with lube. He must've gotten the lubricant when he'd gone to the tent for the sleeping bag. He teasingly rubbed me again, his fingers slowly sliding over and around the entrance to my body. He gave me no more warning than that before he dipped a finger inside me.

I groaned.

Richard sucked harder.

Luke thrust his finger in and out of my ass, going slow at first, then picking up speed, adding his mouth into the action.

I hung my head and squeezed my eyes shut. This was pure heaven. One man thrusting and licking, the other sucking and tugging. So many sensations at once. I was on the edge in no time.

"Fuck. I'm gonna—"

Luke sat up in a rush. "Richard." He sounded desperate.

Richard let go of me. He must've seen what Luke hadn't verbalized, maybe *couldn't* verbalize. "You got it." He moved out of the way, and they both helped me turn onto my back again.

Luke frantically lay over me. There was nothing slow or careful about his movements. He thrust against me, wantonly rubbing his erection over mine, his arms flexing with each push and pull, each rocking movement forward and back.

Richard lovingly laid a hand on the back of Luke's head and watched us for a moment. Then he grabbed the lube and slathered his dick as he moved in behind Luke. In a series of swift moves, he buried himself in Luke's ass. Luke dropped his head forward and groaned.

Richard didn't hold back. He fucked Luke in that signature piston-like style of his, driving Luke against my body, rubbing our dicks together in the most perfect slide of flesh on flesh. I moaned, loud and long, relishing the feel of both of them over me.

But I wanted more.

Someone else did too

Luke lifted up over me onto his hands and knees, Richard moving with him.

"I want you, Matthew." Luke's tone was so serious. So genuine. God, I loved him. With his hand on my face, he drew me to him and brought our mouths together, electric passion passing back and forth between us as the kiss went on and on. Then he lowered me back to the ground, exhaling a shaky breath as if the intensity of that kiss—or the desire racing through him—was too much, too overwhelming. "I've never wanted you more."

Richard handed Luke the lube. With a shaking hand, Luke wet his dick, then my ass. But one look at him and I knew the reaction wasn't out of fear or uncertainty. He was so turned on, he was ready to burst.

I held my legs up and open as he leaned over me again. He sank into me in the same smooth, rapid thrusts as Richard had done with him. No hesitation, no doubts. It was ecstasy.

"Yes! Luke! Richard!"

They both moved over me then. Grunting and thrusting, skin slapping against skin, we were all flying high on the building sensations. The scent of sex rose up around us, filling the night air with that primal blend of carnal need and sweaty male bodies grinding against each other.

All I could do was take what they were giving me.

And I loved it.

Craved it.

This was what we'd been missing.

Lust. Passion. Desire. An uncontrollable rush.

Strange that we'd found it in the middle of the forest.

I should've known, though. It didn't matter where we were. So long as we were all together.

Luke's body shook. "Oh, Jesus." He groaned and started slamming into me harder. "Why the hell was I scared of this?"

"I know," I panted, overcome by the building sensations.

I wanted to hold off until they came, but I wasn't going to last much longer. That was okay. They were right there on the edge with me.

Luke's breath hitched. "Fuck." The muscles of his abs jerked as his body went taut against me, his dick deep inside me. "Fucking hell. Matthew." He shuddered and came, spilling every drop of his release inside me, and I squeezed around him, drawing out one last groan and jerk of his hips as he repeatedly clawed at the sleeping bag beside my left shoulder.

With his breaths still coming in heavy pants and his dick still in my ass, he reached for my cock. He stroked me as Richard started in on his ass again.

With that knowing hand on me, I completely lost it. I grabbed on to Luke's upper arms, my entire body shaking throughout my orgasm, whimpers and cries surging out of me, the sounds so loud I had to have scared off all signs of wildlife. I barely registered the grunts from Richard as he came too, calling out Luke's name, then mine.

When I finally returned to myself, I lay on my back, Luke beside me, Richard on his other side. I stayed like that, watching the twinkling, mesmerizing stars in the night sky above the line of trees. Despite everything else, I felt free, alive in a way I hadn't in a long while.

I could barely lift my head. "That was... wow."

"Uh-huh," Luke agreed.

I couldn't help but laugh. "We totally need to wash up again, and the water's gonna be even colder now."

Luke chuckled with me, but then his voice was full of meaning when he said, "It was so worth it."

"It was."

He reached for my hand at my side and held it in his.

After several deep breaths, Richard sat up and leaned over Luke, tugging me closer so we were all smooshed together. Then he sprawled out over Luke's lower body and laid his head on my chest. He ran his warm fingers over my left pec, higher, along my collarbone, and then up the side of my neck and back down again. "Next time, it's my turn to be inside you, Matthew. It's been too damn long."

"Oh God, yeah."

A few quiet minutes passed.

Richard raised up so he could see my face. "You look relaxed."

"I am."

"Good." He gave me a kiss. "We're going to do our best out here."

"Yeah, we are."

And that was all I could ask for really.

In the end, so long as I had them, everything would be okay.

More than okay.

Richard moved around to spoon me, and I laid my head on Luke's chest. Several minutes later, Richard's breathing grew slow and steady with sleep.

Luke idly ran a hand over the back of my shorn hair. "Looks like we wore someone out."

"All this stress makes him tired."

"Yeah." Then Luke's hand stilled as if a thought occurred to him. "You think he's okay? Physically, I mean."

"Sure. What makes you ask that?"

"He said his grandfather died of a heart attack, and his dad's had some heart and high blood pressure issues too."

"I think he's good. He's in great shape, takes care of himself."

"Yeah." Luke started stroking my head again. "Have I ever told you that I'm really glad you took a chance with two older guys?"

"You're not that much older."

He scoffed. "Eleven years. That's old enough. A relationship like this could've seriously freaked out someone your age."

I held him tighter and shook my head. "I was never freaked out. Not once."

He hugged me back. "I'm glad."

"You sure?" To show him I was kidding, I tickled him.

He wriggled and laughed. "Stop. Stop. You're gonna wake up the big guy. As old as I am, he's way older, you know. He needs his sleep."

I eased up on the teasing but kept my voice light. "That's true. We gotta let him rest after sex like that."

Richard let out a sleepy groan. "Fuck the both of you."

"You already did that," Luke said. "Well, you fucked me. Pretty damn awesomely too."

I laughed more. "Awesomely?"

"It's a word."

Richard groaned again. Then he shifted closer and leaned over me to offer a soft kiss on Luke's lips. "I'm okay, you guys. At my last physical, the doc said I have the heart of a twenty-five-year-old. No worries, okay?"

I sighed. "Okay."

Luke didn't say anything.

"Luke…"

"Yeah, no worries."

"Good. Now"—he sat up and playfully smacked my ass—"let's get dressed and get in the tent, before some wild animal decides to take a bite out of this gorgeous ass."

Chapter Twenty-Four

"You okay?" Richard asked as he ran his warm hand down my bare back.

It was almost midnight. I was lying on top of him, and Luke was half on the sleeping bag, half on me, his cheek plastered against my ass where he'd landed after we'd climbed inside the tent, all of us still naked. We'd washed up in the water, then carried our clothes with us to the tent, but hadn't had the energy to get dressed yet.

"Yeah," I said. "Just hate waiting until morning to start searching again."

"I understand. It's frustrating as hell when something you really want is out of your control."

Luke chuckled, his warm breath tickling my ass cheek. "Trust him, Matthew. He knows about control issues."

Richard reached around me and pinched Luke on the back of the neck.

"Ouch." Luke turned his head and playfully bit my ass.

"Hey," I called out. "I wasn't the one who pinched you."

"You're closer. Pinch him back for me."

I laughed. "No. You pinch him yourself."

"What good is being in a three-person relationship if I gotta do all the pinching myself?" He tickled me along my sides, and I squirmed and laughed. Then he moved up to lie over my entire body, smashing me between them so I couldn't get away.

Richard got in on the action, helping Luke with the teasing.

I laughed harder, wriggled more. "Hey! You guys were the ones who started this. Not me."

"But," Luke said, "it's more fun to make you squirm." Then abruptly he stilled. "No. It's just as much fun to get *him*. Come on, Matthew, we already got him pinned down."

I shifted sideways so we were both lying over Richard, and we attacked him, each tickling along one side of his ribs and his armpits.

Richard bucked up under the assault, almost knocking us off him. "Stop. Stop. I've got something to tell you guys."

I let up on the tickles. "What?"

Luke rolled to his back on Richard's other side and groaned. "Matthew, you fell for it."

"I'm serious." Richard stroked my cheek with the back of his fingers. He cleared his throat, but only silence followed.

Luke snorted out a laugh. "Just say it, big guy."

Richard laughed too as if Luke had read too much into it and whatever was on his mind was no big deal. Yet when he spoke his voice held a note of self-condemnation. "I'm sorry I've been holding back so much."

"Me too," I said. "I should've been clearer with you guys about what I wanted, about what I was feeling."

Silence followed as if we were all thinking that over. Then Luke lifted his head. "Me three."

I laughed, but I cut off the sound as soon as I spotted the pained expression on his face. "We got to this place together," I said. "And I understand why you were both feeling the way you were. I really do."

"I don't," Richard said. "I believed you when you said you'd tell me the truth about what you wanted. I don't know why I couldn't let it go."

"You're allowed to feel things. You're allowed to make mistakes and freak out and be afraid of stuff. We all are. You don't have to try to be so perfect all the time."

"Yeah. You're right."

"He is," Luke said. "I mean, look at me. I'm far from perfect at this relationship stuff, and you both still love me."

Despite the lighthearted way Luke had said the words, there was something strained and melancholy about the expression on his face.

I raised up and propped myself on one arm so I could get a better look at him. "What is it?"

He shook his head. "Nothing."

Richard lifted his head. He and Luke held a stare for several beats.

Eventually Luke said, "It's just... sometimes I still wonder..." He trailed off.

"You wonder what?" Richard asked.

"What it would be like if it were just him and me together, or you and me..." He shook his head. "It would never be the same."

"No, it wouldn't." Richard lay back down, and we all snuggled together again, my head on Richard's chest, Luke on his other side, an arm draped over both of us.

"No, it wouldn't," I echoed.

* * * * *

"If Alex was here," Luke said in a slow, cautious tone, "or anywhere along the river, do you think maybe he drowned?"

We were at our second stop of the day, near where we'd met up with Windtree River again. We'd hiked along the water's edge until we reached a rock formation that Tomas had noted on the map, a naturally formed rose-colored sandstone tower. We took a break and drank some water, sitting at the base of the tower. We were all quiet for a while, surrounded by the soothing natural sounds: the rush of water flowing over rock and the calls of the birds chirping and singing all around us.

Then Luke asked about Alex.

"I don't know," I said.

He waited a moment, like he didn't want to say more. "He could've fallen from higher up, hit his head, and rolled into the water. Maybe his body got caught in some vegetation under the surface and that's why the search dogs never found him."

"But," I said, "then his truck would've turned up somewhere. The sheriff's deputies would've found it in a parking lot here at the park or along the side of a road near one of the trails. Even if he walked from Windtree into the park, his truck would be at the center."

"That's what's been bothering me," Richard said with a grim note to his voice. "How hard did they look if they couldn't find his truck, even out in the middle of the park? We're not seeing that many places where he could've driven off-road."

He was right. If Alex hadn't left town, and he'd been in the park that day, someone would've eventually come across his vehicle. This time of year there were hikers in and out of the park at all times during daylight hours. We'd passed several people on the trails during the past three days.

Luke cleared his throat as if reluctant to mention his next thought. "Maybe he really did take off on his own. Maybe he just packed his bag and left, no note, nothing." He turned my way. "Maybe he was running from something. Or someone."

"What do you mean?"

"What about his wife?"

"What about her?"

"Could she have done something to drive him away? Or done something *to* him? Both Tomas and the sheriff mentioned their argument. It must've been a doozy. Maybe he was abusing her. Maybe she'd finally had enough and didn't want him anywhere near the new baby."

I emphatically shook my head. "No. That's not possible."

He threw me a sorrowful look, then glanced at Richard over my shoulder.

"I hate to say this," Richard began.

"No."

He forged on anyway. "Matthew, some people are good at pretending to be something they're not. You barely knew him and his wife."

I shook my head once more, then watched the river again, mentally running through every possible scenario I could come up with. "Maybe someone moved his truck after he got hurt." Or after he died, but I couldn't make myself say that out loud.

Neither responded to that.

"I don't believe his wife did anything to him, but maybe someone else did, and whoever that was tried to hide what really happened."

Richard's gaze narrowed. "I don't like the sound of that."

And if my theory was even remotely true, he wouldn't want us continuing to look into Alex's disappearance, especially since at least a dozen people in the town of Majestic Falls knew we were out in the park, looking for what happened to Alex.

I met his sharp stare. "We're probably overthinking this. He probably got injured somehow and they didn't look for him hard enough. Maybe he parked somewhere obscure, and they missed his truck during their search."

Richard continued to watch me, a long, grave look, but he didn't say anything more on the subject.

In fact, no one said another word, and it was strange, not our usual comfortable silence. We trudged on amid that heavy lull back to the trail we'd been on that morning. We checked one more of Tomas's markers but came up empty again. We kept going as far as we could until the sun started to set, then found an open area to set up camp.

We ate dinner and then crawled into the tent immediately afterward with no more than a few words exchanged the entire time. After we got situated for bed, silence descended once more, the same solemn stillness that had settled over us after our discussion at the river's edge.

Richard was still sitting up, his focus on the closed door of the tent.

Maybe Luke knew what would happen next. He reached for the portable lamp and clicked it off. "We better get some sleep."

Once the light was off, Richard got under the sleeping bag. A few minutes passed. With their uneven breaths, it was clear neither of them had drifted off to sleep. Then Richard sighed and sat up, reaching across us to turn on the light as he did. He sat facing the door of the tent again, his legs bent, his elbows on his knees.

Whatever he was going over in his mind, whatever he was about to say, I knew I wasn't going to like it.

"I don't trust that sheriff." He turned toward us. "I think you were right, Matthew. Whatever happened to Alex probably wasn't an accident, and I'm guessing the sheriff was involved or he's covering for someone else. Either way, I don't want us tangled up in this for one more second."

I sat up. "But Alex could still be alive."

"The more time that goes by, the less likely that's possible. Besides, I seriously doubt we're going to find anything out here anyway. We don't know how to conduct a search like this. We're not trained for this kind of thing. If we're all honest with ourselves, we're just going through the motions here."

"No." I scrambled past him and out of the tent, needing to move, needing some fresh air. They followed, Luke carrying the lamp. I took several steps away from our campsite, then stopped and turned back, gaping at Richard.

In the dim light of both lamp and moon, Luke looked from Richard to me and then back. When neither of us spoke, Luke gestured at me. "We at least need to try. Matthew needs us to try."

"I know." Richard regarded me with apprehension from where he still stood near the tent. "I know this is important to you, but if something suspicious is going on here, then I think it's best we pack up and—

"No!" My entire body shook as I glared at him. "This isn't your call."

He didn't say anything or try to approach me at first. Eventually he took a step toward me but then stopped as if he didn't want to use physical touch to coerce me. "I really do get why this matters so much to you, but I will not put your safety or Luke's at risk. For anything."

"I don't care how dangerous it might be. I'm not going anywhere until I can at least prove Alex was in this park the day he disappeared." Even as I said the words, I knew it didn't matter. With our speculations about foul play, we'd already crossed a line that Richard couldn't live with, and he wasn't going to back down on this.

But I couldn't leave now. I couldn't walk away after I'd promised Tomas I would help. We were the only ones looking for Alex. There had to be some way I could get Richard to change his mind on this.

Before I could come up with anything, he said, "This isn't just your decision, Matthew. It involves all of us. We are all in this together, and I want us to leave before we find out something that could put us in even more danger."

"No. I'm staying. You can go if you want, but I'm staying. Or are you going to try to make me do something else I don't want?"

As soon as the words were past my lips, I slapped a hand over my mouth. I wanted to take those words back, set them on fire until they burned away and there was nothing left of them, no evidence that I'd ever said anything like that to him. But that wasn't possible. Those awful words were already in the air between us.

Richard staggered back a step, his eyes wide, his parted lips quivering. He looked crushed, hurt in a way I'd never seen him before. I had no idea one look from someone could break my heart.

Luke was carefully eyeing him too. Then he gradually moved toward me, holding out a hand as if he was afraid I was a skittish squirrel who'd bolt the minute he got too close. "Let's all just take a breath." He came in closer.

I shook my head and took an unsteady step back, desperately wanting to sprint away from them, to go out into the night and get lost in the dark. I shook my head again. "Don't."

Luke stopped.

Tears welled in my eyes.

Richard now had his focus locked on the ground before him, his jaw clenched, pain etched on his face. It surprised me more than anything when he lifted his head and met my stare.

"I'm sorry," I said. "I didn't mean that. I just…" I swallowed and forced myself to go on. "I'm going to keep looking. With or without you."

He gave a measured nod. "Okay. Then it's with us."

I wiped at my eyes. "Okay." I turned away from him.

It wasn't long, and I heard one of them approach behind me. I wanted it to be Richard so badly, to feel his solid arms around me, hear that deep voice whisper in my ear, but as soon as those two arms slipped around my waist, I knew it was Luke. He laid a hand over my stomach, and I frantically gripped it in mine.

I heard the tent flap opening behind us.

Pressing his lips to my ear, Luke whispered, "It's going to be okay."

I wanted to believe that. But how could anything be okay when a good father like Alex was missing and I'd hurt Richard so badly?

How could it ever be okay again?

The tent door shifted again. Luke rotated us around as one. Richard stood just outside the tent, not looking any better. No one spoke for a long breath. Then Richard tipped his head toward the tent door. "Come to bed with me."

Luke let go of me, but I couldn't move.

Another grave pause followed.

Richard let out a strained breath as if he had to physically expel the reluctance from his body before he could move. Then he made his way to us. He hesitated for another brief moment before he took my hand in his. "Please."

I nodded.

He led me to the tent and waited for me to get inside before following me in. When I was situated under the sleeping bag, he slipped in beside me. Without a word, Luke did the same on my other side.

I lay completely still, staring at the ceiling of the tent. I'd never felt so uncertain and uncomfortable around them. Not even the night of our first date.

With surprising and sudden urgency, Richard rolled to face me. He pushed the sleeping bag out of the way, scooted down, and laid his head on my stomach. An arm around my hips, his hold firm but tenuous. I wasn't sure if I should touch him or not. I softly laid a hand on the back of his head. Luke settled in on my other side with his forehead pressed to my temple. No one said a word.

With one sentence, I had destroyed everything we'd managed to begin repairing over the last few days.

"I'm sorry," I whispered.

"I know." He turned his head and kissed my stomach. "I know."

Chapter Twenty-Five

We stayed in that position for at least a half hour, Richard's head on my stomach, my fingers buried in his hair. I heard his uneven breaths, felt his restlessness, even though he hadn't moved an inch.

Eventually I drifted off to sleep. I awoke sometime later to find Richard on his side facing away from me. I couldn't tell if he was asleep or not. I wanted to lean into him and snuggle up against his back, but I held still and let my eyes fall shut again.

When I got up just after dawn, he was climbing out of the tent. Luke was gone too, up and outside before Richard. After I slipped out of the tent, I expected that Richard—or even Luke—would encourage us to talk about the night before. Neither said a word.

As soon as we had the tent and other supplies packed up and were ready to go, Richard simply asked me, "You got the map?"

"Yeah."

"All right. Let's see what we can find today."

As we hiked through the park, Luke chatted about the picturesque views and the uneven terrain, but ultimately he grew quiet too.

During our lunch break, we sat on a fallen red oak and ate energy bars, nuts, and dried fruit. Luke occasionally commented on some interestingly shaped vegetation he'd never seen before or the strange squawk of a bird.

Richard still said nothing.

I kept turning on my phone throughout the day but had no signal so I had no way to update Tomas. Which probably wasn't a bad thing. I had nothing new to tell him. The rest of the time, we kept our phones off to save the last of our batteries.

As before, we stopped searching for the day when the sun began to slip behind the horizon. We skipped building a fire. The night air was warm enough, and the park had a regulation against starting campfires anywhere other than at designated camping sites. I gathered together another simple meal of energy bars and dried veggie snacks while they worked on setting up the tent. After we finished eating, they went to check out the nearby stream, and I tugged out my phone to try texting Tomas once more. I actually had a signal this time, but it was weak. I sent a text anyway, and a minute later, a message popped up stating the text couldn't be sent.

I started to retry but stopped when I heard hushed tones coming from the water's edge. With the flow of the stream, they must've thought I wouldn't be able to hear them.

"What do you mean?" Richard asked.

"Why aren't you making him talk about what happened last night?"

"He'll talk about it when he's ready."

"Since when the hell do you wait until we're ready?"

"Luke." Exasperation and heavy sorrow tainted Richard's voice. He breathed deep. When he continued, his tone was soft, sad. "This isn't exactly easy for me. What he said…"

He trailed off, and then there was nothing more from him.

"Yeah," Luke said. "I get it. But you know he didn't mean it, right?"

At first, Richard said nothing more. Then in an even lower voice came, "It was just so hard to hear him talk to me like that. He was so angry and… hurtful. It wasn't like him."

I shot to my feet and strode away from the campsite in the opposite direction of the stream, moving farther into the forest. Nightfall was approaching, and I had no idea where I was going. I just needed to move, needed to get away from the dark thoughts rolling through my head. Just for a few seconds.

I couldn't stand that I'd hurt Richard. Again. I couldn't stand that I'd been so filled with anger and frustration that I'd said something that terrible to him.

As I marched faster, my boots slammed against the dirt ground, the impact reverberating throughout my body, a perfect match for the racing beat of my heart. I couldn't stop moving, couldn't stop hearing myself shout those awful words at Richard.

I tripped over a branch lying on the ground. My ankle twisted as I fell forward onto my stomach, my palms scraping across the harsh dirt and prickly brush. "Goddammit."

Pushing myself off the ground, I got up and cradled my lower leg in both hands until the ache lessened. I tried walking again. A blister had been forming on my right heel for the past few hours of our hike that day, and now my ankle on the opposite side stung with each footfall. The combined pain added to my aggravation.

"Matthew!"

That was Richard. He sounded far off.

I stopped. Where the hell was I? I thought I'd only taken a few steps away from our campsite, but I could no longer see any illumination from the battery-powered lantern we'd left sitting near the tent. The woods around me was now pitch black.

Shit.

I called out, "I'm here."

"Matthew!"

I tried again. "I'm here. I'm okay."

"Where? Say something else." Richard's voice grew louder.

"Over here."

I spotted them to my right. They were coming toward me, Luke carrying the lantern, and Richard storming forward, a look of complete panic on his face.

He stepped up to me, and without so much as a hesitation, he pulled me into a fierce embrace. "What happened to our deal to stick together, no matter what?"

"I'm sorry. I didn't realize I went so far. I just needed a minute to myself."

"Fair enough. But next time, you take your minute within view of the campsite. All right?"

"Yeah."

"You sure you're okay?"

"Just twisted my ankle a bit. I'm fine."

"Can you walk?"

"Yeah."

He kept his arm around me as we started back, Luke beside us, holding up the lantern to light our way.

We'd only made it ten steps before Richard frantically jerked me to a stop.

There, some thirty yards ahead and outside the radius of our lamp, were several four-legged figures, moving across our path, barely visible in the dim light of the moon seeping through the tree limbs.

"Coyotes?" Luke asked in a hushed whisper as he cranked the light off.

"No," I said. "Too big. I think they're..." We were too far away, and it was too dark for me to get a good look, so maybe I was wrong.

"What?" Luke whispered. "What are they?"

"Wolves."

Luke lowered his voice more. "Thought there are no wolves in this part of the country."

The last of the pack stopped directly in front of us. Its head scanned our way. Spotting us, it remained motionless, a living statue with its glowing eyes fixated on us.

"Whatever happens," I said, "don't run. And don't turn your back to it. Do exactly what I do and be ready to back away slowly if this doesn't work."

"Why?" Richard reached out for me. "What are you going to do?"

"Scare them off. Just follow my lead and make yourselves look as big as possible." I raised my arms overhead and waved them in the air, trying to appear as intimidating and menacing as I could. When that alone didn't work, I screamed unintelligible sounds at the creature. Luke and Richard did the same.

The wolf, if that was what it was, startled and then trotted off in a rush. In seconds the entire pack was out of sight.

When I turned back to them, Luke nodded. "Nice."

Richard scanned the trees in the direction the animals had gone. "Will they be back?"

"Probably not." That didn't seem to appease him. "Wolf attacks are incredibly rare. When they happen, it's usually because a human was trying to save their pet dog, or something along those lines. Humans are actually more a danger to wolves then they are to us."

"Still. Let's get back to the campsite." He helped me walk again.

Once at our tent, we slipped inside. I lay back on the makeshift bed as Richard removed my shoes and socks and carefully examined my ankle with his fingertips. He rotated my foot. "Does this hurt?"

"No. There's just a twinge when I walk on it. It's no big deal."

"Well, you stay off it until the morning, and we'll see how it is before we start out."

"All right."

He moved in to lie beside me. Luke was already on my other side. I stared through the mesh ventilation in the tent's roof to the tree tops and stars of the night sky above, grateful we hadn't put the rainfly cover over the tent this time so I had something else to focus on as I tried to calm the anxiety racing through me.

I couldn't hold it in any longer. "I'm sorry," I blurted out. "I'm so sorry."

"I know you are." Richard reached for me and pulled me to him.

I folded my arms around him and buried my face in his chest. "I shouldn't have yelled at you. I shouldn't have said what I did. I just wanted you to stop talking about leaving. I had to say something to get you to stop."

"I know." He ran a hand down my back. "And it's okay. I'm not mad at you."

I tilted my head backward so I could see his face. "But I never should've talked to you like that. I lashed out at you, and I—" I sucked in an uncontrollable gasp. I was instantly back to that moment when my dad first struck me. I sat up and scooted away from them until I was between their feet, my back to the tent door. "Oh my God! Oh my God!"

"What?" Luke asked as they both bolted upright. "What's wrong?"

"I'm just like him." I gaped at them, but it wasn't Luke or Richard I saw. It was the anger etched on my dad's face. "I'm just like my father."

"God, no." Richard slid forward. "You are nothing like him, you hear me?" He held my cheeks in his large hands. "You never could be."

I shook my head, not even sure what I meant by that.

He tenderly ran his hands up and down my arms as he said more. "You were upset. Everyone gets upset at times. It's normal. We all sometimes say things that hurt the people we love. Coming to the park for your interview and Alex's disappearance has brought up a lot of painful stuff for you. It's okay for you to feel angry and frustrated. It's okay for you to make mistakes, Matthew."

"Yeah," Luke agreed. "Mistakes aren't bad. They help you become a better person if you allow yourself to really see what you've done wrong. Trust me, I know."

I nodded. "Yeah. You're right. I just... I don't want to ever be like him. I don't want anything to change between the three of us because of my mistakes."

Richard leaned forward until our foreheads were pressed together. "It won't. Ever."

I took in the feel of him, the scent of him, his warmth, his love for me. I pulled back and searched his face. "That thing I said to you, about you making me do something I didn't want..."

Richard dropped his arms and eyed me for a long breath. "Yeah?"

"You're going to be afraid of touching me again, aren't you?"

"No. I'm done with that. I'm not holding anything back from you. Ever again." He had his hands on my face again, tilting my head up so all I could do was stare into those loving green eyes. "I'm so completely in love with you. I love everything about you, and I want you to feel that in every moment between us." He kissed me, a soft, sweet affirmation of his words.

I looked to Luke. He shook his head, and the reaction worried me until he said, "You're nothing like him. How can you not see that? You're such a beautiful person, inside and out. You're smarter and stronger than you ever give yourself credit for. And you're the sweetest guy I've ever known."

"And addictive," Richard said. "Don't forget addictive."

Luke laughed. "That's right. Sweet and addictive."

I laughed with them, remembering our third night at the Haven when they'd first said those words to me.

Luke kissed me, a replica of that loving kiss from Richard, and I fell into it.

As Richard came forward and joined the kiss, the embrace went beyond affection and adoration. It was breathtaking, loving, then passionate and powerful. They lowered me down onto the sleeping bag, undressed me and each other, and they showed me just what they thought of me, what they felt for me in every caress of my body, every breath they grazed over my skin, every word they whispered over my heart.

It was a sensual, beautiful slide of male body against male body, Richard lying on top of me, gliding our erections together, Luke alongside me, kissing me, my hand wrapped around his length as he thrust against me.

They came one after the other, and when I followed, it was explosive, crashing, a physical affirmation of our words.

In the quiet that followed, we all lay there together, wrapped up in each other.

As if I had drifted to some far-off place during the sex, the nocturnal sounds of the forest and the gentle flow of the stream gradually resurfaced, filling the night air around us.

Without making a move, Richard cleared his throat. "Matthew."

"Yeah?"

"I need you to believe me that I forgive you for what you said, and I'm not going to let it get into my head. I'm not going to let it come between us."

"I believe you." I turned so I lay on my stomach between them, then lifted up onto my elbows so I could see them both. "How we move forward—in our lives and our relationship—is our choice. I will always choose us, over any fear or doubt or anything else."

Richard grinned at me and said again, "I love you."

Luke offered me the same pleased smile. "Who the hell wouldn't?"

Richard snorted out his agreement. Then he added more seriously, "Everyone he met before us."

"Thank God."

"Yep, he's all ours."

"Yep." Luke wrapped an arm around my waist. "Ours."

* * * * *

I had no lingering pain in my ankle the next morning. We headed north from our campsite. The ground leveled off some as we got farther away from the popular trails and trekked deeper into the thick grove of chestnut oak trees, ducking under the overhanging limbs jutting out into the trail and listening to the constant crunch of underbrush beneath our feet.

It wasn't too long before we stumbled upon an opening in the trees to the right of the footpath. A larger dirt path lay past that, wide enough for a vehicle. I stepped out onto it. "This must be one of the access roads the sheriff mentioned."

"Can we follow it?" Luke asked. "It'd sure be easier hiking this than that narrow trail."

I checked the map the sheriff had given me and compared the marked access road to our destination on the other map. "Yeah. This heads north for a while. We should be able to stay on it until it curves in the other direction. We'll be close to the river again."

"Sounds good." Richard gestured ahead. "Lead the way."

We followed the access road for a couple of hours. When the bend in the road was visible ahead, I stopped. "I can hear the river." I checked the map. "The trail comes close to the road here. We should be able to get back to it right through those trees."

We headed that way and came upon the footpath just inside the tree line. We took that for another two hours, until we reached our next search location: the top ridge of a narrow, deep gorge. At the far edge of the gorge sat another waterfall. This one featured a delicate curtain of water that tumbled over a red and orange rock wall. The flow of water gently cascaded into a sparkling pool below. The scent of old hemlock trees sweetened the cool air. It all resulted in a more tranquil, serene experience than any of the previous falls.

"Damn," Luke said, "this one is really cool."

"Yeah," I agreed. "I can see why Alex loved coming here."

We took another moment to admire the sight, then got started on our search.

We examined the upper ridge first. As with the other locations, we didn't find his backpack or anywhere the brush had been disturbed as if someone had fallen into the water below. There was also no way a vehicle could've traveled from the access road to the gorge's edge through the dense grove of trees, or into the valley that led to the river.

I pointed down into the gorge. "Let's take a look along the water." Richard indicated to our left. "There's a path over here."

We started down, the path quickly turning into a zigzagging staircase. Unlike the previous stairs we'd seen, these had been constructed with thoughtful purpose so they'd feel like part of the surrounding landscape. At the base, we searched more. An hour passed, and we still hadn't found anything.

I was about to give up and suggest we return to the trail and make our way to the next location on the map when I saw it.

Back over the ridge of the gorge, above the waterfall, a bright object glinted in the light between the branches of the trees, like the sun was bouncing off something metal or glass, maybe a window or a mirror. "Look." I gestured for them to follow and started the climb back up the stairs to the ridgeline.

"Be careful," Richard called out as he and Luke hurried up after me.

At the top, I followed the edge of the gorge toward a break in the trees where the forest opened up to a meadow. Striking beams of sunshine lit the green field. The grass under my feet was softer than the dirt trails we'd been hiking all week.

But what really stood out was what sat at the far edge of the meadow.

Near a small cluster of oak trees and covered in loose brush and leaves was a pickup truck. Barely visible on the side of the vehicle were the words *Windtree Wildlife Rehabilitation Center.*

Chapter Twenty-Six

"It's Alex's truck!"

I sprinted forward.

The brush had obviously been added to obscure the truck from view, but a couple of the tree limbs had slipped off and now lay on the ground. The canopy of tall oak trees along the far side of the truck most likely kept the vehicle from being seen from above by the search helicopter. Hell, it had been difficult to see the truck from the edge of the meadow. If it hadn't been for the sunlight bouncing off the side mirror, I might've missed it completely.

I ran forward and frantically lugged the debris off the driver's side door. A part of me knew I shouldn't be touching anything, that the police would need to inspect the vehicle, but I couldn't stop myself. I needed to see inside.

The side window was filthy. I couldn't get a look at anything,

I cranked the door open, surprised to find it unlocked. The cab was empty. No sign of Alex. Or his bag. Just a blue Detroit Tigers baseball cap sitting on the passenger seat. Like the hat we'd seen Gus wearing. Same style, color, design.

Had they gone to a game together and purchased the hats at the same time? Or was it something else? Had Gus been there at the truck since we'd seen him two days ago? Had he been the one to cover up the vehicle? Or had he put it back the way he'd found it? And why?

Luke reached the truck and went around to the other side. He cleared the passenger door, then opened it. "The keys are in the ignition."

"Maybe Alex parked it here so he could hike down into the gorge, and he got hurt and couldn't make it back." I glanced toward where we'd been searching along the ridge. "Or maybe it's like you said before. Maybe he fell into the water."

"But why hide the truck? And who did it? Him? Or someone else?"

"I don't know. Maybe he didn't want anyone to know he'd come to this spot. Or maybe someone else covered it up after he left it here."

"Why? Unless it's like you said, and they wanted to hide the fact that he was out here, or hide what happened to him."

"Either way," Richard said from where he now stood beside me, "I'm not liking the picture this whole scene is painting." He ran a hand over my shoulder in a comforting stroke, like he didn't want to say more for fear of upsetting me and arguing again, but he also wanted me to get what he meant.

I nodded. Because he was right. This didn't look good. I told them my thoughts about the baseball hat. "I'm guessing he and Gus just have the same cap."

"Maybe," Richard said.

"Well…" Luke closed the passenger door. "I guess it makes sense that the search teams never found the truck with it hidden like this."

"Yeah," I agreed. "Maybe the sheriff really did do his best. I guess I should call him." But instead of pulling out my phone, I shut the truck door and examined the exterior of the vehicle. The bed of the truck was filled with empty metal cages, a med kit, and a pair of Carhartt overalls.

Luke came around to the driver's side. "What are you looking for?"

"I don't know. I feel like we're missing something." I shook my head. "But I have no idea what." I gave the truck another once-over but found nothing odd. I couldn't put off the inevitable. I got out my phone and turned it on. I didn't have a signal, so I stuffed it back into my pack. "Luke, can I use yours?" His phone was on a different network through his job. He'd had a signal sometimes when I didn't.

He gave it to me.

Sure enough, his phone had a much stronger signal. I dialed, and the call went through. I asked to talk to Sheriff Emerson. Once he came on the line, I told him we'd found Alex's truck. He asked a few questions, including our location.

After I hung up, I told the guys, "We're supposed to wait here. He's sending two deputies. They'll take the access roads as far as they can, but then they'll have to hike out here or try to figure out which way Alex drove his truck off-road to get here. In any case, it'll be a while."

"He's not coming himself?" Richard asked

"He's in the middle of something, but he'll join his deputies here as soon as he can."

"Was he surprised we found the truck?"

"Not sure. He sounded relieved, though."

Luke scoffed. "You'd think that shithead would hate being wrong."

Richard snorted in agreement.

"I don't know," I said. "He sounded concerned when he asked if there was any sign of Alex or his body."

Richard removed his backpack and dropped it to the ground next to the truck. I slipped my pack off too and set it beside his. I opened the driver's door again, then got inside the cab and glanced around, spotting nothing more than the blue hat on the passenger seat.

I couldn't stop the questions rolling through my head.

Why was the truck concealed under the brush? Had Alex come out into the park because he was hiding from someone? Did he not want anyone to know he was at this particular location that day? Or had someone else hidden the vehicle?

Luke came to stand beside me. He indicated inside the truck with a nod of his head. "You probably shouldn't touch anything in there. If something happened to Alex, they'll need to search the truck, check for prints and evidence, DNA, that kind of thing."

"Right. Okay." I was about to get up, but something told me not to go. Despite Luke's warning, I took another look around and caught sight of something sticking out from under the edge of the baseball cap on the other seat. I picked up the hat. Underneath lay a piece of paper. The torn corner of a map. Written on it was one name and a note below that.

"What is it?" Luke asked.

I turned to face him. "It's a letter for Gus." I looked over his shoulder to Richard. "Should I read it?"

"It's your call."

Luke eyed Richard skeptically, but then he sighed as if giving up on the notion that we should leave the scene alone. He flipped a hand toward the paper. "Why not? I still don't trust that sheriff. Whatever is in that letter could get covered up. Just like this truck."

"I don't think Sheriff Emerson would do that."

"You know for certain he wouldn't hold back any information from the family?"

"I guess not."

"There could be something in that letter that Alex's wife and kid should know about."

"You're right." I picked up the paper and swung my legs around to sit on the edge of the seat, facing them.

I read aloud.

"Gus, I need your help. I hate to leave you a note like this, but I can't get a signal on my phone right now. I hid my truck because I didn't want anyone else to find it. But I knew you wouldn't give up on looking for me. I just hope to God I'm right, and you're the one who's reading this.

"I've seen something I shouldn't have, and the people involved are coming for me. I'm hiding in a cave right now, but as soon as it's dark again, I'm going to make my way back to my truck and leave this letter there for you. Then I'll head out of the park on foot. I can't risk driving the truck. They've got a drone, and I'm afraid they'll spot me on the roads.

"I'm going to do my best to get home, but if something happens to me, there are three videos on my phone that will explain everything. I've hidden the phone here in the cave. Natalie will know which one. Tell her it's my favorite cave, the same one we found the first time we went backpacking in the park together. If you somehow get this note and the phone, watch the videos but don't show them to anyone else until you see them first. I've password protected the video files. Natalie can give you that too. It's the same four numbers as our banking PIN. Tell her I love her and Tomas and the new baby very much. I'm sorry I got involved in all this. I never meant to put myself in danger or bring any sort of trouble near her or the kids. Please keep them safe for me, Gus."

As I stopped reading, my hand holding the note fell to my lap. "Someone was after him."

"Yeah." Richard spoke carefully, as if afraid to say anything more to me. "I guess…" He trailed off.

I finished his thought. "If something happened to him, it wasn't an accident."

Richard gestured at the truck and the letter. "Which means all this really is evidence." He gave me a pointed look. "We need to let the police deal with this from now on."

I nodded.

"What if the sheriff's involved?" Luke asked. "I noticed Alex didn't mention taking the videos to Emerson. I wonder why that was."

Maybe Luke was right. "What do you think Alex saw?"

"Nothing good." Richard spun away and took a couple of steps from the truck. He stopped and stared out toward the wooded area that led back to the gorge, his hands on his hips, his back stiff and straight.

I got up from the seat. "We need to see those videos."

Richard jerked around. "No. We don't."

I turned to Luke. "I could call his wife. Find out where that cave is and get the password."

"No!" Richard stormed toward us.

"But we need to find that phone. Maybe he left another note with it. Maybe there's something in the videos that will explain where he went and what happened to him."

"The people chasing him caught him and killed him. That's what happened to him. And that's all I need to know. This entire situation just became a whole hell of a lot more dangerous." He cut off abruptly as if he hated the sound of his own frustrated voice. He tipped his head back and breathed deep, seeming utterly conflicted. "Let's let the authorities figure this out."

"But what if Luke's right and we can't trust the sheriff? Once we give the letter to him and they find the phone, whatever Alex saw, whatever else he might've said to his wife and son, could get destroyed if there's some kind of cover-up going on here."

Richard focused on me again. "I don't care. All I care about is keeping both of you safe."

"Well, I *do* care. Alex could still be alive. Maybe locating that phone will help us find him. I have to do this. For Tomas."

Luke moved in closer. "Matthew, that cave could be miles away from here. This park is filled with all kinds of caves."

He was right. But then it hit me. "I know what cave he was talking about. It's close." I motioned for them to follow and rushed for the tree line. "This way." I heard their footfalls behind me, then Richard's booming voice calling out for me. I kept on going until I reached the ridge above the gorge where we'd searched earlier. I bolted down the path and headed straight for the waterfall. Large boulders blocked the recessed cave's opening from view. I'd have to scale the wet rocks and under the waterfall to get to it.

I started to climb.

"Take it easy," Richard said as he came up behind me, but he didn't try to stop me. He helped me up onto the surface of the rocks.

I turned back to warn them. "It's slippery. Go slow." Then I continued on and was around the massive boulders and at the opening of the cave in no time, Richard and Luke there with me.

"How'd you know about this?" Luke asked.

"From Alex's book. He mentioned finding this when he first moved here. It's called Hidden Willow Cave. I had forgotten it was here."

Luke pulled a flashlight from his back pocket and flicked it on.

The cave was shallow, and we could see all the way to the back wall. "Should we take a look?" he asked.

I had to, but I also wanted Richard to be okay with this. I glanced his way.

He studied me for several breaths, then said, "Just please be careful."

Together we worked our way from the front of the cave toward the back. There were loose rocks and cracks in the walls, but other than that, there weren't many places to search. As we neared the back of the cave, I found a wide crevice behind a rock that jutted out from the base of the wall. Tucked into the opening was Alex's red backpack.

"It's here! Alex's pack."

I tugged it out and slid open the zipper as Luke and Richard approached. I took a look inside. "It's full of money." I spread the bag open so they could see the wads of cash.

Luke pointed at the bag. "That's gotta be several hundred grand."

"Maybe more," Richard added.

"I don't understand." I shook my head. "Where did it come from?"

Richard raised a brow. "Nowhere good, I'll bet."

"Maybe someone was paying Alex for something," Luke suggested. "Something illegal. Or paying him to keep quiet about what he saw."

I didn't like either thought. I checked the front pocket of the backpack. Inside was Alex's phone and a folded map.

The phone's case had a wide crack along the back. I pressed the power button, but nothing happened. I unfolded the map. It was of the park. A corner had been torn off where Alex had written the note to Gus.

On the map were a series of hand-drawn grid lines that covered the park, each grid labeled with a number. It was the map I'd seen on Alex's desk the day of my interview. Maybe he and the rangers used the numbered grid as coordinates to keep track of where they found animals in need of rescue.

"What is that?" Luke asked.

"A map of the park. The phone's dead."

"Let me see." He gestured to the phone.

I handed it over. "They said on the news they couldn't locate Alex by his phone, so they assumed, if he was in the park, that it had been damaged or the battery died."

Luke examined the cell. "Looks like it's only the case that's broken. It'll need to be charged to know for sure."

It was the same type of phone Luke had. "Do you think your charger would work?"

"Maybe. It's a way older model, but I'm pretty sure it uses the same plug. My charger's in my pack back at Alex's truck."

"Let's head back and check while we wait for the deputies." I folded the map and slipped it into my back pocket. "What about the money?"

Richard indicated the crevice where I'd found the backpack. "We should leave it here. Let the cops deal with it."

"Okay." I returned the bag to its hiding spot behind the rocks, and the three of us headed out of the cave and up the stairs to the truck.

Luke searched through his gear and found his charger. "Yeah, it fits." He slid into the driver's side of the truck and turned the key in the ignition. The engine roared to life. He plugged in the phone and examined the display. "It's charging. It'll take a minute or so before it'll turn on, but so far it's working."

I went to my backpack and removed the plastic bag with the photos Tomas had given me, along with Gus's card. I added Alex's map and letter to the bag, and tucked everything into my back pocket for safekeeping. I'd need to give the map and letter to the deputies when they arrived.

Richard and I leaned against the side of the truck as we waited.

"You okay?" he asked.

"I guess."

He examined my profile for a long moment.

I turned to him. I could tell by the look on his face that he believed Alex was already dead. I didn't want to talk about that. "I'm okay, really."

"I wish…"

"What?"

"I wish there'd never been a reason for us to be out here."

"Me too," I said.

"Phone's on," Luke called out.

Richard and I went to stand at the open door of the truck.

"Screen's locked." Without unplugging the phone, Luke tried various combinations on the lock screen.

Richard sighed. "This is not a good idea. That phone is evidence."

Luke shot Richard a skeptical look. "I still think it's weird that they never found this truck. Even hidden like this. I mean, Matthew spotted it all the way through the trees from down inside the gorge. Supposedly they had a huge team out here, search dogs, a helicopter, and they found nothing. We're out here for a few days, and we find the truck, his backpack, a letter, and his phone." He turned to me. "You were right to come out here. I think that sheriff or the park rangers, maybe both, are definitely covering something up. I mean, don't you think it's odd that Alex was able to drive his truck all the way out here? Look at how thick the forest is around here. I bet there's another access road nearby. One that's not on the sheriff's map. Maybe something new, something he didn't want us to know about." He swiped another combination into the phone, but when he still had no luck, he asked, "Should we call his wife and see if she knows the code?"

I nodded, and Luke gave me his phone again. I dialed Tomas's number and put the phone on speaker so Luke and Richard could hear.

Tomas answered on the first ring.

"Hey, it's Matthew. I'm on Luke's phone."

"Did you find anything?"

"I can't really go into it now. I've gotta hurry, and I need to talk to your mom. Is she around?"

"Sort of. We're at the hospital."

"Is everything okay?"

"She was feeling sick last night and then she started having these weird pains."

"Are you there with her?"

"I'm in the waiting room by myself. I've been here forever, and no one will tell me anything."

"I'm sure everything will be fine."

He let out a distressed sigh and offered nothing more for a few seconds. Then he said in a low whisper, "She had a couple of miscarriages after she had me."

"Oh. That doesn't necessarily mean anything for this baby."

"Yeah. I guess it's only a couple weeks before she's supposed to have it." The tone of his voice eased as he asked, "When I see her again, you want me to ask her to call you?"

"Only if she's feeling up to it. Have her call me back on this phone."

"Okay."

"Thanks. Listen, I've gotta go. I'll call you again with more info as soon as I can."

"All right." Sounding reluctant, he said goodbye and hung up. I hated keeping what we'd found from him, but what did I really know at this point?

Richard carefully said, "I'm sure everything will be okay."

"Yeah. I just feel bad that he has to wait there by himself. His dad should be there with them."

Luke gestured for me to hand the phone to him. "I've got an app on my cell that I could use to get the video files unlocked. Another programmer at work wrote the code just to see if he could do it. We know the password's a four-digit pin, so it shouldn't take that long for the app to cycle through the possible combinations. If I can just crack the main lock screen, I could tether the two phones and then let the app handle the password on the videos. I've got an adapter with my charger that should work."

I looked to Richard, then back to Luke. "Do it."

Richard breathed deep again, shaking his head. "Whatever is on that phone, I don't want any of us to know a thing about it." He gripped my shoulders and turned me to face him. "I want you to be able to do what you feel you need to here, but once we see what's on those videos, we can't go back."

"What are you saying? You want me to walk away from Alex's family and just hope the sheriff tells them everything?"

"I want us to walk out of this park safe and sound."

"But I need to know the truth. Tomas needs to know."

Without warning, he pulled me into an embrace. "I know how much this means to you, but whatever Alex saw could've very well gotten him killed. I don't want us near that."

"I know. I don't want that either."

"Then we're waiting here for the sheriff's deputies and letting them take it from here. We'll just have to hope for the best outcome, okay?"

I pulled back from Richard. "What if Alex is still alive, but the sheriff won't do much to look for him again?"

"You really think that's possible, about Alex?"

"I don't know, but I have to find out for sure."

Richard didn't respond to that at first. He searched my eyes, then exhaled another long breath as if steadying himself for what would come next. He glanced over my shoulder to Luke. "Give it a shot, see if you can get the phone open."

Luke got to work again on unlocking Alex's phone.

I hugged Richard. "Thank you."

He embraced me in return, holding me so fiercely it was as if he literally feared what would happen if he let go of me.

"Bingo!"

We refocused on Luke. "You got it open?" I asked.

"Did you seriously doubt I would?"

I moved in to lean against the truck beside him so we could both take a look. The phone's main screen showcased the typical smartphone apps.

Luke browsed to the videos section. "Here are the three locked files. Just give me a minute to get them open." He unplugged Alex's phone from the truck, then connected it to his phone and ran the hacking app to get the correct password.

As we waited, Richard and I kept an eye out for the deputies, even though it would likely take several more hours for them to reach us. Unless they were already in the park and somewhere close by. Or, as Luke had suggested, another access road was near our current location.

Luke held up the phone. "Got it!"

Richard and I moved in close again, and we positioned ourselves on either side of him so we could see the phone, using our bodies to block the sunlight from impeding our view.

Luke hit play on the first video, and the screen filled with a rainy nighttime exterior shot of what looked like a newly constructed rudimentary cabin. A low light was on inside, illuminating a single window on the side of the building. The camera zoomed in closer, and we could make out several people to the right of the cabin.

Whispering, a low voice came over the video. *"What is this place?"*

I pointed at the screen. "That's Alex's voice."

Alex continued. *"There isn't supposed to be a cabin here."* He panned the camera over the cabin's exterior. *"I'm guessing someone built this illegally on park land."*

He zeroed in on the people who were beside the small shelter. Two of the figures stood close. They were a young man and woman who appeared to be in their early twenties. Hikers from the looks of them. Each wore a backpack. They had their hands resting at the backs of their heads like they were being held at gunpoint, but the video was too dark to see if any of the others held a gun on them.

Two of the others, also a man and woman, removed the younger couple's packs and forced them onto their knees. The third person standing behind them raised his arm. A gun was definitely visible now.

"Shit," Luke said around a breathy exhale.

On the video, Alex spoke in a similar hushed tone. *"Oh God."*

I slapped a hand over my mouth in horror as we watched the scene play out.

Both hikers kneeling on the ground held out their arms as if pleading to the others for their lives. It made no difference. The man with the gun fired twice. The hikers dropped forward in rapid succession right as lightning lit up the sky.

The video in the playback window shook. *"Oh my God."* Thunder boomed overhead, and Alex started backing away from the murderous sight before him. The entire time he moved, he kept the camera pointed at the bodies on the ground.

I reached out and hit pause on the phone. "I think I heard about those kids on the news. Just a couple of weeks ago. They were friends, both taking classes at the university. They went missing from their dorm rooms on the same day. No one knew where they went or why. The police suspected they ran off together, but their families said they wouldn't have done that. They were last seen leaving campus with only their backpacks." I pointed at the paused video. "That has to be them."

Luke nodded as if that made sense. "But why the hell were they killed?"

"And by who?" Richard gestured to the phone. "Play the rest."

Luke hit the play button again. The shaking of the video stilled as if Alex had composed himself and stopped moving backward. He zoomed the camera in and got a better shot of the guy with the gun. He panned out over the others who stood near the shooter. The rain came down harder, making it more difficult to pick up any details on the video. Then the woman turned toward the camera. Another bolt of lightning flashed across the sky, providing a better view. She wore a uniform. The same uniform Gus had been wearing that morning.

"That's a park ranger." Luke hit rewind and paused the playback right as the lightning lit up the sky. He pointed to the female ranger, then indicated the man with the gun. "And he's wearing a deputy sheriff's uniform."

"Oh my God," I said.

Richard got a closer look. "You sure that's a deputy? Not the sheriff?"

"I think so. He looks too short to be Emerson."

Luke started the video again. Without warning, the man with the gun turned and looked directly into the camera. Lightning struck again. It was the deputy with the slicked-back dark hair we'd seen at the sheriff's station the other day. He held still for a heartbeat. Then he started right for Alex.

"Shit," Alex said on the video. The camera quickly shifted down and kept recording the ground as Alex's frantic footsteps and heavy breaths could be heard over the beat of rain.

The recording continued on like that for several seconds. Then it went dark.

Luke started the second video file.

We were looking at an exterior shot of another building, older, more run-down, surrounded by lush grass and brush several feet high that obscured much of the structure. Alex's voice came over the recording again. *"Okay, I think it's safe. There was someone here on guard a few minutes ago, but they got a call and left. Maybe to help locate me. You've got to see what I found inside here."* He headed for a dilapidated door, opened it, and entered.

The camera captured the interior, a large open room made up of wood walls, plank floors, and yards of rustic beams overhead, like the interior of a barn. It was cleaner and more brightly lit than expected based on the state of the building's exterior. Wooden pallets filled the room, each loaded with a four-foot-tall wire mesh basket that took up the entire pallet. Every basket was stocked with rocks and small boulders, all about a foot in diameter. It was as if the park service had ordered a delivery of the rocks to use in some kind of landscaping project. Only...

The camera zoomed in on a single rock that had been cracked in two. It was hollow. Hidden inside was a large plastic bag filled with a powdery substance.

Alex spoke again. *"I just found all this. These are fake rocks, every single one I checked is filled with this stuff. I'm guessing it's heroin. I also found several bags full of cash. Whoever left all this here must've done some renovations on the building. The last time I was here, this place looked nothing like this. There's now a generator running electricity, and the whole building is temperature controlled."* He swung the camera toward tables that were set up in the far corner of the room with scales and empty plastic baggies. Then he rotated around, getting a shot of more pallets containing the faux rocks and boulders. The room was jam-packed with them.

"Jesus," Luke said. "That's a lot of fucking drugs. That's gotta be worth a shit-ton of money."

"Where is he?" I asked. "That place looks familiar. What kind of building is that?"

Richard shook his head. "It's hard to tell. Someplace that's been around for quite a while."

Luke stopped the video once more. "That was a smart move."

"What was?" I thought he was talking about something Alex had done until he explained.

"Storing drugs on state land. If the cops or the feds find that stash, the building and the land can't be traced back to a private property owner. It's like when dealers keep their drugs in a stolen car on the street. No way to prove it's theirs."

He hit play again. Alex continued filming more of the building's interior, zooming in on the additional faux rocks he'd opened, the bags with the cash, the temporary power setup, and new lighting fixtures that had obviously been a recent addition.

A loud bang came from behind him. He gasped and spun around. *"Shit. Someone's here."* He lowered the phone and started running again, the camera lens pointed at the floor. He sped out a back door of the building and into the forest.

A minute later the recording stopped.

When Luke started the third video, Alex's image filled the screen. He was crouched inside the cave where we'd found his phone and backpack. He spoke softly but loud enough to be heard over the muted rush of the waterfall outside the cave's opening. *"This is for Natalie."* He glanced down for a long breath, then lifted his head to stare directly into the camera. *"Honey, I don't want you involved in all this, but I know you'll make Gus tell you everything. You'll want to know what happened to me. Please, do not trust the local sheriff, his deputies, the rangers, or anyone else. These guys have almost caught me once already. They saw me recording the murder of those hikers. They were shouting at me that they wouldn't hurt me if I just gave them my phone. I'm going to hide the phone here in this cave so if they catch me I'll have something to bargain with, but—"* He stopped and lifted his head as if he'd heard something or someone outside the cave.

When he refocused on the camera, he talked more quickly. *"I don't think they'll want just the video. They'll want to silence me."* Tears filled his eyes. He breathed deep and glanced down for a moment. *"I'm going to travel at night and hide wherever I can during daylight hours. I wish I could hear your voice before I go, but I'm still not getting a cell signal here. I'm going to do everything I can to make it back to Windtree."* He hesitated, clearly choked up again. *"But if you haven't seen me yet, then I'm guessing something happened to me. I'm so sorry that I can't be with you when you have the baby. Tell our kids I love them. And tell Tomas I'm so very proud of him for who he is."* He raised his head as if listening for something outside the cave again. *"I've gotta go, honey. I love you all very much."* Then Alex reached forward and stopped the video.

A low-battery message flashed on Alex's phone. Then it shut off. Luke fiddled with the phone for a minute, then said, "It's dead. I'll have to charge it more." He turned his own phone off and slipped it into his backpack, then plugged Alex's back into the charger.

I stood completely immobile, saying nothing. I couldn't believe what we'd just seen and heard.

"Matthew," Richard started. "I think…"

"I know. They probably caught him and killed him." I breathed deep, letting that realization sink in.

Feeling anxious and needing to move, I stepped away from the truck. I didn't want to look at the vehicle any longer. Despite having found the truck and the videos and knowing that would at least lead to some answers for Tomas and Natalie, I couldn't help but feel the crushing weight of despair.

Richard came up behind me.

I shook my head, not wanting him to say anything. Frustration rolled off me in waves that I couldn't contain. I had truly hoped—no, I *believed*—that Alex might've just gotten hurt and was still somewhere in the park, injured, but able to keep himself alive as he waited for help. No matter how slim the possibility anything like that could've happened, knowing that someone had most likely intentionally hurt him and that we weren't going to find him alive was almost more than I could stand. Tomas had truly lost his father. "He's really dead."

Richard held me from behind. He kissed the side of my head and kept his lips pressed there. "It looks that way."

What would happen to Tomas now? And the new baby? He or she would never know Alex, never see what kind of person he was.

"I was hoping maybe…" I couldn't form the words. I shrugged. "I wanted to find him before it was too late."

"I know." He tightened his arms around me. "At least Tomas and Natalie will know for sure that he didn't leave them. And maybe they'll find out what actually happened to him. Let's just hope whatever that was, he didn't suffer."

"Yeah." I still couldn't shake my intense disappointment.

We made our way back to the truck. As I stopped in front of the open door, I said, "Maybe the people who were after him took him back to that cabin where they shot the others."

Richard nodded. "They could've buried him there."

"Or anywhere," Luke said as he got up from the truck's seat. "They could've ditched his body anywhere in this park. In one of the rivers or the lake." He stopped and shook his head. "I'm sorry, Matthew. I'm just frustrated. How the hell are we supposed to know who to trust?"

"I don't know." Richard scanned the area around us. "But we need to get away from this truck."

I threw him a startled look. "Do you really think the sheriff's involved?"

"Yeah, I do. I'm betting his search for the doc ended very differently than he told us."

"He didn't seem like the kind of guy who'd—"

Luke interrupted with, "That's because you want to believe the best in everyone. He was an ass. But even if he's not involved, some of his deputies obviously are." He came toward me. "Richard's right. We need to get away from this truck. Now."

"Come on." Richard gripped my hand and got us moving toward the trees.

Luke called out after us, "I'm just going to grab Alex's phone and the charger."

"Hurry up." Richard paused for a second as if he were going to wait for Luke, but then got us moving again.

A few feet from the tree line, I hesitated, and Richard stopped with me.

"You really think they'll hurt us?" I sounded on the verge of panic.

"It's okay." He tightened his grip on my hand. "Everything's going to be fine."

A high-pitched sound whizzed by my head. A small section of bark on the tree beside Richard exploded. Then two more impacts hit another tree to the right of him.

"Someone's shooting at us!" Luke shouted.

Chapter Twenty-Seven

Another shot hit the tree.

Richard tackled me to the ground, his heavy weight pressing down on me. He waved an arm at Luke. "Get down!" More shots impacted in the grass beside us.

He spoke against my ear. "We have to run. We're sitting ducks here."

I nodded.

He yanked me off the ground and shouted, "Luke, run!"

Clasping my arm tightly, Richard practically dragged me with him as we sprinted for the trees. Once we were thirty feet inside the tree line, we hunkered behind the base of a massive red oak tree.

Richard peeked out toward the truck. "Luke!" he shouted again. Then he ducked down as more bullets hit a tree near us.

"Is he okay?" I asked.

"He's inside the truck."

I turned to look.

"No. Stay back." Richard scrambled to pull me behind the tree, but not before the rear windshield of the truck imploded.

"Luke!" Richard sprang up.

Luke rolled out of the passenger side of the truck and raced toward us. He had his backpack in one hand, Alex's phone and the charger in the other. Divots of grass shot up behind his feet as gunshots pummeled the earth. He didn't stop. He ran straight for where we'd entered the grove of trees.

As soon as he was within arm's reach, Richard grabbed him and hauled him behind the tree with us. With both hands, Richard frantically examined Luke's torso and head. "You hit?"

"No." But Richard didn't let up until Luke gripped his wrists to stop him. "I'm fine."

More shots came, and we ducked our heads again. Richard had a hand on the back of my head and one on Luke's, pushing us both down. Then the shots halted right as Luke asked, "What the hell do we do? Make a run for it?"

I didn't like the sound of that. At least behind the tree we had some cover from the bullets flying our way.

I wasn't sure Richard agreed with me. He glanced at our surroundings. "We've got to get out of here. They'll be coming for us." He pointed in the opposite direction of the meadow. "That way. Toward the river." He started to get up but stopped when a booming voice rang out.

"We just want the doctor's phone."

Richard crouched back down.

The voice hollered again. "If you have the phone, throw it out into the grass, and we'll let you walk away."

We were all breathing heavily, no one moving a muscle.

The man called out again. "Just give us the phone. That's all we want."

"Who is that?" Luke whispered.

"Not the sheriff," I said. "He doesn't sound familiar. Maybe the deputy from the video."

Richard took a look out into the clearing again. "I don't think they can see us in here."

The man shouted once more. "You might as well give us what we want. Sheriff Emerson isn't sending anyone to help you."

Richard slapped the tree trunk. "Fuck."

With those words, my head spun. Someone had shot at us, and the sheriff sent them to do it. "You were right."

Luke held up Alex's phone, and Richard immediately shook his head. "We give them that phone, what's to stop them from killing us? It might be the only thing keeping them from actually hitting us with those bullets."

"Right." Luke tucked the phone and charger into his pack and slipped the backpack onto his shoulders.

The distinct whine of a dog came from the meadow.

"Shit." Luke shot a look to Richard. "They've got search dogs."

"Matthew and I left our packs back there. They'll have our scent. Come on." He gestured toward the gorge. "We're getting out of here. Now. You two first. I'll bring up the rear. Stay low and get to the river."

"I'll take the lead." Luke started moving, keeping low to the ground. I followed with Richard behind me.

No shots rang out, but the fear racing through me made it nearly impossible to move.

The fear. And the guilt.

Someone had shot at Luke and Richard. Because of me and my brilliant idea to search the largest state park in the Midwest for clues to a man's disappearance.

What the hell had I been thinking?

* * * * *

When we reached the water's edge, we heard a dog barking behind us. Faintly, but still…

Did the barking mean the dog was on to our scent? Getting closer? Was the dog alerting its handler to our presence?

Richard waved us on. "It's too deep to cross here. Keep going. Follow the river but keep inside the tree line."

Luke led the way again, staying several yards from the water's edge, which kept us well hidden in the trees as we made our way through the forest. We jogged at a quick pace and heard no one behind us, no more bullets or shouts. When we stumbled upon a narrow bend in the river ten minutes later, we paused.

Richard pointed to the surface. "It's shallower here. Let's wade through the water as long as we can, maybe get the dogs off our scent."

Luke and I nodded, and we stepped into the river, making our way through the waist-deep water, over the slick rocks and gravel of the riverbed. Luke held his pack above his head to keep it dry. Once the water rose higher, making the trek more difficult, we headed for the other side and picked up the pace again, racing along the far bank.

Eventually, when we'd run farther from the river and the forest had grown even denser around us, we were so bone-tired we could barely keep going. We stopped to catch our breaths. Luke and I dropped to the ground while Richard remained standing, his complete focus on the way we'd come.

We were all panting heavily, and no one uttered a word for over a minute, as if just discussing our options would make this crazy situation more real.

Luke sat up and reclined against a tree, his forearms on his bent knees. "Why the hell does this shit keep happening to us? I'm so fucking tired of people aiming their guns at us. And shooting at us."

Richard gave him a pointed look. "I'd had enough of that the first time." He kept standing there, watching the forest for another minute. Then he eased up and moved closer to me. "I don't think we're being followed." He asked Luke, "Did you get a good look at any of them?"

Luke shook his head. "What the hell do we do now?"

"We have to call someone for help," I said.

Luke scoffed. "What? 9-1-1? They'll just contact our good buddy the local sheriff and his deputies."

Richard shot a stern look our way. "We get the hell out of this park, that's what we do. Then we'll figure out what's next after that."

Luke waved a hand through the air. "We can't just keep on running and hope they don't catch up to us."

"You got a better idea?" When Luke offered nothing more, Richard added, "We've got to get to one of the main roads. Or back to the Jeep."

"Richard..." Luke gestured back toward the way we'd come. "They're gonna be waiting for us at the Jeep. And we need to stay off the trails. Whoever those guys are, they were fucking hunting us back there. We're talking armed, murderous, asshole law enforcement officers who probably know this park a hell of a lot better than we do. They're not going to stop until they bury this."

Bury us.

"Oh God." I shook my head, barely able to breathe. "We never should've come out here. This is all my fault." I bent forward and gulped in several rapid breaths until I was practically hyperventilating.

Richard moved to sit at my side. He stroked my back. "Take a deep breath. It's going to be okay. Just breathe deep." He asked Luke, "Got any water in that pack?"

"Yeah." Luke handed it over.

Richard held the bottle out for me. "Here. Drink some of this." As I drank, he repeated, "It's going to be okay."

I gave the bottle back to him. "I didn't know someone would—" I shook my head. "I didn't know."

"Of course you didn't."

"You did. You said it wasn't safe. If something happens to either of you because I dragged you out here—" My breath quickened again.

With a hand to my chin, Richard forced my head up. "Everything's going to be fine. We're still together and no one got hurt. That's all that matters. And now, we're getting out of this park. Right now." His confident green eyes remained locked on mine.

He was right. I couldn't lose it now. I had to make sure they were safe. I sat taller. "I can get us out of the park. I know which way to go."

"Without using the trails?"

"Yeah. I'll use the compass and the map to take us a different—" I shot a look back the way we'd come. "Shit!"

"What?"

"The compass and map are in my pack back at the truck. Wait." I removed the plastic bag from my back pocket and took out Alex's map. The bag had kept it dry during our trek through the river. "I have this."

With raised brows, Luke said, "Even if we don't stop, it'll take us two days, maybe three, to get to one of the main roads on foot. Longer than that to get to the cabin. And they're gonna be all over looking for us, probably waiting at the cabin too." He paused for a moment. "We could call the state police or the feds."

I shook my head. "Alex said not to trust anyone."

"Every law enforcement officer in the state can't be involved."

"We talk to the wrong person, and we'll have more people shooting at us."

They both seemed to be thinking that over.

"We should call Gus." I fished out his card and held it up. "Maybe he'll know who to trust."

Neither said a word, and I knew what they were thinking.

"He's a friend of Alex's. He wouldn't be involved in hurting him."

"He's still a park ranger," Luke said. "You saw that video."

"I know. But Alex trusted him. We can too." At least I thought so. I'd made such a bad call where the sheriff was concerned. I didn't want to fuck up again, but I also wanted to trust my instincts. I wanted to believe I wasn't completely wrong about everything.

Richard hesitated as if thinking it over, then finally nodded. "All right. If you think so, I say we take a chance and see what he has to say. If it sounds like we can trust him, then we'll see if he can help. Maybe he knows someone in the sheriff's department who's not in on this. If we don't like what he has to say, we hang up before we tell him anything about where we're at right now. Then we take the battery out of the phone so they can't track us."

Luke dug his phone out, turned it on, and handed it to me. "Go for it."

I dialed, and Richard added, "Put it on speaker."

As soon as I did, Gus came on the line. "Hello."

"It's Matthew. From yesterday. We're in trouble." I explained that we'd found Alex's truck and then told him what had happened to us since.

"Christ. Are you guys okay?"

"Yeah. For now. We think we lost them."

"You sure the sheriff is involved?"

"Yeah, pretty sure."

"And they want Alex's phone? Why? What's on it?"

Richard shook his head, and reluctantly I lied. "We don't know. It was dead when we found it."

"Okay. I've got a friend in the state police. Let me call him and see if he can help."

"Alex said not to involve any police. Are you sure you can trust this guy?"

"Absolutely. I've known him for years."

"All right."

"I'll call you right back."

Luke's phone rang less than fifteen minutes later. I put the call on speaker again.

Gus said, "He and another detective are coming to talk to the sheriff. They'll be here in a few hours."

Luke snorted out a bitter laugh. "To *talk* to the sheriff?"

Richard grabbed the phone. "Did you tell them we were shot at? And that the sheriff and his deputies are in on everything?"

"Of course. The state investigators are going to look into it. If you ask me, they didn't sound surprised to find out Sheriff Emerson was involved in some kind of criminal activity. Maybe they've already been investigating him. They also want to talk to you three. I told them I'd pick you guys up right away and make sure you're safe. Then when they get here you can give them your statements. Where are you?"

Richard reached out and hit mute on the phone. "What do you think?"

Luke shrugged, and they both looked to me.

"I think we should go for it. If we don't have his help, those guys with the guns might catch up to us before the state police get here."

"Okay." Richard turned the phone off mute.

I told Gus about the meadow where we'd found the truck, how far we'd gone since then, and in what direction.

"Okay," he said. "I know where you mean. Stay right there, and I'll find you."

"No," Richard said. "We're still too close to the truck. We gotta keep moving."

"You think they're coming for you?"

"Hell yes. We still have Alex's phone."

"Gotcha. Let me think." Gus grew quiet for a moment. "Okay. Here's what I want you to do." He gave instructions on where to meet him, and I used Alex's map to find the location. "It should take you about two hours to get there on foot. You'll have to cross the river again."

"All right," Richard said. "We'll meet you there."

"Good." He sighed and didn't say anything more for several seconds. Then quietly he asked, "You think they killed Alex?"

I bit my bottom lip, hating having to admit to that possibility again. "I don't know. Maybe."

He let out a ragged breath, then said, "I'll see you in two hours. Be careful." He hung up.

I passed Luke his phone. He hit the power button and removed the battery.

Richard gestured to Luke's backpack. "What supplies do you have in there?"

"Not much. A flashlight, one of the sleeping bags, my clothes, a couple of those energy bars, and another bottle of water. You had the tent in your pack this time."

"Right." Richard stood. "Okay. Let's get going."

I gave a nod, and Luke and I got up. I slid the map into my back pocket, then handed the plastic bag with Alex's letter and the photos to Luke. "Could you put these in your pack?"

"Sure."

When he had everything situated, we headed out, moving as rapidly as we could on foot. An hour later we stopped for rest. The terrain had become rocky again and far more challenging to traverse. We sat on the large boulders lining a creek and had the last of the bottled water. Richard leaned into my side. "You okay?"

"I was just thinking about Tomas. If Alex really was killed, Tomas lost his father because of some stupid asshole criminals."

"But thanks to you, he's going to know the truth. He's going to know his dad was a good man."

"Yeah."

"Even if he doesn't see it right away, that's a huge thing for him."

It was.

We got moving again. Another hour and I spotted the structure Gus had described sitting in an open field. "There it is."

The two-story wooden bird-watching station sat at least fifteen feet off the ground, elevated on stilts. A ladder situated along one of the structure's supports allowed access to both levels. The top level was an open-air deck. The lower section was enclosed, probably so people could stay out of the wind and cold weather and still enjoy the view. On that level, a large opening took up nearly one full wall. With no light on in the station, it was impossible to tell if Gus was waiting inside.

I started forward, wading through the thick vegetation and fragrant wildflowers that surrounded the station on all sides.

Without warning, Luke grabbed me around the waist and tackled me to the ground. "Richard, get down. Now!"

Richard hit the dirt, half of him landing on top of Luke. "What did you see?"

"A police uniform. Could be state police. I'm not sure."

"Maybe Gus brought someone with him," I said.

"Hang on." Richard slowly made his way onto his hands and knees and shot a look over the brush toward the station. He hastily dropped back down to his stomach. "It's a state trooper."

"See anyone else?" Luke asked.

"Yeah."

"Gus?"

"No. The state cop is standing next to a sheriff's deputy. The same guy from the video, the one who shot those hikers. Gus screwed us."

I gaped at him. "No."

"I'm sorry, Matthew. Looks like he wasn't such a good friend of Alex's after all."

Goddammit. I had believed in the wrong man. Again.

So much for trusting my instincts.

My instincts sucked.

Chapter Twenty-Eight

Richard shifted so he lay over both of us. He whispered against my ear, "It's okay. We'll figure something else out." He gave my arm a quick squeeze and moved off us, inching backward on his hands and knees.

Luke and I followed. When we were out of sight from the bird-watching station, we got to our feet.

"What is that sound?" Luke asked.

I heard it too. A faint buzzing. Coming from above. We scanned the sky but couldn't see anything.

"Shit." Luke waved frantically for us to get moving again. "It's a drone."

We raced toward the trees and ducked inside the forest for cover. We didn't stop there, just kept on running. When we were about half a mile from the station, we stopped under a thick canopy of trees, not far from another creek.

Luke searched behind us. "The drone's gone. I don't think anyone saw us."

"Me either," Richard said.

Light-headed, I leaned against a tree. Before I even realized it, I was sliding down the tree, my ass landing on the ground with a thud. Tipping my head back, I stared up at the awning made of green leaves. A brilliant red bird with black wings jumped from one branch to the next. I was completely mesmerized by its movements. With the bird's chirping song and the thin streaks of sun filtering through the leaves that swayed in the wind, the moment had an enchanting quality that was in direct contrast to what was happening to us. I felt oddly detached as the sounds of the forest around me faded from my consciousness.

It was as if everything I'd come to know about myself was all wrong, and I had no idea what to think or feel. So I just kept focusing on that bird that was fluttering, almost dancing, from branch to branch. "That's a scarlet tanager."

"What?" Luke studied me with confusion.

"That bird. It's beautiful."

He came to sit next to me. "Hey."

I rolled my head his way.

"Everything's going to be fine."

"How can you say that? I put us in danger." I squeezed my eyes shut and shook my head. I felt the air shift before me. When I opened my eyes, Richard was crouched in front of me.

"You did what you thought was right. We all did. And nothing is going to happen to us. You're going to get us out of here."

Luke bumped shoulders with me. "Damn straight, you are."

The trust and confidence on their faces had my senses rushing back to me. I once again heard the high-pitched chirping of the birds above, the wind rustling through the trees, felt the cool forest-shaded air sweep across my face. I nodded. "I am."

"All right." Richard turned to Luke. "Your phone still got a charge?"

Luke pulled his phone out of his bag. "Damn." He held it up. The screen was smashed in. He reinserted the battery and tried to turn the phone on but had no luck. "It's junk now."

Richard indicated Luke's pack. "I thought my knee landed on something back there. And Alex's phone is dead?"

"Yeah."

Richard shook his head in agitation. "Fuck." He stood and strode a few feet away, keeping his back to us. "Okay." He spun around. "Here's what we're going to do. Matthew, you'll lead us back to the closest road. We'll try to find a car, a hiker, anyone with a phone."

"Who do we call?" Luke asked.

Richard tapped a hand on his thigh as he thought that over. Luke seemed to be doing the same.

"The feds." I looked to Luke. "You still have the name of that agent from everything that went down with your dad?"

"Yeah."

"Good. We'll call him, report what's going on here. He'll know what to do."

They nodded their approval. I tugged the map from my pocket and reviewed it for a path through the forest that would lead us to the closest public road.

I showed them the way I thought we should go. We all agreed that was the best plan. We took a couple of more minutes to rest. Then

Richard glanced up at the sky. "We better get going. It'll be dark before long."

It was going to be a rough night. Since Richard and I no longer had our backpacks, we didn't have the tent or two of our sleeping bags or our jackets or extra food and water.

"Wait." I held up a hand. "I just remembered... There are several ranger stations out here. They stock them with supplies, use them for emergencies with hikers, that kind of thing. Some have outdoor bathrooms and potable water for hikers." I examined the map again. "Yeah. There's one not too far from here."

Luke threw me a skeptical look. "But we can't trust the rangers. Who knows how many of them are involved in all this?"

"I don't think these remote stations are staffed all the time. They mostly use them for special park events or when they need to take a break during patrols or when they have to spend the night out here for some reason. We could at least check. See if there's a radio, maybe food and water. If the station's empty, it's at least a good place to stop and rest for tonight."

Richard crouched down again and took a look at the map. "Where is it?"

"Here. This symbol means it's a ranger station."

He gave a sharp nod. "I think we should go for it."

"All right," Luke said. "Let's do it. If there's no radio, maybe there's at least power. We could charge Alex's phone."

"Good idea." Richard stood. "But no matter what happens..." He pointedly looked to Luke, then me. "We stay together. And we move fast."

Chapter Twenty-Nine

"Matthew, I think…" Using the side of his boot, Luke swiped at a half-buried tree root that snaked across the ground, then did it again as if he could actually sweep the root aside. He wouldn't make eye contact with me.

Neither would Richard.

"What?" I asked.

Luke finally met my stare. "I think we're lost."

We'd been trudging through the forest for hours, and we hadn't spotted the ranger station yet.

I checked the map once more. "We're not lost. We're close." I surveyed our surroundings again, searching for a clearing in the trees where the station might be located. But it was dark now, the sun long gone. Thunder rumbled in the distance. Even with the flashlight from Luke's pack, visibility was shit. I gestured in the direction we'd been heading. "I think we should keep going this way."

"Sounds good," Richard said.

I had no idea why he was being so adamant about letting me lead. I was losing faith that I knew what I was doing, or that I knew how to read the map correctly. Regardless, I pressed on.

I drew up short when a bolt of lightning lit up the sky. A jarring crack of thunder immediately followed.

"Not good," Luke said.

I motioned for them to keep following. "I know we're close."

Five minutes later, we were all soaked from the downpour, and lightning had come dangerously close to the ground twice. The tops of the trees were moaning and creaking as they swayed in the wind.

"Matthew!" Luke shouted over the beat of rain surrounding us. "We need to stop."

I turned to him. "Not yet."

He pointed at a rock outcropping to our right. The overhang

created a protective canopy, keeping the ground dry below. "Let's stop there and wait out the storm."

I shook my head. "The station's not far."

Richard, who'd been bringing up the rear, patted Luke's back as he passed by him. "Come on. This is Matthew's call. He knows what he's doing."

I threw Richard a smile in thanks and started forward again.

It wasn't long before a break emerged in the trees ahead. I ran for the opening but found nothing except an open field filled with blooming pale bluish flowers, each with a yellow eye that glowed in the light of the moon. I waded through the wet flowers and brush. The flat meadow would be an ideal spot for the ranger station. Maybe it stood beyond the clump of trees in the middle of the field. I sprinted forward.

"Matthew!" Luke called out again.

I shook my head and kept going, the vegetation scraping the sides of my pant legs with each step. If my clothes weren't already soaked, the trek through the drenched field would've done them in for sure.

At the cluster of trees, I rounded an enormous oak, and there it was. A rustic cabin. It sat at the edge of the field, surrounded by trees on three sides. A hiking path was visible on the far side of the cabin. "It's here!"

They caught up to me. Richard stopped at my side, but Luke kept on going.

"Wait." I raced forward and grabbed his arm to stop him. "We should take this slow. Just to be safe."

"Right."

"Although…" I pointed toward the partially overgrown path. "That trail's not on the map. Maybe it's not open to the public anymore. Maybe they won't even look for us here."

Regardless, the three of us cautiously advanced and circled the perimeter of the station. There were no lights on inside and no sign anyone had been there for months. Even through the rain, it was easy to spot the cobwebs that covered the door and every window. The building didn't just look empty. It looked abandoned.

Richard indicated the front door with a tip of his head. He practically had to shout to be heard over the heavy beat of rain on the cabin's roof. "Let's give it a try." He moved forward before Luke or I could. He brushed aside the cobwebs, then turned the door handle. It was unlocked. The door opened with a startling creak.

Luke's eyebrows shot up. "This is really fucking creepy."

I nodded in agreement.

But what choice did we have?

Richard took the flashlight from me and stepped inside. Luke and I followed.

A plume of dust greeted us, disturbed by the opening of the door and the rush of the cool air from the storm. A narrow counter that spanned more than half the length of the cabin was situated near the door as if serving as a front desk. That was all we could make out in the dark.

Luke felt around on the walls near the door. "No light switch."

Using the flashlight, Richard scanned the other walls of the room. "No signs of electricity at all." Which made sense, given the remote locale.

"So much for charging Alex's phone," Luke said.

"At least we're out of the rain." Richard swept the light over the room again.

Brochures for area attractions and maps of the park lined the front counter. Behind the counter there wasn't much. Just a metal desk, a single padded office chair with a Majestic Falls State Park sweatshirt hanging over the back, a fireplace, and a set of metal shelves lining the back wall. The shelves included a few supplies: a sleeping bag, an oil lantern, several metal canisters, a case of bottled water wrapped in plastic, a toolbox, and a first aid kit. A gurney sat propped against the side of the shelf, probably for transporting injured hikers. Layers of dust covered every last item.

Richard paused the flashlight on a two-way radio that sat on the desk. He went to it and hit the power button. There was no indication it was working. He examined it more closely. "No batteries."

Luke took a look inside a second room at the rear of the cabin. "Just a bathroom back here. With water, if you can believe that. Sink has a hand pump. Basin's pretty gross, though." He pointed to a stack of firewood in the corner. "There's dry wood and matches. I'll see if I can get a fire started."

"Check if the flue will open," Richard said. "With the state of this place, it might be blocked."

"Got it." Luke went to work on the fireplace.

I asked, "What if they see the smoke from the fire?"

"I think it'll be okay at night," Richard said. "Especially with the rain. Besides..." He came to me where I stood near the door, water dripping off me. "We need to get you warm. You're shivering." He wrapped his arms around my shoulders and held me close, my forehead pressed against the base of his throat. I reached up and held his face in my palm. His skin felt like ice, even through the rasp of three-day-old facial hair.

I was numb. And not just from the rain.

Richard let go of me to lock the cabin door, then went for the sweatshirt on the chair. He used it to dry my hair and arms.

When I spoke, it was barely above a whisper. "Do you think they'll look for us here?"

"I don't know. With the rain coming down this hard, it should wash away our tracks and make it harder for the search dogs to pick up our trail. We'll keep an eye out, take turns getting some sleep while one of us keeps watch. As soon as the rain lets up, we'll head out again." He tossed the makeshift towel aside. "Your shorter hair dries much faster."

"I feel kinda naked with it like this."

"You look great, but if you don't like it short, grow it out again. It's just hair, Matthew."

"I know." He made it sound so simple. I guess with my hair, it was. It was everything else in my life that was far more complex at that moment. I felt like I couldn't make a right decision if my life depended on it. And right then, all our lives did. "You think it's okay for us to head out while it's still dark?"

"I think we have to."

"We could just hide out here. When we don't show up at home in a couple of days, Kevin and Walter will know something's wrong."

"I don't think we should stick around this cabin for long. Eventually they might pick up our trail and find us here." He ran his hands up and down my arms. "You're still shivering." He crossed the room and grabbed the sleeping bag from the shelves. "Take off your wet clothes and get under this in front of the fireplace."

"Not yet." I faced the door. "That lock's not gonna hold anyone off for long. And it's so dark out, we'll probably never see them coming. We need to set something up so we can hear them if they try to sneak up on us."

"Like what?"

"We could cover the front steps and the porch in twigs. And…" I glanced around the room. There wasn't much that would help keep anyone out. "We could push the desk in front of the door and find something to perch on top of the doorknob so if they try to turn the knob, even with the door locked, we'll hear it fall."

"So will whoever's trying to get in. Then they'll know someone's in here."

"Yeah, but at least we'll have some warning. Maybe that and the desk will give us enough time to climb out one of the back windows."

"Good idea. I'll take care of the front steps. Why don't you look for something to use on the door?"

"Okay." Before he was gone, I spun to him. "Be careful."

"I will. Be right back."

It took him less than five minutes, and he was back inside. We used a hammer I'd found in the toolkit to make a rudimentary alarm system on the door. It took some finesse to balance the hammer over the circular doorknob, but we made it work. Then we pushed the desk in front of the door. We also made sure we could open one of the back windows in a hurry. The cabin butted up against the trees so we'd have immediate coverage if we could get outside fast enough. We'd just have to hope that if anyone looked for us here, they wouldn't have enough people to surround the place.

"Now," Richard said, "get out of those wet clothes."

I didn't think, just did what he told me and started to strip. Then his words really sank in, and I threw him a halfhearted smile. "You're just trying to get me naked."

He returned the smile. "Well, who wouldn't?"

After I had my shirt off, I gestured to his drenched clothes. "You need to get warm too."

Luke finished building the fire, and we all got down to our underwear, hanging our clothes over the table and chair as best as we could so they'd dry out. We sat before the fire, the two of them on each side of me, one sleeping bag open under us, the other from Luke's pack wrapped around us.

I raised my knees to my chest and stared into the flames. "I can't believe all this is happening."

Richard laid a warm hand at the back of my neck. "We're going to be fine."

"Yeah." Luke inched closer and slid one leg along my opposite side so he held me from behind. He ducked his head and kissed the side of my neck. "Richard and I are both too stubborn to get hurt."

I laughed as I leaned back against him, my mind and body starting to relax. With them, I always felt safe, comfortable in a way I never did before them. Even with armed, angry cops and rangers chasing us down.

But with that one thought, a flood of anxiety returned.

As if sensing the shift, Richard slid his arms around both Luke and me.

Before he could say anything reassuring, I shook my head. "You only gave in and stayed in the park because of our fight, because of what I said to you about forcing me to do something I didn't want. And now..." My breath hitched, and I couldn't get the rest of the words out.

Richard held us tighter, and I leaned sideways to lay my cheek on his shoulder.

"You went against your instincts. If anything happens to us, you'll never forgive yourself. Or me."

"That's not true." He shifted us around until all three of us were lying together before the fire, his arms wrapped around me. "Nothing is going to happen to us. Just try not to worry and get some rest." He kept stroking my back as Luke sat up and drew the sleeping bag over us.

Luke took the first watch while Richard and I stayed by the fire. Exhausted, I fell asleep quickly, despite the anxiety still rushing through me.

I awoke sometime later to the sound of rolling thunder and the rhythmic beat of rain hitting the cabin's roof. I so didn't want to move. My leg muscles were sore from all the walking—and running—we'd been doing, but I was dry and warm, nestled against Richard's back.

I breathed deep and forced myself to roll to my other side. Luke sat in the desk chair by the window, keeping watch through the slit between the wooden shutters. He was dressed again. Even without a phone or a clock, I could tell from the glowing embers in the fire that it was long past time for him to get some sleep.

"Hey," I whispered. "Why didn't you wake one of us?"

He shrugged. Without turning to me, he said, "Figured I couldn't sleep anyway."

"Come here. I'll get up now. You need to rest too. It's going to be a lot of hiking tomorrow."

He didn't move or say anything.

I slid out from under the sleeping bag and slipped on my clothes, then went to him, laying a hand on his bare back. "What's wrong?"

He looked at me over his shoulder and smiled. It wasn't a lighthearted grin. He went back to focusing out the window.

"Hey." I knelt beside him. "What is it?"

He shrugged again. "Just thinking."

"About what we should do next?"

"No. Not that."

I kept my gaze locked on his profile, really hoping he'd go on before I had to convince him to say more.

Finally he spoke again. "I just..." He shook his head. "Never mind."

"What?"

He kept his focus on the window. "I have this awful feeling something horrible is going to happen to you out here. Or maybe to him." He gestured to Richard.

I bit my bottom lip and looked back at where Richard slept. When I returned my attention to Luke, he was watching me with a penetrating, meaningful stare, like he thought it might be the last time he'd ever get to see me like this.

"We're going to be fine," I said, repeating their words to me earlier. "I'm not going to let anything happen to us."

He offered a wistful smile. "I know." He gave me a kiss. "I think I'm just tired. Guess I'll try closing my eyes for a bit." He gave me another kiss, then got up and headed for the fireplace to lie down beside Richard.

As I watched him get settled, I thought over what I'd said. I wasn't exactly sure how I would do what I'd promised, but after dragging them out there, I had to do whatever I could to keep us safe.

I also had to get back to Tomas so I could tell him the truth about his father.

Chapter Thirty

I took the next shift on watch, rotating between keeping an eye out the front window toward the overgrown dirt trail, and the back windows of the cabin. I tried to stay out of sight as best as I could while checking out the perimeter.

Settling into the chair near the front window once more, I finally had a better view since the rain had begun to let up some. I found nothing suspicious along the trail or near the cabin.

With the crackle of the fire filling the room, I couldn't keep my thoughts from floating back to the night I'd been sitting across the campfire from my father, the night he'd told me his dad had died. After we'd packed up our gear the next morning, he led us toward the most famous waterfall in the park, Eagle's View, the first one Luke, Richard, and I had visited. My dad and I spent much of the morning there, snapping photos and sitting on the rocks above the falls.

Where had those pictures gone? They'd been tucked inside a photo album on our coffee table for a while after the trip, but I hadn't seen that book since my dad left. I'd forgotten all about the pictures we'd taken.

Wait. *Pictures.*

I bolted upright in the chair. "Oh man. Why didn't I see it before?"

I went to where Luke and Richard lay before the fire. They had the sleeping bag draped over their lower halves. Richard had his head on Luke's chest, an arm around Luke's middle. Not too long after Luke had first gotten situated under the sleeping bag, Richard had rolled onto his side and held him. Even in sleep, he couldn't refrain from reaching out for us. I adored seeing them snuggled together. It wasn't often just the two of them were in bed without me between them.

As quietly as I could so as not to wake them, I knelt on the floor before the fire and reached for Luke's backpack. I removed the map. It had gotten wet in the rain, but it was mostly dry now and was still readable. I also got out the photos from Tomas. I flipped through them and found the ones I wanted. Keeping only the relevant pictures, I put the rest back into Luke's bag. Then I laid all the photos out on the floor face down and compared the numbers on the back of the pictures with the numbers on Alex's map.

Bingo. The number on each photo matched one of the grid coordinates on the map. I dug a pen out of Luke's bag and circled the grids that paired with the photos.

I followed the path the pictures made. "Where were you going, Alex?" I turned over the photos so they were right-side up and reviewed each one again, and then I saw it. I rechecked the dates on the back of each photo.

Holy shit.

I reviewed the map and pictures again, and it all came to me.

"What are you doing?"

Luke's voice startled me. He still lay before the fire, watching me. One of his arms was tucked behind his head. His other hand was raking through Richard's short hair in a contented, loving stroke. I wasn't sure Luke was even aware he touched Richard like that. That only made the gesture more beautiful.

"I figured something out," I said. "I'm pretty sure I know where Alex was when he made that video of the building with the drugs."

"Where?"

"Not too far from where we are right now." I pointed to the photos. "The pictures Tomas gave me weren't only of Alex's favorite spots in the park. I think Alex was tracking something when he took some of these photos."

"Tracking what?"

"Those hikers that were killed. I think I know where he found the drugs. I'm also guessing that the cabin in the video, where they shot those college kids, might be somewhere near there. I want to see if I can find it before we leave the park."

Luke stilled his hand on the back of Richard's head.

I turned to sit facing him, my legs tucked underneath me. "I bet that cabin's where they took Alex. Maybe we could find out what actually happened to him. Or maybe…"

"What?"

"I think he might still be alive."

Luke's eyes widened, then closed for a brief second. "Matthew…"

"I know you guys don't think that's likely, but maybe they caught him and took him back to that cabin."

"Then he ended up just like those hikers."

"But maybe not. Maybe he escaped. He could've gotten hurt when he was trying to get away from them, and he knew he'd never make it out of the park on foot, so he's hiding out somewhere until his injuries are better. He'd know how to find food and water. And there are a lot of caves out here. He could be lying low in one of them."

"But if he's hurt, then he probably couldn't—"

"I know." It took a moment to say more than that. "I know it's not logical. I just have this really strong feeling that I have to check. I have to find that cabin and see if there are caves near there or anywhere else he could be hiding, or maybe where he could've left another note for his family. I just *have* to see for myself."

"Okay. Take it easy." Luke studied me for a moment more. Then he tapped the side of Richard's head. "Wake up."

I gave him a pleading look. "Please."

Luke shifted his upper body, jostling Richard. "Get up."

Richard grunted and rolled off Luke onto his back. He blinked several times. When it was clear he remembered where he was, he sat up like a shot. "What's wrong? Someone here?"

"No. Matthew wants to change directions and head off to see if we can find where the doc was when he made that video of the cabin."

I gave in and repeated my thoughts to Richard.

He stayed quiet the entire time, carefully listening to me. I knew he didn't want to push me on anything because of the horrible way I'd spoken to him the other day, but I didn't want to think about that right then. I needed to do this for Alex and Tomas.

Richard said nothing for several seconds. Then he got up and got dressed. As he was doing up his pants, he asked, "What makes you think you know where to look?"

I showed them the pictures I'd been reviewing. "See those hikers?"

Richard took a seat on the floor beside Luke. "Where?"

"Way in the background."

"All right. I see them."

"They're in quite a few of the pictures Alex took. I think those are the two people who were killed in the video."

"You can't tell that for sure. These were taken from too far away."

"I know it's them, and I think Alex was watching them. Not only on that day but for several weeks. Or maybe he didn't know they were in some of the pictures when he first took them. Maybe he spotted them later when he got a good look at the photos after he had them printed. And then he knew something was up, so he went out into the park to see what they were doing."

Luke asked, "Why would he assume something was up? They just look like they're out hiking."

"Look." I turned over two of the pictures. "They're all dated, with the time too. These two pictures are from a week before Alex disappeared, taken on the same day, only a couple of hours apart." I flipped over the photos so they could see the young couple in them. "Do you see it?"

Luke took a closer look. "What are we supposed to be seeing?"

"The backpacks. They were carrying different packs when they left the park than when they entered." I picked up another set of pictures. "These are from a few days before. And these, the week before that. Same thing."

Richard took the pictures from me. "Yeah, those are different packs."

"And check this out." I showed them more photos. "There are three more college-age couples in these pictures. All wearing backpacks and all taking the same route through the park that the first couple did. I've marked it here on Alex's map. Each photo has a number that coordinates with the grid."

Richard shook his head. "I don't get it."

Luke snapped his fingers. "They hired these kids to take the heroin out of the park on foot."

I nodded. "Not sure why they were killed, but I think I know where that building is with all the drugs." I laid the map out on the sleeping bag between us. "From what I can tell in the pictures, those couples were in this grid when they switched packs, near the old mill. I'd bet a million bucks that's where Alex was when he found the heroin on the video."

"What old mill?" Luke asked.

"It's this abandoned mill along Windtree River. I kept thinking the outside of that building looked familiar. I thought I'd seen it before, but I couldn't remember from where. Then it came to me. I hadn't *seen* it. I'd read about it. Alex mentioned the mill in his book."

Richard carefully examined the map. "There's no indication of a mill on here."

"It's pretty remote, and the park service doesn't publicize it so they can keep tourists from trying to get there. It's pretty run-down. There's been a push in recent years to restore the mill, so they've left it standing for now."

Luke asked, "If it's not on the map, how do you know where it is?"

"Alex described the location in his book. I'm pretty sure it's not too far from where we are right now." I pointed to the grid area on the map again. "If I take a look around this area here, I know I can find it. And also find the cabin where those hikers were killed. I bet it's not too far from the mill. There has to be a road or a path, something that leads to the mill, probably to the cabin too. Maybe something that's not in use anymore, like the trail here at the cabin. There had to be some way they originally brought in all the drugs and supplies to set up their operation."

Richard seemed to be considering that. When he spoke his tone was deliberate but cautious. "Matthew, we need to get out of this park and get help. And when we do, we can tell the feds everything you figured out about where Alex was and why. Then they can go take a look at the mill."

"I know I'm asking a lot. I know this is a huge risk, but I can't wait. I need to find out if Alex is still alive."

"Matthew..." Richard was shaking his head. "The chances that he—"

"I get it. I don't know how I know, I just do. I think he's still alive."

He sighed. "These people are incredibly dangerous. They killed that young man and woman, maybe because the two were stealing from them or they wanted to get rid of any loose threads or maybe just for the hell of it. And if they find us with the phone, they're going to kill us too."

I knew he was right, but I couldn't shake the feeling that I had to do this, that it was up to me to figure this out before it was too late.

But too late for what? Did I really think there was a chance Alex was alive?

I did. But why did I have to do this myself? If we stayed in the park any longer, it could be too late for *us*.

"Okay," I said. "Yeah. I know you're right. I don't want anything to happen to either of you." I couldn't even fathom that. Hearing Luke vocalize his fear that something awful might happen had been bad enough. "We'll keep going for the road."

Richard eyed me for a long moment as if he wasn't sure if I was really on board with that plan.

I nodded in reassurance but said nothing more.

After another quiet beat, my stomach growled.

Luke gestured toward the shelves at the back of the cabin. "I checked those tins earlier. They're filled with granola bars and trail mix." He retrieved one of the containers and several bottles of water. "Most of it's expired, but I say we chance it."

We ate the stale granola bars and trail mix and drank the water.

Luke stuffed four extra bottles in his pack. "We should hide Alex's cell phone somewhere in here. Just in case…"

In case we were caught, but he didn't say that. He was right, though. It would give us something to bargain with.

"Yeah," Richard said. "Good idea."

Luke got up and meandered around the room, indicating several places where we could stash the phone. There weren't many options that wouldn't be obvious if the cabin were searched. We all settled on the best spot: shoved down in between the seat and the back cushion of the office chair. The phone wasn't visible, and Luke had it lodged in there so well if someone moved the chair around or took a seat in it, the phone would stay put.

As we neared the end of the granola bars, Richard said, "We should get going. I think we're just going to have to make our way in the rain. It doesn't seem like it's going to stop anytime soon." He went to take another bite of his bar but stilled with it halfway to his mouth like he'd just thought of something.

"What is it?" I asked.

"Shh." He held still and listened.

Snap.

The twigs on the front steps.

Richard met Luke's stare. "Someone's outside."

We all hurried to get up.

I was hastily gathering up the last of the photos when the hammer fell from the doorknob. "Shit."

"Go." Richard pointed to the back of the cabin. "Now!"

Chapter Thirty-One

Luke tucked the map and photos into his pack, and we raced for the rear of the cabin. Richard cranked the window open and climbed through first. I knew what he was doing. If they were already surrounding the place, he wanted to be the first one shot at.

No shots rang out.

I rushed out after him. Then Luke did the same. We quickly made our way into the trees behind the cabin.

Right as we ducked into the tree line, we heard the cabin door burst open, then the desk being shoved aside. A voice filtered out from the open window behind us. "They were here."

"Go." Richard grabbed my arm and Luke's and thrust us in front of him.

Lightning lit up the sky. The stinging rain came down harder as we wove our way deeper into the forest, racing around giant chestnut oak trees and leaping over fallen limbs. My drenched boots repeatedly slipped in the wet, muddy brush. I had to focus on every step to keep from falling flat on my face.

"Faster," Richard said. "They're right behind us."

We trudged on, farther and farther away from the cabin, all of us breathless, the rain beating down on our backs. We had nowhere to get out of the weather or attempt to hide.

After several minutes, I pointed to our left. "I think I can get us to the main road if we go this way."

"How do you know that?" Luke asked.

"I went over the map back at the cabin. We've been going north since we left there, and we just passed Angel Wings rock formation a few minutes ago, which means if we turn and head due west, we'll eventually run into the main road on this side of the park."

They both gave a nod, and I led us that way.

The wind kicked up, whirling the rain and rotting remnants of last year's fallen leaves through the air, limiting our visibility. It wasn't long before I'd lost complete sense of where we were. For all I knew I was leading us in circles, and we were headed in the opposite direction of where we needed to be, but there was no way I could stop to review the map and get my bearings. I had to trust that I was on the right track. Besides, all that mattered right then was getting us away from the murderous gun-toting cops and park rangers.

So I kept going, traipsing through the heavy brush as fast as I could. I had no idea how much time had passed when Richard pulled me to a stop. "Ease up. I don't think they're behind us anymore."

I nodded and slowed down so none of us would trip and fall in the dark. I didn't want to stop altogether, though. I was determined to get us to the road. And I would too. That was if I hadn't completely fucked this up and gotten us lost.

The wind howled through the air and whipped the branches of the trees around like they were nothing more than paper streamers blowing in the breeze. The brutal rain and wind made it harder to keep an eye on the ground before me. I tripped right as I came upon an embankment that led down to a wide rushing stream. I caught myself before I toppled down the steep hillside, then tried not to ruminate for long on how I'd almost fallen like I did when I was a kid.

When Richard and Luke caught up with me, Richard gestured at the stream. "Let's follow the ridge and see if we can climb down somewhere safer."

I started hiking again but halted when a loud crack tore through the air above our heads. A heavy branch came crashing to the ground five feet from me. I jumped with the jolt of the impact. My boots slipped on the muddy ground, and I landed on my hip, sliding headfirst down the embankment, mud kicking up as I attempted to grab for purchase.

"Matthew!" Richard called out from somewhere above me.

I managed to flip to my stomach and tried digging my fingers into the ground to stop myself, but that just got the rest of me slick with mud and also descending faster toward the stream and the rocks at the water's edge.

No time to do anything else, I ducked my head and flung my arms up as I tried to turn my body before impact. I came to a crashing halt, my right shoulder blade smacking into a massive rock. Stabbing pain radiated down my side and back.

I couldn't move for several breaths. Then the pain started to recede. Before I could even think about trying to get up, Richard and Luke were there.

Richard gripped me around the waist. "Easy does it."

"I'm okay," I said. "I can get up myself."

That didn't stop him. He kept his arm around me and held on as I got my feet under me and stood. Mud covered me from head to toe. I spit to clear my mouth and then wiped at my eyes.

"You sure you're okay?" Luke asked, practically screaming to be heard over the roar of the wind and the rain smacking the surface of the water beside us.

"Yeah, I'm fine. Guess we should cross the stream here." I laughed, but it wasn't a humor-filled sound.

Luke smiled tentatively in return. "Sounds good." He handed me a T-shirt from his pack. "Here, wipe your face on this."

Richard shook his head. "We're not going anywhere right away. You're resting here for a minute." He still had an arm around my waist.

I shrugged out of his touch. "I said I'm okay." I threw the soiled shirt at Luke and went to take a step away. My right boot slipped, and I almost hit the ground again, but Luke caught me.

"You're not okay. You need to take a break, Matthew."

I backpedaled several steps. "Don't tell me what to do. I *am* okay." He flinched at my tone.

I hadn't meant to take out my frustration on either of them. I spun away from him and glanced out into the forest on the other side of the stream. "We're probably heading in the wrong direction anyway."

"I don't think so," Richard said.

I shook my head, not even sure what I meant by that.

He came up behind me and laid a hand on my shoulder, lovingly sweeping his thumb over my taut muscles. "Let's wait until the rain lets up and we can see better."

"No. We have to keep going." Before they could argue more, I started across the stream, wading through the knee-high water, navigating around the larger rocks that jutted up out of the surface. I dipped my hands into the cool water to aid the pelting rain in washing away what I could of the mud from my face and arms. Richard and Luke followed, but I didn't wait for them. I started hiking along the bank.

"Stop!" Luke caught up with me and grabbed my arm, pulling me to a halt. "You need to let up before you get hurt."

I was vibrating with anger. At Luke's words. At the men chasing us. At the storm. At myself for falling down the embankment like I'd done all those years ago.

If it hadn't been for the tender way my father had treated me after that fall, for all those good moments alone with him—the camping, the video games we used to play, the movies, the laughs—I might not have been so fucked up about the way he beat me, about his leaving, or about Alex's disappearance. I might not have forced Luke and Richard to head out into this park and put them in jeopardy.

"Goddammit!" I bent for a rock that lay at my feet and chucked it through the air. The rock bounced off a nearby tree, hit the ground, and rolled to a stop before me, right where it had started.

Luke and Richard wore matching concerned expressions. Like the night I'd come home drunk. I couldn't stand seeing those looks from them again.

I shook my head. "We never should've come out here. We should've hired someone experienced to look for Alex. I never should've put you in danger." I started pacing between two trees, moving back and forth in long, agitated strides, going nowhere but needing to move. "I was so obsessed with doing this myself, I didn't think about what could go wrong. And now look what's happening. You could get hurt. Or worse. I didn't think about your safety. Or what was the right thing to do. I just *had* to do this myself. And look at me now. I'm still trying to do things that could get you hurt." Just like my father. His choices and actions hurt me, when he was supposed to be the one protecting me. I kicked at a branch in my way and kept pacing.

Richard stepped into my path. "You did think of the right thing to do. That's what you've been doing this whole time, that's what you're still doing. Helping someone in need. That's what you always do. It's who you are, Matthew. And I love that about you. I may not like that we're out here, I may not like that we're in danger because you wanted to help Alex, but I don't for one second think you did the wrong thing."

Luke pointed at Richard. "Right. What he said."

I barely choked out, "Then why?" The anger at myself for how I'd handled the search for Alex had morphed into the fury and despair I'd kept buried beneath the surface for far too long.

Richard's brows drew in. "Why what?"

"Why did he do it? If I'm such a good person, why did he hurt me? Why did he hit me?" I spun away. I didn't want to see the pity-filled expressions from them any longer. Once again, my boots slipped, and this time I didn't try to stop myself. I dropped forward onto my hands and knees in the mud. "You hurt me."

Richard knelt beside me. He laid one hand on my back, the other across my stomach. "Your dad?"

I shook my head. I didn't want to talk about this now. We had far more important things going on, but I couldn't stop the words, couldn't focus on anything else. I sank back on my haunches. "I was just a kid. I'd go to bed scared, crying, bruised, a split lip, trying to figure out what I could do to stop it from happening the next time, like I had some control over that part of my life." I reached for the rock that I'd thrown earlier and gripped it in both hands. "But I had no control. You took that from me. You hurt me every time you drank. Every time you hit me. And when you walked out the door without a word, it all changed who I was, who I became. I'll never know the man I could've been. Maybe I would've been more confident, more certain, more... I don't know. Just more. More of a man."

I sounded mad, talking to a person who wasn't there, who hadn't been there for such a long time.

The rain had stopped, which made the tears streaming down my cheeks all the more obvious. I wanted the rain to return. I couldn't take back the words, but maybe with the rain, Luke and Richard wouldn't see the flood of tears.

Luke came to kneel in the mud on my other side, his arm around my shoulders, his lips pressed to my temple. Richard shifted to kneel before me. He was all I could see.

He held my face and tipped my head up. "You're absolutely perfect the way you are."

Luke spoke without removing his lips from my skin. "You are."

"Then why?"

Richard gathered me up and pulled me into his arms. He stroked the back of my head and held on to me. "None of what he did to you was your fault."

The tears came harder, and I let it all out. The pain, the humiliation, the betrayal, the anger, the heartbreak.

For the first time since that night my dad had started hitting me, I let myself grieve for the loss of the father—and friend—I'd once had.

Luke moved in so he was eye level with me where I had my head pressed against Richard's chest. "You were a good son. It wasn't your fault."

"I know." I wiped at the tears. "I know that. I do." I sat up taller and faced them. "I guess I just needed to say all that out loud. Just once." I considered my words, and in that moment, I wondered if I needed more. "I wish I knew what to do, what the *right thing* was to do."

"About finding your dad?" Luke asked.

"Yeah. I want him to know how much he hurt me. I feel like I need to say it to him."

"I get that. I do, but..." He sighed as if he couldn't bring himself to argue with me about this.

"I want to know why he wouldn't stay and get help."

Richard stared at the rock I held. Without glancing up at me, he said, "Whatever you decide, whatever you need, we'll be there with you."

Luke nodded. "Yeah." He reached for my free hand. "Whatever you need."

"But maybe that's not what would be best for me." I shook my head. "It doesn't matter right now. We don't have time for this." I released a trembling sigh as I let the rock in my other hand fall to the muddy forest floor, then tilted my head back. The gray storm clouds were clearing. The sun was beginning to rise in the east, creating a brilliant orange arc above the hills and trees on the horizon. "Being out here isn't about him. Or me." I stood. "I have to look for that mill and the cabin. I'm going to find out for sure if Alex is still alive, find out if he left another message for Natalie and Tomas."

"What?" Luke staggered to his feet. "No. We came out here to find his truck and prove he was in the park that day, and we did that. Why do you feel like you need to do more? The chances that they kept him alive are minuscule."

I thought about that for a moment, then glanced at Richard where he still knelt in the mud. "Have you ever heard the saying that a man is never truly a man until his father dies?"

Cautiously, Richard stood. "Yeah."

"The way things are now, I'll never know when my father dies. He could already be gone, and I just don't know it. I don't want Tomas to grow up and never feel like a man."

Luke stepped in front of me. "Fuck that. It's a bullshit saying, Matthew. It doesn't mean shit."

Richard signaled for Luke to ease up. He took one of my hands in both of his. "You continually sacrifice your time and energy to give to others and to help animals in need. In my book that makes you more of a man than most guys. Than your father or your grandfather. Than me."

Luke nodded. "And me."

I sighed. "Then why can't you understand why I *have* to do this?"

I could see the arguments forming.

Before either could say anything, I added, "I can get us to that mill and find the cabin. I know I can." I took a step back. "If there is even the slightest chance he's still alive, I can't just leave him out here. I can't."

Richard kept quiet as if giving what I'd said serious thought. "You know, with all the drugs and money, they'll likely have that mill heavily guarded. And that cabin was new. It's probably their headquarters. They'll be guarding that too."

"But maybe not since they're searching for us."

When they said nothing, I offered, "We won't go near either place. We'll just find where they are and then check for any caves or recesses nearby, someplace Alex may have hidden, where he may have left something behind."

Richard remained quiet for another ten seconds. Then he said, "Okay. But the minute we see anyone—and I mean anyone—we take off."

"Agreed."

Luke stepped in between us, facing Richard. "Have you lost your goddamn mind? We could walk right into the path of those psychos."

"We'll be careful. Keep out of sight." He indicated my way with a nod. "He needs to do this. And we need to help him. Maybe if he does this for Tomas, then he won't feel so helpless himself, so lost." He looked over Luke's shoulder at me. "He won't feel like that abused, abandoned kid anymore."

I rounded Luke so I could see both of them at once. "I have to do this."

Luke searched my face. "I just don't want anything to happen to you or Richard."

"I know. I don't want that either. But I need to do this."

He studied me for another long moment. There was a spark of understanding in those blue eyes. "I get that. I do." He tugged the map out of his pack. "Which way?"

Chapter Thirty-Two

It was an hour past daybreak when we found a narrow dirt road that I was pretty sure, based on my memory, wasn't one of the access roads on the sheriff's map. Various tire tracks covered the surface, deep enough that even the heavy rain hadn't washed them away. We stayed back from the road, and instead hiked out of sight, using the trees for cover. The thick vine-laden brush on the ground made each step difficult. Still, I didn't want to slow down or stop for a break. We had to be getting close.

Then I heard something.

"What is it?" Luke asked as he caught up to me.

"I can hear the river." The road ahead vanished as it curved into the forest and was engulfed by the trees. "Come on. Around that bend." We continued on.

When I came to an abrupt stop after the curve in the road, Luke almost walked right into me. "What—"

"Shh. That's it."

A hundred yards ahead, alongside the river, sat a dilapidated wooden structure. The old mill. It was nestled back off the dirt road, nearly shielded from view on all sides by overgrown grass and weeds.

We slowly started forward, scanning the surroundings in search of the cabin and anyone on guard near the mill.

When we approached the edge of the open area where the mill sat, I stopped dead in my tracks again.

"What is it?" Richard whispered as he came up behind me. "You see someone?"

"Not someone." I pointed toward a mound of dirt situated between two trees to our right. We moved in for a closer look.

"That's a grave, isn't it?" I asked.

"I think so," Richard said.

"Maybe it's not Alex. It could be the hikers."

"Could be."

Frozen in place, I couldn't turn away from the haunting vision of piled earth loosely covered with half-dead foliage. The reality of where we were and why slammed into me so forcefully I wavered back a step. What a stupid, idiotic, fucked-up thing for us to do, coming out there to search for... anything. Why the hell had they listened to me? Because I'd been crying and carrying on like a madman.

"We need to go." I backed away from the grave. "We need to get out of here right now. Before someone finds us."

"You sure?" Richard asked.

"Yeah. Let's go." I turned away from the unmarked grave but stopped when a low, muffled groan came from somewhere to our left.

"Shit." Luke gestured for us to hunker down in the brush.

Richard grasped my elbow. "Come on. Back this way."

Then came another moan. It was followed by a call for help.

I pointed north. "It came from that way." I barreled toward the sound of continued groans, wading through the knee-high grass to a nearby cluster of trees. I rounded the trees and found another open area. There sat the cabin from the video. Smaller than the ranger station but definitely a newer structure. Visible on the other side was a rudimentary path consisting of two strips of trampled brush, far enough apart they had to have been made by a vehicle. The makeshift driveway probably led to the access road.

An arm came around my waist. Richard hauled me back against his chest. He whispered in my ear, "We're not going near that cabin."

"But that could be Alex."

"Help," came the same cracked voice, only louder now. It was definitely coming from inside the cabin. "Someone. Help. Please."

"That's him. That's his voice. That's Alex!" I sprinted for the building.

"Matthew!" Luke called out. "Wait!"

I didn't stop until I reached the back of the cabin. I had to get a look inside, but I wanted—needed—their help. I waited for them to catch up.

Luke gripped my forearm in a firm hold. He had no intention of letting me take off again. "What do you think you're doing?"

"We have to help him."

"You have no idea who's inside there with him."

"If he's calling out for help, there must not be anyone close by."

Without a word, Richard stepped past me and shot a glance around the corner of the building. "There's a window on this side. It's open a crack." He looked torn. Like his instincts were telling him to both protect us *and* go see who needed our help. "I'll take a look. You guys stay here."

"No." I pointed a finger at him. "We stay together. No matter what." Although that wasn't exactly what I'd been doing. I had charged forward several times now without waiting for them.

A swell of nausea landed in the pit of my stomach. If anything happened to them because of my decisions, because I'd taken chances with all our lives...

No, I couldn't think about that now. Alex needed our help.

We were getting him out of that cabin and taking him to safety. Nothing was going to happen to any of us in the process.

Nothing.

Richard hesitated, then gave a nod. The shock on Luke's face was almost comical, if it weren't for the fact that we were standing in the exact location where a crooked sheriff's deputy had murdered two people.

Richard gestured toward the corner of the cabin. "We'll have a look in the window. That's it."

I nodded, and Luke reluctantly did too.

Richard carefully peeked around the corner again. He inched forward. Luke and I followed, shuffling behind him with our backs against the side wall of the cabin, trying to stay out of sight and not make a sound.

When he got to the window, Richard darted a look inside. He jerked his head back.

"What did you see?" I whispered frantically.

"Just one person." He slowly got another look, then moved to stand before the window. Luke and I joined him.

Inside, in the middle of the one-room cabin, which was set up as both an office and a living space with several cots, sat Alex.

His ankles were secured to the legs of a chair with duct tape, his wrists similarly taped to the arms of the chair. He had his head down, his chin on his chest. His eyes were closed, but his chest rose and fell with each breath.

I advanced, reaching for the window to open it the rest of the way.

"Fuck!" Luke grabbed me and tugged me backward, out of view from the window. He gestured for Richard to step back too, then spoke low. "What the hell is wrong with you two? You're gonna get yourselves killed." He pointed at the window. "Someone could show up here any minute. Someone dangerous. With a fucking gun. We need to go get help."

"No." I emphatically shook my head. "I'm not leaving him here." I tipped my head to get another peek inside the window.

"Shit," Luke said under his breath, but he didn't stop me.

I tapped the window. Alex's head shot up. His face was severely bruised, his eyes swollen, his lower lip cut. It was obvious some of the damage was new, but most of it was days old, maybe even weeks. Despite his appearance, the expression on his face lit up when he spotted me in the window. A cloth was tied around his face, pushed low over his chin like he'd managed to get it out of his mouth. *Help me*, he mouthed.

I signaled that I was going to open the window.

Alex nodded and spoke louder. "You can open it. I'm alone right now."

Once I had the window pushed up, I asked Alex, "You sure no one else is here?"

"Yeah," he croaked out. "They left. But they'll be back soon. They always come back."

"Okay." I turned to Luke. "Lift me up."

Luke sighed and stepped forward.

"Wait." Richard laid a hand on his shoulder to stop him. "I'll go keep an eye on the driveway in case someone comes back. Help Matthew with Alex and then you three get the hell out of there. I'll be right behind you."

Luke's brows furrowed. "Didn't we just say something about sticking together?"

"I'll stay right there at the corner of the building. You'll be able to see me from the window."

"All right."

Richard turned to me. "Get Alex untied and get him out of there. Nothing else."

"Got it."

Richard took off for the front corner of the cabin while Luke lifted me up into the window. I helped pull him through next. When Luke had one leg over the windowsill, I rushed to Alex and dropped to my knees before him.

His features were gaunt. He'd lost at least fifteen pounds. "Are you okay?"

"Mostly. I've been locked in here for days, weeks, I don't know how long."

Luke removed the multi-tool from his pack, then flipped open the blade and began sawing at the tape around Alex's wrists as I said, "You've been gone for over three weeks."

Alex dropped his head back. "Oh God. My family…" He lifted his head. "Are they okay? Did anyone hurt them?"

"They're okay."

When Luke had Alex's arms free, Alex fell forward and grasped my shoulders. If he hadn't, he would've toppled over. He was weak, barely able to hold his own weight. "Thank you," he whispered. Then he searched my face while Luke worked on the tape at his ankles. "Why are you here?"

"We were trying to see if we could figure out what happened to you."

"You sure my family's okay?"

"Yeah. They're fine."

"The baby?"

"As far as I know, she hasn't had it yet."

Luke said in a rush, "We'll catch you up on everything later. We gotta go." He grasped Alex by one arm and hauled him out of the chair.

Alex wobbled on shaky legs. I shifted around and held on to him at his other side.

He gave me a slight smile. "I'm okay."

"Let's go," Luke said, tugging on Alex to get him moving.

The sound of a car engine came from the direction of the path out front.

Richard reappeared in the open window before we'd made it across the room. "Get your asses out here. We're not alone anymore. A car's coming down the path." He helped Alex slip out the window first. Then Luke gestured for me to go next. When we were all out, we hightailed it for the trees, Richard providing support for Alex. We kept our heads low and moved as fast as we could, which wasn't all that quickly since Alex was unsteady, physically weak from his captivity.

We hadn't gone fast enough.

"Stop!" came a voice from behind us. A shot rang out, smacking into a tree five feet to our right, the bark splintering on impact.

Not again.

"Jesus Christ," Luke muttered.

The shot was close. Too close.

My adrenaline kicked into high gear. Determination flowed through me. There was no way I was letting anything else happen to Alex. Or to Richard and Luke.

I moved to Alex's side opposite Richard, lifted Alex's arm over my shoulders, and jerked him forward. "Everyone, move!"

Chapter Thirty-Three

"I think we lost them." I shifted Alex's arm higher on my shoulder. "We need to stop for a break."

Since we'd taken off from the cabin twenty minutes earlier, Alex had been sagging against Richard and me more and more with each step. The rain had started up again, coming down harder than earlier, darkening the sky overhead. The storm, as well as our zigzagging route, had likely aided our escape through the forest, but the almost torrential rainfall also seriously impeded our progress. It was nearly impossible to keep the rain out of our eyes or to hear if anyone was following us. At least the lightning was holding off this time.

"All right," Richard said. "I don't think they're behind us, or they'd have shot at us again."

"Yeah," Luke agreed. "But let's not stick around here for long."

"Okay." I pointed toward a downed tree. "There." The substantial log lay at the base of another tree. The pair would give Alex a backrest, and the thick limbs above would provide some cover from the rain. We started toward it, Alex stumbling on his last step. Richard caught him before he went down and then eased him onto the makeshift seat. "You okay?"

"Yeah." Alex leaned back against the upright tree. When he was settled, I sat beside him.

His soft smile was full of relief. "Are these your partners?"

"Yeah. This is Luke and Richard." I indicated each in turn.

He gave a nod to one, then the other. "It's nice to meet you. Thanks for saving my life."

Luke snorted out a laugh. "That was all Matthew. He had this crazy idea you might just be alive out here. Everyone else thinks you're dead or you took off."

"I wasn't sure," I said. "I just had this strong feeling that I had to find the cabin that we saw in your video."

"You found my phone?"

"Yeah."

"You got it with you?"

"We hid it once we realized there were people that would kill us for it. We didn't want to have it on us if they caught up to us."

"Good. That's good." His eyes fell shut.

I turned to Richard. "He needs to rest. We should stay here for a bit."

"No." Alex's eyes shot open. He shook his head so emphatically I thought he might hurt himself. It was the most animated he'd been since we'd gotten him out of the chair at the cabin. As if that movement alone had been too much for him, he tilted his head back to rest on the tree behind him. Deep breaths poured out of him as he spoke again. "You need to keep going. You should leave me here, and you guys go for help."

"We're not leaving you anywhere. What if they find you and take you again? And this time they kill you?" I looked to Luke and Richard.

Luke got the last partial bottle of water from his pack and offered it to Alex. "Here. Drink this."

When Alex had finished off the water, he handed back the empty bottle and then closed his eyes again. A minute later, he was barely awake.

Richard turned away and kept his back to us as he scanned the forest the way we'd come, looking for someone who might've found us.

When he faced us, I said, "He needs more to drink and something to eat."

Luke checked his bag. "I've got nothing left."

"Matthew…" Richard started.

"I know. He won't make it back to one of the main trails, much less the road out of the park."

Lightning struck overhead, followed by an enormous crack of thunder.

Richard examined the sky. "We should get moving. This looks like it's just going to get worse."

"But where to?" Luke asked. "Matthew's right. Alex can't go much farther."

"I can make it." Alex held his eyes closed for a moment more. Then he met my stare. "I can. But we can skip the trails. They'll be looking for us on those. You got a map?"

I pulled out his map and held it out for him.

"If we head due west, eventually we'll end up here." He pointed to a location along the main road on the west side of the park. "And then it's only five miles until we're out of the park and at Windtree."

Richard examined him. "We gotta keep moving or those friends of yours will find us. They've got search dogs."

"I'll make it. I have every intention of seeing my son and wife again, and meeting my new baby."

Richard nodded. "All right. Then let's get going."

I helped Alex stand, but he didn't last for more than a second. He fell forward to his knees. I caught him before he landed face-first in the mud.

Richard and I got Alex up and on the downed tree again. "You okay?"

He shook his head. "I don't feel so well. My stomach…"

"When did you last eat?"

"Maybe yesterday. Or the day before. They usually fed me once a day, but I haven't had anything lately. They only gave me enough to keep me alive." He took in a couple of deep breaths, really struggling now. "I think you might be right. I don't think I can walk much farther."

Luke looked to Richard. "Can you carry him?"

A deep voice came from behind us. "I'll do it."

We all swung toward the voice. It was Gus, wearing his uniform and the same Detroit Tigers baseball cap we'd seen him in earlier.

Richard bolted in front of Alex and me. "Don't come any closer."

Gus glared at him in surprise. "What the hell?"

"Thanks for sending your pals after us at the bird-watching station."

"I didn't send anyone after you. No one was at the station when I got there. I waited there for you for hours, tried calling you, but it just went to voice mail."

"Sure."

"Listen…" Gus started forward.

Richard held up a hand. "Stay back."

Gus stopped. "I don't know what the hell's going on here, but I'm going to check on my friend." He started forward again. As he did, Richard tugged me out of his path. It was clear Gus wasn't going to give in until he talked to Alex.

Gus crouched down in front of him. He expelled a slow breath of relief as he took in the sight of the other man. "Damn, it's good to see you, old friend. I thought you'd died out here."

"I almost did."

"You look like it. What the hell happened to you?"

"Long story. How's Natalie?"

"She's good. No baby yet."

"You've seen her? Tomas too?"

"Yeah, almost every day. She had to go to the hospital yesterday, but it was just false labor and some cramping. They kept her for a bit to make sure everything was okay, but she's back home now."

Alex lowered his eyes in relief, then opened them again. "I knew you'd take care of them for me."

"Absolutely. I gotta say, though, it wasn't easy. When you first went missing, Natalie wanted to hike out here and search for you herself. As big as she is, I was surprised I kept having to remind her she was pregnant and about to give birth."

Alex snorted out a laugh. "She's stubborn, that's for sure."

Richard stalked to them and stood beside Gus, towering over him. "So you just happened to come across us out here in the middle of nowhere?"

"Yeah. Been looking all over for you."

Richard scrutinized him with suspicion. Luke too.

I knew what they were thinking, but were they right? Was it too much of a coincidence that Gus had found us not long after we'd located Alex, not long after we'd been shot at by his ranger pals and the deputies?

Richard asked him, "Did you call anyone after you talked to us?"

"Only when you didn't show up. I started asking around. The sheriff said you'd found Alex's truck, but when his deputies got there, they found no sign of the truck or you. He's got his deputies and several park rangers all out looking for you."

"I'm sure he does. If they're the same crooked cops and rangers as the ones that are behind Alex's disappearance, then they're not here to help us. They're trying to kill us. We weren't lying to you about that."

Gus looked from Richard to me, then to Alex.

Alex nodded. "People from both agencies are helping drug traffickers use the park to store and distribute heroin."

Luke approached the group and asked Gus, "Do you have a phone? Or a radio?"

"I've got my phone, but I don't have a signal here. I stopped nearby on the trail to try calling Natalie and check in, but I couldn't get through. That's when I heard your voices."

"There's a trail near here?" Richard asked, clearly nervous we were so close to a marked path.

"Yeah. Not far that way." Gus pointed into the trees to our right.

Richard told me, "We've gotta get moving."

Luke held out his hand to Gus. "Let me take a look at your phone first. Maybe I can come up with a way to boost the signal."

I doubted that was true. My guess was that Luke wanted to see if Gus was lying about not being able to make a call.

Gus appeared to come to the same conclusion, but he said, "Sure," and handed over his phone.

Richard turned to me. "Let me see the map." After I gave it to him, he faced Gus. "Show me that trail you were on." They moved into an opening in the trees under what limited daylight there was and inspected the map together.

I knelt down before Alex and spoke low so only he'd hear me. "Is that your Tigers hat that Gus is wearing?"

He looked to Gus. "No. We both got the hats at a game last summer. Mine is more faded than that."

"Do you trust him?"

"Gus? With my life."

"He wouldn't do anything to hurt you, then?"

"Absolutely not."

"What about the rest of us?"

Alex studied me with dismay. "He's not working with those people."

The clouds grew darker overhead, and the rain shifted to sharper, stinging drops.

I said, "I had a feeling I could trust him when we first met him, but I don't think Luke and Richard agree." They were both talking with Gus now, Luke using his body to try to block the rain from soaking the map. Then Richard folded the map and tucked it in his back pocket.

He approached us. "Gus said his truck's parked just off an access road near that trail he was on. We'll head for the truck."

"It's not too far from here." Gus crouched beside me so we were both facing Alex. He dug into his pack and removed a bottle of water and a protein bar. "Think you could make it about a mile?"

"Yeah." Alex swallowed a gulp of water and started in on the protein bar. "This'll help."

"Once we get on the trail, it'll be easier going."

Richard shook his head. "We aren't taking any trails."

Gus gaped up at him. "I've been on them all day and haven't seen a soul. No one's out in this weather."

"No trails." Richard reached down and gripped my arm. "Come here." He gestured for Luke and me to step aside, far enough away that Gus and Alex couldn't hear us. "I don't trust this guy."

"Me either," Luke said. "We should tell him to get lost, that we'll be fine on our own."

"No," I said, then hesitated. Was I right about Gus? Was I wrong to trust my possibly faulty instincts when it came to reading people? The only answer I could come up with was that if I didn't trust my gut, I would regret it. "I think we can trust him."

"He works with the assholes who shot at us," Luke added in a raised whisper louder than the beat of rain smacking the ground all around us. "For all we know, he could be the one in charge of this whole operation."

I glanced back at Alex and Gus. Gus was still crouched before Alex, removing the wrapper from another protein bar. He passed it to Alex.

"We can trust him. I know we can." Although, I'd also thought that about the sheriff, but I forced that thought from my mind.

Richard sighed. "Gus could have people waiting for us at his truck."

"How about this?" Luke said. "We skip Gus's truck altogether, find someplace else to rest up, and take a different approach when the rain lets up."

"Wait." I gestured for Richard to give me the map. "I know what trail Gus was talking about. It leads to the Windtree Valley Caves." I opened the map and showed it to them. "See." I returned to Alex and Gus and held the map out for Alex, pointing to a particular spot along the trail. "The caves that are located here. They're made up of a series of tunnels, with multiple entrances, right?"

"Yeah."

"And there's a little shack outside one of the entrances?"

"Right. For the park employees. They do tours through the caves a couple of times a month. The booth wouldn't have power, but…" He shot a knowing look up at me. "It should have a radio. I've seen them using it."

"We can call for help and hide out in the caves while we wait." I nodded, calculating how far we'd have to hike.

Alex must've got what I was thinking. "I can make it that far."

"You sure?"

"I'll make it."

"Okay." I looked to the others. "I say we go for it."

"All right." Richard approached Gus. "In the meantime we're holding on to your phone."

"Why?"

"Because you didn't think to tell us about that radio and you must've passed right by the booth outside those caves."

"So you don't trust me because I forgot about a damn radio in the woods?"

"Yep."

Gus scoffed in irritation but then gestured to Luke. "We should check my phone for a signal as we move."

"Sure," Richard answered for Luke. "We can do that for you. You're going to stay in front of me where I can keep an eye on you the whole way."

"Fine. But when we get there, I'm still going for my truck. You're not going to stop me from getting my friend to a hospital."

"There'll be no need. We're going to find that radio and call for help long before you can get to your truck."

With that plan in place, I knelt before Alex again. "You ready?"

"I think so." Despite his words, he seemed unsure.

I gave him a nod of encouragement. "We got this. Together." Gus and I helped Alex stand. "We're going to get you back to your family."

He gripped the hand I had on his arm. "Thank you."

I offered another nod in response, then faced the others. "Richard, you and Gus take turns carrying Alex. Luke, you stay behind Richard so you can be on the lookout for anyone following us. I'll take point."

Luke raised his eyebrows. "Point?" He shot a stunned look to Richard. "Guess we better stop calling him *kid* if he's gonna be this bossy."

Richard laughed. "Maybe." He waited until Gus had Alex lifted in a firefighter's carry, and then Richard tipped his head at me. "Okay, lead the way."

Despite everything, I couldn't help but smile to myself as I got moving in the direction of the caves. I'd always loved that they called me *kid*. Which was funny considering how much I still felt like a kid sometimes. Although when they said it, there was nothing about the gesture that made me feel naive or inexperienced. It was a sign of their affection for me, and it always reminded me of the night we met.

They'd been right when they said I was more of a man than my father ever was. I didn't give up on people. I hadn't given up on Alex, and I wasn't giving up on us—or myself.

Chapter Thirty-Four

When we arrived at the main entrance to Windtree Valley Caves, a curtain of rain pummeled the forest—and us—stronger than ever, demonstrating the true power of nature and making the last steps of our journey a frigid struggle. Thunder continually rolled through the air above. Day had almost turned to night as the sky had grown eerily dark, and the temperature had dropped at least ten degrees.

We checked out the shack first. No radio. Just a battery-powered lantern, first aid kit, and brochures for area attractions similar to what we'd seen at the ranger station. Since no more than two of us would fit in the booth, I grabbed the lantern and we headed inside the main cave to get out of the rain.

A short, narrow passageway led into an open room.

Luke pointed to two other passages at the far end of the cave. "Where do those go?"

"More caves," Gus said. "And exits." He got Alex situated on an outcropping several feet from the main entrance. There Alex could sit off the ground with his back against the cave wall.

Luke shot a quick glance into the other passageways. "Guess that's better than getting trapped in here with only one way out."

"Yeah," I agreed. "I think it's our best option right now."

Richard nodded. "Me too."

Luke began examining Gus's phone. He'd checked for a signal before we'd entered the cave but had no luck. I couldn't imagine he'd get anything within the confines of the rock walls. He gave the phone a closer inspection while Richard remained near the front passageway, standing off to the side, out of sight but close enough to keep watch for anyone approaching.

I wanted to ask Luke what he was doing with Gus's phone. I had a feeling he thought Gus did something to disable the cellular signal in a way not easily detectable, but I didn't ask so as not to alert Gus to anything odd.

Gus dropped to sit beside Alex. "How you feeling?"

"Better."

"Yeah? Because you look like hell, man."

Alex chuckled. "Thanks."

"I want you to stay here and rest with them. I'm going to head to my truck so I can go for help. We gotta get you out of here and get you home." He hesitated before standing up. Alex was staring at the floor of the cave. "Alex?"

He didn't answer Gus. Instead he asked me, "Why did you really come out here?"

"To see if we could find you. Or at least your truck or your backpack. We wanted to locate something that would prove to the sheriff that you didn't leave town. Then he'd have to take another look for you."

Alex searched my face. "Why would you think to do that?"

"Tomas came to our house and asked me for help." Which had me wondering... Why hadn't Tomas gone to Gus? Hadn't he trusted Gus? Was I wrong about the man?

Alex dropped his chin to his chest and breathed a long sigh of relief. "Then Tomas doesn't think I left him?"

"No. He thought you got into an accident out here in the park. He never believed you just left without saying anything. Even though that's what most everyone else believes."

"And my wife?"

Gus answered. "She knows you didn't leave too."

Tears welled in Alex's eyes. Gus laid his hand on Alex's shoulder in a sign of support. Alex nodded and swallowed down the emotion.

Luke had given up on Gus's phone and was helping to keep watch by standing near the back entrances to the cave. "So tell us, Alex, they held you captive all this time?"

At Luke's question, Richard turned to face us, obviously as interested in hearing the answer as the rest of us.

"Yeah," Alex said. "They wanted me to tell them where I'd hidden my phone. A deputy sheriff named Baranski knew I'd made a video of those hikers that he murdered, and he wanted the footage."

Gus's jaw dropped. "Baranski killed someone?"

"Two people. He wanted to know if I'd made a copy of the video, backed it up to the cloud, or sent it to anyone. He came out to the cabin every other day and beat the shit out of me, tortured me, but I wouldn't give him anything. I kept waiting for him to just get it over with and kill me. Or to use my family against me, but he just kept pounding on me. He wasn't giving up until he had my phone. I thought I was going to die in that cabin. After a couple of rounds of him clobbering me, I lost track of time. I was so delirious I thought I kept hearing wolves howling." He let out a bewildered laugh. "I've always loved wolves."

Luke and I exchanged a look. His brows rose.

"What happened before they caught you?" I asked Alex. "What made you follow those college kids?"

"I was out taking pictures one day when I saw them hiking. I'd seen the two of them in the park before, but that time, something about them seemed off, so I followed them, snapping more pictures. Then I got a call about an injured swan, so I had to leave. Later when I went through the pictures I'd taken that day, I spotted them in more of the shots, and I knew something wasn't right with those kids. And it wasn't just them. There were more hikers their age, taking the same paths. It didn't seem like they were out there for the view, more for a specific destination. I started documenting their movements.

"The last day I saw the original couple, I followed them again. Just before they got to the old mill, several others approached them, all rangers and sheriff's deputies, all armed. They led them off the trail into the forest. I followed and started filming. When they got to a cabin I'd never seen before, they made the hikers kneel down. Then Baranski shot each of them in the back of the head." He stopped, the raw emotion of what he'd seen overtaking him.

The heavy rain thudding against the ground outside the cave and the rumbling thunder overhead sounded louder now, despite that we were out of the storm's direct onslaught.

"But I guess you guys saw that last bit on the video." Alex's next words caught in his throat. He had to breathe deep for several seconds before he could continue. "I didn't have time to do anything to stop it. And then I just ran. I headed toward the mill. I hadn't been there in over a year, but I could tell right away that something was different about the place. I waited until the guy on guard left, then went inside and found it loaded with landscaping rocks. I thought it was odd that the park officials would order something like that. I took a closer look and saw that the rocks were fake and stuffed with drugs. I filmed that too. Took some of their cash in case they caught up with me. Figured I'd need a bargaining chip. Then I heard someone coming, so I ran again."

He took another short breather. "They'd seen me filming them, and I thought they'd kill me if they caught up with me." Alex turned to Gus. "Baranski knows I can ID him. At least one other sheriff's deputy and two park rangers are in on it too. I think they're being paid to look the other way and deal with any obstacles that come up."

I nodded. "We saw them on the video. Plus some state police are involved too."

Alex asked, "Where did you hide my phone?"

Richard gave a barely visible shake of his head. He didn't want Gus to know where the phone was.

"It's somewhere safe," I said.

Luke asked, "So what about Sheriff Emerson?"

Alex shook his head. "I know what you guys said, but I don't think he's involved. I never saw him with the others, and all this really doesn't seem like him. But... I guess I don't know for sure."

Luke looked to Richard. "Maybe his deputies lied to him."

"Or maybe not. Maybe he's the one running the whole show."

Gus harrumphed, the incredulous sound echoing off the cave walls. "Emerson's not smart enough for something like this."

Luke gestured to me. "Maybe you were right about Emerson from the beginning."

Was I? So far it seemed like I might be right about trusting Gus. But something in my gut told me I wasn't seeing things as clearly as I should. What was I missing?

Alex shared more of his story. "After I made the video, I headed for my truck. I wanted to get out of the park and get help, but the guys with the guns were everywhere, searching for me, using a drone to track me down. I hid in a cave nearby that night. The next day, I left a note for Gus and took off on foot again. They ambushed me not long after that. I figured I was dead, but Baranski wanted to know what I'd seen and if I'd been recording him as he assumed. I told him about the video on my phone. Thought it might be my only chance to stay alive. The guys running the drugs wanted their money back, but Baranski... he wanted that video. I guess they let him keep me alive and do his thing so long as there was a chance he could get me to tell them where I'd hidden their cash."

Richard said, "It's weird they didn't use your family against you."

Alex nodded, wincing with the move. "I thought the same thing. It's like Baranski figured that was going too far. Or maybe someone threatened him to stay away from them. Maybe it was the sheriff. Maybe he's involved after all. I don't know." He dropped his head forward and pressed the heel of his hand to his forehead.

Gus laid a hand on his back. "You okay?"

"Yeah, just a little dizzy." He sucked in a sharp breath and went on. "When they first had me tied up in the cabin, I could hear the search dogs and a helicopter. I thought if I just held out for a while, someone would find me. But no one came to the cabin."

"Maybe," Richard said, "because the sheriff was the one directing the search." He glanced my way. "Which means we should still try to get in touch with the feds like we planned."

Luke nodded. "We get to where we can get a signal on Gus's phone, and I'll make the call."

"Shh." Richard held up a hand to silence everyone. He listened for a minute, then turned toward the passageway at the front of the cave and scanned the area outside. "Shit." He ducked sideways out of view and then rushed toward me. He grabbed the lantern and clicked it off. "Someone's out there."

Crouching low, Gus moved to the front entrance. "That's them. I see two of them."

Luke made his way to the other passages at the back of the cave. "This way's a no go too. I can hear them coming."

"Luke!" Richard called out. "Get back here."

Luke crossed the cave in the dark and stopped beside me.

"They're armed," Gus said as he got another look out the front of the cave. He faced the rest of us. "There's no way we're getting out of here."

"We have to." I scanned the cave walls, my eyes adjusting to the darkness now that there was only the dim moonlight seeping in from outside. I frantically tried to think of a plan but came up empty.

Shit. What had I done to us?

The moment I made eye contact with Richard, the panic subsided. There was no way this was going to end with their deaths. I wouldn't let that happen. We were going to negotiate. The phone and cash for our release. "We're all getting out of here. Alive."

Gus turned to the opening of the cave once more. "No, Matthew." He spun back around. Despite the low light, there was no missing the handgun he held in his right hand. "You're not going anywhere."

Chapter Thirty-Five

"No." Alex stood, wobbling on unsteady legs. "Not you, Gus." Luke went to his aid and helped Alex sit on the rock again.

Gus glanced their way but kept the gun aimed at me.

"Gus." Richard's voice was filled with barely restrained rage. "You better fucking point that thing somewhere else. Right now. Or I'm going to end you."

"Fine by me." Gus turned the gun on Richard instead. "You will do as I say, and no one will get hurt."

The two men stared each other down.

I couldn't believe this was happening. "I trusted you. *Alex* trusted you. He's your friend."

Gus didn't respond with anything. He just kept his glare—and the gun—aimed at Richard. He'd take the shot if Richard made so much as one wrong move. I couldn't stand seeing Richard in such a vulnerable position, that weapon pointed right at his chest, at his heart. I pictured the scar he had under his shirt. A knife wound from a hateful time before I knew him. He'd survived that.

And he was going to survive this.

I wanted to charge Gus, beat the hell out of him until he dropped the gun and let us all go. Until Richard and Luke were far away from him and safe again.

As if mimicking the mood in the cave, the wind outside kicked up again, creating an eerie whistle as it blew through the cave's opening.

Without taking the gun off Richard, Gus tugged a two-way radio from his jacket pocket. He clicked it on and spoke to whoever was on the other end. "All clear. You can come in now." He slipped the radio back into his pocket. "They just want to talk to you."

Alex shook his head in dismay. "Why would you do this?"

Gus wouldn't acknowledge him. He kept his focus on Richard. He thought he had us all figured out. He thought Richard was the biggest threat to him. I wasn't so sure. Luke had Gus locked in his sights. He was trying to figure out how to get that gun off Richard and get us the hell out of there before whoever was on that radio came barging in. All I could picture was Luke lunging for Gus and getting shot in the process. I could barely breathe through the fear.

Agonizing seconds ticked by as no one made a move. Then came activity at both the front and back of the cave. Baranski, the deputy from the video, barged through the front first, semiautomatic pistol in hand. Another deputy sheriff and two park rangers, including the woman from the video, were at the rear entrances. All had guns drawn, the rangers carrying shotguns. To say the two rangers looked awkward holding deadly weapons would've been an understatement. Maybe we could somehow work that to our advantage.

They, as well as the cops, were soaked and appeared as exhausted as the rest of us.

"Good work," Baranski told Gus. "I didn't think you had it in you. We've been trailing you forever, waiting for you to make a move. The phone and the cash?"

"Not here. They hid them somewhere."

"Hid them? Goddammit. You said you'd take care of this."

"I said I'd try. I warned you it was time to close up shop and get those fucking drugs out of this park, but you wouldn't listen to me."

Baranski scoffed. "That's not the problem. They are. If we don't handle this and get that money back, those men who hired us to ensure shit like this didn't happen are definitely going to make us all pay. With our fucking lives." He charged forward and grabbed Richard's arm. He whirled him around so they were facing the rest of us, the gun jabbed into Richard's side. "Everyone's going to do exactly as I say or he's going to die. Right here."

"No!" I lunged for them. The female ranger turned her weapon on me, and I stopped.

"It's okay, Matthew," Richard said with a quiet calm I had no idea how he was pulling off. "Just do what they say, and everything will be fine."

Baranski signaled to the others. "Secure them."

The ranger removed the pack from her back and got out several zip ties. She and the second deputy sheriff secured our hands behind our backs. Then they did the same to Richard.

Baranski gestured to them again. "You three, search the cave." He motioned Gus's way. "Help me get them outside. They'll tell us where everything is one way or the other."

"And then what? They can ID every one of us."

"I have a way to keep them quiet. I just need that video first."

Gus grabbed Richard by the upper arm and led him outside. Baranski forced the rest of us to follow. Alex stumbled with every other step, but he managed to stay upright. They stopped us thirty feet from the entrance to the cave. We stood there in the pouring rain, waiting for the inevitable, the sky flashing bright with each bolt of lightning, a nearly constant creak coming from the tree limbs overhead.

Baranski made no move to encourage us to talk. The other deputy and the two armed rangers returned.

"The cave's clean," the woman said.

"All right." Baranski gestured to us with his gun. "Everyone, on your knees. It's time for a chat."

Richard and Luke shot each other far more panicked looks than I'd ever seen from either of them. I knew they were desperately trying to figure out if they could overpower our captors. What the hell were we going to do?

Baranski spoke again. "Get down. Now!"

The second deputy charged behind Richard and clocked him on the back of the head. Richard groaned and dropped to his knees in the mud. Luke and I instinctively moved toward him, but we were stopped by the other two goons. They forced the rest of us onto our knees.

"Richard." My voice shook. He had his head hung low, his chin against his chest, but at least he hadn't fallen face-first into the mud.

"I'm okay," he said as he lifted his head. He was clearly not okay, but he was conscious and talking. That was something.

Baranski stepped forward to stand before Alex. In an odd move given the circumstances, he holstered his gun and folded his arms over his chest. "Where's your phone?"

"I don't know."

"Yes, you do. You talk, or these people are going to die. Because of you."

"I don't know where it is."

"All right." Baranski shifted his gaze to the man standing directly behind Luke. "Start killing them. Clean shots to the head. One every five minutes. Eventually one of them will talk."

"Wait!" I shouted. "We hid it, but not here."

"Matthew." Luke spoke my name with deep affection, despite his next words. "They're going to kill us anyway. No matter what we tell them."

Baranski came to me. "Where is it?"

"You won't hurt them?"

"I won't."

"You'll let us go?"

"I will. If I get that phone."

"It's in a cave."

"You'll have to be more specific."

"Hidden Willow Cave, the one under the waterfall near where we found Alex's truck. There's a rock jutting out along the south wall inside the cave. It's tucked in behind there, inside a red backpack. With the money." Of course the phone wasn't there, and I hadn't believed him when he said he wouldn't hurt us, but I was hoping he'd wait to silence us for good until he had that phone. If I could just buy a little time, maybe one or all of us could escape.

He just grinned at me for the longest time. The eerie smile never faded as he took several steps backward, reaching for the gun on his belt. Just as he had it in his hand, a high-pitched howl filled the night air. The ominous sound continued on, morphing into a lower octave. It was the howl of a wolf.

Baranski's eyes widened. "What the fuck is that?"

A second wolf joined the first, then a third, their howls blending into a haunting chorus.

Baranski shook his head. "That can't be."

Although the howls were coming from far off, he backed away from the sound—and us.

Thank God for those wolves.

"I'm so sick of this goddamn fucking park." Baranski looked toward Gus and the two rangers. "I'm getting out of here and going for that cave." He waved the gun our way as he kept moving backward. "Kill them all. Burn and bury the bodies."

I gasped. "No."

"Sir?" That was the female ranger to my left. She didn't sound keen on being the one to murder someone this time.

Baranski shot back with, "The men who hired us want them disposed of. If we don't, they'll take us out—and our families—without a second thought. So you do it, or we're all dead." He spun away and took off, the other deputy trailing along behind him.

The two armed park rangers reluctantly got into position behind us. Apparently, it was either them or us.

We fought our restraints. Richard tried to stand, but he was far too unsteady after the blow to his head. Luke managed to get to his feet. The ranger behind him struck him on the back of the head with the butt of his weapon and then shoved Luke back down to his knees. The blow hadn't knocked him out, but it kept him on the ground.

"Don't do this, Gus," Alex begged.

Gus hadn't moved from where he stood before us.

"Please. I'm the one who found the heroin, who made the video and took the money. Just let them go, and they won't say anything. They'll keep quiet if you let them go."

"We will," I said. "I promise, we will."

Gus held up a hand, signaling to the other park rangers to hold on. He kept his gaze locked on Alex but spoke to the rangers. "Why don't you two take off?" He tipped the barrel of his gun at us. "I've got this. No sense all of us getting our hands dirty."

The other rangers were quick to lower their weapons and move several feet away from us so they were standing off to the side, but they also seemed reluctant to go far without completing the task they were ordered to do.

Gus looked just as hesitant. Or furious. I wasn't sure which. He stalked several feet away, then turned to face Richard. He raised his gun and aimed it at him.

Luke and I shouted, "No!"

He fired.

There was no slow motion like in the movies. Everything happened fast. Too fast.

The gun went off, and Richard flung backward, landing with a thud on the ground, his head smacking into a puddle of mud, thick black water splashing up all around him.

"Richard..." I scrambled forward, trying to get to my feet with my arms secured behind my back. I slipped in the mud and fell to my knees again. Gus barreled forward, grabbed me by the back of my shirt collar, and tugged me backward, slamming me onto my side.

Luke got to his feet again and charged for Gus. "I'm going to fucking kill you!" One of the others lurched forward and tackled him to the ground. He secured Luke and zip-tied his ankles together.

Everything slowed down then. The sound of the rain, the wind on my face, my own heartbeat. I waited for Richard to move. To see some sign of life. To see his chest rise and fall and know he was still breathing, but there was nothing from him.

Nothing.

Gus grasped my arm and yanked me up to a kneeling position again. He held the gun to my temple. I didn't care. I couldn't tear my focus away from Richard, one very still, lifeless Richard.

This was all my fault.

I made him come out here. I made him stay after we knew the situation was dangerous. And now...

I couldn't breathe. Couldn't move.

No. This wasn't happening.

He was fine. This was all a dream.

Another nightmare.

It had to be. We couldn't lose him.

We were three. Always three.

Three men. Three lovers. Three partners. Always.

Forever.

How long was forever?

I thought it would be so much longer.

How naive. Foolish.

No. This was just a dream. A goddamn nightmare.

Only...

Cold, stinging drops of rain pummeled my skin. The trees kept creaking in the wind. Another howl from a wolf filled the air.

This was no dream.

Luke had stopped struggling as soon as the gun was at my head. "Don't. God, please don't. Not both of them. Please."

Without taking his eyes off Luke, Gus ignored his pleas and spoke to the rangers. "You guys get going. Help Baranski find that phone and the money before someone else does, or else we're all fucked."

The rangers, who now seemed eager to get the hell out of there, took off.

Luke pled more. "I can pay you. My family's rich. I can get you a shit ton of money, more than those drug dealers are giving you. Just let him go, and I'll get you whatever you want. Please, God, just let him go."

"I don't want any more money." Gus threw an irate look toward where the other rangers had left, but they were long gone. He raised the gun.

Not at me. Not at Luke. He pointed it at the sky and squeezed off three shots. Without another word, he let go of me and went to Richard. He knelt beside him. "You okay?"

Richard's eyes sprang open. He started to sit up, a difficult move with his hands bound behind him. Gus helped him up.

There was no blood. No bullet hole visible anywhere. He was breathing normally. He was alive.

He met my gaze. "I'm okay." Then he did the same to Luke. "I'm not shot. I'm okay."

My head swam with relief. "You're not shot?"

"No."

"You're not dead?"

He gave me an affectionate grin. "I'm not dead. I'm okay."

Gus pulled out a pocketknife and cut the zip ties from Richard's wrists as he told him, "I was hoping like hell you could read that look I gave you." As soon as Richard was on his feet, Gus went to Alex and untied him. Then he moved on to Luke.

Richard spoke to Gus but walked straight for me. "When you winked at me, I figured you had something planned. I fell back out of shock more than anything, but I stayed down and tried to play dead, hoping you knew what the hell you were doing." He helped me to my feet. "You almost blew it when I heard you had the gun on Matthew."

"Good thing my fellow rangers aren't that versed in seeing someone take a bullet, or they might not have bought our act. They might've seen that shot hit the ground behind you."

The minute Gus had Luke free of his restraints, Luke jumped up and lunged for Richard. "You asshole." He tackled the larger man to the ground and straddled him, slapping at his chest over and over again. "Don't ever scare the crap out of me like that again. I thought you were fucking dead."

Richard reached up and grabbed Luke by the wrists, putting a halt to his flailing. He pulled him down so their lips were almost touching. "I promise. No more scaring you."

Gus cut the ties from my wrists, but I couldn't move, couldn't take my eyes off Luke and Richard where they lay together on the wet ground. "You're not dead?"

Richard got up, helping Luke off the ground at the same time. Then Richard came to me. He cupped his hands over my cheeks. "I'm right here. Everything's okay. We're all okay. Just take a deep breath."

I tried, but I couldn't stop the rapid pants pouring out of my chest.

"It's okay, Matthew." He lowered his forehead to mine. "Just breathe with me."

"You're not dead?"

"I'm fine. We're all fine."

"Okay." I sucked in more air. "I'm so sorry."

"Stop. You didn't do anything wrong."

"He's right." Luke stood at my side. Richard grabbed him by the back of the neck and tugged him close so all three of us had our heads together. We stayed like that for several breaths, until Gus spoke.

"Sorry to break up the party, but we gotta get out of here." He had returned to Alex and was assisting him off the ground.

Alex shoved at Gus. "Get the fuck away from me." With that move, Alex lost his footing and almost ended up on the ground again.

Luke went to him and helped steady him. "You better start explaining yourself, Gus."

"We don't have time for this."

Alex glared at his friend. "They think you just fucking shot us to death. We can take a minute. Talk."

"I've been working for them for months."

"Why?"

"They came to me and offered a boatload of cash if I just looked the other way and helped to steer people clear of their operation."

"Why would you agree to do that?"

"I didn't think anyone would get hurt, and I needed the money. I went way over budget on the new house, and I was scared we'd lose it. But the minute those hikers disappeared, I knew what had happened, and I was done with it. I wanted nothing to do with hurting anyone, shooting at people, killing people. Then when you disappeared, I just wanted to find you. I knew they'd built a cabin out here, but I had no idea where it was. I'd never seen it."

Richard snorted. "It was near the mill."

"I didn't know that."

"Sure. If you really care about your friend, then what was today all about?"

"I played along so I could save him, save all of you. I had no other choice."

"Why didn't you tell us all this when you first met up with us the other day?"

"I was hoping you three would search for a bit, then give up and go home. I didn't want you out here in the park. I knew you'd be in danger, but I couldn't tell you the whole story."

Alex scoffed. "But you should've told me after you found us today."

"I wanted to, but I needed you to trust me. Otherwise I was afraid you'd turn me away, and I had to come with you. I knew that if you got into trouble, I was the only one who could get you out of it. I was going to get you back to your family, no matter what." Gus's posture sagged as if everything he'd done was just sinking in. "Not long after you first went missing, Baranski made it sound like they'd already killed you. I tried to get back into the organization, get deeper inside, so I could find out what happened to you, find out if they really had killed you, who did it, and where they left your body." He stopped as if he needed a moment to let the emotion pass. "I swear, when I started this whole thing, I never thought they'd hurt anyone."

Alex didn't say anything. It was clear on his face that the sting of betrayal battled with the relief that we were all still alive.

I was right there with him.

Richard took my hand in his and led us toward Gus and Alex. "We need to go."

"Yeah," Luke said. "Let's get the hell out of this park. Because I've decided... I really fucking hate camping."

Gus gestured into the woods. "This way. My truck's pretty well hidden so it should be safe." He asked Alex, "Can you make it?"

I moved to Alex's side, looped his arm over my shoulders, and held some of his weight. "He'll make it."

Alex gave me a warm smile. "Thanks to you."

Chapter Thirty-Six

I exited the hospital room and walked down the nearly empty corridor in a daze. So much had happened. So much to process. I stopped and glanced back through the open doorway.

Tomas stood beside Alex's bed, talking a mile a minute to his dad, the smiles never fading from their faces. Natalie was there too, sitting in a wheelchair beside the bed as she listened to her son and husband. She held their new baby, Ayda, in her arms. She'd given birth a few hours after Alex had first gotten to the hospital the night before. A nurse had helped him make it from his room to the maternity ward, where he'd gotten to witness his daughter's birth.

I couldn't help but smile as I took in the sight of the reunited family.

Although I knew Alex was still distraught over one thing: the arrest of his friend.

In all likelihood, Gus was going to be charged with aiding in the trafficking of heroin, but his testimony would help reduce his sentence.

Back in the park, after we'd gotten to the truck, Gus had driven us straight to the closest FBI field office. There, he had confessed everything and also named the others who were involved. Federal DEA agents had raided the old mill. They found Baranski and the others trying to move the evidence out. The feds seized the heroin and distribution paraphernalia, as well as a slew of rifles, handguns, and bags of cash. Baranski, along with several sheriff's deputies, park rangers, state police, and members of the drug trafficking ring, had been arrested. More than a dozen people in total.

Baranski was also charged in the murder of the two college kids. He'd confessed that he'd shot them as he'd been ordered to do once they said they were done helping transport the drugs out of the park.

Sheriff Pat Emerson hadn't been involved in any of it. He'd been lied to and manipulated by his own deputies and was cooperating fully with the investigation into his department's corruption.

"Hey." That was Richard's voice.

He and Luke were approaching down the hall. I went to them and wrapped my arms around Richard's waist. Laying my head against his chest, I listened to the beautiful, steady beat of his heart.

"You okay?" he asked.

"Yeah."

He propped his chin on the top of my head. "You did a good thing here, Matthew."

Luke ran a hand down my back. "Yeah, you did."

Without letting go of Richard, I wrapped an arm around Luke and drew him close. "It wasn't just me. We all did it."

Luke hugged me in return, and Richard tightened his hold, his arms around both of us now.

I relaxed into their embrace.

"Excuse me."

I let go of them and turned to find Tomas grinning at us.

"You guys are so cute together."

I laughed. "Thanks." I stepped toward him. "Is everything okay?"

"Yeah. It's awesome. I just... I wanted to say thanks for believing me about my dad."

"You're welcome."

He hesitated, then forged on. "I'll never forget what you all did."

"It was totally worth it. Your dad's a great guy."

"He is." Tomas looked me in the eye. "You are too."

"Thanks. That means a lot."

He gave a sheepish nod, then motioned behind him toward his dad's hospital room. "I better get back. I'll see you next week?"

"You bet."

"Okay." Tomas waved goodbye and headed back down the hall.

When he was gone, Luke asked, "What's next week?"

"Alex still wants me to work at the center." I paused, unsure what they'd think or say about that after everything that had happened to us in the park. But I knew what I had to do. "I'm going to take the job."

Richard smiled at me. "Yeah, you are."

"You're okay with this?"

"Now that those piece of shit, nut-job, gun-toting crooked cops and park rangers are gone? Yeah. I think you'll do great things there."

A dopey grin spread across my face. They smiled back at me just as wide.

"One of the first things Alex wants us to do is to track that pack of gray wolves that have apparently moved into the park."

Richard's eyes narrowed in concern. Not for me this time. "What'll happen to them?"

"Since it's odd for them to be in this part of the country, they might attract a lot of attention, too much attention from people like trophy hunters, especially if the wolves wander outside the park. So Alex said he'll push to get them relocated to protected land farther north or out west."

"Good." Richard nodded. "I'm glad. If it weren't for them, Baranski would've shot us himself. The sound of those wolves scared the shit out of him. He just wanted to get the hell out of the park after that."

Luke huffed out a laugh. "I think wolves just became my favorite animal."

I laughed with him. "Mine too."

Richard studied me. "You know what you're going to need now, don't you?"

"All I need is the two of you."

He pressed a sweet kiss on my lips. "But you're also going to need a car for work." He paused, examining me again. "Are you going to let me buy you one?"

I thought that over. "Yeah, I am."

His eyes widened in surprise. Luke's did too. I got why. I'd been so reluctant at first to accept Richard's help with my tuition.

"I really want to work at Windtree, and there's no way for me to get there. No bus route that goes anywhere close to the park. I can't take a cab or borrow your car all the time. I need my own car, but even with what I'll be earning, it'll take me months to save up enough for something reliable."

He smiled at me, looking utterly pleased.

"So," Luke said, "tomorrow we're going car shopping?"

"Yeah," I said. "I guess so."

Richard tugged me into his arms again. "Thank you."

I snorted out a laugh. "You've got that backward. Thank you for helping me make this possible."

"You're more than welcome."

"Come on, you two." Luke gestured toward the exit door. "Let's go home."

Chapter Thirty-Seven

Outside the hospital, Richard slid into the driver's seat of his car but didn't start the engine right away. I got in the middle of the back, and Luke took the front passenger seat. None of us moved a muscle or said a word. We all just sat there, staring off into space. We were only a few minutes from our house, but driving even that far seemed like too much to contemplate.

When we'd gotten home from the hospital the night before, all we'd managed to accomplish was showering and then crashing in bed for twelve hours. Yet we were still exhausted, emotionally spent after the ordeal we'd been through.

Only for me, it was even more than that.

"You could've died."

Richard eyed me in the rearview mirror. "I didn't."

"You don't blame me for making us stay? For trying to find that cabin? I feel like it was all my—"

With sudden urgency, Richard cranked open the driver's side door and got out. I gaped after him. Where was he going? Luke seemed just as shocked that Richard had left while I was right in the middle of a sentence.

Then Richard opened the back door of the car and slipped in beside me. "I don't blame you at all. I want the truth from you, more than anything. You gave us your truth out there in the park. More than I think you ever have. I will never regret that. Or regret that we helped save a man's life."

"But you said on the big decisions that we all need to agree. I didn't really listen to you out there. I was determined and reckless. I kept pushing and taking chances."

"You took chances because you wanted to find Alex. It's not a bad thing to take a chance—even one that could possibly hurt you—when you've got a good enough reason."

With his overprotective streak, I knew how hard that was for him to admit. I wrapped my arms around him. I could barely form more than a whisper. "Thank you." He held me in return, until I pulled back to ask Luke, "What about you? You had a feeling something bad was going to happen."

He shook his head. "I have that feeling a lot. It's a remnant of having a creepy-ass stalker criminal for a dad." He laughed.

Richard and I joined him, and the relief rushed through me with such intensity I actually felt dizzy for a moment. For the first time in days, the anxiety and fear started to drain away.

Luke gestured to Richard. "The big guy hit the nail on the head. I'll always be glad for everything that happened at Majestic Falls. I think it was an important trip for you, in a lot of ways, and it reminded me not to take anything—especially the two of you—for granted."

"Same here." Richard studied me, a grin on his lips.

"What?" I asked.

"You were right about the sheriff. And Gus."

"No, I wasn't! I should've listened to you guys about Gus. You knew we couldn't trust him."

"That's the thing. No matter what he'd done before we met him, you were right to believe we could trust him right then. You saw how much he cared about Alex. He saved our lives. If he hadn't been there, I don't think we would've made it out of that park."

"I hadn't thought of it that way."

He laid his hand against my cheek and ran his thumb over my skin. "You have good instincts, Matthew. You need to trust those."

"Yeah, I think maybe I finally can now."

"You also need to stop striving for perfection."

Luke snorted out a laugh.

I did too.

"Yeah, I get it," Richard said. "Pretty funny coming from me. But I've learned a lot in the last year. It's okay to make mistakes. It's okay to want things that turn out not to be the right move for you and then change your mind about them later. It's okay to do and say things that turn out to be the wrong call, to even trust the wrong person sometimes. We all do that. The important lesson is to forgive yourself and focus on what's right for you in that moment."

I searched his bright green eyes. How did I get so lucky to have him—both of them—in my life? "You're pretty smart. Where did you learn all that?"

"From you."

"Me?"

Luke laughed again, nodding his agreement.

Richard caressed my cheek once more. "You are such a good person, Matthew. I think lately you've just needed reminding of what you already know, deep down. It's time to let some things go and move on."

He was right. "I don't know what I'd do without you guys."

"Good thing you never have to find out." Richard leaned in and planted a kiss on my cheek. I turned into it, not wanting him to go, desperately wanting to be close to him right then, both of them, wanting to kiss them, touch them, love them, feel how alive we all were.

From the first second our lips met, there was a new vulnerability and intensity to his kiss. He parted his lips and dragged me closer, plastering our bodies together, deepening the kiss with every second.

Luke was right. I'd never take this for granted.

Ever.

Then Richard gripped me by my hips and tugged me forward, laying me out on the backseat and going down with me, never breaking the enticingly sexy press of our lips.

The feel of his hard body over mine and the wet slide of our tongues had desire blazing through me. I spread my legs, and he settled his hips in between them, kissing me harder, more passionately. I stroked him everywhere I could reach, and he rocked against me, unabashedly moving with an erotic rhythm that already had me on edge.

I basked in how very alive he felt in my arms. How very alive I felt.

Lifting my knees higher, I wrapped my legs around him, and he surged forward, pressing his groin against my ass, humping me like there were no clothes in the way and he was already inside me.

I threw my head back as he kissed a path down the side of my throat. The words surged out of me. "God, I want you. Never wanted you more. Now! Please!"

Richard shot a look over his shoulder at Luke. "Get us the hell home."

Luke laughed as he slid into the driver's seat and started the car.

Richard rolled us around until he sat with his back to the seat and I was straddling his lap. "You need to put your seat belt on."

"Yeah. You too."

He didn't. He dived in for another kiss. I held his face and kissed him in return with as much fervor, grinding my body against his. I wanted him so much. He still hadn't fucked me yet, and I desperately needed to feel him pounding into me, taking my ass over and over again, to feel that primal urge from him, that loss of control.

When we parted, we were both panting, desperate.

He shook his head. "Shit. I don't want to stop."

"Me either."

"Get your fucking seat belts on," Luke called out from the front seat. "In case you haven't noticed, I'm already driving and about to pull onto the freeway."

Richard laid his forehead against mine and blew out a long huff of air. "Okay." He helped me move off him and deposited me on the seat beside him. He reached across me for the seat belt and tugged it over my body, avoiding making eye contact or even looking at my face.

Once he had me buckled in, he got his seat belt on in the center of the backseat. The stare he shot my way was intense, those green eyes smoldering with heat. He laid a hand on my left knee. He slowly ran that hand up the inside of my leg, his fingertips lightly, teasingly grazing my thigh. He stopped before he reached my dick. "You're going to feel my hands all over you soon."

I nodded.

"Luke too." He inched his hand up higher, his fingers brushing my cock as he headed for the top of my jeans. He popped open the button on my pants and slid the zipper down. "You want me?"

"Yes!"

"You want Luke?"

"Yes!"

Luke glanced back at us. "Ten more minutes."

I shook my head. "I don't want to wait. Luke, come back here."

Luke choked out another laugh. "This car's not automated. Someone's gotta drive it."

Richard leaned into me and took my earlobe between his lips as he pushed my seat belt as far out of his way as it could go. "We have to wait. Can't fuck in a moving car. Gotta be safe." He slipped his hand inside my underwear and rubbed my cock. Then he freed the top of my erection from the fabric and ran the pad of his thumb over and around the head, focusing on the ridge at the base of the crown.

My breath came in heavy pants. I squeezed my eyes shut and grasped his forearm, needing to feel more of him in any way I could.

He stilled at my touch. "You want me to stop?"

I threw my eyes open. I expected to see that look of concern he'd sported so often lately. There was nothing like that on his face. He had a teasing look in his eyes as he waited. He wanted to hear me beg.

"Please don't stop. Ever. I need you. And Luke. Touching me. Fucking me. Loving me." I whimpered. "Please."

Richard drew his hand away and licked the length of his palm. He grasped my cock again, and I cried out in relief.

"Shit, you two," Luke said. "You gotta stop this, or I'm gonna have to pull over and jerk off right on the side of the goddamn road."

"Sure. Whatever you say, Luke." Richard massaged the top of my erection, mercilessly, relentlessly, stroking my length as much as possible with my pants and underwear in the way. I moaned, and a quick grin hit his lips, as if getting me to make that noise had been his intent.

He leaned in so our lips were almost touching. "Damn, that is a beautiful sound." He rubbed the head of my cock with more vigor, his harsh breaths spilling out over his parted lips onto mine. "I want to swallow you down and let you fuck my mouth until you scream out my name."

"Jesus," Luke hissed. "Driving as fast as I can here."

I threw my head back and arched up into the touch. The seat belt dug into me, but I didn't care. "Please, Richard. Need you. And Luke. So much. Never needed you two more."

He nodded. "Same here." He kissed me, hard and fast, dominating the kiss at first and then letting me do the same in return. He spoke against my lips. "I want to pull you on top of me and let you ride me until I come."

"Yes. God, yes!"

"Then I want to jerk you off while I'm buried in your ass, my cum held inside you." He stroked me faster.

I moaned an uncontrollably loud sound right as the passenger door beside me swung open. I hadn't even felt the car stop.

Luke crouched beside the open door. He clasped my face in his hands and turned me his way. He kissed me, the touch warm and wet and ravenous all at once. I felt Richard's hands on me as he removed the seat belt and did up my pants.

When Luke and I parted, he exhaled a long breath. "God, I love you."

Richard shot out of the car on the other side. He rounded the front end. Grasping Luke by the arm, he yanked him up and shoved him against the side of the car. The move wasn't out of anger. He smirked at him the same way he'd done to me. "Look who can't stop telling us how they feel."

"You've got me all flustered. That was a hell of a show."

"You were supposed to be paying attention to the road."

Luke snorted. "Then don't distract me."

"We saved the best part for the bedroom. You're going to get an amazing show once we're inside."

"I'm counting on it."

Richard hesitated. His voice turned far more serious. "You should've told me weeks ago how you were feeling about being with him. *Months* ago."

"I know. I was hoping it would fade on its own."

"Has it gone away?"

"Yeah. For you?"

I tried to hold still, to wait for Richard's answer, especially after the horrible way I'd talked to him in the park, but I couldn't take waiting another second. I tore out of the car and slipped in between them. I flung my arms around Richard's waist and pressed my cheek to his chest. "I won't ever let you think I want something that I don't, not ever again. I promise. I'll always tell you both the truth. Always."

Richard held me. "I know." He dipped his head down so I'd look up at him. "I know." Then he yanked me off my feet, planting one hell of a kiss on me as he pushed me backward into Luke and settled his weight against me until all I could feel was them, the two of them surrounding me, holding me up.

Luke laughed. "Come on. Let's move this inside." He slid out from behind me and shut the car door. He tugged on my arm as soon as Richard set me down, and then grasped Richard's arm too, turning us toward the house. "I'm so not spending the night in jail because you two couldn't wait two more minutes to fuck."

Once we were inside the house and had the door closed behind us, Luke backed me against the hall wall and kissed me, continuing right where Richard had left off beside the car. Richard moved in and pressed his groin against Luke's ass, pinning Luke between us.

Just like our first kiss the night we moved in together, standing in that exact same spot.

As if Richard had no desire or capacity to wait, he turned Luke's head his way the moment our lips parted. Then he kissed him, a passionate, erotic openmouthed swipe of lips and tongues.

Luke abruptly pulled back. "I swear if you ever fake die again..." He glared at Richard.

"I won't."

"And you better not even think about really—" His breath hitched.

"Hey." Richard came around so they were eye to eye. He cupped a hand at the back of Luke's head. "I won't. Not for a very, very long time."

"Good. Because you promised me." Luke's voice faltered on his last word. He swallowed hard. When the emotion seemed to have passed, he offered a cocky grin. "Sex and lube at eighty."

Richard's eyes brightened as he smiled back at Luke. "You got it." Then he threw the same look to me. "Come with me." He took my hand, then Luke's, and led us toward the staircase.

Despite that action, Richard halted at the base of the stairs. We all stood there facing one another. None of us made a move to get back to where we'd been headed, and I wasn't sure why. Was Richard nervous? Was I? Was there anything I had left to be anxious about?

Of course there was. The box I'd hidden away in our bathroom upstairs. I still hadn't told them about it.

But I couldn't think about that right then.

I tugged on their hands and repeated Richard's words. "Come with me." I skipped heading upstairs and instead led them through the kitchen and down the back stairs to the basement. Neither man protested.

I opened the door to our playroom, and they followed me in. At the cabinet in the corner, I grabbed a bottle of lube and set it on the nightstand. "On the bed, Luke. Richard, get naked."

They just stood there watching me for a shocked moment. Then Luke scrambled for the bed, tugging the blankets off and tossing them aside so all that was left was the fitted sheet. He lay on his back in the center of the mattress. I sat beside him on the edge of the bed. "Give us a good show, Richard."

He snorted out a laugh. "You're driving me crazy here, kid."

Luke held a finger to his lips. "Shh. Don't talk. You're supposed to be getting naked." He looked to me. "He doesn't listen very well."

Richard tipped his head back, and a deeper laugh bellowed out of him. When he shot another look our way, it was smoldering, penetrating, all the humor gone from his eyes, replaced with complete desire. He reached for the hem of his T-shirt and pulled it over his head, flexing every muscle in his arms with the move. He tossed the shirt aside and then purposely made his pecs jump. Luke and I let out simultaneous sighs of appreciation.

Richard ditched his pants and underwear next, and then he stood before us in all his tanned, toned, muscular glory.

"Now," I told him, "get Luke naked."

Richard stepped forward, and I held up a hand to stop him.

"But you can't use your hands."

His eyebrows rose. "You want me to use my teeth?"

I shook my head. "You can't touch him in any way. You can only use your words. And don't just get him naked. Get him hard and wanting, begging us for more."

He cracked a smile. "Perfect." He refocused on Luke but remained standing where he was, sporting a burning stare that spoke volumes about what he wanted to see from Luke. "Snake a hand up under your shirt."

Luke sucked in a ragged breath but then did as instructed.

"Run the tips of your fingers over your nipple."

Speechless at the sight before me, I nodded. It was a genius idea. Luke loved having his nipples played with. Seeing him do it himself was epic.

Luke slid his right hand toward the nipple on his left side. He gasped as his fingers made contact.

"Pinch it."

The moment Luke's fingers squeezed his flesh, he arched up and groaned.

"More. Don't stop."

Luke kept toying with his chest, writhing under his own ministrations. It was a stunning sight, seeing him fully clothed, one hand under his shirt, his body on fire, alive with explosive need and lust.

"Stop," Richard demanded. "Lie still."

Luke whimpered but did as he was told.

"Take your shirt off."

Luke stripped the T-shirt off and flung it onto the floor.

"Undo the top button on your jeans."

Once he had that done, Luke slid his hand lower to cup his own cock through his pants.

"Don't." Richard's voice had dropped lower. "The next person who touches you there will not be you."

Luke let go of himself, took several deep breaths, then nodded.

"Take off your jeans and underwear. But don't touch your cock or balls."

Luke sat up and carefully shed the rest of his clothes. He lay back down. I couldn't take my eyes off the two of them. They were amazing together. Even with the physical distance between them, they were so very together in that moment. Both had gone from half-hard to fully erect from the simple exchange of words, Luke touching only himself.

As if he heard my thoughts, Luke rolled his head my way. "Please. Come here. Touch me."

"No." Richard shook his head. "Not yet."

"Then let me touch Matthew. Let me suck him off. Something. Anything." As if Luke had no control over his actions, he reached for his dick again. He gave a long stroke. The flesh at the tip peeking out through his closed fist was flushed and stretched taut. Instinctively my mouth fell open. I licked my bottom lip, wanting to taste him so badly.

Richard looked to me where I sat on the edge of the bed. "Didn't I tell him he's not supposed to be touching himself there?"

I laughed.

Richard grinned at my giggle. "What do you think, Matthew? Should we let him keep going?"

"Maybe."

Richard watched Luke again. "It is pretty damn hot how turned on he is."

"Just from you telling him what to do."

"Uh-huh. Hands above your head, Luke. Grab the headboard." To me he said, "You know what gets him even hotter?"

"Maybe." I stood and crooked a finger at Richard. "Come here."

He rounded the bed to stand before me.

I gestured that he should come even closer so Luke wouldn't hear. "Tell me."

He leaned in and whispered, describing exactly what I'd thought.

"He does like that, doesn't he?"

"Oh yeah," he said. "It drives him insane. Every. Single. Time. And I love watching it."

"Take a step back." I wanted him to have a better view of the bed. "Stay right there." I slipped off my jeans and shirt, then my underwear and socks. I got on the bed facing Luke and slid a leg over to straddle him, positioned just as Richard had described.

Luke shifted his hips, seeking out friction with my body, all the while keeping his hands clasped around the slats on the headboard. I laughed and bent over him so our lips were only a couple of inches apart. "You want me?"

"God, yes."

"Do you want me to kiss you?"

"Yes." The word was nearly swallowed up by his whimper. "I fucking love your kisses."

I offered him my lips, erotically rocking my hips over him, shamelessly rubbing my body along his. I loved the scent of him, the hard, eager feel of his body under mine.

The kissing, the frottage, it was driving Luke absolutely crazy, just as Richard had said.

But it wasn't only that physical connection that was getting to Luke. When our lips parted, his blue eyes were locked on mine, telling me so much without words. This moment was meaningful for him in a way that had nothing to do with sex.

He looked... almost scared. Vulnerable like I'd never seen him.

I halted my movements. "Luke, it's okay. We're all still here. Together."

"I know." He let go of the headboard and ran his palm along my cheek. His hand shook as he swiped his thumb over my lower lip. He leaned in for a soft kiss. "I know. I've just waited so long for this, for us. I don't want to lose it."

"You won't. Ever."

Another kiss, and I could feel the unease slip away. He grasped the headboard again as if he could no longer deny Richard what he'd asked of him.

Richard's breathing had sped up a notch as he'd watched us from beside the bed. I wasn't sure if it was the sexual contact between Luke and me or the tender exchange that had gotten to him.

No, I knew which it was.

I sat up and turned toward him. "Come here."

I didn't have to tell him twice. He dived for the bed and knelt beside us. "You two are incredible together." He ran a hand across Luke's bare chest. Then he bent down and gave a soft swipe of his lips over Luke's.

Luke lifted his head and deepened the kiss, his body shifting beneath mine as his arousal kicked up even higher. Both of us touching him at once always did that for him.

When Richard ended the kiss, Luke's knuckles lost color as he gripped the headboard tighter. "When the hell are you going to fuck him?"

"Oh, Luke, no matter what's been going on here, you and I aren't the ones leading this show. Matthew is." He met my stare.

I reached out for him, needing to feel his lips on mine, his bare body pressed against me.

The searing kiss was explosive, sending a rolling need surging throughout me. As if Luke knew what else I needed, he let go of the headboard, and then his hands were all over me, over Richard too. It was like he couldn't merely watch the way he sometimes did. He had to be a part of it.

With every second, Richard's kisses became more forceful, deeper, harder, his body more on fire against mine. In one swift move, he pushed me down onto the bed on Luke's other side. He straddled me, then reached back across Luke, trying to grasp for something. He fumbled around for several more seconds but couldn't find what he wanted. "Shit."

Luke got in on the act, seeming as frantic and uncoordinated as Richard. He finally seized the bottle of lube and held it up. "Here." He tossed it to Richard.

"Thank God." Richard snatched the bottle. He shifted back and off my legs. "Spread your thighs."

I opened myself up for him. In every way. He bent forward and took me into his mouth, kissing and licking along the length of my shaft, stroking me with his wet, warm tongue as he slid his lubricated fingers along the crack of my ass, dipping them inside me when he finally reached the spot where I ached for him to be.

He teased and stroked, went slow, then sped up, caressing my cock with his mouth, fucking me with two fingers, driving me insane.

He hadn't done anything like this since the night I'd flinched from him.

I threw my head back and moaned, my feet restlessly shifting on the sheet.

Luke chuckled as he came forward and kissed me. "You're gorgeous, Matthew."

Richard sat up and gave me one final, deep stroke with his fingers, then tugged them free. He dropped down to his back beside me and pulled me onto him. I sat up, positioning myself over his hard shaft as he held his cock up for me. He ran it back and forth so the tip repeatedly brushed against my asshole. "You ready for me?"

"Always."

He pressed the head of his dick against me. The touch sent white-hot explosions pulsating throughout me, a burning need racing through me, igniting that primal part of me that craved more. I shifted my body, and the tip of his cock slipped inside. He groaned, loud and long, holding me still with a fierce grasp on my hip.

I didn't let him get used to the sensation, I slid my body down farther onto his length, his full, thick shaft spreading me open, filling me completely.

Nothing—*nothing*—in the world felt like that.

"Fuck." His body trembled beneath mine.

I wanted him to move, needed him to take me with everything he was.

I braced my hands on each side of the bed beside his head. "Do it." I practically growled the words.

His eyes narrowed, and in a single sharp move, he flipped us around so we were closer to Luke again and I was on my back, my legs splayed over his muscular thighs, his body draped over mine, his cock still buried inside me. He didn't delay. He slammed into me, fucking me with unbelievably swift jabs that stroked my ass in the most intense, mind-blowing way.

This wasn't gentle lovemaking. This was a carnal need we'd waited too long for.

The slap of our bodies, the grunts he let out with each jerk of his hips, the firm muscles of his arms jumping with his every move as he held himself over me—it was all exactly what I needed from him.

His thrusts grew wild, wanton. He had to be close. He shifted back for a new angle, his hands on my hips, slanting my ass just right, my legs over his shoulders now as he plowed into me again and again. "Luke. Now."

"Yeah," Luke groaned out. He got on his knees, moving into position so he could reach around my leg. He took my shaft in hand and slid his lips over my erection.

The wet heat, that perfect pressure of his mouth engulfed me.

Their rhythm of push and pull, suck and thrust was intoxicating. I was flying high, an almost unbearable release building inside me.

I threw my head back and arched up under them. "Oh God. Oh God."

Richard plunged into me over and over again, and Luke swallowed me down, his hot mouth giving me no respite. I was gone. To that single-minded place where my orgasm was close, so very close, and I was chasing it down like a sprinter out of the blocks on the last leg of a race.

Luke picked up the pace on my dick, bobbing his head with more vigor, sucking on my shaft like he had to get me to come or he'd lose me forever.

Richard's thrusts became erratic. He gripped me tighter and groaned, the sound raw and desperate.

That almost sent me over the edge. My entire body tensed.

"No." Richard stopped. Everything stopped. He shook his head. "Not yet. I want you still hard when I come in your ass."

"Oh God." That was from Luke. He'd pulled off me at Richard's words. He rolled onto his back beside me and stroked himself as he watched us again.

Richard hooked his hands under my knees and raised my legs higher as he dropped down to lie over me, my knees nearly at my shoulders. It felt amazing to be in that position again, to feel the strength and power of his body over mine, to feel him so close to losing it inside me.

He circled his hips, grinding our bodies together in a deliberate move that had my every nerve ending on fire. Then he kissed me, a delectable wet swipe of lips and tongue. "Shit, I could stay buried inside you forever."

I nearly came from that declaration alone.

He reached for my hands where they were fisting the sheet beside us. Lifting my arms over my head, he wrapped my hands around the slats on the headboard. "Hang on. It's gonna get wild."

"Oh God." I grasped the headboard, and he lifted up, my legs lowering some with the move.

"Luke. Feed him your cock."

I nodded emphatically. Both of them filling me? "Yes!"

Luke sat up and moved in close. The skin covering his cock was even more taut and flushed than earlier. He was ready to burst. Holding it out to me, he slid the sleek head between my lips, and I sucked him in without delay, stroking him with my tongue. He leaned over me, and I took him deeper and deeper, letting him fuck my mouth as Richard drove into my ass again and again, even harder, faster than before.

It was electric, unrelenting.

Beautiful.

I squeezed my ass around Richard and tightened my mouth around Luke.

"Oh shit." Richard jerked forward. "I'm close. So close."

Luke withdrew from my mouth and gave Richard more room. But instead of going to town on me, Richard pulled out, his chest heaving. He caught his breath, then said, "There's something else you want."

"Me?"

"Yeah."

What was he talking about? I breathed deep and let my eyes fall shut, and then I knew. I opened my eyes and nodded. He shifted farther back to give me room. I flipped over and sat on my heels, my back to him. "Luke, slide over."

Luke's eyes widened as soon as he got what I wanted from him. "Fuck, yeah." He shifted into place, legs lifted high.

I heard Richard opening the bottle of lube behind me. Then he reached around and stroked my cock with slick fingers, getting me ready. I hissed and gripped his forearm to stop him. "Too much." I was so damn close to shooting all over Luke before I even got inside him.

"Right." Richard let go of me. He pressed into my back and spoke against my ear. "All together."

"Yeah. All together." I propped myself over Luke with one hand on the bed. With the other hand, I guided my dick to his ass. I didn't mess around. None of us were going to last much longer. I pressed inside him, the tight heat of his ass swallowing my cock inch by inch.

Luke groaned as I filled him. He arched up and grabbed the headboard the same as I'd been doing a minute before.

Once I was bent over him, buried deep, I paused. Richard had his hands on me, spreading my ass cheeks as he sank into me once again. He didn't hesitate. He drew back and thrust in, grasping my hips, moving me with him so I was well and truly fucking Luke.

Luke and I groaned in concert.

We repeated the move again and again. Forward and back. Moving as one. Luke angled up to meet each stroke, pumping his own shaft now. We sped up, the bed squeaking under us, the headboard banging against the wall, our heavy breaths and uncontrollable grunts filling the basement as we soared together, chasing down the ultimate release. Not as three. But as one.

My body shook right as Richard's hold on my hips tightened. "That's it," he cried out. "Shit. Matthew! Gonna—fuck!" With a shuddering breath, he drove into me one last time and came, cursing under his breath, groans of pleasure pouring out of him.

I held still and clamped down around him, trying to give him every ounce of sensation that I could.

He stayed buried deep inside me throughout his release. Then he collapsed against my back, keeping most of his weight off me so I didn't fall onto Luke. "Holy shit." He breathed deep and kissed my bare shoulder. "That was…"

"Amazing."

"Yeah. I want to do that again. Soon. Very, very soon."

I nodded. "Uh-huh."

He whispered his next words against my ear. "Fuck him good." With urgency he withdrew from me. He shifted to lie on the bed beside Luke. Then they were kissing before me, that sensual, desperate battle of lips and tongues.

I rocked my hips, thrusting in and out of Luke, the two of them kissing with more vigor.

Without breaking the kiss, Richard grasped Luke's cock and stroked his length, squeezing to the tip. Luke dropped his head back to the bed, his eyes falling shut as that large hand worked him over.

Then Luke's eyes shot open, a confidence visible in his smirk that reminded me of the Luke we first met at the Haven. He turned his head and reached for Richard once more, planting another potent kiss on his lips. "I want you."

Richard nodded. "You got me." He shifted down to lie alongside us, his head at Luke's groin. I raised up to give him room, then watched as he licked his lips and took Luke into his mouth, offering him the most eager, consuming suction. I knew that technique well. I could practically feel his mouth on my dick, which only intensified the grip of Luke's ass.

A string of curse words spilled from Luke as I sped up, slamming into him now with nearly the same force Richard had used on me, losing control in that same exquisite way.

"Luke!" I cried out. My body went tight as I pummeled into him again and again, my orgasm racing like fire throughout me, deep, intense.

That did it for Luke. He followed me into that blissful heaven, exploding down Richard's throat, his hands no longer on the headboard but fisted in Richard's hair. I kept my cock inside him as he rode out the orgasm.

Richard took in what he could, but some of Luke's cum spilled from his lips, dripping down Luke's cock to his balls, sliding down the crack of his ass to the base of my dick where we were still joined.

When Luke had given Richard all he had, he dropped his head and hands to the mattress, his entire body going slack.

I pulled out of him and let his legs fall to the bed too. Then I slid down to lie between his spread thighs. I laid my head on his stomach, running my fingers over his flesh. He did the same with his hand on the back of my head, as if in awe of what we'd just done. Or that I was still there with them, maybe that we all were still there together.

Richard shifted up the bed and settled in beside Luke, spooning him, his hand on my head too. Three sated bodies. Three men in love.

Then Luke frantically clasped on to Richard's hand. "Don't ever leave us. Ever. You got that?"

"Hey." Richard lifted up to look down at him. "I won't. I promise."

"Good." Luke patted my head. "You either."

"It's a deal."

With that, Luke relaxed once more. Richard lay back down and held him, both of them cradling my head again.

Chapter Thirty-Eight

We stayed like that for several minutes, just basking and sighing and stroking, featherlight touches that seemed to say more than we ever could with words.

Eventually we got up, lingered under a hot shower together, and then spent the afternoon in bed, snuggled under the blankets. We napped, laughed, talked, laughed some more, and only crawled out of bed long enough to gather sandwiches and chips for a snack.

A few hours later, after Walter and Kevin had dropped Trixie off, we reluctantly agreed it was time to see about making dinner.

I wandered into the living room and sat on the couch beside Trixie. I gave her some love and a kiss on top of the head. "I missed you so much, baby girl."

She leaned into my side.

Luke stepped into the room, his hair wet from the second shower he'd had that day. Richard was behind him. He stopped and leaned against the doorway, watching me.

Luke flopped down and sprawled out on the couch with his head in my lap. "God, I love this couch." He reached across me and scratched Trixie behind one ear, then rolled onto his side, grabbing one of my thighs in both hands and snuggling in like he had no intention of moving for a week. Maybe longer.

Despite all the rest we'd gotten, we were still tired. And relieved. The week could've ended very differently than it had, and I didn't even want to contemplate what things would be like for Luke and me right then if Richard had been shot and killed right before our eyes.

"Come on, you two." Richard tipped his head toward the stairs. "Let's just order pizza and head back to bed."

Luke stretched his back. "God, yes. I love our bed." He got up and crossed the room to Richard.

"Matthew?" Richard asked. "You coming?"

"Yeah, but there's something I need to do first." I went to the fireplace, retrieved the lighter from the mantel, and sat on the floor. Luke knelt at my side. "What is it?"

"This." I removed the piece of paper my mom had given me from my pocket. "It's the number for my dad's divorce attorney."

Richard had been right.

I was more of a man than my father ever was. I didn't need to see him to prove anything to myself. I just needed to be me. I was exactly who I was meant to be. Despite him and all he did to me, I had learned to trust. And to love. Who could ask for more than that?

Richard got on the floor on my other side and ran a hand down my back. "You sure about this?"

I nodded. "I don't need anything else from him. I can move past what he did to me and how he left us on my own. With you guys at my side." Without an ounce of reservation, I lit the edge of the paper and tossed it into the fireplace. The yellow flames swallowed up the paper and then burned away to nothing. I looked at Richard, then Luke. "I have my family. One I'm very proud of. You were right when you said sometimes taking a chance is the right move." I got up. "Wait here. I have something for you guys." I raced up the stairs and into our room and retrieved the hidden case from the bathroom drawer. I rushed back to the living room and knelt before them.

Once I had the plastic case open, I removed two of the three small black jewelry boxes tucked inside. I held one out for each of them.

They stared at the little boxes for a shocked moment. Then Luke opened his first.

I held my breath as I waited. Neither man said a word. For a panicked moment, I worried I'd gone too far, but then every ounce of anxiety faded away. This was something I had to do. I was being honest with them about what I wanted. I could handle whatever their reactions were.

Luke lifted his head, a huge grin on his face. "Really?"

I nodded. "I got one for me too. That's why I put in all those extra hours at the kennel last semester. I wanted to pay for them myself."

Richard opened the lid on his box next. He was silent, his mouth hanging open as he took in the sight of the gold band inside. Some of the best moments of my life were when I made him speechless.

I took one of Luke's hands in mine, then Richard's. "I love you both. And I want to spend the rest of my life with you. Will you marry me?"

"Matthew." Adoration filled Luke's voice as he kept his gaze locked on the ring. "Never before in my life have I ever wanted to wear one of these. But now…" He lifted his head. "I've never wanted anything more."

"Really?" My voice shook with that single word.

"Are you kidding me?" He lunged forward and wrapped his arms around me, both of us laughing as we fell backward, Luke kissing my cheek over and over again.

"Is that a yes?" I asked.

He rushed to sit up, pulling me with him to straddle his lap. "Goddamn, yeah. That's definitely a yes."

Richard shifted closer. He said nothing as he scanned my face. I wasn't sure what he was looking for. He seemed at a loss for what to say or how to say it.

So I said, "I know it won't be legal but—"

He put a single finger to my lips. Then he kissed me, a deep toe-curling kiss that sent heat and passion and love racing through me. When he pulled back, he smiled at me. "Yes, I'll marry you. Both of you." He pressed our foreheads together. "Do you know how long I've been waiting for you to ask us this?"

"What?"

"I knew it was something you wanted. I wanted it for us too."

"You did?"

"Absolutely. I almost asked you guys. So many times. Been thinking about it for months now. When I was going over the idea of getting a new house, I kept picturing a ceremony in the backyard with all our friends and family." He looked Luke's way. "But I didn't want to freak you out. I never thought you'd say yes."

Luke's eyes widened. "Me?"

I laughed, and Luke turned his shocked expression my way.

"Hey, I've done everything you two have in this relationship right alongside you guys. Every step of the way." He stopped as if he just heard his own words, then shrugged. "Well, okay. Sometimes maybe a step or two behind, but I still did it all."

"Yeah, you did," I said.

Richard grew serious once more. "I don't think it's any surprise that I already think of the three of us as a lifetime commitment. A part of me feels like we've already made promises to each other in every way that's important, but I also really like the idea of making them in a formal way, to make sure you know how much I mean them."

I reached out and laced my fingers with his. "We know."

He lifted my hand and peppered kisses across my knuckles. When he lowered our hands, we both turned toward Luke.

He was staring down at the gold band he now had out of the box.

He read the inscription on the inside. "Forever." He grinned at the ring.

"Luke..." I said.

"Yeah?" He kept his focus on that ring as if it would disappear if he glanced away.

"I don't just want us to wear the rings. I want a ceremony, vows, witnesses, the whole thing."

He lifted his head, not a single sign of panic in those blue eyes. "Yeah, I know."

"And you're okay with that?"

"I am." He scrutinized me. "You didn't expect that from me either?"

"I don't know."

He placed the ring back into the box, closed the lid, and set it aside. He reached for me, cupping my face in his hands, tenderly caressing my cheeks with his thumbs. "What I want is to be with you, to live here with both of you for as long as you'll have me. I want to help you, support you, be your partners. I guess that's what it means to be married. And truthfully, I like the sound of it. I like thinking of you guys as mine forever, and I don't want to hide that from the world." His eyes lit up with the smile. "So let's make it official. In front of our family and friends."

It was my turn to lunge for him. I tackled him to the floor, laughing as the joy nearly burst from my chest. Richard joined us, positioning me between them.

I held on to both of them. "I was so afraid to bring this up. I thought asking for everything I wanted would be too much. I thought it might mess things up for us if I pushed too hard."

Richard pressed his lips to my cheek. "We always want to know what you want. That's not being pushy."

"I know." I shook my head. "I think it was just a part of me being afraid of losing the people I love."

"Are you still afraid of that?" Luke asked.

"Not anymore."

We lay there wrapped up in each other for several breaths. Then Luke lifted up onto his elbows. He stayed like that for a moment, staring off into space as if contemplating something. Then he sat up the rest of the way and folded his legs under him, facing us, his focus on me.

"What?" I asked him.

"I've been thinking about something all day. You said before that Richard was the one who held this relationship together in the beginning. Then you both said the other day that it was me. But that's all wrong. It has always been you, Matthew. You're the light that Richard and I gravitate toward. I think, whether consciously or not, we knew from the beginning we didn't want to live without that light in our lives."

Richard sat up and laid a hand over Luke's heart. Then he pulled him forward, pressing a soft kiss on his forehead. "I couldn't have said it better." He reached for me and tugged me to them. "It's that light we both fell in love with."

I offered each a long, luxurious kiss. "You're right."

Luke snorted out a laugh. "Of course we are."

"I meant you're sort of right. We're not together because of you or Richard or me. We're here together because of all three of us. Not anything any one of us said or did. It was all of us. Together. It always has been. Always will be."

Richard nodded. "Always."

I traced his lips with my forefinger and then stroked the side of his face. "I love you." I looked to Luke. "I love you both. I can't wait to marry you." I drew them to me and we kissed. Three men, three sets of lips, one beautiful kiss.

"Well, then…" Luke wrapped an arm around my waist and tugged me back down onto the floor with him. He spooned me and kissed the back of my neck. "Let's get started planning this shindig."

I'd never heard him sound more excited.

"All right," Richard said as he lay on my other side, both their arms encircling me now. "Who are we going to invite?"

I couldn't contain the grin.

I settled into their embrace, loving the feel of my men—my fiancés—surrounding me, their strong arms holding me close, their love for me as real and vibrant as ever.

No, more than ever.

* * * * *

*Sign up for **Sloan Parker's free newsletter** at sloanparker.com to get all the latest news about her book releases, reader giveaways, current discounts, and more.*

ABOUT THE AUTHOR

Award-winning author Sloan Parker writes passionate, dramatic stories about two men (or more) falling in love. She enjoys writing in the fictional world because in fiction you can be anything, do anything, even fall in love for the first time over and over again. Sloan's greatest moments in life are spent with her family, her friends, and her characters.

To contact Sloan, find out about her other books that are available for purchase, and read free stories, visit: www.sloanparker.com. If you'd like to be notified of new releases and get exclusive sneak peeks, be sure to sign up to receive Sloan Parker's newsletter via her website.

Other Titles by Sloan Parker

More (More Book 1)
More Than Most (More Book 2)

How to Save a Life (The Haven Book 1)
How to Heal a Life (The Haven Book 2)

Breathe
Take Me Home
More Than Just a Good Book
Something to Believe In
I Swear to You
The Break-In
Swept Away
A Lesson in Truth